PRAISE FOR

ALL THE MEN ARE SLEEPING

"Such great and captivating fluency with the physical, the natural and most particularly with the human realm of events. These wonderful stories have been a revelation to me, as well as a needed assurance that there are great writers working long and patiently to get things right and who suddenly (or so it seems) break forth to amaze us. Mr. MacDonald is an extraordinary writer."

—RICHARD FORD, winner of the Pulitzer Prize

"The fifteen stories in *All the Men Are Sleeping* are eloquent and poignant. MacDonald manages to move the heart while jangling the brain. . . . [The] stories should be read on their own, savoured and considered and admired before moving on to the next. MacDonald's work insists on such careful scrutiny and criticism, and any work on the reader's part is richly rewarded."

—*Vancouver Sun*

"MacDonald . . . said he set out to write short stories that were a match for the best among those he'd read himself. *All the Men Are Sleeping* is further proof that he's achieved that ambition."

—*The Chronicle-Herald* (Halifax)

ALL THE MEN ARE SLEEPING

ALSO BY D. R. MacDONALD

Eyestone

Cape Breton Road

ALL THE MEN ARE SLEEPING

SELECTED FICTION

D. R. MacDONALD

ANCHOR CANADA

Copyright © David MacDonald 2002
Anchor Canada edition 2003

Anchor Canada and colophon are trademarks.

National Library of Canada Cataloguing in Publication

MacDonald, D. R.
All the men are sleeping / D. R. MacDonald.

Short stories.
ISBN 0-385-65890-7

I. Title.

PS8575.D6295A76 2003   C813'.54   C2003-900635-2
PR9199.3.M23A66 2003

Several stories in this collection were previously published in *Eyestone*, Pushcart Press,
1988, Penguin Books, 1989. In addition, these stories originally appeared in the
following publications: *Canto* ("Holy Annie"), *Southwest Review* ("Eyestone,"
"Whatever's Out There"), *The Sewanee Review* ("The Flowers of Bermuda"),
Sequoia ("Work"), *Epoch* ("Of One Kind," "Vikings," "Meat Cove," "The Snows,
They Melt the Soonest," "Ashes"), *The Seattle Review* ("Sailing"), *TriQuarterly*
("Green Grow the Grasses O"), *The Threepenny Review* ("All the Men Are Sleeping").
"The Flowers of Bermuda" was reprinted in *Pushcart Prize XI: The Best of the Small Presses*.
Lyrics from "The Flowers of Bermuda" by Stan Rogers.

Cover image: The Special Photographers Comp / Photonica
Cover design: Adapted from a design by Paul Hodgson / pHd
Printed and bound in Canada

The characters in these stories are fictional creations and
are not intended to represent actual persons living or dead.

Published in Canada by
Anchor Canada, a division of
Random House of Canada Limited

Visit Random House of Canada Limited's website: www.randomhouse.ca

TRANS 10 9 8 7 6 5 4 3 2 1

To the memory of Murdock D. MacDonald, Margaret MacLeod MacDonald, and Isobel MacDonald Peterson

Fois Anama

CONTENTS

Trì nithean brèagha: long fo sheòl, craobh fo bhlàth,
duine naomh air leabaidh a bhàis.

*Three beautiful things: a ship under sail, a tree in bloom,
a holy man on his deathbed.*

GAELIC PROVERB

THE FLOWERS OF BERMUDA

Bilkie Sutherland took the postcard from behind his rubber bib and slowly read the message one more time: "I'm going here soon. I hope your lobsters are plentiful. My best to Bella. God bless you. Yours, Gordon MacLean." Bilkie flipped it over: a washed out photograph in black and white. *The Holy Isle. Iona. Inner Hebrides.* On the land stood stone ruins, no man or woman anywhere, and grim fences of cloud shadowed a dark sea. So this was Iona.

"You want that engine looked at?" Angus Carmichael, in his deepwater boots, was standing on the wharf above Bilkie's boat.

"Not now. I heard from the minister."

"MacLean?"

"He's almost to Iona now."

Angus laughed, working a toothpick around in his teeth. "Man dear, *I've* been to Iona, was there last Sunday." Angus meant where his wife was from, a Cape Breton village with a Highland museum open in the summer, and a St. Columba Church.

"It's a very religious place," Bilkie said, ignoring him. "Very ancient, in that way."

"Like you, Bilkie."

"I'm the same as the rest of you."

"No, Bilkie. Sometimes you're not. And neither is your Reverend MacLean."

Angus's discarded toothpick fluttered down to the deck. Bilkie picked it up and dropped it over the side. Angus never cared whether his own deck was flecked with gurry and flies. Nor was he keen on Gordon MacLean. Said the man was after putting in a good word for the Catholics. But that wasn't the minister's point at all. "We're all one faith, if we go back to Iona," is what he'd said. And nothing much more than that.

As Bilkie laid out his gear for the next day's work, he heard singing. No one sang around here anymore. Radios took care of that. He stood up to listen. Ah! It was Johnny, Angus's only boy, home from Dalhousie for the summer. He had a good strong voice, that boy, one they could use over at the church. But you didn't see him there, not since college. No singer himself, Bilkie could appreciate a good tune. His grandfather had worked the schooners in the West Indies trade, and Johnny's song had the flavor of that, of those rolling vessels . . . "'He could smell the flowers of Bermuda in the gale, when he died on the North Rock Shoal. . . .'" Bilkie stared into the wet darkness underneath the wharf where pilings were studded with snails. Algae hung like slicked hair on the rocks. He had saved Gordon MacLean under that wharf, when the man was just a tyke. While hunting for eels, Gordon had slipped and fallen, and Bilkie heard his cries and came down along the rocks on the other side to pull him out, a desperate boy clutching for his hand.

Bilkie's car, a big salt-eaten Ford, was parked at the end of the wharf, and whenever he saw it he wished again for horses who could shuck salt like rain. At home the well pump had quit this morning and made him grumpy. He'd had to use the woods,

squat out there under a fir, the birds barely stirring overhead, him
staring at shoots of Indian Pipe wondering what in hell they
lived on, leafless, white as wax, hardly a flower at all. Up by the
roadside blue lupines were a little past their prime. What flowers,
he wondered, grew on Iona?

The car swayed through rain ruts, past clumps of St. John's
Wort (*allas Colmcille* his grandfather had called them) that gave a
wild yellow border to the driveway. His house appeared slowly
behind a corridor of tall maples. In their long shade, red cows
rested. Sometimes everything seemed fixed, for good. His animals, his life. But God had taken away his only boy, and Bilkie
could not fathom that even yet. For a time he had kept sheep, but
quit because killing the lambs bothered him.

Bella was waiting at the front door, not the back, her palm
pressed to her face. He stopped shy of the porch, hoping it wasn't
a new well-pump they needed.

"What's wrong?"

"Rev. MacLean's been stabbed in Oban," his wife said, her
voice thin.

Bilkie repeated the words to himself. There was a swallows nest
above the door. The birds swooped and clamored. "Not there?" he
said. "Not in Scotland?" A mist of respect, almost of reverence,
hovered over the old country. You didn't get stabbed there.

"Jessie told me on the phone, not a minute ago. Oh, he'll live
all right. He's living."

Over supper Bella related what she knew. Gordon MacLean
had been walking in Oban, in the evening it was, a woman friend
with him. Two young thugs up from Glasgow went for her handbag, right rough about it too. Gordon collared one but the other
shoved a knife in his back.

"He's not a big man either," Bilkie said, returning a forkful
of boiled potato to his plate. He had known Gordon as a child

around the wharf, a little boy who asked hard questions. He had pulled him from the water. He'd seen him go off to seminary, thinking he would never come back to Cape Breton, not to this corner of it, but after awhile he did. To think of him lying in blood, on a sidewalk in Oban. "Did they catch the devils?"

"They did. He'll have to testify?"

"What, go back there?"

"When he's able. Be a long time until the trial."

Bilkie felt betrayed. A big stone had slipped somehow out of place. Certain things did not go wrong there, not in the Islands where his people came from. Here, crime was up, too few caring about a day's work, kids scorning church. Greedier now, more for themselves, people were. But knives, what the hell. There in the Hebrides they'd worked things out, hadn't they, over a long span of time? It had seemed to him a place of hard wisdom, hard won. Not a definite place, for he had never been there, but something like stone about it: sea-washed, nicely worn, and high cliffs where waves whitened against the rocks. He knew about the Clearances, yes, about the bad laws that drove his grandfather out of Lewis where he'd lived in a turf house. But even then they weren't knifing people. Gordon MacLean, a minister of God, couldn't return there and come to no harm? To Mull first he'd been headed, to MacLean country. And then to Iona, across a strait not much wider than this one. But a knife stopped him in Oban, a nice sort of town by the sea.

From his parlor window Bilkie could see a bit of the church in the east, the dull white shingles of its steeple above the dark spruce. *We all have Iona inside us,* the man had said. *Our faith was lighted there.* Why then did this happen?

Bilkie had asked such a question before and found no answer. They'd had a son, he and Bella, so he knew about shock, and about grief. Even now, thinking of his son and the schoolhouse could suck the wind right out of him. The boy was born late in their lives anyway, and maybe Bilkie's hopes had come too much to rest in him. Was that the sin? Torquil they called him, an old name out of the Hebrides, after Bella's dad. But one October afternoon when the boy was nine, he left the schoolhouse and forgot his coat, a pea coat, new, with a big collar turned up like a sailor's. So he went back to get it, back to the old white school-house where he was learning about the world. It was just a sum-mer house now, owned by strangers. But that day it was locked tight, and the teacher gone home. A young woman. No blame to her. His boy jimmied open the window with his knife. They were big, double-hung windows, and you could see them open yet on a warm weekend, hear people drunk behind the screens. But Torquil had tried to hoist himself over the sill, and the upper half of the window unjammed then and came down on his neck. Late in the day it was they found him, searching last the grounds of the school. A time of day about now. The sash lay along his small shoulders like a yoke, that cruel piece of wood, blood in his nose like someone had punched him. . . .

Bilkie barely slept. He was chased by a misty street, black and wet, and harrowing cries that seemed one moment a man's, the next a beast's. He was not given to getting up in the night but he dressed and went outside to walk off the dreariness he'd woke to. A cold and brilliant moon brightened the ground fog which lay-ered the pasture like a fallen cloud. The high ridge of hill behind his fields was ragged with wormshot spruce, wicks of branch against the sky. As a boy he'd walked those high woods with his grandfather who offered him the Gaelic names of things, most of them forgotten now, gone with the good trees. One day he'd told Bilkie about the words for heaven and hell, how they, Druid words, went far back before the time of Christ. *Ifrinn,* the Isle of

the Cold Clime, was a dark and frigid region of venomous rep-
tiles and savage wolves. There the wicked were doomed to wander, chilled to their very bones and bereft even of the company
of their fellow sinners. And the old heaven, though the
Christians kept that name too, was also different: *Flathinnis*, the
Isle of the Brave, a paradise full of light which lay far distant,
somewhere in the Western Ocean. "I like that some better," his
grandfather had said. "Just the going there would be good. As for
hell, nothing's worse than cold and loneliness."

As he moved through the fog, it thinned like steam, but
gathered again and closed in behind him. Suddenly he heard
hoofbeats. Faintly at first, then louder. He turned in a circle,
listening. Not a cow of his. They were well-fenced. Maybe the
Dunlop's next door. But cow or horse it was coming toward him
at a good clip and yet he couldn't make it out, strain as he might.
Soon his heart picked up the quick, even thud of the hooves,
and when in the pale fog a shape grew and darkened and then
burst forth, a head shaggy as seaweed and cruelly horned, he
raised his arms wildly in a shout of fear and confusion as the
bull shied past him, a dark rush of heat and breath, staggering
him like a blow. Aw, that goddamn Highland bull, that ugly
bugger. Trembling with anger and surprise, he listened to it crash
through thickets off up the hill, the fog eddying in its wake,
until Bella called him and he turned back to the house.

On the porch of the manse Bilkie waited for Mrs. MacQueen to
answer the door. The porch Rev. MacLean had built, but the
white paint and black trim were Bilkie's work, donated last summer when his lobstering was done. He'd enjoyed those few days
around the minister. One afternoon when Bilkie was on the ladder he thought he heard Gordon talking to himself, but no, he
was looking up, shading his eyes. "It's only a mile from Mull,

Iona," Gordon said to him. "Just across the Sound. So it's part of going home, really." Bilkie had said yes, he could see that. But he wasn't sure, even now, that he and the minister meant home in the same way. "Monks lived there, Bilkie. For a long, long time. They had a different view of the world, a different feel for it altogether. God was still *new* there, you see. Their faith was . . . robust."

Mrs. MacQueen, the housekeeper, filled the doorway and Bilkie told her what he would like.

"A book about Iona?" She was looking him up and down. She smelled of Joy, lemon-scented, the same stuff he used on his decks. "I don't read the man's books, dear, I dust them."

"He wouldn't mind me looking. Me and himself are friends." He rapped the trim of the door. "My paint."

"Well, he could have used some friends in Oban."

Mrs. MacQueen showed him into the minister's study, making it clear she would not leave. She turned the television on low, as if this were a sickroom, and sat down on a hassock, craning her ear to the screen.

Wine-colored drapes, half-drawn, gave the room a warm light. Bookshelves lined one wall, floor to ceiling, and Bilkie touched their bindings as he passed. He hadn't a clue where to begin or how to search in this hush: he only wanted to know more about that place, and maybe when the man returned they could talk about what went wrong there. But he felt shy with Mrs. MacQueen in the room. A map of Scotland was thumbtacked to the wall. The old clan territories were done in bright colors. Lewis he spotted easily, and Mull. And tiny Iona. On the desktop, under sprigs of lilac in a small vase, he saw a slim red book. In it were notes in Gordon's hand. With a quick glance at the housekeeper, he took it to the leather chair close by the north window, a good bright spot where Gordon must have sat many a time, binoculars propped on the sill. Bilkie put them to his eyes instinctively. Behind the manse a long meadow ran down to the shore. Across the half mile of water his boat rocked gently in the light swells. Strange to see his yellow slicker hanging by the wheel, emptied of him. Moving the glasses slightly he made out Angus standing over his boy, Johnny hunched down into some work or other. Good with engines, was Johnny. Suddenly Angus looked toward Bilkie. Of course his eyes would take in only the white manse on the hill, and the church beside it. Yet Bilkie felt seen in a peculiar way and he put down the binoculars.

Aware of the time, he turned pages, reading what he could grasp. That Iona's founder, St. Columba, had sailed there from Ireland to serve his kinsmen, the Scots of Dalriada. That he and his monks labored with their own hands, tilling and building, and that in their tiny boats they spread the faith into the remote and lesser isles, converting even the heathen Picts. That even before he was born, Columba's glory had been foretold to his mother in a dream: "An angel of the Lord appeared to her, and brought her a beautiful robe—a robe which had all the colors of all the flowers of the world. Immediately it was rapt away from her, and she saw it spread across the heavens, stretched out over plains and woods and mountains. . . ." He read testaments to St. Columba's powers and example, how once in a great storm his ship met swelling waves that rose like mountains, but at his prayer they were stilled. He was a poet and loved singing, and songs praising Columba could keep you from harm. His bed was bare rock and his pillow a stone. During the three days and three nights of his funeral, a great wind blew, without rain, and no boat could reach or leave the island.

Bilkie was deep in the book when Mrs. MacQueen, exclaiming, "That's desperate, just desperate!" turned off the soap opera and came over to him.

"You'll have to go now," she said. "This isn't the public library, dear, and I have cleaning to do."

He would never talk himself past her again, not with Gordon away. He returned the book to the desk and followed her to the front door.

"Did you ever pray to a saint, Mrs. MacQueen?"

She crossed her arms. "I'm no R. C., Mr. Sutherland."

"I don't think that matters, Mrs. MacQueen. The minister has a terrible wound. Say a word to St. Columba."

"He's healing. He's getting better and soon might be coming home, is what I heard."

The next morning the sun glared up from a smooth sea as Bilkie hauled his traps, moving from one swing to another over the grounds his grandfather had claimed. By the time Bilkie was old enough to fish, there was a little money in it. But you had to work. Nobody ever gave it to you, and the season was short. He had started out young hauling by hand, setting out his swings in the old method, the backlines anchored with kellicks, and when he wasn't hauling he was rowing, and damned hard if a wind was on or the tide against you. He had always worked alone, rowed alone. Except when his boy was with him, and that seemed as brief now as a passing bird. He preferred it out here by himself, free of the land for awhile, the ocean at his back.

This season the water was so clear he could see ten fathoms, see the yellow backline snaking down, the traps rising. His grandfather told him about the waters of the West Indies, the clear blue seas with the sun so far down in them it wouldn't seem like drowning at all, for the light there.

He gaffed a buoy and passed the line over the hauler, drawing the trap up to the washboard where he quickly culled the dripping, scurrying collection. He measured the lobsters, threw a berried one back. But after he dropped the trap and moved on, he knew he'd forgotten, for the second time that morning, to put in fresh bait. To hell with it. On the bleak rocks of the Bird Islands shags spread their dark wings to dry. A school of mackerel shimmered near the boat, an expanding and contracting disturbance just beneath the surface as they fed. He cut the engine, letting the boat drift like his mind. He hummed the song of Johnny Carmichael but stopped. Couldn't get the damn tune out of his head. Sick of it. He picked a mackerel out of the bait box and turned it over in his hands, stroking the luminous flow of stripes a kind of sky was named for: a beautiful fish, if you looked at it—the smooth skin, dark yet silvery. Gordon MacLean said from the pulpit that a man should find beauty in what's around him, for that too was God. But for Bilkie everything had been so familiar, everything he knew and saw and felt, until Torquil died. He took out his knife and slid it slowly into the dead fish: now, what might that be like, a piece of steel like that inside you? A feeling you'd carry a long while, there, under the scar.

Astern, the head of the cape rose behind buff-colored cliffs, up into the deep green nap of the mountain. He had no fears here, never in weather like this when the sea was barely breathing. Still, he missed the man, the sound of his voice on Sunday. The last service before he left for Iona, the minister had read Psalm 44, the one, he said, that St. Columba sang to win the Picts away from their magi, the Druids . . . *O God, our fathers have told us, what work thou didst in their days, in the times of old. . . .*

After Bilkie lost his son, he'd stayed away from church, from the mournful looks and explanations, why he should accept God's taking an innocent boy in such a way. His heart was sore, he told Bella, and had to heal up, and nothing in the church then could help it. But a few weeks after Rev. MacLean arrived, Bilkie went to hear him. Damn it, the man could preach. Not like those

TV preachers who couldn't put out anything much but their palms and a phone number. A slender string it was that Gordon MacLean couldn't take a tune from. And only once had he mentioned Torquil in a roundabout way, to show he was aware there'd been a boy, that he knew what a son could mean.

As Bilkie turned in toward the wharf that afternoon he saw three boats in ahead of him. Above Angus's blue and white Cape Islander the men had gathered in a close circle, talking and nodding. Only Johnny Carmichael was still down below, sitting on the gunnels with his guitar. Bilkie approached the wharf in a wide arc, trying to discern what he saw in the huddled men and the boy off alone bent into his instrument. He brought his boat up into the lee and flung a line to Angus who was waving for it.

"Bilkie, you're late, boy!" he shouted.

"Aw, I was feeling slow today!"

When the lines were secured, Angus called down to him. "Did you hear about it?"

"About what?"

"The minister, Bilkie, for God's sake! He's passed away! It was sudden, you know. Complications. Not expected at all."

Bilkie's hands were pressed against a crate he'd been about to shift. He could feel the lobsters stirring under the wood. He looked up at Angus. "I knew that already," he said.

Instead of going home, Bilkie drove to a tavern fifteen miles away. He sat near a window at one of the many small tables. Complications. Lord. The sun felt warm on his hands and he watched bubbles rise in his glass of beer. The tavern was quiet but tonight it would be roaring. Peering into the dim interior he made out Jimmy Carey alone at a table. Jimmy was Irish and had acted cranky here more than once. But he seemed old and mild now, back there in the afternoon dark, not the hell-raiser he used to be. And wasn't St. Columba an Irishman, after all? Bilkie raised his glass and held it there until Jimmy, who looked as if he'd been hailed from across the world, noticed it and raised his own in return. Bilkie beckoned him over. They drank until well past supper, leaning over the little table and knocking glasses from time to time. Bilkie told him about St. Columba, about the monks in their frail vessels.

"You know about St. Brendan, of course," Jimmy said, his eyes fixing on Bilkie but looking nowhere. "They say he got as far as here even, and clear to Bermuda before he was done."

"Bermuda I know about." Bilkie tried to sing what he remembered. "'Oh there be flowers in Bermuda, beauty lies on every hand . . . and there be laughter, ease and drink for every man. . . .'" He leaned close to Jimmy's face: "' . . . but there not be joy for *me*.'"

On the highway Bilkie focused hard on the center line, thinking that Jimmy Carey might have bought one round at least, St. Brendan be damned. To the west the strait ran deep and dark, the sun just gone from it as he turned away toward home. Bad time to meet the mounties. He lurched to a stop by the roadside where a small waterfall lay hidden. He plunged through a line of alders into air immediately cool. The falls stepped gently through mossed granite, down to a wide, clear pool, and he remembered Bella bending her head into it years ago, her hair fanning out red there as she washed the salt away after swimming. He knelt and cupped the water, so cold he groaned, over his face again and again.

As he drove the curves the white church appeared and disappeared above the trees. When he came upon it, it seemed aloof, unattended. Cars were parked carelessly along the driveway to the manse, and Bilkie slowed down long enough to see a man and woman climbing the front steps, Mrs. MacQueen, in her flowered apron, waiting at the door. Oh, there'd be some coming and going today, the sharing of the hard news. When he felt the schoolhouse approaching, he vowed again not to look, not to bother what went on there. But he couldn't miss the blue tent in the front yard, and the life raft filled with water for a wading pool. This time he did not slow down. Too often he had wondered about the blow on the neck, about what his son had felt, and who, in that instant, he had blamed . . . something so simple as a window coming down on his bones. There. In a schoolhouse.

Bella had not seen Bilkie drunk like this in years, but she knew why and said nothing, not even about Rev. MacLean. She could not get him to come inside for supper. He reeled around angrily in the lower pasture, hieing cows away when they trotted toward the fence for handouts of fresh hay. He shouted up at the ridge. Finally he stalked to the back door.

"Gordon was going to Iona," he said to his wife. "He could check the fury of wild animals, that saint they had there. Did Gordon no damn good, eh?"

"You've had some drink, Bilkie, and I've had none. I'm tired now."

He stepped up close to her and took her face in his hands. "Ah, Bella. Your hair was so pretty."

She made him go to bed, but after dark he woke. He smelled of the boat and wanted to wash. Hearing a car, he went over to the window. Near his neighbor's upper pasture headlights bounced and staggered over the rough ground. They halted, backed up, then swept suddenly in another direction until the shaggy bull galloped across the beams. Loose again. A smallish, wild-looking beast they'd imported from Scotland. Could live out on its own in the dead of winter, that animal. You might see it way off in a clearing, quiet, shouldering snow like a monu-ment. The headlights, off again in pursuit, captured the bull briefly but it careened away into the darkness, and the car—a

Dunlop boy at the wheel no doubt—raked the field blindly. Complications. A stone for a pillow. His own boy would be a man now. Passed away, like a wave.

It was difficult for Bilkie to get up that day. He had always opened his eyes on the dark side of four a.m. but now Bella had to push and coax him. He sat on the edge of the bed for a long time staring at the half-model of a schooner mounted on the wall. His grandfather had worked her, the *Ocean Rose*, lost on Hogsty Reef in the Bahamas with his Uncle Bill aboard.

"You don't get up anymore. What's the matter with you?" Bella said. He took the cup of coffee she held out to him, nodding vaguely. Squalls had lashed the house all night and now a thick drizzle whispered over the roof. "You know Rev. MacLean is coming home this day, and tonight they'll wake him."

"I can't go," Bilkie said.

"What would he think, you not there at his wake with the others who loved him?"

"He's not thinking at all anymore. That's just a body there, coming back."

"Don't be terrible. Don't be the way you were after Torquil."

"They could have buried him over there. Couldn't they have? Near where he wanted to go?"

"He was born *here*, Bilkie. Nobody asked, I don't suppose, one way or the other."

He could see that she'd been crying. He put the coffee down carefully on the window sill and took her hands in his, still warm from the cup. "Bella, dear," he said. "You washed your hair in that water. It must have hurt, eh? Water so cold as that?"

Gusts rocked the car as Bilkie crossed the bridge that joined the other island. He was determined to take himself out of the fuss, some of it from people who would never bestir themselves were Gordon MacLean here and breathing. Above him the weather moved fast. The sky would whiten in patches but all the while churn with clouds black as the cliffs by the lighthouse. There was a good lop on the water, looking east from the bridge, and when the strait opened out a few miles away the Atlantic flashed white against an ebbing tide.

In the lee of the wharf the lobster boats were surging like tethered horses. No one was around. The waves broke among the pilings beneath him and the timbers creaked. He walked to the seaward end where Angus had stacked his broken traps. Across the roughening water the manse looked small, the cars tiny around it. Every morning his grandfather would say, old as he was, *Dh'iarr am muir a thadhal.* The sea wants to be visited.

He threw off his lines and headed out into the strait, rounding up into the wind, battering the waves until he checked back on the throttle. In the turns of wind he smelled the mackerel in the bait box, the fumes of the engine. But as he drew abreast of Campbell Point, a gust of fragrance came off the land and he strained to see its source in the long, blowing grass of the point. It was quickly gone and there was nothing to account for it but what had been there all along—the thin line of beach, the grass thick as hay all the way back to the woods. To the west, on the New Skye Road, he glimpsed St. David's Church, a small white building behind a veil of rain, set in the dense spruce, no one there now but Bible Camp kids in the summer.

The sea was lively at the mouth of the strait where wind and tide met head to head. He bucked into the whitecaps, slashes of spray cracking over the bow. The waves deepened as the sea widened out but he'd ride better when he reached the deeper water where the breaking crests would cease. He had a notion of the West Indies, of his grandfather under sails, out there over the curve of the world and rolling along in worse weather than this. Hadn't the Irish monks set out in their currachs of wickerwork and hide, just for the love of God? They had survived. They reached those islands they sailed for, only dimly sure where they were. But maybe you could come by miracles easier then, when all of life was harder, and God closer to the sea than he was now. Now with no saints around, saints who could sow a field and sail a boat, you had to find your own miracles. You couldn't travel to them, could you, Gordon, boy?

He would have to go back. He would have to stand at the wake holding his hat like the rest of them, looking at Gordon who'd come dead such a distance. Bilkie watched the rhythm of the waves. He needed a break in them to bring his boat around and run with the sea. But then he wasn't hearing the engine anymore, and the boat was falling away, coming around slowly with no more sound than a sail would make. Columba. A dove. Strange name for a man. *Colmcille. Caoir gheal*, his grandfather called waves like these. A bright flaming of white. The sea had turned darker than the sky, and over the land the boat was swinging toward, clouds lay heavy and thick, eased along like stones, dark as dolmens. "Ah!" was all Bilkie said when the wave rose under him, lifting the boat high like an offering.

GREEN GROW THE GRASSES O

A suspicion had come down that Kenneth Munro was using dope in the house he rented above the road. "Harboring drugs" was the way Millie Patterson put it.

"I don't think he's that kind," Fiona Cameron said, in whose parlor Mr. Munro was being discussed. She had seen him coming and going, a thirtyish man with dark gray hair nearly to his shoulders. It was the only extravagant thing about him, how the wind would gust it across his eyes. He had left St. Aubin as a tot and returned suddenly now for reasons unclear.

"Drinking's one thing," Millie said. "But *this*."

"This what?" Fiona said. She was curious about him too, but in a different way. And Kenneth Munro, after all, was not just any outsider. His family was long gone but still remembered.

After some coaxing, Lloyd David, Millie's son, described how Munro's kitchen had been full of the smell the day he'd dropped by to cut the high wild grass out front. "There's no other smell like it," he said.

This expertise got him a hot glance from his mother. Millie missed no opportunity to point up the evils of drugs.

"But Millie," Fiona said, "a smell in his kitchen is hardly criminal."

"Fiona dear, you have no idea." Millie, a nurse for twenty-six years, recalled with horror a young man the Mounties brought into the emergency ward last winter: "In that weather, crawling down the highway in his undershorts, barking like a dog." Lloyd David chuckled, then caught himself. "He was that cold," Millie went on, "he was blue." She paused. "Marijuana." But the word came out of her mouth erotically rounded somehow, lush and foreign.

"But we hardly know Kenneth Munro," Fiona said. She knew he often stood shirtless on his little front porch late in the morning, stretching his limbs. He'd just got up, it was plain to see. He was brown from the sun, though he'd brought the brown with him. Fiona could not imagine him crawling along a highway or barking either. What she could imagine she was not likely to admit. She was from the Isle of Harris in the Outer Hebrides but had lived in Cape Breton all her married life, nearly twenty years. Her eyes were an unusual pale green, peppered with colors you couldn't pin down, and they looked merry even when she was not. No, Millie would not easily let go of this matter. Kenneth Munro. And drugs. They had come to Cape Breton like everywhere else, and of course people saw on TV what drugs out there in the world could do. Marijuana? Just a hair's breadth from heroin, in Millie's eyes, whereas alcohol was as familiar as the weather. Hadn't there been a nasty murder over in Sydney where two kids on drugs stabbed an old man for his money? That shook everyone, murder being rare among Cape Bretoners, despite a reputation for lesser violence. Fiona glanced out the front window: she hadn't seen Munro all day. His bedroom window was flung high and the curtains, green as June grass, whipped in the wind.

"He's got a telescope in the backyard," Lloyd David said.

"What's he up to?" Millie said.

"Well, that's the point." Fiona took a sip of tea. It was cool. "We can't say."

"He seems like a nice fella." Harald, Fiona's husband, had come in from haying and stood stout and perspiring in his overalls. "Fiona's right," he said from the doorway. "Yesterday he was asking me about the bobolinks."

"About the *what?*" Millie said.

"Birds, Ma. Tweet tweet?"

She glared at her son: she hated his Oakland Raiders T-shirt with the insolent pirate face on the front.

"Well," Fiona said. "He's just over the road. We'll have to find out about him. Harald, won't we?"

At a table by the west window of the Sealladh Na Mara Restaurant Kenneth Munro took in the postcard view. Whatever he saw he measured against the descriptions his father had given him years ago. He could see a good portion of Goose Cove and the mountain behind it whose profile darkened the water this time of the afternoon, calming the bay. Terns squabbled on a sandy bar. The waitress, whom he fancied and who, he felt, was ready for a move, came up behind him, her slender figure reflected in the glass. In her unflattering uniform—a bland aqua, the hem too long—she seemed all the more pretty. She'd worn her fine brown hair unfashionably long down her back when he had seen her walking along the road, but now it was clasped in a bun.

"Ginny, suppose I was to take you to dinner some night soon? In Sydney?"

"Oh, I don't know. You're older than I am, by more than a bit." Ginny had graduated from McGill this summer and was back home, pondering her future. She loved the country she'd grown up in but knew she would work in a big city before long.

"I can't deny it," Munro said. "I'm up in years. I expect your parents wouldn't approve."

"No. No, they wouldn't much. And they've always known just about everything I've done around here." She looked over at two elderly women picking daintily at their lobster salads. "There's no need they should keep on knowing."

"I'll get you home early," he said. "Early as you like."

"I suppose we could. I'm thinking we might." She went off to another table and stood with her back to him. Munro drank from his water glass, running the ice around his tongue, and smiled comfortably at the immobile brilliance of the bay, its surface inked in shadow.

That was the kind of light he imagined in his special afternoon, an ambience like that.

They ate in a steakhouse too open and noisy, but after a bottle of wine they talked freely in raised voices, discovering that they might be distantly related through a great-grandmother, and that brought them a few inches closer. Munro told her about his carpentry work in San Francisco, cabinetmaking and remodeling, and how he liked working for gays because they paid him well and were particular. Ginny told him about Montreal and how she always tried to speak French there because she got to know the people. She asked him why he was living alone over there in St. Aubin with hay and woods all around him.

"Only for awhile," Munro said. He took a photograph out of his coat and laid it on the white tablecloth, moving his face closer to hers. "That man there is my father, Ginny. The women I don't know."

"I'd say they like him, eh?"

"Something more than that going on. Look at his face."

"Is he your age there, your dad?"

"About."

"I like your gray hair. It's a bit long. His looks black."

"And very proud of it he was. Vain, even."

"He's dead?"

"He is." Munro tapped the photo. "But not here. Here, he is very much alive." He touched her hand. "Would you come with me to a field like that? Would you be one of those women, for an afternoon?"

Ginny laughed. He looked so serious in the smoldering light of the candle jar. But the people in the photograph, the man and the two women, seemed happy, and she felt quite good herself after three glasses of wine.

"You mean like a picnic?" she said.

On the way back to Rooster Hill Munro pulled off the highway near South Gut so they could take in the bay. Along the mountain ridge the lost sun threw long red embers. In the evening water below them, still as a pond, lay the blackened timbers of an old wharf.

"My father had a picture of that," Munro said. "From back in the twenties when he was a kid. There was a schooner tied up to it. Looked like another century. Here, you want a hit of this?"

He proffered what she thought was a cigarette. She stared at it.

"Am I shocking you?" Munro said.

"I've run across it, and I don't shock easy as all that."

He was afraid he'd blown it with her, but he was in a hurry, and for him puffs of grass were part of almost any pleasure.

"You *are* a woman," he said.

"At home here, I am still a girl."

"Well, then." He made to stub out the joint but she grabbed his wrist and took it from him, drawing a long hit.

"God help us if the Mounties come by," she said through the smoke. "And you with relatives here."

"Never met any. One afternoon of my own is all I want. With the sun out, and a warm wind coming up the field. And women like those in the photo, at their ease. That's what I came for—to take that back with me."

"I don't want to be a woman in a picture."

"Ah, Ginny, you'll be more than that."

They kissed in the car as it idled by her mailbox, once quickly like friends, then again with a long deep taste of something further. After Ginny got out, she kissed the window on the passenger side. The fierce twilight made her reckless. Through the rosy smudge on the glass, Munro watched her walk up the hill to her house, twirling her bag.

Fiona parted the parlor curtains: Kenneth Munro's car was turning slowly up his driveway, its broad taillights reminding her, in the foggy dark, of a spaceship. Wee men would be coming out of it, heading for the scattered houses of St. Aubin. *Feasgar math,* she'd say, I've been waiting. *Fuirich beagan.* Certain feelings had no shape in English, and sometimes she whispered them to herself. Harald was not a speaker above the odd phrase, but Gaelic came to her now and then like old voices. *Traighean.* The sands of Harris, the long shell-sand beaches that even on a dour day opened up white like a stroke of sun, still warm to your bare feet after the wind went cold and the clouds glowered over the gusting sea. Those strange and lovely summers, so distant now— brief, with emotions wild as the weather, days whose light stretched long into evening and you went to bed in a blue dusk.

"Harald," she said, "is it time for a call on Mr. Munro?" But Harald, pink from haying, had dozed off in his chair. A rerun of *Love Boat* undulated across the television, the signals bouncing badly off the mountain tonight. Fiona loathed the program. When she turned off the set, Harald woke. He kissed her on the cheek, then wandered upstairs seeking his bed.

So why not go up to Munro's? Yet when she thought of him opening the door, her breath caught. Of course she could phone him first, but that was not the same thing, was it?

Fiona had shared a life with Harald for a long time, here in the country. She'd left Harris for a small farm in Nova Scotia because she loved the man who asked her away, the seaman she'd met in Stornoway where she worked in a woolen shop. Love. *An gaol.* Yes, she had no reservations about that word, and all it carried, never had. She loved his company, even when he was dull (and wasn't she the dull one too sometimes, shut into herself, beaten down by a mood?). The two of them together had always seemed enough, and although they liked other people, they never longed for them. Small delights could suffice, if you were close in that way you couldn't explain to anyone else: it was the robin who nested every summer in the lilac bush at the front door, huddled in the delicate branches as they came and went, always aware of her, pleased that she didn't flee, and the families of deer they watched from the big window at the foot of their bed, grazing elegantly one moment and exploding into motion the next, and every day the Great Bras D'Eau, the different suns on its surface, the water shaded and etched by tides, stilled by winter, the crush of drift ice, and the long mountain in autumn, swept with the brilliance of leaves. And just the day-by-day work of living seemed to have a reason that lay in their being together, but they could never have said what it was. A meal, a task, a domestic calamity—who could say what made them glad for having it? They talked about some things, but left most unsaid. She loved . . . what? Harald's presence? Was that the word, *làthair?* In some way that no one else could embrace? It was like a bit of music that was always there, behind everything, often too faint to be noticed, but there, and sometimes powerful. He knew her, and he loved her, without question. She had not yearned for any different thing between them.

Yet something shocked her out of sleep now and then, her heart galloping hard until the dream yielded to the bedroom, to the familiar window, and she knew again where she was. An impossible longing came on as she lay there in the dark, whether was there a bright moon out, or snow raging or flickering down, or a deep rain drumming on her nerves as she waited for thunder. Harald would mutter on in his own dreams. She wondered if they were anything like her own. He never said. And why anyway? They were his, he needed them. But in some dreams, she made another man care about her: his attentions were utterly new and like that first keen love when everything is on the tips of your fingers. Each time, in whatever dream place, the feeling was the same: rich in sensation, strange, like none she knew in her waking life, and there were no words for it in Gaelic or English either.

Munro's front light burned in the fog, a gathering coolness on her skin. In Harris as a girl, mists had sometimes frightened her because of the tales she'd heard and because sights would suddenly appear in her path, ambiguous shapes in a gray sea, and as she approached Munro's house, she thought maybe that was why he looked out his window a moment before disappearing from it fast. She rapped on his door. What had she seemed like to him? A specter? *Tannasg?* He was slow to answer. She stamped her feet lightly though the wind was not cold.

"Did I scare you?" she said, pleased to have that edge.

"I don't get many callers, not at night. Mrs. Cameron is it?"

He looked tense but he ushered her inside, smiling. There was an odd smoke in the air and she blushed.

"Am I interrupting you? Harald's asleep. Tired to the bone." Was she rattling on?

"Something to drink?" he said. "Rum and ginger ale maybe?"

"Well I think I will. A wee one. Thank you."

Munro pried an ice tray from his snowy freezer, scattering frost on the floor. He jabbered on about bobolinks in the hayfield. Wouldn't the tractor mow through their nests, the females drab but the males decked out in cream cravats? Were the fledglings gone, was that it? He held ice cubes in his hands.

"Oh, yes," she said. "They've flown by now."

He poured rum into a glass. The ice crackled.

"I've seen your husband cutting hay," he said. His face was pleasantly creased, as if he'd spent time outdoors, but comfortably, skiing or swimming perhaps. His long hair looked recently trimmed.

"He sells it. Three thousand bales." She smiled. At the tips of her cheekbones she felt spots of red. Like rouge, but hot. "I used to help him."

Munro handed her the drink, then peered out the window. "I'm glad it was you coming out of that fog," he said. "Jumped out of my skin."

"Nothing to harm you here."

"I know. Sometimes I'm sensitive to surprises." He sat down at the wooden table he used for a desk. "This little house is fine for me. The roof leaks a bit, in the kitchen."

"A family of seven lived here once. Less than fine." She had taken a good swallow and could feel the rum in her blood. She was startled to see her white knees crossed at the hem of her skirt since she'd intended to wear slacks. "I'll send Lloyd David over. He'll patch your roof."

"Lloyd David's mother showed up here this morning," Munro said as if it had just come back to him. "She asked me if

I knew about the Knox Church and would I like to attend." He laughed. "She was really looking me over. I said no thanks, and she said it was only what she expected. What do I make of that?"

"Millie is just concerned about your soul, Mr. Munro. Some people here feel a kind of responsibility toward you, and they don't know what you're like."

"Because I was born here?"

"Your father grew up here, your grandpa too. He's buried over in the churchyard." She nodded toward the small white church that on a clear night could be seen from the kitchen. "That's part of why Millie came to your door."

"And you?"

"It wasn't for church, Mr. Munro. I'm not a deep kneeler myself."

"Folks don't usually care about my soul, especially strangers."

"You've got kin around here, if you want to know them."

"Really, I don't." He bent a gooseneck lamp low to the table. "That is, I have something I want to live, or relive, while I'm here. It doesn't involve cousins. Just myself, and two others."

She set the glass down on the carpet, most of it gone. The rum made her bold.

"Has it anything to do with what I smell in the air? Mind you, I'm only asking."

He went still and looked at her. There was a touch of smile in his voice. "Asking's plenty, at this point."

"I'm not snooping."

"And I'm not dangerous. Every Presbyterian is safe."

"It doesn't matter, believe me. Not in my book."

"Would you come here to the table? I'll try to show you what I'm after, something I missed a long time ago."

A photograph was arranged under the table lamp like a document. "I never saw my family except in snapshots," Munro said. "My father would lay them out and tap a face or a house or a field somewhere, places I'd never seen. Bits of a puzzle, to me. People posing in kitchen chairs out back, gray shingles behind them, in Cape Breton. St. Aubin, other places. You know what I mean . . . a guy standing by a horse with his hand on its nose, and my father would say, 'Now that's Cousin Murdock John Rory, and he's nearly a hundred.' And my mother would chime in, 'And isn't that Donald's Heather when she was small, with the dog Uncle Freddie left behind?' She knew all the pictures by heart. But not this one. I found it in the lining of his suitcase, after he died. No, my mother never saw this. She would have said, even though she isn't in it."

His father, shirtless, lies on his back in an unmown field. Closed in delight, his eyes are directed toward the camera through a veil of summer grass into which he seems to be set-tling. His smile is one of self-conscious bliss, unfeigned. A plump woman with dark hair hugs him, her cheek pressed to his bare chest as if she is listening to his heart, while a second woman, younger, her light blond hair pulled tightly back, sits in a sidesaddle way beside his head, her hand playing in his hair. Her smile, pursed with mischief, would warm any man near it. Fiona can see that. Her shorts have cuffs and her tucked-back legs are pale but pretty. It is like the photos Fiona grew up with, in its black-and-white tones of the past. Behind the father and his two women, neglected fields recede toward gray water. Shy spruce trees stand singly in the far reaches of meadow, awash in wild blond grass. Visible at the edge of the picture is a boarded window. The old house lists like a grounded ship.

"The farm was long abandoned by this time," Munro said. "Granny was dead. The land is going back to woods, slowly, and my dad didn't care. He'd had to stay home into his thirties, being the youngest. Had to see to his mother. But you see, he was cut off, for years, there in the country. No electricity. No plumbing. Nothing to tune into. A caretaker, a nurse. And Granny was hard to live with sometimes. So when he was free of all that, he took off west. He only came back here once, and this is it, I know it. On a whim he's come out to the old place, with two women. There's something he has to taste, one more time, and it's all in the air of that afternoon."

"And who *took* the picture?" Fiona said.

Munro looked the question off, his eyes still on the photograph. "I'm trying to *see* this, you understand, to get inside it. An afternoon like this one, just once. No camera has to record it, only me. And the two women."

"And what happens when that day dies down and you all have to go home?"

"I'll still have the day. And I can enter it whenever I wish." He showed her a stubby joint from his shirt pocket. "This helps me. Does that make any sense?"

"Portions of it." Fiona could see right into that old house: the lamps were dry and the cold air was damp with absence. She could smell the mildewed cushions and clothes and bedding, on the beds or in the drawers. And that man in the grass, he would never be back. The women touching him were neither his wife nor his wife-to-be. What was he like? What kind of man had he been?

"But why do you need help from that?" she said, pointing to the roach in the palm of his hand. "I'm sure I sound naive."

"It helps me see things I've missed. And it makes me high." He smiled. "Are you going to evict me?"

"You're not noisy. Your rent's paid. And it's only you up here, isn't it?"

"You do understand what I'm after here? A kind of re-enactment?"

"And where will you do all this?"

"At my grandmother's old place, of course. Nobody's there. Are they?"

"No." Fiona looked to the window that faced the strait and the mountain. "But I have to tell you that your grandmother's property is gone for a gravel pit. There's little of it now but a bare cliff. I'm sorry."

Kenneth Munro spread the tripod legs and focused his telescope on the bare brown scar across the water: dust blew about it like smoke, and yes, it was mostly cliff now, gravel mounded for hauling at the base of it. He could just make out the monotonous grind of a stone crusher. A dump truck rumbled off with a heaped load and disappeared into the dense green mountainside.

When Harald's tractor started up the hill from the road, Munro hailed him and waited in the row he was mowing. Harald stopped and got down, leaving the engine running.

"I wanted to ask you," Munro said, offering Harald the photo and nodding toward the mountain. "How could they do *that* to *this?* How is it legal?"

Harald doffed his cap and wiped his startlingly white scalp with a red bandana. He studied the picture. "It was fallow, you know, your grandma's place, a long while. Nothing coming out, nothing going in. Just deer and hunters. So, goes for taxes. Goes for what money might be made of it."

"Gravel?"

"Gravel. God, they took ton after ton out. All under the highway now."

"Where I live you could fight that."

"Fight what? We had nice farms all over here once. The place was full of people. Lots of trees now, as you see it, everywhere."

Harald patted the hood of his tractor as if it were flesh. "You liking it up here, in the house?"

They both looked at the house. Lloyd David was kneeling on the roof wielding a thick black brush. He waved.

"It's fine. Look." Munro brandished the photo. "Is there a meadow like this anywhere over there, on the other side?"

"Look east a bit. That patch. I used to cut hay for the old widow but she's gone. It's clear yet, I think. Funny how trees don't come back into certain places, just don't. Further up lies a stone house, what's left of it. We didn't build with stone. Plowed up too damn much, I guess."

"Is it grassy there?"

"Old hay and whatever." Harald yanked a stalk from the ground. "There's no single grass called hay. It's a mixture, varies from place to place. Over at the stone house, I can't recall." He blew on the timothy in his hand. "See that powder? Pollen."

"Flower tops," Munro said. "Them I know about."

He glanced back at the roof. Lloyd David flashed him an ambiguous peace sign and then put his forked fingers to his lips. Munro ignored him.

"Look through your scope there and you'll see the spot I'm talking about." Harald climbed up into the tractor seat. "Or is that just for stars?"

"There's a comet due pretty soon. Next Friday, I think. Come up and have a look."

"Can't stay awake for a comet, Mr. Munro. That time of night I'm sawing heavy wood." He looked toward his house where Fiona had come out. "Now, Fiona, she'd love to. You show her the stars." Harald released the brake lever and fell instantly into the rhythm of mowing. The man would keep it up until dark, and if the weather shifted, he had other things to do. Had he noticed how lovely his wife looked?

Down by her lilac bush, Fiona was taking in the morning, her face up to the sun, or so it seemed, a mist of lavender still left in the branches behind her. When she saw him, she crossed the road and came slowly up the field, the wind in her clothes, billowing her pale green skirt. She stopped short of him and shaded her eyes. The sun warmed her honey-colored hair.

"There's a stone house over there I'd like to go to," Munro said.

"I heard it's dangerous." She was a bit out of breath and her cheeks had reddened. "It's falling in."

"I suppose there's some danger, sure," he said. He looked down at her white house and the green shutters. The barn, the big doors of its threshing floor thrown wide, was painted and trimmed the same, neatly. All of a piece. "Why did my father hate his own farm so much he let it be ground up into nothing? The fields have been hauled away in trucks."

"He wasn't happy there," Fiona said.

"He was at times. At times."

The sound of the tractor was fading out beyond the rise.

"I guess you've been to the stone house," Munro said.

"I never have. I know it's there."

"Do you like comets?"

"How couldn't I?"

At the big rock behind his house he helped her up to the telescope, his hands shaping her waist. Fiona looked into the eyepiece where the stone house was supposed to be. He watched her looking, her hands on her bare prim knees. Something in the tension of the skin there made him want to touch her.

"It fair puts you right there, doesn't it?" she said. She tapped the barrel of the scope. "That could find mischief far and wide." She looked down at him. "Why the stone house?"

"My afternoon lies over there. Would you come along? We'll have a look."

Harald was returning over the hill. Lloyd David had hauled his ladder down and stood smoking a cigarette. He grinned at Munro as if they both shared some secret.

"But," Fiona said, "how would I fit into an afternoon like that?"

"Just fine." He gave her his hand and she hopped down off the rock. A strap of her blouse slipped down and Munro plucked it quickly back in place. "You see," he said, "I know the mood of that day. My father could go away again any moment he wanted to. His mother wasn't in the house anymore, cranky, dying." Munro looked at the tall, almost platinum grass beside his house, beautiful as a woman's hair. He'd told Lloyd David not to cut it, to leave it as it was. "My father had the smells of summer in that grass, that air. The women felt it too. So could we, I think."

A breeze rushed through the old maples along the hayfield, a warm sound in the leaves. The ripe hay shimmered. Crows roamed the stubble like portly deacons. Down on the road a red Lada crept past, Millie hugging the wheel.

"When?" Fiona said.

Since there was an old path, she let Munro and his excitement lead the way through the foothill woods until they stepped out into a meadow, clear except for a sprinkling of wild apple, gnarled and stunted by browsing deer.

"Up there!" Munro said. In the upper boundary of the meadow sat the ruins of the house, its stones the color of damp sand. It seemed to be merging with the ground. All these years and Fiona had never seen it: strange to look upon the open gut of it, all tumbledown, massed, grassed in, tufted with wildflowers. But then she had had no cause to come here before. Harald came haying but how would he have known she'd take an odd pleasure in beholding a stone house half broken back to where it came from? Munro pulled her away to a pair of apple trees so old they knelt, their trunks extending out like thick branches, and he sat her down in the tall, fine grass.

"My father's trees were straighter," he said. He was flushed and proprietary, as if all he saw were his. "These are hardly breathing. Leaves, but not a fruit on them."

"Och, they needed pruning and propping in their later years, and who was here to do it?" Harald tended their own small orchard, and Fiona loved the apple blossoms in June, the white perfume of a new summer. Rain scattered the petals like snow.

"This can be the place," Munro said. "I know it, I feel it."

"It is a place already. People worked here, lived here."

"I'll borrow it for a day. That's all right, isn't it?"

"If there's ghosts, I doubt they'd mind."

Munro was lighting a joint as if it were no more than a cigarette, his eyes absorbed in the flame.

"They might well mind that, though," Fiona said.

"You mean they never got high, these people? Can't believe it."

"I didn't say that. But I wouldn't think you'd need that stuff up here," she said.

"My father had a bottle up here." Munro hissed more smoke from the joint and blew it out in a long sigh. "Background music, Fiona. Here, try a little. We'll see things the same way."

"Thanks, no. I'm seeing fine."

He was on his feet and striding toward the ruined house. That smoke changed him, she could see that clear enough: he took a little turn of his own and left her a step behind. What was it like? She had to wonder. She liked his eyes, but they were too light sometimes, like water in a swimming pool, and she could imagine him leaning against a palm tree. But that was unfair. His long hair suited him somehow, carefully trimmed, and the rough clothes too, the denim shirts and jeans that made no distinction between leisure and work.

She followed him up the hill, drawn more to the house itself than to Munro's investigation. She knew stone houses, growing up in Harris they were all she knew. But here she had never seen one like this, rude as an old hearth. Two of the walls, thick with stacked stones of many sizes, were nearly intact, their outer surfaces sealed in a layer of rough mortar (some crude version of harling?), but the inner ones exposed like a tall fence of fieldstones, weathered and stained from rains and the earth they'd been pulled from (but chosen with the patient eye and hand of a stone setter), smaller ones (pebbles even) wedged between larger, all to complete this solid unwavering puzzle, this wall. At the corners, broken or joined, the stones had been dressed to fit flat. The lintels of the low, cramped windows were long, chiseled blocks. Never fancy, this house, but Highland skill and labor had formed it. The roof had long ago pitched itself into the living space, atumble with split timbers, gray as driftwood, and with broken stone. Among them grass and hardy flowers sprouted from sod clumps. Rubble from the collapsed sections had spilled into the fruitcellar, a cell-like pit lined with stones dressed into neat blocks like the lintels. But all was collapse now, a giving in. It must have been dark indeed, but she could attest there was nothing like two feet of stone between you and the world, a kind of safety, coming as she did from an island of wind. Wind cowered her mother's flowers, but howl as it might, the house did not budge. Only neglect could bring it down—an open roof, and no one caring.

"Look!" Munro was running his hands over an outer wall where lichen blossomed in bits of ochre. "Feel the *mass*. It's not like a wooden house going down at all, is it. See that?" Faint marks in the mortar. "Bird tracks."

She touched the wall. Odd what things stones had in them. St. Clements. On Harris, the church in Rodel so old it was worshipped rather than worshipped in. When she and her friend

Morag visited there, awed by its stone mysteries inside and out, it was two sculptures that forced their glances as they wandered the wild grass of the grounds, the tombs and graves: high above a door in the east wall were two lewd sandstone effigies, a woman squatting to display her unmistakable cunt (as plain as that) still swollen after four hundred years of blurring wind and water, and balancing her out was a male also embedded in the wall stones, gripping rigidly his huge implement as if he had hold of life itself. What was this lurid couple doing high up the wall of a church, papist though it had been, burial place of MacLeod chiefs? The devil put them there, if you ask me, Morag had said, and Fiona only laughed, knowing better.

"But what bird walks on walls?" Fiona said.

"There are birds you don't know about, my dear Fiona."

His eyes had taken on that abstracted, detached look she noticed the other night. The stones felt cool, like cave rock. She shivered. Munro brought his face close and when she didn't move, he kissed her mouth, her chin.

"They must've been lovely cozy in that house," he whispered.

"How lovely we'll never know," she said.

"We might, we might." He smiled and moved away into the foliage that hugged the ruins. She listened to him pushing through branches. "They must've had a garden or something here," he called back, his voice muffled in the trees, a different voice than he'd come up the hill with. She wished she had said no, had let him come alone, even that she had come herself alone, for she liked this place, liked the day, the feel of it. She hadn't kissed him, he had kissed her. She liked his mouth and that warm moment before the kiss, his eyes soft and blind, taken up with what was coming, a look she had not seen in so long she wasn't quite sure it was there. Kenneth was younger, a desirable man, a mystery of sorts—and yet not. How could she say what she was after in him? It was something beyond him, something maybe impossible, even unwise, to reach for. She caught again that smoke: a whiff of burnt grass.

Munro called out to her, "Yes, there has been a garden!" He was shaking the branches of a tall shrub. "See? Lilac!" At the tips of its bony, dead-gray stalks were dry but visible blossoms, and yes, it was in leaf. Lost in the slender fir trees they found a spindly rose bush too tall to be wild, and further away a single apple tree, hoary but filled with tiny green fruit. "They had flowers here," Munro said, "no doubt about it." Then they nearly stumbled over a low stone wall, disguised by grass, much of it, and what they could make out here and there showed it as an enclosure within which the wild trees had checked their growth, the birches almost thinly decorous, the spruce lightly branched and airy. "How strange," Fiona said. A walled garden behind a small farmhouse like this, in this country, walled not to keep anything out but just to define a place, to contain pleasure. No vegetables in this space, their potatoes and turnips would have ripened elsewhere. How strong the scent of flowers must have been in the midsummer air when the people of the house came walking here, the same people who hauled and chiseled and hoisted those great stones ten feet up for windows and walls. It would have been peaceful, for the men as well as the women, with the fields cleared, the wind off the water. She sat down on a mossy patch of wall and imagined the garden without the invading trees. Daisies bloomed at her feet. What other flowers of their own had they put in the ground? Was it the women of this stone house who planted them? She wanted to think it had been a man, the kind of man who, after grappling with stones in those hard days, would have, with a splayed finger, poked tiny seeds into the dirt of a flower garden.

Munro had knelt behind her and was parting, as he might a curtain, the back of her hair. He kissed her nape, and that was all she felt, just that sensation, unexpected, its surprise moving warm like wine into her face. She closed her eyes and turned her mouth to his. They slid down into the grass outside the wall. His fingers smelled of balsam, and very faintly of the lilac that had brushed him. Yes, the garden, and a coppery evening sun, the wind down, the flowers tense, waiting for night, birds merging into trees and leaves. She felt the warm sun on her legs, and then his fingers, almost cold so that she tensed and gave into him at the same moment, and it seemed they were sinking gently into the grass, she whispering to him but not words, his mouth hot through the cloth of her blouse as his breath moved down her waist. Then he stopped, his muscles hardening and he sat up out of her arms: "Someone's coming." Her own breath stopped, then she pulled her skirt down and smoothed it over her knees. Who was the someone coming? She didn't move. To flee would look more foolish than lying in the grass, a man on his knees next to you. In her daze she nearly laughed: oh Millie, turning her tongue on them both, fiercely, first at this suspect man who had surely tricked Fiona into the trees, and then at Fiona who would have to be some kind of a thing herself to lie down in the weeds with him in the middle of a working day. Lord, the racket in the teacups, sipping her name, and his, and Harald's. Fiona sat up but stirred no further, nor did Munro while feet tramped nearer and took the forms of Lloyd David and a pal, a taller boy Fiona didn't know, their voices preceding them, earnest but unintelligible in the noise of leaves and snapping branches as they ducked and staggered through the trees. Lloyd David was holding in his fingers a cigarette butt like a captured bug and the boys paused long enough to share its smoke, taking it gravely to their lips in turn. They were not look-ing for anyone, were headed elsewhere, heads down, intent, guileless, the woods just something to be got through. They passed within a few yards of Munro and Fiona, stumbling on, oblivious, their blue-jeans fading out into the thicker trees.

"He had a bottle in his back pocket, that squirt," Munro said. "God, I thought he was working with Harald."

"He was, this morning. He comes and goes."

Fiona brushed off her skirt and redid two buttons of her blouse, her fingers cool and clumsy. Over on a wall of the stone house a tree shadow swayed like a flame. She stood up: something had both happened and not happened. Munro lay back in the grass, his shirt open. There was a silver medallion in the thick hair of his chest.

"What was it my father used to say?" he said. " 'Hot as Scotch love'?"

She saw in his closed eyes, in their fluttering lids, something of the father in the photo: something that had to be satisfied, but never would be.

"You're looking pleased with yourself," she said. "Does it not bother you a wee bit?"

"Does what?" He got to his feet and climbed on the stones so he could see down the hillside.

"I'm married," Fiona said. "You do know the man. You have met him."

"I like Harald. He's a worker, he is. But what have we done, you and me?"

"Half what we would do, I suppose. Isn't that part of your 'afternoon'?"

"We don't have to make love . . . if you'd rather not."

"You're an arrogant man, you are. You know I like you, and like the feel of you. But there's an ache I'll carry home with me. I don't think you know anything about that. Do you feel it at all?"

"Feel what?"

"Guilt, they call it around here."

"Over *this*?"

"Somebody could be hurt over this."

"Nobody knows, nobody will. Lloyd David and his buddy were stoned blind." He jumped off the wall and put his face close to hers. "You have beautiful eyes, extraordinary eyes. And listen: I'll be gone in a month, less."

Munro went off down the hill to pick a spot for the next visit. The wind had turned and the weather with it, chilly out of the east, the sun gone behind rolling gray clouds. Fiona hung back. She picked up a chip of stone. How cold and damp this house must have been at times, here where the winters were so much colder than in Harris, deep frosts and blizzards. The night Harald brought her to St. Aubin it was winter and deeply cold, colder yet to her, a stranger. Harald soon put a fire in the old coal stove and she ran outside yelling into the snow, snow so cold it had bits of blue in it, and she stood there, panicked: a fire like that in a wooden house, wood from sills to rooftree? All she could think of were flames, creeping, then roaring up the walls. She soon enough felt the freezing air, Harald at the back door calling to her, laughing. Wood and paper, she'd thought, that's all this house is. But he came out into the windy snow and put himself around her like a cape. He said you're warmer now, aren't you? Aye, she said, let's go inside.

Munro beckoned to her from a heap of fieldstones in the meadow. "We'll have a picnic down here! Look at the soft grass!" He brushed his hand through it. Fiona wandered down, the chip in her fist.

"In the photograph," she said, "weren't they lying under an apple tree?"

"We're not slaves to the photo. It's the spirit we're after, Fiona. Besides, I've got to have a hand in it. I'm scripting this play. The original afternoon was as easy as living. Anyone can live. The hard part is ours."

A sweep of wind up the hillside brought a few hard, cold drops of rain.

"There were *two* women, in that picture," Fiona said.

"I have the other one," he said. "She's perfect."

Ginny was at the roadside, waiting against a tree. In a full red skirt and white blouse, there was a touch of peasant about her that he liked, the way she hailed him as she shouldered her bag: he might've been driving a bus. Beside him on the seat she was all talk and faint perfume, happy to be released from the restaurant, the duties of food. "Do I smell like a kitchen?" she said, brushing her rich brown hair. He said no, that she smelled like something he had never tasted but had always wanted to.

"You've been smoking, haven't you?" she said.

Munro smiled. He described the stone-house meadow as he drove, how perfect it was, the very place.

"And what happened to your dad's then?"

"Dug up and dispersed. There might be some of it under us right now."

"Gravel?"

"Gravel."

"Kenneth, I'm not sure who I'm supposed to be in this," she said. "The women in the picture were older than I am."

"But not prettier. I consider it a bonus. And you don't have to *be* anyone but yourself. The day will do the rest."

"But I'd like to visit the spot first."

Munro touched a fold of her skirt. "Of course. We'll go up there today."

Ginny said nothing more until they had turned onto the main highway at South Gut, passing the big motel that looked up the bay. Its restaurant's windows were cluttered with tourists and they reminded her somehow of busy chickens, feeding away, packed into that one place and cocking their heads now and then at the country around them.

"I should've worn jeans," she said, "if we're going in grass."

Munro accelerated up the mountain highway, praying the weather would hold.

Perfect? What did he mean?

Maybe he had said it only to get a rise out of her.

Fiona had not seen Munro up at his house since yesterday. Tonight the comet was due. Was he there and she'd missed his car? She picked up the phone. No. A foolish schoolgirl, wanting to hear his voice, thick with sleep even this late in the morning. What did other women do when a certain man set them wondering? Dream it out?

She set about dusting the parlor, but suddenly she flung the feather duster to the floor. What a silly object, and how silly she felt bustling around with it. Was there really another woman in this? Did he mean beauty? Youth? Someone more inclined to be the way he wanted? When they had parted that day, Fiona said yes, maybe she would meet him again at the stone house when the weather was to his liking, and it would be another step, her life into his. But a kind of acting, for a day, part of a day. And what would she say afterward, to herself, to him? Something would be altered for good. She liked being in his arms, no lie there. He was a different man and she could not get the details of him out of her mind, those she knew and those she might. Two days since they talked and she missed him, even the complication the sight of him brought.

But this other woman? Where? Fiona could not conjure her up. Why did he insist on this fantasy when common sense would tell him that his father was not out sporting with two women that afternoon, that surely there had been another man behind the lens of the camera? He couldn't wish him away, though perhaps he could smoke him away.

Kenneth had told her what the comet might look like, but her anticipation was not celestial. They would be up there alone. She would know before long whether she would go with him down below the stone house and be arranged in the grass according to an old photo, where Kenneth would be hoping to find what he was after, old moments he knew little about.

From the kitchen window she could see Harald starting in on the lower and last field, the felled hay a wake of darker green following him toward the shore. She knew the look he would be wearing: absorbed, contented, a slight smile as he rocked along in the sun, calm as a boatman. By the time he was done for the day it would be near dark, and later she would spot him up in the hayloft, the bare light bulb throwing shadows around him.

Did Kenneth mean the *two* of them, to have herself and that nameless woman, both . . . ?

Fiona went out to her flower bed and weeded furiously, panting with amazement, trying to will images out of her mind before they dizzied her daft. My lover? *Mo gràdh?*

After lunch she walked up to the mailbox. Millie pulled up slowly in her car and spoke out the window.

"They caught a bunch of smugglers last night," she said, out of breath as if she'd been running instead of driving. "Along the north shore. Drugs, bales of it."

Fiona sorted through letters. "Anyone we know, Millie?"

"They were Americans, wouldn't you know! The ones behind it. And mainlanders."

Fiona could feel what was coming. Her cheeks were already hot and she ripped open an ad for weedkiller instead of looking at Millie.

"Well, anyway," Millie said. She revved the engine a little. "What about that Munro fellow over there? What did you find?"

Fiona nearly said I found your son in the woods and he wasn't hunting rabbits. "He'll be going home soon, Millie, so don't concern yourself."

She took her anger into the house, anger with herself, with everything. Not the day to have run into Millie Patterson. She banged around upstairs, cleaning their bedroom that did not need it. This was a big house but why did it seem so small, so cramped? Soon she was standing at the picture window: its view was clean and wide and took in miles up and down the strait. The water lay out blue and sheer on a slack tide. Without meaning to, she was staring at that part of the mountain where she had been with him. She could see the patch of field, and some flicker of movement there, deer, or dogs. She reached for Harald's field glasses, the powerful ones he spotted ships with. She moved the circle of vision up and down until she found them. Kenneth, for sure. And a girl with him. Kenneth was jogging ahead, towing her along by the hand. They'd soon be breathless at that clip. But she was young. And he young enough yet to take a hill on a beautiful afternoon. She watched them tumble into the grass and lie there like children, their arms flung open to the sky. Was he handing her something, like a flower? It was not a flower. Fiona was aware of her own eyes against the glasses, of the weight of them in her hands, and she set them back on the sill. Munro and the girl were up and running now, flecks of color on the green hill, but she didn't care to look at them any closer again. They'd be heading for the stone house, for the lovely ruins of the garden. You're making a mistake, she wanted to tell this girl, you don't know that man at all. But how stupid: Fiona did not know him either, and the girl was free to be foolish if she wished. And what did that girl, so much younger than herself, see in Kenneth Munro? What made her take his hand and disappear into the trees of that mountain? When they parted, what would she take away? Humbled that she had no answers, Fiona stepped back into the shadow of the room, a vague ache in her chest. Along the shoreline, Harald's tractor was passing against the strait, rocking like a boat over the uneven ground, while, unknown to him, Lloyd David danced a distance behind, spinning in circles, flinging cut hay into the air like flowers.

"Are you coming up to Kenneth Munro's? The comet is on." Fiona stood over Harald in his easy chair. "It's a right clear evening for it." She half wanted him to say yes because that might make things easier but he said no, and her heart shifted.

"I'm whacked out, dear. Anyway, what's come of your investigation up there? Was the man inhaling terrible fumes or what was he doing?"

"There's nothing there Millie need fash herself about, or anyone else either," she said with more heat than she'd intended.

Harald smiled. "I just wondered where the comets might be coming from."

"That's more than I can say. Where do they usually?"

"Oh, I guess there's all kinds," Harald said, getting up.

Fiona glanced through the curtains. "That comet, it won't come around again for sixty years," she said.

Harald kissed her as he passed. "Then we'll both miss the next one. Eh?"

She skirted the house where he'd left his lamp on, briefly annoyed that he would carelessly burn a light all day while he was off with the girl who was perfect. It illuminated the table by the front window where he did his reading and snacking, and smoking too, no doubt. Out back on the big rock the telescope waited, a spindly silhouette in the deep blue of the night. He had aimed it where he figured the comet would appear, not in the direction of the stone house but somewhere over the westerly woods. The smell of the mown grass lifted with the wind. Frogs in the spring pond chirped like sleepy birds but they were well awake. In the humid nights of the last week she had heard them shrill at the fitful corners of her sleep. The telescope trembled on its thin legs and she steadied it, startled by the cold metal. He wasn't coming.

She tried the back door and of course it was open. Hadn't she herself told him you needn't lock up here like you would in San Francisco? She moved slowly through the darkened kitchen and its spicy smell she didn't recognize, into the lighted living room where his things lay about as he'd left them, trench coat tossed across the sofa (it smelled of the rain he'd worn it in), a few empties of Old Scotia Ale on the table, reeking of stale malt, a dinner plate holding two bits of butt-ends (how could he have smoked them to nubs like that? She flicked her tongue over her lips). She thumbed through his bird book, noted the kinds he'd checked off in the index. Had he really seen a Tennessee Warbler? She had never heard of one, but then he saw things here that she did not, perhaps could not, without smoking those leaves. There was visible dust on the bureau and she ran her finger through it, tempted to write him a mischievous message but realizing she had passed that stage with him. She hefted the walking stick he had whittled from a driftwood branch. Stacked neatly were letters in a woman's hand but she did not disturb them. A magnifying glass, a book about stargazing, a jar of peanuts uncapped. Harald would distrust this sort of leisure. What Harald was not using he put away in sheds or chests or closets. He would never surround himself with things as idle as these. There were no leavings of his pleasure for others to peruse. But Kenneth's were all over this house. And there was the photograph.

Stretched out in the grass, stripped to the waist of his baggy trousers, the father looks somehow naked. The women's bare legs are sexy in a way now lost, Fiona thinks. A bottle of liquor is propped against the apple tree. The tree needs pruning badly. All those years he had been under his mother's stern and jealous eye, but today no one watches him from the house. And the land, now his, is turning wild. He is free to drink inside the house or out, to play in the unruly grass of his own fields, to ignore the decaying roof, the spoor of hunters (surely that's their work—the splintered door, the riddled pail), the stealthy trees new in the distance. He's free, as dusk comes down, to steal back toward his old bedroom where wind sighs through shot-out windows, his shoes crunching over glass, a finger to his lips, mocking his mother's prohibitions. Drink, drink, drink, he wants to shout in the dark hallway, the woman behind him hugging his back, giggling with a fear she hardly understands, there in that summer twilight that smells of damp and age. He cups his ear. He pretends, for a laugh, that his mother lies listening down the hall. And of course she does, even now; years after her death she is still in this house, and even on the slashed stuffing of his old mattress, in a desolate smell of winter and wet cotton where he makes the kind of noises he never dared, like love in a storm, he feels her hard rain on his back. And this his son will never know, will never see.

Fiona turned out the light.

On the rock, she put her eye to the telescope, holding down her skirt. Kenneth said it would have no fizzing tail, it wasn't that kind of comet. Far from flashing across the sky, its motion seemed little more than a waver, like a star, just brighter, more restless and low in the sky. Wasn't just the word charged with speed and color? Was it something like that he got from his smoke, from that brittle smell? The comet flared, south of west. She let her skirt go, the gusts took it away from her legs and whipped it about. If she turned the telescope toward the stone house, she wouldn't see anything now but the cold, yawning walls, heavy as dreams.

When she got into bed, she lay looking out the big window at the end of the room. Harald stirred beside her. "Did you see it?" he said. Fiona could tell from his voice that he'd been sleeping.

"The tail was magnificent. Fiery. The way you'd think it would be."

"Streaked across the sky, did it?"

"No," she said. "No, it took longer than that."

Harald touched her face, then turned back into sleep.

She remembered waking one cold, cold February morning, unaware that Harald had wakened too. From their pillows they could see that the water of the Great Bras D'Eau had vanished, become a long white field. The men had not laid down a bush-line yet but someone was crossing the new ice anyway, a woman, making her way slowly over the rough snow of the surface, her trail as fragile as a bird's. Her danger seemed to enter the room, and they watched her, she and Harald, saying nothing about her, this dark, tiny figure. They never saw where she came ashore, and they never found out what woman she was, coming so early, and finding her own way across.

THE CHINESE RIFLE

D. J. was never afraid of anyone. He wouldn't back down from King Kong, I remember thinking, the time we stayed with Aunt Sadie, his mother, one summer after World War II. In Boston on the way up my mother had bought me a loud sportshirt which I refused to wear in Glace Bay, a Cape Breton mining town of some size. Though only eleven, I knew that a shirt of yellow palm leaves on a sky-blue background would, along the dirt streets of the New Aberdeen Colliery, be akin to carrying a flag that said, "Please Taunt Me! Please Call Me Names!" D. J. was nineteen and had grown up in the dark company houses a short distance from the pithead. He played rugby and hockey in high school and was to me in every way a man, despite the glasses he wore. When we'd walk out in the evenings, he'd exchange remarks with hard-looking boys lounging against faded picket fences, or he'd ignore them, depending on how he felt about them. I was comfortable with him (there were names like mine in Glace Bay and a network of relatives) and he was good about conducting me around: in the tiny store across the street (no more than a converted parlor in a miner's house) we'd play the pinball machine with funny Canadian nickels, or we'd go swimming at the base of a steep cliff where sometimes the ocean foamed dangerously over the plank diving board bolted into the rock (he told me there were miners miles away out there, working deep under the sea). Our weekly showers (company houses had no bathrooms) we took at the colliers' wash house, a huge place empty of miners that time of night, their street clothing, to keep it from dust, tied on the ends of ropes and clustered high up against the ceiling as if it had risen there on its own.

But finally my mother insisted I wear the bright shirt: she knew it had been a mistake but with characteristic stubbornness she made me bear the burden. "It's a perfectly good shirt," she said, buttoning me into it, but I felt I may as well be naked. At least I wouldn't have to endure it alone. D. J. was taking us to a movie down on Commercial Street with the two-dollar bill I'd won for the best pinball score of the week and I was proud to be treating him. As we walked to the bus, he told me how his dad, a colliery mechanic, had, that afternoon, wired back together the broken peg leg of an ex-miner, how years ago the man had lost his real leg when it slipped between the spokes of a mine car wheel, the wheel tumbling him along until it twisted his limb off at the knee. "I'd rather lose my life than my leg," D. J. said, and I nodded glumly. We passed a pond layered with coal scum and I thought I might dip my shirt in it a few times or simply fall into it myself. I stayed close to my cousin as if he might diffuse the colors a bit, but only too soon I heard a shout: "Hey, Sundown!" The sharp brogue, readymade for jeering, cut deep. My face burned. Before, I had blended in and now I was being scorned, all because of a ridiculous shirt. I walked faster, hoping only to survive. But D. J. had already turned back. My tormentors—his age or older, most of them—were gathered under a tree by the roadside, cawing and hooting and bored enough on this hot summer evening to be mean just for the hell of it. I could see their lean faces in the streetlight, hands cupped to their mouths. Suddenly I heard D. J.'s voice rise above them: "You want to say that again?" he said. "You want to lose some teeth?" I was stunned. This was no D. J. I'd seen before, my congenial cousin who'd been uncondescending to me, whose mild blue eyes seemed incapable of anger. Now I envisioned this mob of boys swarming over us, ripping my foolish shirt to rags and leaving us bloodied in the dirt. Yet, there was D. J. standing in front of them, his chin out and his hands in fists, and apart from sniggers and whispers nobody ventured out of the shadows to meet him; not until we were well down the road did they dare to yell again. I knew then that D. J. already had a reputation, and that in a town of tough colliers and tough sons, he had earned it by deeds. He could, as the saying went, stand the gaff. I felt great, part of something powerful.

I thought, though how could I say for sure (who of us knows much of anything about suicide?), that Karl, D. J.'s son, had this image too of his father: a kind, soft-spoken man who nonetheless need never be menaced by anyone or anything, and from whom you yourself could take strength.

I was delighted two years later when D. J. came down from Nova Scotia to live with us in Ohio. Like other Cape Breton men, he was after work on the lake boats, decking on Great Lakes' ore freighters. My dad was a mate and helped him find a berth, and my mother boarded him as she had his older brother and three other cousins before him. When he laid up that winter and came home with my dad, it was like having a brother around. He told me about his stint as a cadet with the Mounties (he didn't like the long restriction on marrying). He made me a gift of his brown and gold rugby shirt after showing me snapshots of the pitch he'd played on in Glace Bay—a dirt field—and of his fellow players, all sporting bloody knees. There have been times I wished I still had that shirt, but when you're a kid you let things like that get away from you. Underneath his photograph in his yearbook it read: "His limbs were cast in manly mold/ For hardy sports and contests bold." He could lie flat on the floor with a tumbler of water balanced on his forehead and slowly stand up without spilling a drop. I had to get his biscuits at mealtime because his hand was too wide for the mouth of the jar. We boxed, he in a deep crouch, just parrying. We listened to Red Skelton on the radio and, being a fair mimic like my dad, I did imitations for him of the punchdrunk prizefighter and the mean little kid. When my mother was away one night, he introduced me to beer, pouring me a glass with great ceremony and making me a salami and raw onion sandwich to go with it. But then he bought himself a 1942 Buick Special with a pushbutton radio and hydramatic and I saw much less of him. He was pursuing the ladies (on certain afternoons he met a married woman in a motel), a pastime I had no sympathy with, and he would roll in late from bars. Sometimes I'd find him gruff and hungover at the kitchen table, my mother icily silent as he sipped his coffee like castor oil. But he did come to the YMCA with me one morning where we shot baskets in the old gym. In the pick-up game D. J. was keener to get us working as a team than he was to shoot his set shot. But his sharp passes and his presence made me play above my head. At home he collapsed on the couch, coughing, laughing. "I'll be sore tomorrow, boy. I'm too old for this."

But for the Korean War he was just the right age and they drafted him that spring before he could report to the Lakes. Of course, he could have returned to Glace Bay and avoided the draft altogether, but he intended to do better than the mines and a secondhand Buick. We were all concerned about him. There were stories of undertrained G. I.s being rushed into combat and prisoners shot in the back on capture or tortured in horrible cells. The Chinese had come in on the North Korean side and driven the Americans back below the 38th Parallel; *Life* magazine showed us pictures of soldiers scattered dead along frozen ditches, hands bound behind their backs. The winter war in Korea seemed particularly cruel and harsh. D. J. tore a photograph from the newspaper and pinned it up in his bedroom: a kilted Highlander, part of the British contingent, in battle dress, a dirk strapped to his leg. "I'd sign up for that outfit if I could. I wouldn't mind Korea so much, being piped into it."

He didn't need a piper. Almost from the first day of basic training he was put in charge of others, going from platoon leader to corporal in a few weeks. From there on he advanced as quickly as the army could oblige. When he came home on leave he was already a staff sergeant assigned to the engineers. We were glad because chances were he'd be serving behind the front lines. In his Eisenhower jacket and trousers bloused over his glossy combat boots he looked every inch the stripes on his sleeve. Since I was too young for his Buick, he turned it over to my sister Peggy who drove it to Cleveland where she worked. But D. J. promised me something from overseas and I knew he would come through. When he reached Korea he was a first sergeant, and a master sergeant by the end of his first year in the army.

His letters, which he signed "love and stuff," were an event for me. In his neatly slanting hand he wrote about his duties in a place called Sopa, about turning down a commission because he preferred the authority he had to that of a lowly lieutenant. He unofficially adopted a Korean boy ("There are so many orphans around here it would make you sick"), paying for his upkeep (he was also keeping a Korean woman, I learned only later, he not wanting to scandalize my mother or his), seeing the kid was fed and clothed and went to school. I was not a little jealous since the boy was about my age, and he was there amid the dangers of war receiving favors from Master Sergeant D. J. MacKenzie while I trudged off to Park Junior High. But a letter arrived that lit up my attention: D. J. and a buddy had found two slightly damaged Chinese rifles near the front lines. He cannibalized parts from one to fix the other. "It fires fine now," he wrote, "but ammunition is hard to come by." It was earmarked for me and he would try his best to bring it home. I dreamed of that rifle, of carrying it in my hands, an amorphous weight without features or utility but yet a connection to my cousin, to a strange place and what he was doing there.

When he came home on leave a year later I was too shy and excited to meet him at the door. Home sick from school, I feigned sleep on the couch until he came into the room. Standing over me he seemed even bigger, his garrison cap cocked to the side; he'd grown a red moustache. I knew he'd moved far ahead of me and there'd be no more tricks in the kitchen or pick-up games at the Y. But there was the rifle: he held it out to me, its metal dull, the wooden stock dark and weathered. "Buried," he said, "two of them, covered with cosmilene. I don't know why they were there." It looked scarred, foreign, nothing like the hunting rifles I had seen or the ones soldiers carried in the movies. "Coming stateside," he said to my mother, "we had to exchange our clothes and there I was standing buck naked in a line holding *this.* Some thirty-day wonder tried to take it away from me but I had the papers and he finally said keep the goddamn thing." I was fascinated by the slender bayonet that folded back flush against the muzzle, unlike the kind G. I.s carried in sheaths and affixed to their rifles on command. To me, Chinese had been quiet men in silk, their hands clasped harmlessly beneath baggy sleeves. What would a Chinese sergeant yell? D. J. had filed away the identifying marks but there remained a faint ideogram or two. On the barrel I could make out a hammer and sickle and I touched it with awe: in my youth it was a symbol of evil, imbued with an almost mystical danger. That night D. J. showed me how to break the rifle down, advising me not to fire it empty because that was hard on the pin. "It kicks like a horse," he said.

In shop class at school I made a pair of wooden mounts and hung the rifle above my bed. "If that ever fell, it would kill you," my mother said, not liking guns from the start. But I had no shells for it and so she got used to seeing it on the wall. I'd take it down sometimes to show my friends. Alan up the street wore one of those gaudy silk jackets we all coveted, a fiery dragon embroidered on the back of it along with the name of his brother's unit. But it was no match for a Chinese rifle. Now we all knew about the human wave attacks used by the Chinese troops—masses of yowling men in earflapped hats and quilted clothing, surging toward you over a field of thin and crispy snow.

We heard less often from D. J. There were rumors of a truce and he thought he might stay in the army. But one cold and rainy night my sister went into a skid in his Buick, slamming into a tree at the bottom of a steep hill. Suddenly our house became a turmoil of alarm: her internal injuries were critical and threatened her life. I shuddered every time the phone rang. My mother's tears, which I had once expected might be shed over a distant D. J., were shed for my own sister, her condition immediate and close and frightening. I felt for the first time the fear of grief, as if I were becoming unmoored, growing lighter: love had weight and losing any of it could set you adrift. But after weeks in the hospital Peggy came home and recuperated in a rented hospital bed in our den. Because her pelvis had been badly fractured, her left leg would be shorter than the right. She cried over that at first, but said to me one evening as we listened to the radio:

"Boys my age died in Korea, lots of them." D. J. told her to forget about the car, totalled and uninsured. "It's just a lump of metal, girl, and you're alive."

Although he was weary of Korea after the truce, he signed up for another hitch because the army promised him a transfer to Germany. He wrote to me occasionally while I was in high school and college. "I live pretty well here and I can travel, so it's not a bad life for a sergeant." He involved himself with a foster home whose orphans had been maimed or crippled in the war, taking them on excursions and being "ein Onkel." But there were hints that he was getting restless in the army. To stay in, he said, he would risk turning into a sergeant he knew, "fat and cynical, an alcoholic lifer." Besides, he had been going with a German woman, Katrin. Just before he finished his tour of duty they married and I lost touch with him.

The year I left graduate school I came home to find my room done over, the rifle gone from the wall. Knowing I would never be living there again, my mother had reclaimed the bedroom. I went to the basement where the rifle lay on the toolbench, solitary in the cleared space my dad, away on the Lakes, used only in the winter. In spring, he left everything seaman-neat, racked and stowed. But the rifle was not his (he was not a hunter and owned no guns), and so he had set it out here apart as if it required some kind of decision. The cellar was damp and cobwebby, the fearful grey spiders safe for the summer in their mossy nests. The rifle had once seemed heavy, resting in my hands, but now it was light, its barrel cold in the cool basement. I aimed it at the window above the bench, at the pane dirty with rain-splashed dust, and pulled the trigger. I flinched at the pin's snap but the only kick was in my imagination: a Chinese soldier had fired this and I knew nothing at all about his mind, about what he thought when he fixed an enemy in his sights. Had he been swept along in one of those human wave attacks, running with comrades who carried not this weapon at all but maybe, as some did, only wooden rifles, their lives cheaper than guns? Did he write to a son, brother, cousin in those oddly beautiful ideograms of love and war? Did he bury it in that shell hole, or fling it away in dying? But here it was in a darkened basement in a town on the shore of Lake Erie, the butt-plate cold against my shoulder, and I knew I would never shoot it even if I had the ammunition. I pulled back the bolt and laid the rifle on the bench. I could see D. J. in Korea, scooping away the dirt with his hands, exposing maybe the stock first, the wood, or the machined gleam of the barrel, then lifting it carefully, brushing it off, sighting it into the sky. It would have smelled of the ground it came out of.

I was hired into the editorial department of a small publishing house outside of Boston. I enjoyed the work—devising and editing ESL texts—although the publisher himself seemed capricious and eccentric, the result, I was told, of his having been indulged by a wealthy aunt and of his affection for Jack Daniels. But down the road he saw big things for his small company and he urged me to be a part of it all: he found me promising. I was ambitious enough to take this to heart, and so I was busy those early years determining clear ways to present tense-aspect systems and modal auxiliaries, returning home for infrequent visits too brief to include D. J. and his wife. A quick study as a carpenter, he'd become a construction foreman with a company that built freeway bridges around Cleveland. Katrin had two miscarriages but he never mentioned them in his rare and laconic letters. Ohio was drifting away from me, and the country became enmired in a war I was too old to go to. We were beyond that sorry conflict, D. J. and I, at least directly. Viet Nam did not lay a hand on us the way World War II or Korea had: we didn't wait for telegrams, and there was no souvenir from the place I could imagine wanting. "I'm glad I'm out of it," D. J. wrote the week of the Tet Offensive, "and besides Katrin just had a boy. Some problems, but they're doing well." He asked me to be godfather, but I was about to depart for Japan and had to miss the christening. I sent Karl John a silver cup engraved with his name and the MacKenzie coat of arms.

In Tokyo I learned Japanese etiquette and landed ESL contracts that put the company, for the first time, well into the black. At a sumo match my thoughts wandered to my new cousin: would he be flower and iron like his dad? Who would he need to be afraid of? On the way back I nearly bought him a tiny Hawaiian shirt in Honolulu but ended up with one my size which I wore bravely on the street and then stuffed into my suitcase.

My father died, and then my mother, events so close together that I was still staggering a little from the first one. On a trip home to settle the estate, I roamed through the house just before it was sold, lamenting the work my dad had put into it all his winters home, soon to be lost to us. In the basement a few tools lay about but not the Chinese rifle. Somehow I wanted to see it, to recall its details. I picked up a hammer and a stray nail and drove it flush into the bench. Upstairs, bare except for some pieces of furniture nobody wanted, the rooms sat nearly blank. We had come here from Nova Scotia, from Cape Breton, my family, all of us just before World War II. In the New Aberdeen Colliery there were still MacKenzies, and in the country my dad was from, MacLeods and Corbetts. But in this town we were extinguished. Nothing of us would remain with this place but two small, almost anonymous gravestones that would go unvisited in a burial park where no flowers were allowed.

My sister arrived and we drank instant coffee in the living room, sitting on two kitchen chairs. Our voices echoed as they had the first day we'd moved in. Peggy had divorced and was moving to Chicago. She wore a slightly elevated heel you hardly noticed when she walked. In the allocation of things she had given the Chinese rifle to D. J.

"I think he hunts, doesn't he?" she said.

"I doubt that he'd hunt with that, dear."

"Besides, he asked about it, if it was still here in the house."

I had never considered taking the rifle. It didn't seem to belong to me, and I would never bring anything down with it. Even firing it was inconceivable anymore—its sound, the notion of its bullet entering man or animal or even falling harmlessly to earth.

"Just as well D. J. has it," I said. "You're looking good, Peggy."

"I have bad headaches but apart from that. . . ." She sipped her coffee. "You're not a marrying man, I guess, John."

"Married to my work, it seems. I have what I need."

Through the stripped and yawning window I saw two black teenagers, a girl and a boy, walking the middle of the street in a way none of us, my pals and I, would have done, never with that air of possession.

"You knew D. J.'s boy had another operation on his legs."

"For what?"

"He was born with deformed legs. He's had several operations already, difficult ones. He has to recuperate for weeks and weeks in a body cast. I hear he's very brave about it."

I wrote to D. J. expressing my concern but he was vague about the matter, clearly not keen to discuss it. "He's a fine kid but he gets down on himself sometimes, naturally. It's a tough world to be lame in."

Over the following years as Karl grew up, it was my sister who kept me up to date on his struggle to keep walking. I wondered where they went off to together in that city, he and his dad. Did they play pinball somewhere? Did they swim in dangerous places? Yet on a Christmas card D. J. spoke of one day returning to Cape Breton, not to Glace Bay but somewhere in the country where our mothers were from. He didn't say why but I felt Karl had something to do with it.

Apart from holiday messages we had no contact for some years. I was senior editor at Rowland House and had long been looking forward to a partnership with the publisher, had in fact, between his more serious bouts of drinking, been encouraged in such a hope—a reward for the contracts I had brought in and the promised bonuses so long deferred, as well as for my indispensability, my discretion. I was one of the best editors in the business now, but I was beginning to realize that I had labored too long for a man who was both blundering and lucky and who sometimes looked at me as if I were a pane of glass between him and something he desired. Behind the orderly exterior of Rowland House there was often chaos while a near-mutinous staff tried to contain his latest binge of bad decisions. But the sporadic successes of his company (we had just come out with an ESL teacher's text that would be the bible for years) only deepened his conviction that his genius had brought them about, an opinion he could charmingly project, when it mattered, to interested listeners.

While in Frankfurt that fall I heard a rumor that he intended to sell the company. I remember breaking out in a sweat and leaving the restaurant: it was like news of a family disaster—stunning, disheartening.

I flew home from Germany and confronted him on a lovely October afternoon when I could see the splendid maples turning color in the window behind his desk. I was wearing my Hawaiian shirt, its bright collar open wide against the pinstripes of a dark three-piece suit. I thought, good God, this tall, stoop-shouldered, shambling man in bluejeans and a tweed coat is only a few years my senior, but I allowed my future to be placed in his fluttering hands without any specific promises, without any legal contract or obligation, and now his word is vanishing before my eyes. He denied it at first, then, as guilt can make you do, he began to bully and rave. His eyes grew dull: I was ungrateful, disloyal, disruptive, and he could fire me on the spot. He waved his arms toward the wooden cabinet on his wall where expensive shotguns were racked. I'd always known he was a little crazy but I had ridden with that, even been amused by it at times. But now I was no longer his valued editor who brought money to his company and cleaned up his messes but just someone who might stand between him and a great deal of profit, a nuisance, dispensable. He sneered at my shirt. "Maybe there's an opening in Tonga," he said. I told him he would have to kill me before I would leave the room, that he had turned into a lower form of life. He leapt for the cabinet, pulled out a shotgun and yelled, get out, get out. I did. I wished I had the Chinese rifle right there in my hands and my madness might have matched his own. The ugliness of that scene I could never forget, and what it taught me it taught me too late. Three months afterward he sold Rowland House to a big New York publisher and all of us who worked there received a lesson in the magic of the marketplace: not only was his profit considerable, he was hired as a consultant at a high fee while his employees were set adrift without so much as severance pay. The new company offered me a position, but it meant a move to New York City to work under others, a move deeper and harder than any I'd made. I felt beaten up, but unwilling to give in. I took time off to find my way. I wanted to visit my cousin D. J., the man who had said, you want to say that again? You want to lose some teeth? And I wanted to see his son.

They lived in Lake Village, an older suburb near the shore. I was relaxed that day, released somehow as the taxi took me through the streets. What struck me about the neighborhood were the trees: tall and narrow and, considering the houses, dense, high in the air. Up above, it was like a thinned-out woods, but below, the homes were arranged conventionally along the blocks. The light that fell through the leaves that afternoon reminded me of a Sunday when I was a boy and went with a pal to see *All Quiet on the Western Front.* All day the light had been strange even though no one said much about it: it was like looking at the world through yellow cellophane and it gave me an odd feeling, as if something were wrong but the only clue was the light and no grown-ups seemed alarmed. And then the movie too was an unusual shade—not black and white but brownish—and so bleak and alien, with no speaking, just subtitles. The soldier reaching for the butterfly at the end came back to me in dreams, his cupped hands reaching out while the French sniper fixed that young German's death in his gunsights. When we came out of the movie—not like any movie I had ever seen—the sky had turned a deep amber that permeated everything with a strange dreariness, not of coming night but of something utterly unfamiliar, and now I could feel the unease around us as people stopped on the sidewalk and gestured toward the sky. On Monday a nun at my pal's school told him and his classmates that the weird light of the day before signified that the world had started to end and that they ought to mend their ways. Our neighbor said it was the atomic testing and that, high up, the air itself was beginning to burn. But a few days later we found out there'd been a huge forest fire in Canada and the smoke had drifted hundreds of miles, tinting the atmosphere that disquieting color, like film yellowing. This information set our world right again, but the fear and mystery never went away.

When I arrived they were gathered—all but Karl—in the backyard, Katrin, D. J., and Katrin's father visiting from Germany. "It's his last," she told me. "He's eighty and won't come again." Her eyes were a deep brown, her blonde hair cut short. She looked young but thin and nervous. D. J. was a supervisor now in the construction company, the only supervisor without a college degree, Katrin added. His build had thickened, his wavy hair gone iron grey, and there were bifocals in his glasses. But I was so pleased to see him, to hear his voice, it seemed that everything around us was dim and diffused, out of focus. From somewhere in the house a bagpipe record was playing but not loud. The father spoke no English, nor did his goddaughter who'd made the trip with him because he wasn't well, a woman in her sixties, plump and self-effacing. Her hands folded in her lap, she stayed in a chair by the fence pretending to sun herself until she rose with a smile to help in the kitchen. We sat around a small white table on the lawn and Katrin translated for Herr Schrader, but the conversation soon grew awkward, her dad speaking to me but looking at her. He wanted to place me in the family, to know how I figured in the equations D. J. had altered in Germany. He didn't like sitting for long, Katrin explained, and soon he got up and paced the yard. He walked with a slight limp and would stop and stare into the high trees whose tops moved restlessly in the afternoon wind. "He used to be so easy to please." Katrin said. "He gets cranky now."

"He's waiting around to die," D. J. said. "I'd be cranky too."

"No, not you," I said.

The father had fought on the eastern front when already a middleaged man. Captured by the Russians in a vicious winter battle, he'd spent hard time in a p. o. w. camp. "It was terrible," Katrin said, looking at him in the corner of the yard where he stood with his hands in his pockets, his back to us. I felt I had dropped into the center of something I could not understand but that yet I needed, that in this chair under these trees, things might work out for me. I drank two German beers quickly. D. J. stood up and I knew the boy had come out of the house.

From the waist up Karl could have passed for a small, young version of his dad—his arms and chest muscular, his hair curly and dark. But his legs were withered under his jeans and bowed in at the knees. He held his back ramrod straight to counter the sway of his walk.

"Karl, meet your cousin," D. J. said. "John and me had some fun years ago."

Karl took my hand firmly. Behind his glasses he had his mother's eyes, but up close I could see some hurt there, something brightly defiant and guarded.

"You used to stay with him at home, in Glace Bay, my dad said."

"Oh, it was good there. I enjoyed just being around him. He was a tough hombre, your dad, so I always felt safe."

"Safe from what?"

I laughed. "Well, from everything that's out there, when you're a kid."

He hooked his thumbs in his jeans and waited as if for elaboration. I assumed that D. J., like any dad, had recounted exploits to his son, and he had more than a few to offer.

"D. J., remember the time you were home on leave?" I said. "You told me about the guy in your barracks, the weightlifter who was always needling you about your accent?"

"I got the drop on him is all," he said, almost shyly. He and Karl stood a few feet apart. With his thumbnail D. J. peeled the label from his bottle of lager. He sighed. "Oh, he was up in the top bunk mouthing off . . . it was dark. I just waited for his feet to hit the deck, and then. . . ."

I didn't heed his frame of mind and I pushed on, thinking Karl would like it, that we shared this much at least.

"When he was living with me, your dad went into a bar one night, all dressed up. Sportcoat, tie. On your way to a date, eh, D. J.? This guy playing pool with his buddies starts calling your dad Mr. Peepers and won't quit. D. J. thinks to hell with this and leaves, but this character follows him outside, comes running after him into the parking lot all the way to his car. Your old man finally wheels around and puts this fellow down, boom boom. Two overhand rights."

Karl glanced at his father quickly, appraisingly. "You told him that, Dad?"

D. J. shrugged. "Could be. I was young then. What's a fist good for anymore? A jerk like him would have a gun."

I almost asked him, then what would you do, but I held back. I didn't want his answer to matter.

"Karl, would you like a coke?" Katrin said.

"That's okay. I'll get it."

"Sit and talk."

"I'm fine."

As he moved off toward the back door I noticed his shirt-sleeves rolled up to his biceps. D. J. could have taught him a punch or two, I thought, with arms like that. We were all watching him.

"He's had so many operations," Katrin whispered, turning to me. "He thought they were over but he has to have another one soon. He'll be all right. He knows we love him. He knows that."

"He doesn't want it," D. J. said. "'I won't go through another one.' He's never said that before. Hell, he's the one who used to cheer *me* up."

Katrin leaned forward in her chair. "He just got his driver's license, John. The car has special controls. He looks so good in the car, doesn't he, D. J.?"

D. J. seemed to slump for a moment. "Yes, yes, he does. But driving isn't what he thought it would be."

I wanted to contribute some wisdom to this discussion of their son, but I knew almost nothing about Karl or about kids in general. In the house the bagpipe record stopped.

"D. J., do you still have that Chinese rifle, the one you brought back from Korea?"

"Sure. Peggy gave it back to me. She said you wouldn't mind, since you'd left it there."

"I thought it meant more to you, that you might want to pass it on."

"No, no. I keep it in my closet. It's all cleaned up though. You want to see it?"

"Did you hunt with it? Bring anything down?"

"I quit hunting after Karl was born. I lost my taste for it."

When he was gone into the house, Katrin said, "Karl was teased cruelly in school, you know. All the way along. So many times he'd come home and I could tell he'd been crying but he wouldn't cry in front of me. Oh, I never told D. J., never once. I was afraid he'd go after them, or their fathers. You see, he never acted tough in front of Karl, never talked about that even. He didn't want Karl to . . . to feel weak, to feel he had to be strong the way his dad was. I don't think he ever saw D. J. make a fist, let alone use it."

The goddaughter approached with a tray of sandwiches and set them in front of us. We thanked her, me in English, Katrin in German, and she smiled and stepped back like a servant. The odd light of the afternoon altered the garden, the tone of leaf and petal. The beer was strong and I drank it greedily. The treetops were dark as cut-outs against the saffron air above them. Suppose as a boy I had been lame? How would we have walked those Glace Bay streets? Cliffs would have been forbidden. The merest venture would have been dangerous and assessed by everyone. Near the fence, the goddaughter and Herr Schrader talked, their faces incomprehensible in the shade.

D. J. returned holding the rifle at his chest, not in a soldierly way but as if he had just unearthed it and together we would decide what it was. Karl came out behind him and stood watching as his father set the rifle in my lap. He had refinished the stock so that the grain shone with oil, and the polished barrel gleamed. My hands hovered over its brightness: there seemed no way to hold it properly. I sniffed the different oils, the faint scent of gunpowder that still clung to it. I wished later that I had taken the rifle up and told him, this is mine, D. J., you gave it to me, a gift from the war, and I must have it back, I want to take it away with me wherever it is I'm going, hang it on a wall where I live. But I did not. Because no consequence seemed obvious that day—for any of us—I allowed him to put it back in the closet behind his clothes. Karl said nothing, just leaned over and ran his fingers along the bayonet.

"Did your dad tell you how he brought this home?" I said. I held the rifle out to D. J. who took it and worked the bolt open and shut. "Did he tell you about the bitter cold? About how it kicked when he fired it at the sky?"

"I told him," D. J. said. "We've fired it. That's one story he knows."

And what of the other stories, the ones he *had* to know?

"Karl, sit. Please."

Despite his mother's urging, Karl would not. He said he'd like to drive his car for awhile, if it was all right.

"Don't get too tired," his father said. "Don't go too far until you're more used to it. Okay?"

"Remember your old buick, D. J.?" I said. "That was a hefty car, or Peggy wouldn't have survived. My pal Alan and I would sit in it at night and listen to that big radio, glowing there in the dark. We drank a few of your beers too, I have to confess."

"Go 'way with you, boy."

"I wasn't too sure about that first beer you poured, but it wasn't long after. Lord, you could put that stuff away."

"I prefer bourbon now. The beer is Grandpa Schrader's."

"A man I worked for once liked that kind of whisky. Me and my Budweiser he used to make fun of."

I drank off the beer in my hand and opened another. I wanted Karl to drive off in the car for awhile because what I had known with his father a long time ago I wanted to know again: a kinship I didn't have to seek or work for, it was just there, a given. That was what I needed that particular day of my life. I did not know what Karl needed, not then, I had no real idea at all. Did anyone? We had spread out so far, the family, all of us. Who would catch us as we fell?

But Karl sat down in a lawn chair, watching us as if he expected, in this little gathering of relatives, something worth the wait. I didn't know what to say to him. I was never able to chat with kids. But I felt him listening nonetheless. His father was smiling at me as he had when I mimicked characters on the radio.

"D. J., do you remember the night I scared you?"

Katrin laughed as if this were absurd. I had not recalled it myself for years until that instant. She looked over at her son. Karl had put on sunglasses for driving, so I could not read his eyes. I just wanted to keep talking. The light and the beer made me want to hold something together even though I was no longer sure what it was.

"Oh, you remember," I went on. "My mother was away, seeing dad on the boats. You were waiting to leave for the army and you came home late, a bit smashed. The house was dark as a pit because I'd turned off all the lights. But you knew I was in there and you let yourself in and came up the stairs very quietly in the dark. I was hiding behind your bedroom door I'd left partly open, but you didn't know just where I was. I heard your footsteps, real slow, in the hall. God, I was a kid, I was scared then too but I wanted to see you jump, to see you grab your heart. But you said, 'I know you're in here, John. Goddamn it, if you jump out at me I'm going to floor you. I mean it.' There was a little night-light in the baseboard, so I could see you dimly through the crack. You had your fist cocked tight and I could hear you breathing hard, like you'd been running. I knew you meant it. If I had roared or screamed, you'd have come undone. You *would* have busted my jaw. So I yelled, 'I give up!' and put on the light. When you saw me, you grinned, like you hadn't been scared at all."

"I'd forgot that," D. J. said, "I was headed for Korea. I didn't know where I was going." He stared at the ground. "You're right, John. That kind of surprise I didn't like. There was a mine explosion in Glace Bay a couple years ago. Did you know? No. 26 Colliery, ran out from the old New Aberdeen. Thirteen dead. One was a cousin of ours, you wouldn't know him I don't think. But down there you always expect some sort of disaster, and when it comes it's no terrible surprise, like it would be to us. We get older, we want to know what's in the dark. It's not something that will answer to a fist."

I didn't want to hear that, not from him, not now. I groped for a fantasy that would draw us together again: I imagined D. J. and Karl and myself taking on a bar someplace, the three of us wild, nuts, superhuman. Maybe the beer was involved somehow in the vision of it: a myth of our vanquishing, without rifles, all who would offend us, anywhere, that the mere fact of our kinship made us frenzied and invincible.

"Needles," I said. "Do you still have that phobia?" I turned to Karl. "Your dad couldn't stand the sight of a hypodermic. He'd faint. He did faint, once in a dentist's office and once in the army. Show him a needle and he was gone, boy, all two hundred pounds of him."

"Is that true, Dad?" Karl said.

"Years ago. All this was years ago. You're the man who can take the needles, eh? Are you all right? Are you going for a drive?"

His son settled back in the chair, his face turned up toward the trees.

"In a while," he said.

There was something faintly alarming in the way he lay back. "Cripple," I thought. The word tore through me. I wanted desperately to tell him something. "When I was in Glace Bay with your dad, he took me to see the pit horses. They weren't much good in the light after working in the mines for months on end, they couldn't see well. I'm not sure why but it was such a pleasure to watch them, all nicked and scarred, knowing where they'd been. They looked so peaceful that day, grazing in the pit yard while the miners were turned up for a short vacation. The horses didn't act blind. They moved about calmly but we were fascinated, your dad and I, because we knew how they lived. It must have been terrible, eh? Deep under the earth like that, never any sun, never a breeze like we're feeling now?"

"I'm not sure," Karl said.

A quiet descended around us. We seemed suspended beyond talk, there in the yard, in our places, all waiting for different things. The Chinese rifle lay on the white table beside the tray of food as if it had fallen there unnoticed. I was aware of the grandfather standing beside me, this restless man whose foot had frozen at Stalingrad. He was looking down at Karl who shaded his eyes from that light above the trees.

"*Bist du müde?*" the grandfather said to him, tenderly.

Karl did not respond at first. Then he inclined his face toward him and smiled. "*Em wenig, Grossvater,*" he said. "A little."

SAILING

I tell my father to watch his step. He is ascending the small deck that leads to the wooden tub of hot water. He is nearly eighty and it is dark here under the long redwood branches. "If I can't climb this, I'd better turn in my ticket," he says. He was a seaman on the Great Lakes for forty-one years, as long as I have been living. His ticket is his masters papers. A wet February wind gusts through the limbs above us and I think of all the weather he has had in his face, the storms and the ice.

He hisses at the heat, but with a deep sigh settles slowly into the water where I am sitting. He told me his future is waking one morning at a time, he's at that point in his life. Somewhere a cold, dark wave has been rising, he said without melancholy, and it will arrive probably by night and sweep him away. I said I didn't know you were ill. I'm not, he said, it's just a feeling. I want to ask him about this but we have no tradition of such asking.

"More rain coming," he says. "It won't last." He reads the weather easily. We had a storm recently that broke up a string of days he considered weatherless, a picture book of sun and blue sky. He believes, I think, there is a connection between such days and the way I live, with no course, no destination. He was amused at how people on the street looked harried, as if the storm were not a natural occurrence. By nightfall there was heavy wind and rain. Great whooshes rose up through the trees and some came down, their roots not used to such buffeting. My father paced the living room. "Look at that!" he'd say, his grin lit by lightning. The power went out. We played pinochle with two ten-cent candles burning between us while a half-cooked chicken sweated grease in the oven. "People around here never think about disaster," he said, not smugly, but just to let me know he knew the truth.

I too sailed on the Lakes. That was the closest my father and I have ever been, those years I worked my way through college decking and coalpassing on the big ore freighters. We were not such strangers then. I was moving away from him and closer to him at the same time. Because I had gone sailing we had, in the winter, things to talk about. But I left and came to live differently over the years. For him, routine is still the framework of life, a seaman's sense of work and hours. My employment is sporadic and I wake late. He rises at six-thirty and could sleep no longer unless drugged—as unlikely for him as it is likely for me. What kind of dreams does he wake from? Does he always know they are dreams or does he sometimes, for a moment, feel he has sailed over the edge of the world?

Over the Pacific in the west faint lightning trembles. I suggest we go back into the apartment but my father says no, nothing to fear from lightning like that. A soft drizzle works down through the redwood's needles and cools our faces. The air is brighter now with reflected light, like that of an overcast winter afternoon. Ivy glistens through the warm mist. My body feels torpid, weightless. I can see trees towering nearly leafless above the house like bare hedges against the sky. Trees of Heaven. Here autumn and winter merge. A few leaves still cling like snared birds. "I read somewhere people have expired in these things," my father says. I assure him we are far from danger. He shrugs, rubbing water over his shoulders like liniment. "I would not want to die here," he says, "like a child in a bath."

One evening we happened upon some Cape Breton fiddle music on a small FM station. My father, who was a grown man before he left Cape Breton, got out of his chair and did a few soft steps, heel and toe. "Oh I used to step out with the best of them," he said. He sat down and we listened to the host of this Celtic program—a woman with Irish affections and a mind full of political mist—interview a young man who was, apparently, versed in Cape Breton folk music. But, strangled either by ignorance or stage fright, he could not locate Cape Breton very precisely. "It's west of Ireland, isn't it?" The woman said helpfully. "And east of Quebec?" After a long delay, the man said, "yes," which was true but not useful, and there Cape Breton remained. But my father enjoyed "Donald MacLean's Farewell to Oban" and "Miss Lyle's Reel." He told me suddenly about having pneumonia when he was three years old, an illness often fatal in those days, especially in the country, and how his dad made him a small wooden mallet so he could rap the headboard when he needed anything or was afraid. For the rest of the evening he was quiet.

I do things for him my mother once did, when he was home for the winter. I mix him a whiskey in the afternoon and again in the evening when we talk. I bake Bisquick biscuits, cut cheese, cook, ask him if he's comfortable. I do this because he can take care of himself, not because he cannot. Around the corner from us there is a convalescent home and his first day here my father saw a frail old man babystepping by our window with a walker. I had to smile when he said, with real sympathy, "Poor old fella," as if there were years between them. Last night, halfway through his second whiskey and feeling good, he remembered a country party ("Long before *I* was married"), a wedding reception back in Cape Breton. A lot of people came to this cold house on Cape Dauphin, stamping snow at the door, December be damned, and there was dancing and boozing, horses packed flank to flank in the barn. A pal of his got sick from drink, but before going upstairs to find a bed he searched around the yard in the dark, finally yanking out of the snow an enamel creamer to set by his bedside. Not until morning, after he'd thrown up in it twice, did he discover the bottom of the creamer was rusted out completely. My father likes reminiscences like this and laughs easily, shaking his head at how vivid they remain. But after the funny part he said, almost casually, "Your mother was there," and the timbre of his voice changed, just slightly, just enough to notice.

I remember one December when I waited with my mother at a Cleveland dock during a bleary hour of the morning and watched his ship ease like an iceberg into her moorings. Freighted with tons of ice, she had gone down dangerously on her marks because of the added burden. My mother knew about the storm and had been worried. My father, bundled up like an Arctic explorer, waved to her from the Texas deck and she gave him the okay sign. Later that winter, at home, my father and I walked along the shore of Lake Erie, our eyes and mouths drawn tight against a wind so cold it pained. We squinted across a jagged icescape which, rough as rockslides and fluted with windrows of snow, had been repeatedly broken up by storms, freezing again and again into new shapes. Beyond it the water seemed calm and green in the distance. We passed a shed built along the lines of a little house and layered with several inches of translucent ice. Beside it a tree crackled, wind-driven spray having turned it as bright and brittle as crystal. Too chilled to bring a hand out of his pocket, my father nodded toward the shed. "Somebody forgot to keep the home fires burning, eh?" he said. He and my mother argued sometimes during the long winter months. She accumulated grievances in her loneliness and sometimes shut herself away in her room after he left. What they quarrelled about I cannot recall. Little things which, I suppose, the strains of separation made larger. It no longer matters, not to him, not to anything. There is probably nothing more he can add to what I know of him. We walked in the wind that day until we could barely speak.

"In a ship," he says, "out there at night . . . it's sometimes like you're at dead center of everything, the works." There are breaks in the overcast now. Clouds tear slowly into pieces and drift off like floes in the dark sky. My father watches them, then points. "The brightest star, there. Sirius. And there, Eye of Taurus." Wherever I am, he has told me, I like to get a bearing. All I know about him are bits and pieces like this. He never talks about himself directly, never did. He prefers stories that entertain—anecdotes, mimicry. Some stories I have heard before, like familiar waters we sail over. I wish we could descend beneath them, that he could reveal things under the surface before it is too late. When he is feeling down he is merely politely silent. Yet I admire his reticence: it seems dignified in a land of public blubbering where people yearn to be heard. At my mother's sudden death a year ago he was, as I expected, stoic, although the shock of her absence had tightened his face. She died next to him in bed, on a normal morning when he rose early and waited for her to come down to breakfast. When he looked at the clock later on, an ordinary day turned into something vaguely expected but never prepared for. "I climbed those stairs like I weighed a ton," he told me. She was already blue and cold. It troubles him that he did not become alarmed sooner, that he might have reached her in time.

The first night he arrived I passed his room and was struck to see him down on one knee beside his bed, whispering prayer. I had forgotten he prayed that way and I was briefly embarrassed, as if this was senility. No. Like other things about him, it is simple and private, as sincere as a Jew at the Wailing Wall or a Moslem on his mat. I wondered if he had prayed beside his bunk when he was a deckhand, how he found the chance or if he feared the jibes of his shipmates. What now does he ask for? What does he expect from God?

He has marvelled at the flowers in February. He left the sidewalk one morning to stand among the branches of a tulip tree and touch the pale lavender cups of its blossoms. "You live in a garden," he said. At home he took over my mother's roses and put in peonies of his own, and marigolds. A sudden show of flowers makes him smile, almost shyly. He missed so many summers at sea, and they seem to strike at the heart of his youth when he knew them in the country.

Yesterday we were hit with an earthquake. Still in bed, I woke certain that this was the Big One and I did not want to meet it hungover and naked. I stumbled to the doorway of the living room where a hanging fern swung like a pendulum. My father, half-crouched in front of his chair, had spread his arms like a wrestler—a reflex from years of steadying himself on pitching decks. We stayed as we were, our eyes fixed on each other, until the rolling passed and the house stopped shaking. At the front window my father looked down at the street, his face close to the glass as if he were back in a wheelhouse. "Not the same as a ship," he said. "It's like being thrown off the earth." Then he smiled and raised his voice like a preacher's: " 'If I take up the wings of the morning, and dwell in the uttermost part of the sea. . . . '" He lowered his voice to a murmur, " ' . . . even there . . . '"

The moon appears in the southwest. Its light turns the water darkly clear, the way it might be on Lake Superior streaming out a deep green against a wake white and crisp. We can see the pallor of our skin. My father sighs, a habit of his now, though usually no words ever follow. The last months his wife was living she would not enter a dark room. At the threshold she would step back and wait while he went ahead of her and put on a light. At the funeral he looked at her in that casket for a long while, and finally he said, to no one: "Where is she *now?*" I was of no use to him in this matter. I do not know how we move after death, or where.

In our old neighborhood back home five widows have been good to him. They observed his birthday, they bring him meals, invite him to their houses for cards. One has taken to calling him dear, a familiarity he does not encourage. He has named her The Star Widow, but when she calls him darling, he says, he will have to cool her off. "I have old feelings to think about. I don't need any new ones." After my mother died, he burned her letters. My anger puzzled him. "Letters are for the living," he said.

In the Twenties my father wheeled on a small Canadian freighter whose captain, a reckless alcoholic, took her foolishly into a Lake Michigan storm. Her wooden hatches, weakened by boarding seas, were carried away and she soon foundered. He and three other men made it to the wooden raft lashed atop the wheelhouse. All night in the darkness they were swept from it time after time, clawing their way back aboard where they huddled like lovers in the cold. It was November and the water was not much above freezing. A man would stop talking for awhile and then he wasn't there, having slipped quietly into the sea. By dawn when the wind had abated, only my father remained, half-conscious and hallucinating. A bearded man kept appearing on the edge of the raft warning him not to eat the ice he'd been nibbling from the lapels of his coat. He heard his dead shipmates calling to him from shore offering him sandwiches. "Go easy, I'm not dead," he said to the Coast Guardsman who'd lifted him like a corpse. He lost two toes and the tip of a finger. "I survived," he told me, "because I was young."

Vapor rises faintly through the moonlight, climbing into the boughs above us whose shadows flash in the steam. I see my father's spare gestures, his pale form. And the occasional spark of his gold tooth, quick as an atom, so contained it seems all I know of him, that tiny glint. He bought that tooth in his bold and single days, just after lay-up, a bonus in his pocket and an aching bicuspid cracked in a fight with a redneck oiler. It always embarrassed my mother, fearful he would grin in church or pick it in a good restaurant. But I like it because it reminds me of his youth about which I know little. In Gaelic, a language his parents spoke, his name means sailor or mariner. As he grew up, I guess he merely eased into what he'd been christened, and that was his life.

We have been up to San Francisco once during his visit. He likes to call it Frisco, a city he has always wanted to see. Indifferent to cities, I take us on a sketchy itinerary of sights. I look for a Scottish bar I've heard about but we soon end up, by mutual consent, in a dark Irish pub where we talk quietly in the cool malty dusk of our Guinness. Outside, people hurry past in the sun. We swap stories about the Lakes, boats we both knew, men we'd worked with, as if we're ashore for a few hours while our ships unload. Later, reluctantly, we stumble out into the glare of the afternoon in time to board the ships docked at the Maritime Museum. We clamber around an old steam schooner, the sort of working ship my father understands immediately. In the fo'c'sle he sniffs a tarry smell. "Oakum," he says, grinning back to that tooth that can still surprise me. We inspect every accessible compartment and only the wheelhouse remains. It is perched high and solitary like the wheelhouses on the old Lake freighters that are no doubt gone by now. We climb to it but the door is locked. No public permitted. My father peers through the glass for awhile, hooding his eyes and cataloging the equipment inside. Then he turns and I snap a picture of him looking older in the cold wind. We hang around the piers. I know he doesn't want to leave. He sees a sloop plunging through the choppy currents off Alcatraz Island and tells me about a skiff he had as a boy, how he rigged a little sail and put rocks in the bottom for ballast. As we drive home, the Guinness seeps ruthlessly from our spirits and I recall how harshly the sun struck us when we stepped into it. We are silent all down the Bayshore where nothing generates talk. I turn on the radio. On our little FM station Pete Seeger is singing . . . "Sailing down my golden river, and I was not far from home. . . ." I look over at my father. He seems dozy. Perhaps his thoughts are somewhere on water, on the cold dark sea of Lake Superior.

He makes swimming motions with his hands. The water ripples and whitens behind him. I remember only one summer when he swam. His boat laid up because of a steel strike and in the afternoons we would catch a bus down to the lake. He would swim out a long way by himself, slowly and carefully, where there were no other swimmers and float for minutes on end, his face a mask on the water. I was too young to follow him, but I knew, anyway, he wanted to be alone. Summer at home was a strange time for him.

He knows that I am still drifting. "A man needs some place to tie up to," he said in the Irish pub. It troubles him that I have lived in so many places, that next year I may have another address. Quite likely it will not have this warm bubbling sea in the back-yard. I work on and off as a technical writer. I don't know where this will lead. In the spring my father was always gone as soon as the ice broke. A different ship but the same places. "Never mind," he told me, wiping Guinness froth from his moustache. "The company gave boats to younger mates and put me mate with them so they wouldn't screw up. I never got my own ship. You had to kiss their ass for that." He looked across the bar at a woman in a slit skirt. "I was into my middle years when Paul came along, Kenny." Paul is my much younger brother back in Ohio, a carpenter. He kept looking at the woman and nodding his head as if considering what Paul's coming along had meant. Finally he said, "Just don't have anything to do with business. It's not in our blood." We touched glasses and finished our Guinness.

Once a bunkmate and I devised a game. Running up Lake Superior in hard weather, we opened the porthole in our cramped, below-decks cabin and climbed into our bunks. We lay there naked and uncovered, rigid as mummies, listening to the bow smash and split the heavy seas. Which of us would feel the first fiery lash of water so cold it could kill you in minutes? We heard the seas break along the shipside, rise to the porthole's rim, splattering the top of our metal dresser, and we knew that inevitably a good wave would collide with the bow and swell upward. We tensed, our jaws clamped tight. Soon there was the sound—a growing hiss, a roaring whisper—and then a thump of spray shot through the darkness, striking one or both of us with a chill that jerked the body like an electric shock. Whoever yelled first lost. We played until wet bedclothes threatened our sleep. I thought of my father on that raft, that I was he. But I did not think of death: death was too distant, like the bottom of that dark sea two hundred fathoms beneath us, so cold it never gave up the drowned men who drifted there. As I closed the porthole, I was sure I would live forever.

"Too hot," my father says. He rises, emerges from the water. I reach out a steadying hand he does not need. He towels himself slowly, in that careful way of old men, as if briskness would be unseemly. He was never a big man but now he has diminished into age. I think of the only time I saw him in the act of his work. Our ships had tied up at adjacent docks in Toledo and I could see him stepping smartly along the main deck over hatch cables and dock wallopers' shovels to chew out a crewman for fouling a winch. I was surprised: he seemed such a different man, one a gold tooth might well belong to. I envied him. No one on that ship would question anything he said, and I hoped that one day I could gain that kind of respect. But I will always somehow remain an amateur. I have been an amateur in nearly everything of my life, and I am one now. Everything in my mind and in my hands seems uncertain, half-formed. But my father was a professional, skilled in those countless ways that make good seamen, and bring them other good seamen's respect. That part of him was not passed on to me, that ability to find your way, deeply, into what you are good at. When I first went sailing, I knew the ore freighters, having as a boy roamed their cold iron darkness during winter lay-up, but I did not know their work. I felt homesick and inept. But for my father, I tried at least to be a reliable deckhand, for that would get back to him. What didn't get back was the hot summer night I got thoroughly and limply drunk on cognac, me and the other two deckhands, cleaning up ore leavings deep in the cargo holds. Between alcoholic fits of energy, we leaned on our shovels and sang. We dodged the backing bulldozer and the first mate's glances from the hatches above, we flirted with the Hewlett's big iron teeth as its shadow descended over us. When the heat and the cognac struck home around two A.M., I crawled along the side-tanks all the way to my bunk and passed out. As penance, the mate put me to work at sunrise hauling up five-gallon buckets of heavy red mud and dumping them overboard. I felt sick enough to die. I hated every motion of the ship and the dull line of the horizon. I wanted to jump at the next port. But I endured it and said nothing because of the watchman. His name was Gunderson, an ex-gunners mate with bleeding ulcers, huge hands, a frightening set of false teeth, and identical square-riggers tattooed on both wrists. He came up to me while I was waiting for my bucket to be filled in the hold below. I must have looked grey as the sea, my jaws tight with nausea. "You know," he said, "I been with some sons of bitches, but your old man is a fine mate. He was a deckhand once too." I could have told him, no, he wasn't, they made him a wheelsman right off when he said he'd been a seaman in Nova Scotia, he never had to do this. But I was grateful to Anders Gunderson. I knew then that to feel homesick was foolish, that I was not in a strange place.

I will never forget a photograph my father gave me when I was young. He proffered it without comment one evening after I had pressed him for details about his shipwreck. I took the old clipping to my room where I pored over it more keenly than the pornographic cards we passed around at school. Something in its atmosphere I could not understand, cannot yet. The corpses of nine seamen are laid out in a morgue, the undertaker in his galluses posing at one end of them, his assistant at the other. A railroad ferry had sunk in December during one of Lake Erie's fearsome gales, and these men, the only crewmen ever found, had frozen solid as stone in a battered lifeboat. Their faces, grotesquely calm, skin like putty in the incandescent glare of floodlamps, have been shaped by the mortician into the contours of troubled sleep. For the benefit of cameras they lie in a parallel row, heads slightly raised on makeshift pillows, sheets pulled snug to their chins. You can see the outlines of their arms folded across their waists. But something disturbs the almost Victorian dignity of their arrangement: there is one man, Smith the cook, whose belly is so swollen its girth has lifted the hem of the sheet, exposing the deadwhite flesh of his buttock. It is clear that all of these men are naked. A copy editor has crudely penned on each sheet the surname of each man. My eyes went slowly up and down that row so many times the order of their names became a kind of poetry. Steele. Shank. Allen. Smith. Ray. Hart. Thomas. Hines. Squars. What my father wanted me to learn from this stark picture I do not know. If he wanted me only to remember it, I have.

My father has dried himself and wrapped a big white towel around him toga-like. "At home there's ice now," he says. "Clear across to Canada." He waves. I hear his feet on the wooden steps. He disappears behind the trellis of ivy.

The wind is gone. The moon, its crescent snagged on strands of cloud, filters down through a tracery of branches. Ivy, which has climbed above the fence and found nothing to grab but air, turns back into itself, forming a pitchblack whorl that seems depthless. I do not understand the heavens or their arrangement as they move through the seasons of the skies. Put my father on a dark and empty sea and still he will not be lost. I think he has never been lost. I must memorize the constellations, learn to guide myself through these winter nights. I stare into the vortex the ivy makes and imagine that black hole my father will wither into, gone beyond the skies that helped him, hindered him. All I know, for certain, is that we are sailing.

OF ONE KIND

A deep voice, bursting loud from behind her screendoor, startled Red Donald, his mind still charged with the flight of a deer he'd surprised in her orchard—huffs and snorts, then the tail up stiff and white as the doe cut quickly into the woods. He turned toward the house. She was playing one of her tapes for the blind, things recorded from a New York paper or some magazine you wouldn't see in Cape Breton. He knew that, but the sound, sudden when he'd been hearing only his feet in the grass, set him back, this voice that spoke the way her dead husband had, using words like you'd wear a fine suit. Was the woman going deaf as well? He stopped to rest in her front pasture, the rifle drooping from the crook of his arm. Why should he be catching his breath now so she wouldn't hear him winded from the long climb? He was nothing to her. A handyman, a fisherman. Seventy years to her sixty-five, besides. What mattered to Mrs. MacKay except that he fix the loose board, the cracked pane, fetch her things from town? He had seen her but once, briefly, since that afternoon of her fall. And she had mentioned nothing about it, one way or the other. He took a deep breath and walked on towards the voice. The deer could wait. From the tall, swaying maple beside her stone chimney a hawk moved slowly away into the darkness of the mountain. Above the long ridge that ran as far as you could see, the day was dimming fast.

Red Donald laid his rifle and flashlight on her steps, then crossed the porch quietly and put his face to the wide bow window. There she lay on the couch, her long slender fingers tapping idly on her breast as she listened. He took in her yellow-white hair, her softly-lined face, the brown unseeing eyes. She looked the lady, even now. He liked to study her this way, brazenly, as he would never have dared before. Maybe sometime he would tell her, "I've watched you from the window, Mrs. MacKay." Let her think on that, let her wonder.

He rapped loudly. Why did she leave her door open? Indian summer was ending.

"I could've been an intruder, Mrs. MacKay," he said as he stepped inside. "Somebody bad just walking in."

She raised her head. "You're bad enough, Red Donald. I knew it was you. I know your knuckles on the wood."

He waited for an offer to sit but she lay back on her pillows. That was like her. Save her life or not, she'd make him stand there like an ox. The tape machine droned on. Someone murdered in an opera house. Or was it a story about a murder in an opera house. Probably a New York man, the man speaking.

Red Donald said, raising his voice, "I saw a hawk in your tree there. When Malcolm Gunn had this house, a hawk would keep his distance."

She raised a hand preemptorily and inclined her ear at the machine. Red Donald shrugged and looked around the large den, furnished as it had been before her husband's death. But there were bits of untidiness now: a stocking shrivelled on the rug, orange peels strewn in the cold firegrate, dropped ashes from her cigarettes everywhere. Red Donald had seen the pine panelling darken over the years, the wallpaper yellow like newspaper and stain with winter damp when she was off to Baddeck staying in the hotel. Darkening too over the big stone fireplace was the portrait of her husband, listing slightly, with his movie actor's moustache, looking the big shot he was in the New York water works. MacKay. A good name and it belonged here, but he'd been an outsider, this MacKay, a yank through and through. Red Donald turned to the door.

"Go on with your listening, Mrs. MacKay. I know how you like it."

She reached for the small table beside her and turned the voice low like someone she was unwilling to silence.

"I'm not sure you have any idea what I like, Red Donald MacKillop." She sat up, touching her hip tenderly. "I look like hell. I need my hair done. But then I don't get many callers, do I?"

"I come up to see what you need, if you need anything."

"Took you long enough. Are you out jacking deer?"

"I'm going to Baddeck tomorrow." So what if he did jack a deer in the broken-down trees of her orchard? He was older now, he needed an edge.

"I hate the hunting season. I hate that first shot from the woods," she said.

"I brought you venison."

"I didn't ask for it. I wouldn't ask you to hunt down a deer for me."

"Well, the season's not come yet."

"Lean beef. That's what my doctor says and that's what I'll eat."

"I'm after losing my appetite. Could live off the skin of a snake."

The black birch cane he had given her stood against the table. "How is the hip faring?" he said.

"Sore but mending," she said curtly, reaching for a packet of Rothman's. Proud. Too damned proud. He knew she had a bruise big as your fist, a bad sprain. He watched her fingers ferret out a wooden match. She lit a cigarette, her eyes wide, and blew out a sigh of smoke.

"Can you get me bananas?"

"If they have them. Sometimes they don't."

"I need the potassium, so the doctor says. And since he's a nice man, I'll do as he asks."

A *nice* man, Red Donald mimicked to himself, echoing her Norwegian accent. He moved about the room touching objects with a familiarity she would not like.

"You can get earphones for them machines," he said. He had the urge to break it, stomp it into the floor.

"Why? Who hears it but me?"

He toyed with the finial of a Tiffany lamp on top of the grand piano.

"I remember when this house was boarded up," he said. "Wood over every window. Dark as the grave." He pulled the chain slowly, lighting the lamp. "Couldn't get rid of it, Malcolm. Too far from the road."

"But that's the beauty of it. And the views. I still see them in my mind."

Red Donald looked out the picture window that framed the black piano. He'd put that in for them so they could gaze at the mountain rising steeply in the near west. When he went home for the day he was done with the outdoors until morning. But his sister had died suddenly in the spring and he didn't care to sit in the house much now.

"Shouldn't be leaving your door open like that, you here alone."

"I've nothing to fear. I've heard hunters sometimes going through the grass, heard their voices. But they always go on. And sometimes kids in the summer. They drive up and shut their engines off. Then I don't hear them until they leave." She seemed to consider this for a moment, turning her face toward the window through which Red Donald had watched her. "Oh, they're just out there necking or whatever. I don't care. I envy them."

He came nearer the couch.

"Suppose you was to fall again."

"Stupid, that was. Carelessness. Never again."

Her eyes were wide and dark and behind that faint smile, he felt certain, stood the memory of that afternoon. She might have lain there for God knew how long had he not happened by and heard her calling out. Through the window he had seen her trying to raise herself off the floor. She cursed and fell back whimpering. But he had waited, feeling his mouth go dry, until she cried out again. Then he'd come inside and lifted her up, with ease, and brought her to the couch, her arms about his neck as if he might've been her husband, the man she loved. But once she was safe and seen to, he was just Red Donald again, the man who aired out her house in the spring, who freed from her chimney a trapped bird that had kept her from sleeping. Didn't she know he could have turned and walked away, left her there helpless?

"It's cold in here. I'll build you a fire," he said.

"Close the door if you're cold. I use the furnace now. I'm afraid of sparks."

"I'll watch it. I'll keep an eye on it. I'm good at that, you know."

"But you wouldn't be here to see it burn out, would you?"

Red Donald laid a hand on the cool round stones of the fireplace. He'd hauled these stones up here in his dumpcart years ago, clear up from MacDermid's shore where they rolled around like big marbles when a storm was on. Carried them in, every damn one on a hot and muggy day while her husband gave orders the way he always did those early summers they came up from

New York, Red Donald doing the labor, MacKay pointing, put it here, there. But there'd been the times too when she was alone, when, wearing but a housecoat, she'd leaned near his face one morning as he showed her the rotting posts under the porch. I'll wait for the right time, he'd thought then, for to see clearly the drift of her.

"You shouldn't be smoking then," he said.

"What are you, the doctor?"

"It's fire I'm thinking about."

"Do you know what Mackay means, Red Donald? 'Son of Fire.' Charles' father told me himself. 'You're my favorite girl,' he'd say, take me on his knee."

She blew out smoke slowly, elaborately, as if to see the way it curled into the cool air of the room. A big city habit. She had a lot of them, even though she hadn't seen New York since MacKay died nine years ago. But she would speak about that city when she brought out her scrapbook. Red Donald knew its contents too well, and the stories attached to them. How she had come from Norway to study in New York, how, later in life, she had met MacKay, an older man, while working in a library. How he'd offered to take her anywhere she liked for a honeymoon. Because Cape Breton reminded her of home, they drove here, fell in love with it, bought the house for summers. Red Donald remembered the evening she appeared at his front door, tall in a dark green dress, her hair the color of wild oats. Like no woman he had ever seen, she was.

He wandered over to the piano, its surface dulled with dust, not polished and streaked with light as it had been on summer evenings when MacKay ran his fingers over the keys. The music had carried a long way then because the land was cleared and trees didn't swallow the sound. You wouldn't hear it beyond the front pasture now. Red Donald struck a black key softly, once, twice.

"What are you walking about so much for?" she said suddenly, her eyes seeking him. She had punched the recorder off. The room was hushed except for the wind hissing outside, spreading like surf through the last leaves of the maple tree.

"Seems like I have to keep moving," he said. "Can't sit around."

"You make me nervous. Have a glass of sherry."

He winced. Why the devil couldn't she keep a little rum in?

"You having it too?"

"We'll have one together. For old times."

Old times? Her sherry had been for guests and he had never been a guest. But he knew where she kept it and so ignored her instructions as he headed for the pantry and the stemmed glasses. He noticed her hands had missed a stain on the countertop and the pantry's little window was dirty as a barn's. He tucked this away in his mind. Maybe one day he would tick them off for her, shoot some holes in that stubborn self-reliance. "I rather like living alone," she said once. How could she, he'd wondered. On his way back to the den he ducked into her bedroom, a forbidden place, but ever since her blindness he'd stood and sniffed in every forbidden corner of the house. He looked at the underclothes hung on the headboard, at the dishevelled bed. Bad dreams, by the look of it. Shouldn't be rolling around in there by herself. There was a smell he could not quite place, like sweet candy . . .

"Donald?"

He returned and sat down in the big chair beside her, filled a glass and led her fingers to it. "Here you are, Mrs. MacKay. Take the chill out."

"Well, yes, that's nice," she said. She took it and sipped without waiting. He watched her purse her lips and swallow.

"Nice it is." Red Donald upended the bottle. Aw, it was sweet stuff but he guessed it would do if you swilled it enough.

"The winter will be hard, I'm thinking," he said.

"And how would you know?"

"No wasps in the ground this year. Bark is thick on the trees."

"You're awful superstitious, Red Donald, like most of your people. Narrow-minded too, a number of them."

He shut his eyes and took another swig. "And in the city their minds are wide, are they?"

"People aren't into your business there. You can't keep a secret in this place, even with the new telephones."

And what secrets did she have? He'd like to know a few of them. He knew she enjoyed the raw story, the blue joke, so his sister had told him. Worse now than ever she was, that way, Sadie had said.

"I remember the night you came here," Red Donald said. "Mr. MacKay stuck in the driveway."

She laughed, looking away toward the back of the room where the piano sat. "We were too tired to do it that night. But there was plenty of time later."

Red Donald's mind snagged on the word "it." He took a long pull of sherry.

"I guess it is you're used to a quiet life now."

"We came here for quiet, yes, we looked forward to it. But things were lively in New York, lots to do, lots to see." She pressed the side of the glass to her cheek. "You could get fed up with it, of course. But that's where the life was. Oh, yes."

"New York City," Red Donald said, as if he understood. But to him just the name reverberated with noise and danger. If he were to come at it from the sea, slowly on some windy morning, and see the skyline rise up in the distance, then he could take it. But no further. Still, that she had lived in that place gave her some advantage he could never seem to counter. "A man gets trapped in the city, all them alleys and streets and concrete."

"You have to know your way around. It's only getting from place to place, just like here."

"I'm never lost here, never in the woods even. I make my own paths if I don't like the other ones."

"I do miss the excitement of the city. Nothing like it really."

"Then why have you kept yourself here so damned many years?"

"Don't get hot, Red Donald. I stay because Charles is buried down the road. And for the beauty and serenity."

Byooty and serenity. He hated it when she used words that way, like she was waving a lace fan at him.

"I'll fill your glass, will I?" he said.

She raised her palm to him. "Too much of this gets my heart going."

"Aw, it's Friday. Folks are dancing. Hearts are going." He held the bottle above her glass.

"All right. One more."

He filled it and she looked over the rim of the glass. "So you've been busy?"

He let the question drift. She took him for granted, always had, expecting him one day or the other. But he'd stayed away this time and let the memory of her fall keep her company. Had she forgotten so soon? The day he had lifted her up off the floor he had just chanced to come near on his way up the mountain. Hadn't they been close for a minute or two, she against his body? She hadn't seen the heat in his face or heard the queer catch in his throat as he asked after her.

"I get busy for spells," he said. "Traps to build, things to mend."

"I was only wondering if you'd look into the attic. I've been hearing sounds up there."

He nodded at the side window where the maple's broad trunk, darker than the moonlit field behind it, moved slightly in the wind. A branch dragged over the roof like fingernails. "Could be your tree. Or ghosts, eh?"

"Another bird, if you ask me. Squirrels maybe."

"I've known ghosts to knock around."

She leaned forward, smiling. "You're serious, Red Donald, I do believe."

"Am I grinning? I've seen strange things, yes, I have, myself and others. Lights in the woods, heard sounds what shouldn't have been there. Tonight the moon's out. Fairies dance on nights like this. Up along the mountain there's a clearing. Certain nights there's a light too, and shadows moving, like dancers. Saw them, I did, and my dad too. Aw, they come back with the woods, happenings of one kind or another."

She reached out for the tape recorder and ran her fingers over it familiarly.

"Woods don't frighten me. Charles and I walked through them, often, after dark. Ghosts and fairies are in the mind, not my woods. Not my attic either."

"No," Red Donald said, pressing toward her. "Too many's after seeing them. Not the young ones, they're blind to it. But us people, yes. Now that just might be the mischief up in the attic, eh? Old Malcolm staggering around up there."

Her face tightened and she drew back against her pillows. But as if aware he was watching, she smiled.

"There's been no mischief in this house for a good while, spiritual or otherwise."

"Well, you'd want to watch out for the *Each Uisge*. Terrible bad, he is."

"Is he?" She laughed. "I've never heard of him."

"The Water-Horse. He could come up this far easy, if the woods don't put him off. A black horse, sleek, a good one you'd want to ride. You'd want to have him. But soon as your legs were 'round him you'd be stuck there fast, and he'd dash you away into the sea, down deep in the strait there where he'd devour you. Only your liver'd be left in the morning, on the shore, or a bit of your heart maybe, there on the rocks."

"My liver he's welcome to."

"Been known to come as a handsome man as well, to take a form like that, the Water-Horse."

"If I'm to be devoured down in the dark sea, give me the man then. You can keep the horse, Red Donald."

"It's not for me to say, what an *Each Uisge* does, or any of the others. You can hear him whinny in the night, that I know. Man or beast, he'd kill you."

She thrust out her glass and he poured sherry into it, holding her wrist steady.

"Your hand is cold," she said.

"Always cold where the blood don't go, eh?" he said.

Wasn't she loosening up with him now? Hadn't her husband sat like this, in this very chair, the fire crackling at his feet? Red Donald filled his cheeks with sherry, rolled it around, swallowed. He winked at MacKay above the fireplace. Maybe later he'd get up and knock that picture crooked a couple more degrees.

"He liked his drink, your husband. Liked his whiskey, if I remember."

"Socially," she said coolly. "Just socially." She stared into the sherry in her hand. She seemed to slip off somewhere else quite often now, as if everything was behind her eyes, not in front of them. She'd go for minutes like you were not in the room at all. Well, he could wait. His eyes drifted to a photograph framed on the wall near her couch. Before she lost her sight he had never looked at it closely but now he could study its detail freely from where he sat. She was standing on a deep lawn and glancing off to the side, her outstretched hand resting gently on the bark of a broad-trunked tree. Her hair was that rich blonde, like it used to be. In the lower corner of the print a shadow intruded. MacKay, probably, manning the camera. Red Donald wondered how that day finished out after the sun went down. Did they go inside that big brick house in the background? He could see her stepping out of the wool skirt, see her loosening the thick, coiled braid of hair in an upstairs bedroom. But the husband would be there too, standing behind her maybe, laying on her bare shoulders those thin white hands that danced over piano keys, hands that never smelled of fish and gurry. Why had she rehung that picture near her? It used to be above the mantel with the small painting of a nude child beholding, on tiptoe, a wave breaking, delicate as china, upon her feet.

"How bad *is* your sight then?" he said with boldness that made him flush. He held his breath. She raised her chin at him.

"I'm not as blind as you think, Red Donald. I see the shape of you there. Not your details, but I know what you're like."

His cheeks felt hot. Just what did she see of him? She never looked him in the eyes anymore. He let the sherry bottle slide down between his thighs and clasped his hands behind his head, leaning back the way MacKay had when he was comfortable here, she on the couch there adoring him, but upright then, clear-eyed and listening.

"Things closed in on you like, eh?" he said. He wanted to know more about her than he dared ask, more than thumbed photos and clippings in a scrapbook.

"I know what's beyond the windows. That's as clear as if I was seeing it now."

Red Donald narrowed his eyes almost sleepily but they were running from her face to her feet. Small feet, and slim ankles that suggested her hips had not always been broad.

"You're due a visit to the doctor soon, eh?" he said.

"I've already been. Last week. Sally Elliot drove me."

That stung him. In the past he had driven her. It was him she always called, just as her husband had called when his car needed hauling out of the mud, MacKay off to the side biting on his pipestem, the knees of his trousers soaked with clay where he'd fallen, shouting orders Red Donald ignored even if he understood him. Never could fix a goddamn thing, that man. Held a hammer like an ice cream cone. Red Donald had brought him a fresh eel once, a good eel big as your wrist, and the man went pale. Son of Fire? A wet wick.

"Sally's a Jesus driver," he said, swinging the bottle to his mouth.

"She drives as good as you, and a damn sight faster. Anyway, it was a new doctor, a young man. Nice man. Pakistani or something. Said I was pretty fit, all said and done." She straightened her back. "My breasts are as firm as a seventeen-year-old girl's. He told me that."

Red Donald's face burned. Christ, she was getting foolish. And what a thing for a doctor to say. If Red Donald put his hands on them, he'd tell her no lies either. He set the sherry on the floor and stood up. The room reeled under his feet.

"I'll have to use your bathroom," he said.

"Ah, you old folks. Always running to the toilet."

He glared at her, then walked away a bit unsteadily, his boots heavy on the wooden floor. The sherry had a wallop he hadn't expected. As he stood at the toilet he could look directly through the dining room to the den. She sat stiffly, poised, her glass partway to her lips. He left the door open wide, unzipped, and pissed loudly into the center of the bowl, watching her. When he was done, he zipped up his fly with a sharp rip. He watched her quickly drain her glass, pat the table for cigarettes. As he returned, she extracted a Rothman's and dangled it in the corner of her mouth. He liked that, something dangerous in that. But it was a city touch too and he felt the distance again, like someone stepping between them, someone he'd have to shove out of the way. Seeing her grope for matches, he picked them up from the floor and struck one. She shied away from the flare, then drew near it, carefully. He too leaned close.

"Can you see me now?" he said.

The match burned between them.

"Your hand is trembling. I can see that."

He touched the flame gently to the tip of the cigarette. She took a soft puff and brought it down from her mouth.

"It's a lonely time of life, this," he said, his voice low. He had taken her hand between his palms and was pressing it firmly. "I know that. I know that right enough. My sister gone. Nights like this don't you feel . . . ?"

"No," she whispered. "I can't. I don't want to be touched anymore."

"But it's me here, look at me. Me, Red Donald."

"No . . . no, I can't see you. And your hands are cold."

"Don't say it, don't tell me that. Blood's beating here, girl. Believe it now. Why do we got to freeze up just because . . . ?"

"Red Donald, what do you mean? My husband is dead."

He squeezed her fingers.

"What about the day you washed your legs at the spring, sat there with your long white legs in the water? What about the jokes, eh? The jokes!"

"Come, come, behave yourself. The sherry's talking."

"*I'm* talking. Me."

She had been afraid for a moment and he had been prepared to seize that fear, to bring it tight against him. But she withdrew her hand and he was left clasping his own, feeling the chill of them.

"That was years ago," she said. "It's not enough to tell me you were there when my legs were naked. That's no memory for me. And that spring is dry, Red Donald."

He stepped back as her hand swam over the recorder. She stabbed the on-button, catching the volume quickly and reducing it to the murmur of a man talking in another room.

"Wherever did you get an idea like that?" she said wearily, so low he could barely hear her. "Some of us don't mind being alone. Not now. Not anymore."

He put his back to her. "I'll have a look in that attic before I go."

She said nothing. He listened to her smoking, to the hiss of her breath.

"The flashlight is in the kitchen," she said.

"I don't need it. I don't want any lights."

He climbed the stairs to the dark landing and felt along the cool wall for the door, climbed the brief steps and stood in the cool sooty smell of the attic. A square of weak moonlight defined a window at the far end. He liked attics. An attic was like the ribcage of a big animal where you could hear it breathing, hear it labor through the weathers of the year. Vague, sheeted outlines of stored objects grew slowly visible. The maple branch dragged like a crippled leg overhead. He reached out and felt the clothed surface of a chest of drawers. "She don't know the woods," he said. "None of it." He lunged at the chest, wrestling it over with a thud that shook the rafters. He waited, tasting the raised dust. When his breath was calm, he went back down the steps.

She sat with the scrapbook open on her lap, its pages of mementoes smudged and askew from her stroking fingers.

"Nothing up there to worry you," he said.

"But the noise! What the devil was that?"

"Nothing there. No squirrels or birds or nothing."

"But good Lord . . . !"

"I'd say it's in your mind."

She gave him a wan smile. "All right, Red Donald. All right."

He turned to the window behind Mr. MacKay's piano, kneading his large hands, warming them, goddamn it, he couldn't warm them anymore. The trees swarming down the mountain slope seemed to rise taller with the night, the long high ridge poised like a great dark wave above the house. Had she forgotten the fall entirely, the boards under her face, the helplessness, him taking her up—not rough like he'd haul a trap or something but with gentleness there, like she was someone he cared for, lightly lifting her, just a slip of a thing really, carrying her, pale and tired, to that couch. She had feared night would come and find her still on the floor with no lamp lit, the ridge darkening, the trees going black, but no, he had brought her to her bed and set her down. . . .

"Have I showed you this one, Red Donald?" she said, almost sweetly.

He went to her and stared down at the page she had found with her fingertips, a photograph of MacKay gazing heavenward in his World War I uniform.

"And why would I care to look at a damned picture of him?" he said.

She moved on, her fingers turning and skimming a page in one motion. "I want things . . . not to change anymore." She spoke quietly, not looking at him. "I want to keep what I have."

He looked up at the ceiling and nodded dumbly. "I'll be leaving now," he said.

She closed the book and listened to him cross the room. He put his hand on the doorknob. In the pasture he'd come through, solitary trees pitched their shadows toward the house, clumps of them conspiring at the edge of the woods further back. He thought he could hear them whispering in their dark huddles.

Turn your back and they'd be upon you, the devils. They had so much time on their side.

"The trees are on the march, Mrs. MacKay," he said.

"What? What are you talking about now?" She frowned, her eyes jumping wildly for something to fix on. Red Donald hummed an old hymn deep in his throat. He opened up the door.

"Aw, yes, Mrs. MacKay, they're coming up. You can't see the water at all anymore, not a patch of it. Did you know? Just a wall of trees now, moving up. Won't be long till they knock at your window."

She lay slowly back against her pillow, her eyes roaming the ceiling as if it were sky.

"Trees can be cleared away, Red Donald," she said, her voice faint. "Cut them and clear them away."

"Too many now, dear. Aw, a great many. And slash is so ugly, you know, all grey and scorched looking. It ruins the view. And don't they always march back? Woods for the Little Men? They'll be dancing out there some night. You'll hear them. And the hoofbeats. They'll drum right up to your door. You have a lot of hearing ahead of you, Mrs. MacKay."

"You, Red Donald," she whispered. "You'll be listening too."

He slammed the door as he left, but allowed himself a backward look through the window. She lay with her arms across her eyes. Even with the door closed he could hear the voice, so loud was it now. He fetched his rifle and started down the long overgrown driveway that ran like an old road through the newer woods. He switched on the flashlight but its feeble ray was no use. He didn't care about the deer. Maybe he would never shoot another, not by jacklight, not by the moon or the sun. But he stopped short, released the safety, and fired twice into the air. The shots, loud as cannon, rippled away up the mountain. He fired again, wildly, feeling a shudder in the nearby trees. They seemed so high and thick now, the trees, wind seething through their growing branches. He shivered and hurried away home, waving the flashlight like a wand.

MEAT COVE

When Sara got up from the bed, her skin in the windowlight made him say, "You don't know where that name comes from." He hated the sound of her hustling already into her clothes, in the corner away from the moon. Her pale breasts disappeared under a dark sweater and Clay felt cold.

"What name?" she murmured. She could indulge him a bit. They were separated legally and they had just made love or whatever you called it now.

"That place you were born, down north." He lay on the tousled sheet, one leg drawn up, the other stretched toward her.

"I didn't grow up in Meat Cove." Sara zipped her jeans and pushed her hands through her dark blonde hair. Where was his mind rummaging now? "That's you, Clay. Plucking something out of nowhere."

"Do you know what happened there?" He saw her hand on the doorknob.

"Not much, in my life. My kin told me what a hard place it could be. Hard winters, hard weather." She was glad he was not living here anymore, that she would hear his truck rumble down through the trees and then the house would be hers, quiet except for her own sounds. She wouldn't tell him tonight. Let Knox do that. "It was the end of the world, Clay."

Clay sat up.

"Gangs of hunters showed up there once, in ships. After the moose, see, and there was moose all over those wild mountains. They hunted them for months, just for hides, for their noses. Can you beat that? That's all they were after. Slaughtered whole herds, hundreds at a go. Ten thousand carcasses, up there where you were born. Scattered all over the ground, for their skins. Did you know that? Got so bad the ships smelled it passing off Cape North, the stink. Meat Cove."

"Who told you that?" Sara said.

"An old fella. Or maybe I read it."

"Listen, you got a job on the bridge, if you can keep it. You're back home with your aunt. What makes you talk like this?"

"You want reasons for everything."

"I've got reasons for everything. Are you hanging out with George Lamont again? You over there on that rock? That's what you sound like."

"It happens I'm not, no." Clay gathered the warm sheet over his belly. "What kind of sound *is* that anyway?"

"Drinking. Smoking pot. That sound."

"I'm never drinking when I come here. Am I?"

She sighed. "I think you shouldn't come again, Clay. Let's make tonight the end of that. It was nice, but it's the only bit of nice that's left."

She was gone into the hallway. He listened to her down in the kitchen, the muffled clatter of dishes. She was bitter with him. Rather be on her way to a kid's room, to a child crying because the moon, cold enough to feel, had frightened him. But he and Sara had no baby to contend for, at least. Clay had stayed out too often and too late, and that last wild summer with George Lamont was the clincher, yes. And now he wouldn't be back. God, he'd put some work into this house, hadn't he, floor to shingles. It had been a bachelor's house, her old Uncle Gord's who'd built it years ago by himself when rooms came small and one oil lamp lit them, and he'd lived in it and died in it, alone.

Clay stood in the window rubbing the moon over him like water. He pressed his hand to his ribs, a reflex now, like a man with a bad heart. Before the bridge job he'd driven a big dump truck, gravel, stone, fill, and he'd liked it up there high in that cab, kissing a car ahead of him on the curves down Ross Ferry Road where the Mounties wouldn't see him. He'd come up in a guy's mirror fast, put his grill there like teeth: nowhere to go on that two-laner but straight ahead. It was that momentum he couldn't resist, a noise like flying in his ears, six yards of fill clanging over ruts and tar lines, toeing those airbrakes *chee chee*, tons of stuff behind his head trailing dust like hair, his muscles tight on the wheel. But one morning bright taillights surprised him before he kicked the brake pedal, the airhorn's blast and the deep grunt in his chest fusing as he swerved hard over, rode her down so quick his mouth was just beginning to yell as a wave of dirt broke red over the cab, over the grass of a ditch. His eyes never closed, his mind kept running. It didn't seem like dying, not that fear and strangeness he thought he knew about. A woman leaned down into the cab to help him. She was pale but calm. His breathing hurt badly and she said, I was afraid you'd been killed, your ribs are maybe broken. Her mouth seemed poised for a kiss, and he heard a truck wheel revolving, the crackle of its bearings. His breath came in pains, and later, after he was taped up and stitched up, Sara told him what a sight he looked, that she knew it would happen.

Now she wouldn't linger with him. Hot skin and kisses, but she didn't want him to hold her in her sleep. She didn't want to hear the things he talked about. You're young and you talk like an old man, she would say. But she'd never been up on The Rock. What did she know about talking?

Gord's old hayrake sat in the deep grass below, tines curved like graceful claws. Strange as a spaceship now, waiting to travel. No hay here anyhow, or horses. All sorts of horses in the world, George said one night. Find the right one and he'll take you anywhere you like. Clay had not seen George in many months but his name aroused a taste, a thirst. Up on The Rock they would pop another beer and they would smoke some smoke. Talk? Jesus.

Smelling coffee, Clay dressed. He made the bed, tucking the spread neatly around the pillows, smoothing it out. He leaned down and kissed the spot she had got up from. He was a little afraid, he had to admit that. Sara had melted away from him somehow, right here.

The next morning was Saturday and Clay squatted in the cubbyhole under Aunt Jo's house cursing the water pump he'd promised to fix. Moisture beaded his face like the sweat on the pipes. The earth was dark and sharp in his nostrils, or maybe it was himself he smelled, the beer. The pump kicked in and he studied it dully. Killing time. That's what this was, what all work was, George Lamont believed. Must be something better we can do with time and I think we're doing it, Clay, boy. The pump began to chatter and then he spotted the leak, smelled burnt wire. He shut off the switch and laid his head on the cool dirt. Bare as when it was dug. God, he could sleep here. Those moosehunters were drunk, weren't they, when they brought those animals down like cows and butchered them? What did they do with the noses, for Christ's sake? Aunt Jo's weight compressed the floorboards overhead and then she was calling him.

Knox Robertson, at the foot of the porch steps, was twirling a sprig of lilac in his fingers. "This bush came from your mother's place, over in Jersey Cove," he said to Jo, nodding to Clay who had no lineage there. Bald now, with incipient emphysema, he ran an easygoing law practice, having returned from years out west. "Not much fragrance left, but lovely," he said. "Sara likes it, if I recall."

"I gave her a cutting last year," Jo said. "Don't know if it took."

"She likes roses better," Clay said. At night the lilac bush woke him, a troubling fragrance in his window.

"Clay, have you seen your pal George? His house seems to be neglected in all ways and I'm afraid it will be pounced on for taxes." Knox's father had been a minister and he had that pulpit voice. "There are interested, inquiring parties."

"I haven't since last summer. When the commissionaires let him go."

"Ah, the fish hatchery incident," Knox said. "Pity. Best job George was likely to have anymore."

"George doesn't care."

Knox squinted at him, a habit left over from cigarettes. "How about you, Clay? Do you care?" Then he smiled. "I am sorry about you and Sara."

"Why sorry?" Clay said. "People split up every day. You'd know all about it." Knox had four children strewn randomly over his life but he was not married anymore.

"Split. Such a hard word. And Sara's a lovely girl. Sensible. A man can talk to her."

"Sometimes."

"She's working in that bookstore in Sydney now," Jo put in quickly, pushing faster in the weatherbeaten rocker Clay had painted white.

"George could lose his house for taxes?" Clay said, stepping in front of her.

"Could," Knox said. "If he isn't careful."

"He's not a careful man."

"Ah, no, he isn't. I've never known him to be careful about anything." Knox stepped back onto the grass. His breathing was gravelly and deep. "Clay, Sara's retained me. She wants to file for divorce."

Clay heard Jo's sharp hiss of breath. He felt oddly embarrassed, as if strangers had crowded into his bedroom. "Well, Jesus. I guess she can talk to you right enough."

"Don't be bitter, Clay. It's not revenge."

"What then? It's an ax coming down, any way you look at it." He had thought they would somehow limp along until something got repaired. Until . . . what?

"She wants to be fair," Knox said. "She isn't angry."

"All my fault, is it?"

"We'll have to talk about it, Clay."

"Not this morning."

"Some morning. Soon."

Knox bid Jo good day. Jo leaned out, the way she had when Uncle Charlie was a ferryman, and watched as he negotiated the steep hill.

"I hope he doesn't fall," she said. "His lungs are terrifying."

"He doesn't walk on his lungs."

Jo brushed away a bee. "You know, we've got no water in the house."

"I'm getting to it, Jo."

She rocked a few times, then stopped. "I knew it would come to this," she said.

Clay's head seemed to pound. He clenched his teeth against it. "You don't know what's coming to anything," he said.

He wandered out into the knee-high grass. There was The Rock, a dark hunk of outcropping, bold as a chin. And George's house down below, half-hidden by trees. The sun warmed Clay's face. He wanted a beer. "I want beer," he said, because it sounded funny, Jo on the porch. Someday the water would not run at all. Did she know that? The pump or nothing would work and they'd all be back where they started. The electric lines would sag like old rope. Then what? The Rock might shudder like something heavy had gone by, but it wouldn't slip or crack or go anywhere at all.

"He's down there, is he?" Clay said.

Aunt Jo swept back the curtain, revealing the dark rain-smeared window. She touched her glasses. "Kerosene lamp, that's all he has. I don't know how he gets on down there. Never paid the electrical. He'll walk up to it one day gone, somebody else in the window. Or it burned to the stones."

"I think I'll walk down." Was it not Saturday night and George with a case of Keith's, at least, in his coal shed? Lord Jesus.

"You have to walk down there?" Jo pursed her mouth. "God knows what you'll find."

Clay said nothing back. She had no say anymore. They looked at the TV's sunstruck screen. Clay could not recall what show it was. Trapped without color, bleached figures swam back and forth. Laughter came on and off like a bad lightbulb. Born under sinful circumstances, Clay had been raised by his aunt and his Uncle Charlie. Charlie, bless him, was dead, and Jo had been happy to see Clay marry a nice girl and help her fix up old Gord's house for their own. But here he was back in the tiny parlor sitting again on the sofa, his wife on the other side of the water, wide as the ocean now. Jo loved Clay but this was not the way she wanted him home. He was not a bachelor anymore, he was something far more difficult, something new. But the TV washed out all difficult talk, of him, of Sara, of George Lamont who was back on the hill. Let the rain hiss on the window. No, she did not want Clay to walk down that hill where a yellow smudge of light burned in the trees. Before he was married she would tell him, Stay away from that man, good Lord he's twenty years older if a day, in ways you don't need to know about. But Clay was past twenty-one even then and he didn't have to listen, and she never knew George like he did anyhow, up on The Rock. Still, Clay wanted to break the cold feeling in the air, wanted Jo to say, Go on down then, see your chum if you have to, you've had bad news today. But she wanted to tell him, You and George last summer, you wrecked your marriage with it barely begun, carrying on up on that rock night after night, and don't start it again. Yet she could not say that, only wish it.

"The rain's chilly tonight," Jo said. "You can catch cold, you know."

Clay glanced at the books tumbled underneath her chair. Paperback romances, all hot breath and throats and half-shed garments. Once with a few beers in him Clay had read a random page out loud, whistling at the steamy gyrations it described. Jo snatched it away and said calmly, It's okay what they're doing, they're married. Would Uncle Charlie have agreed, or jammed it in the coal stove? Clay could not imagine what kind of love had been between them, how Jo's silly books touched on it, if they did, or what they touched on at all. She and Charlie were already old, many years married, when they took him in. In the marriages around them, divorce was only someone else's problem.

"It's July, Jo. I don't think I'll perish."

"You could have perished in that truck," she said. "You had a chance to, and you'll have a chance again."

The path to George's curved down below The Rock, a granite prow in the hillside. The Rock Bar and Grill. George would have hollered to him by now were he up there waiting, Get out of the rain, b'y, we're open for business. Rain had never mattered that summer. Jo would hear them singing and shout down before she went to bed, Are you daft or what? But she never came out to The Rock, the path too steep and narrow. Yell into the night? Yes, they had done that, all sails full and flying.

He lost George's light in the young spruce where he roused a sleeping bird, a small alarm of wings and raindrops. He'd have to hack some branches here, the path was after closing in. But there was the kitchen window, hardly enough to see by. Back from two marriages in Boston, George had claimed the family house three years ago, the last of these Lamonts. Clay banged on the door. A bad gutter streamed water over the steps.

"Oh, Jesus, it's himself." George stood in the dim doorway rubbing his face. "Thought it was the police."

"I heard there was a hot bar in this neck of the woods."

"Heat we could use." George waved his hand vaguely at the room behind him. Clay was struck by the clutter, the obvious domestic failure. George had always been neat. The lamp, its chimney soiled with soot, the wick coiled like an eel in its amber pedestal, smelled of kerosene. The house seemed reduced to this kitchen, to a clinging odor of winter damp.

"What're you staring at? I look like a squatter or what?" George said. His bitter tone caught Clay off guard. "There's talk, I know."

"Maybe a little rimracked," Clay said, unsure of the footing, wanting to kid. "Who cares?"

"Jesus, Clay. Every soul who's left around here cares." The table was littered with cereal boxes and dirty bowls. "You'd think a twice-married man could do better than this, eh? But you, Clay. Married to a nice girl, and up on the bridge now, I heard. Good boy yourself."

How did Sara get into their gab already? She had never been in it up on The Rock, Clay had seen to that.

"I like the bridge, sure. Up high's fine."

"No pot puffing there, b'y. Eh?" George's smile was flat and mirthless. "Lord Jesus, you'd fall like a stone. Got any on you?"

"Would I come down without it?"

Clay fished out a joint, passed it lit to George's eager fingers. There was that few seconds of private silence while they both held smoke. Clay thought he could hear a leak somewhere in the rooms above.

"Wife doesn't like it, I bet?" George said, passing it back.

"Not a problem," Clay said.

"Jesus. A married man without problems."

Clay stubbed out the roach in a tea-stained saucer.

"I don't even have a bottle of beer to give you," George said. "Sorry."

Hurt, Clay shrugged. A beer and the promise of many more was the next step in a dance. He had beer up the hill, sure, but fetching it would be a stoned nuisance. "Whatever you've got then," he said. "Long as it isn't water."

George waved his hands over the table like a magician. "They expect a man to come back better than he left. Remember that, laddybuck, when you go someplace you need to come back from." He held out a bottle of clear liquor.

"Christ, vodka." Clay hated its medicinal blandness, something you'd hand to a sick man. Nothing like the sheer cool volume of beer washing through you, the wet cold bottles going back and forth. But he took a mouthful and the taste, sparked by pot, seemed to score his throat. When his voice returned he asked George what the hell that was, you could run a chainsaw with it.

"Cape Breton silver, b'y."

"Lead, more like it. You drinking this stuff all the time? You working anywhere?"

George fiddled with the lamp wick, curled back the smoke until the yellow light burned steadily. His hair was cut badly, high on the sides like he'd done it blind. His wide shoulders hung like a hanger under his shirt.

"I was painting over at the mall," George said. "I got me foot in here and there for something better."

Something better? Clay nearly laughed. George had had good jobs since he returned from Boston, so good that people were stunned when he lost them. He looked good in a coat and tie. That afternoon he climbed up to The Rock in his navy blue commissionaire's uniform, he looked like someone important, his white hat raked over his brow like a captain's. That had been a job men would kill for. Security, pension. But George never invoked those magic words, and Clay had admired him for that—how lightly he regarded things that mattered so much to other people. Don't give me a beer, I got to have breath like a baby's, he told Clay. I start watchman tonight over at the hatchery.

"Now the bridge," George said. "Job for life, that. Got kiddies on the way?"

"Got nothing on the way, if you need to know." He didn't like George's tone, or that Sara was somewhere behind it. He set the moonshine where George could reach it. Was the bridge a job George had wanted? They'd never have touched him, not after the hatchery.

"You been so busy, I suppose. You been clean out of sight," George said. He took a good pull from the bottle and gave a little whoop, wiping his eyes.

"Me?" Clay said. "Hide nor hair of you around here."

"Was in Sydney. Been there all the time. You could've found me."

"I'm supposed to go looking for you? I had a life to lead."

"You led one last summer all right."

"No. It seems I didn't."

"You could've fooled me, boy."

Fooled him? George had been on duty at the hatchery but three weeks when Clay smelled breath on him that was not a baby's. There's duff on your hat, George, he told him, and I'd look to that necktie. George turned his eyes to him and they were not eyes for a night watchman. Call in sick, Clay said, a man's got a right to be sick. That night a fisherman casting for escaped trout tied his skiff to the fish pens and George put his flashlight on him as only George could do and ordered him in salty terms to leave. Eagles dive for the damn trout all day long, the man said, and George said, here's wings for you then and punched him in the jaw. By the time the Mounties arrived George was sitting with his bare feet in the water, hat and coat discarded behind him, watching a quart bottle bob above the fish. He was back on The Rock the next night, saying, what can they do to me I can't do to myself?

"Steady work, steady money. That's the bridge," Clay said. "It's not the end of the rainbow."

"You have to turn in early, eh? Mind your p's and q's?"

"I can't work shitfaced, can I?" Clay's face flared. It wasn't the job itself he liked so much as some feeling of being up there above things—the way they'd been on The Rock, other lives flowing by below. "Got any music around here? We need some noise, boy. My God, last year we'd be on The Rock by now."

Below them this house would be roaring with light. George was older, sure, but he had ridden a high like a longwinded horse.

"You know, you don't hear the music like you used to. Not a fiddle in a kitchen, no," George said, his voice gone dreamy.

"Jesus, we had a cassette player, George. Remember? Don't you listen to anything here?"

"Ah, laddie, what would you know?"

"Sit down, George. You make me jumpy."

But George suddenly dipped his head in a pail by the sink. He rose up, water streaming from his face.

"That's better. Hot in here."

"You could use a wash," Clay said.

"Don't talk to me like that."

"Like what?"

"Like you just bumped into me in a bar."

George dropped into a crouch and cocked his wide bony fists. Clay saw how thin and white his wrists were. He'd boxed in the army, and up on The Rock he and Clay had sparred harmlessly, laughing.

"That the Billy Martin punch?" Clay said. He wasn't in the mood. When George lived in Boston he'd enjoyed Martin's public scrapes, the ones in bars, not on the baseball field. "He's a sucker puncher," George said, "I'm sure of it."

"He got his finally, didn't he, old Billy? Some young guy busted his teeth."

"False teeth," George said. He danced his fists in the lamplight, shook water from his hair. "You get to be sixty and you're still a prick, it's going to catch up to you. Your Aunt Jo, she doesn't approve of George, does she. I'm not as welcome as I was."

"Who cares anyway? Look, I'll go get us a carton of Keith's, and I got another joint here. Damn it, it's Saturday!" Clay listened to the urgency in his own voice—like blowing on ashes. Would Sara smile, seeing this kind of need? She could spot needs easily, and last summer he would not have cared one way or the other. He did not move to get up.

"Sure," George said vaguely. "Sure." He opened the back door and stared into the noise of the spattering gutter. The rain was merely steady, dense and light, misting into the room. "I'm feeling a little moosey tonight," he said, testing an old line, tuning it. "Wool, hair or feathers, I'd fuck it."

For a few panicked moments Clay thought George was talking to someone on the steps and that surged through his heart with complex possibilities, good and bad, and then subsided.

"George? Shut the door, eh? Nothing out there we don't know about."

"You're sure?" He closed the door softly. On the back of his brown Woolco trousers a store label was still affixed, a detail Clay found so sad he didn't know how to mention it.

"You ever been to Meat Cove?" Clay said, sucking on the charred roach until it burned his fingers. "Up that way?"

"I wouldn't go way up there unless a woman was waiting. Look, I went to Boston and I had it good. I had wives and houses and cars. What else is there in this world? But I fucked it up. People don't forgive that. I'm not as welcome as I was."

"To hell with that," Clay said, squeezing his hands, wanting a beer, several nicely within reach, their cold graspable necks. "You know about the moose they wiped out up around Meat Cove? Gristle and blood all over those mountain fields, and this tremendous smell whirling out to sea."

"Just meat," George said. "Like the name says. Don't get lost up there, Clay. Your head wanders sometimes."

George picked up the lamp and raised it toward the wall where he'd tacked a yellowed calendar.

"Now here's something to fix on. Found this in a closet. 1942. God. Look, it shows the moons. The full ones solid black. War moons. War all over the world. I came along under this one, Clay. Right upstairs. Midwife. Bella Corbett. You wouldn't know her. Friday. That same moon. My dad was off at a dance. He wasn't much of a dancer but Jesus he could fight." George set the lamp back on the table, his face an agony of shadows above it. "You ever notice there's always some arsehole who *thinks* he can stepdance?"

"Every time. Never fails. I met Sara at a dance."

George stood over the table swaying faintly. Frowning, he regarded Clay. "A dance down at the old ferry wharf, I heard. It's on now. We could go. You and me."

Clay saw too vividly the summer folks and their kids milling about, and a few locals who would know him. He did not want to explain himself, not in the smallest way, not stoned. "We're not fit to drive. Or walk either, come to that. This the only lamp you got?"

"Scared? Need more light?" George sat down across from him. He drank from the bottle, then shook it. "You're a kid. I forget that."

"Well forget it again. When did it matter?"

"It always mattered, Clay." George turned his ear to the ceiling. "Hear them? People lived here a long time."

Clay laughed but a tingle cooled the skin of his neck. "So what?"

"Walk all night sometimes, they do. Footsteps. Up the stairs, down. I hear them in the hall outside my door. They stop and I can tell they're just standing there, listening. Or maybe they're hugging each other for all we know, or some long kissing going on. Eh? Oh, I don't see them. Just hear their steps. Talk's not part of it and they want me to know that. Talk's not important where they are."

"I'm hearing rain, George. That and your goddamn gab."

"What they want *you* to hear, you haven't the ears for."

"You could lose this house for taxes, George. Knox Robertson told me. Fuck the ghosts."

"Fuck Knox Robertson. I won't ever lose it."

"Sure."

Clay felt his jaw clamp tight: he suddenly wanted to hurt George, to cut him. But he didn't speak. It would pass, and there was no fun in that anyhow, those stoned moments of sharp meanness. If you didn't swallow them and keep them down, you could kill an evening, or worse.

"Anything left in that bottle, George?"

"Not a spider."

The hatchery lay in woods along a deep cove, quiet and back from the strait, low prefabs and pens lit by lights spaced like street-lamps. Too much slack time there, that was the trouble, nothing for George to answer to but a string of time clocks and by that night they had already betrayed him. He asked Clay to drive him there. He wanted him to see the fish pens, enclosures of submerged mesh where the trout thrived. The catwalks, laid on floats, moved sleepily under their feet, tiny waves scissoring the reflected light. George aimed his flashlight into the water where the trout were raised on corn raining down on them at certain times of day. Waiting for corn isn't much of a life, George said. The fish hovered aimlessly in the dusty shaft George swept over them back and forth, their flanks flashing as they slowly turned and turned again in the light. They're different in a river, he said, they even taste different. You can always tell. Sometimes I watch them till the batteries burn out. That's George all over, Aunt Jo said when she heard he'd punched himself out of the commissionaires, and there you are over there on that rock howling your life away with him, he had good things and he threw them away like trash.

But what were the good things? The liquor fumed in Clay's brain. "Jesus Christ, George! My wife is divorcing me. She's got Knox working on it. Knox, the man who got you out of jail that time."

George sat back and grinned. He held the bottle up like a trophy. "Welcome to the club, Clay, b'y. In the morning this is the only thing on my mind. The one and only thing."

Club?

"You're free, a free man!"

Clay squinted at him. "I don't *feel* free."

"Listen. Grow up. Some of us aren't made for it. Took me two wives. Two."

"And then what, George?" Clay looked slowly around the kitchen. "This?"

George waved him away. His head had begun dipping and bobbing, his eyes losing focus. "My summerhouse, Clay. Just for summer."

"Summer, sure, fine. Jesus!" Clay was surprised by his own anger. He felt like screaming. Let's get some sunshine around here, let's make a little racket! He grabbed up his uncle's sou'wester, patted his pocket. They had to make a move, now, before George was banged out for the night. He couldn't hear any rain. But George's head drooped and his talk collapsed quickly into mere sound, his words mashed into cadences, the brogue he'd grown up with just a melody now of incoherent talk.

Clay sat on The Rock, a chilled bottle in his hand, a carton of Keith's at his feet. The evening had turned so fine it pained him to be here alone. The light in George's window had dimmed out. Bats swirled like dark leaves out of the cold chimney. Christ, it had been like a bad date, so sure was Clay they could pick up that summer again and shake it into life. He drew on a joint, the only fire he could feel. The moon was cool and white and high, washing cleanly over a deer-gnarled apple tree. Oh, that tart fruit, as a kid he'd bit it and spit it out. From out on the water he could hear the clank and splash of a scallop dragger, the tired shouts of its crew. Late at it, and in those played-out beds. Work. And marriage. Was that all there was? Were they really the main things, and if you lost them, life was no good? George didn't care a damn, that was plain. Before, it had seemed just a way with him, something he wanted to make a point about. But now there was no work for that man, any-where. Was there a woman? A bat dipped close to Clay's face but he didn't flinch. In your hand they were like fierce mice, harmless, teeth too tiny to break your skin. Divorce. A peculiar word, effem-inate, high-toned and tawdry at the same time. Clay hung his legs over the edge, a cold jut of granite. Maybe George would be okay in a day or two. Him on the bridge? Lord, Clay could see him falling, not like he had one night from here, ten feet down, laugh-ing drunk, but from the platform whose height Clay knew so well: a body tumbling slowly toward water, shrinking, gyrating like a dummy in a movie, its entry a faint splitting of wood.

Clay stood unsteadily in spirea leaves, his hand raised to tap the parlor window, Jo sunk in her stuffed chair, bifocals cocked at an open book a stranger might have thought was the Bible. No, he wouldn't scare her, he'd done enough of that. She was old and he was drunk and this wasn't his house anymore. Sara would be over on the other side now, alone in that house. Her house. In bed sometimes Clay had reached up and touched the old wall-paper, feeling the woodgrain underneath. *Was* she alone? That she might not be came hot into his face. But they were separated. And soon they would be cleaved by divorce. What could he say to her? If another man wasn't there now, he would be. Matter of time. Sex and jealousy. So simple, so easy, Clay wished he could blame them. But the wrong between him and Sara lay somewhere else. In Meat Cove the cliffs leaned back from the sea, she said. There were jagged rocks down there in the water. She remembered that. Well, it could have been worse, growing up with all that old bone in the ground, that blood, a mountain high up your back and that gray rage of sea in your face.

When Clay arrived, most of the crew had already slipped under the bridge to the platform. Wind, crazy with sun, blasted about the latticework and Clay was sure they'd be knocked off before noon. Kevin Burton and his pal Tommy, huddled in orange coveralls, remained on the bridgewalk, their backs hunched to the chilly air in that pose of boredom. They'd be handling paint cans and hoses but Clay would be messing around underneath, helmeted like an astronaut, sweeping blood-red primer over joists and braces like the undercarriage of some great truck. He grinned at Kevin since Kevin disliked him so much. Tommy MacQuarrie was rubbing his hands and doing a little dance.

"You're getting later every day, "Kevin said.

Clay spat toward the roadbed. "For what?"

"You look shaky, boy," Tommy said. "Pale, like."

Clay ignored him. Tommy pushed a lit cigarette at him and Clay took a drag, letting the smoke drift from his mouth.

"Your job could be in danger, boy," Kevin said.

"I'll give you danger. I'll fling your arse off this bridge."

"Easy," Tommy said. "They don't like that talk here."

"Fuck them."

"Saw your Sara go by," Kevin said, brazen, like she'd just strolled by a second ago. Clay looked quickly down the bridge. Sometimes she did drive past and it chuffed him, even yet, her eyes fast on the road but catching, he always hoped, a sidewise look at him, her pretty face fixed so seriously on the road because she didn't like the sudden gusts of wind. He had loved that face and it hurt to think of it, the skin his lips felt, the closed eyes he'd kissed. That she might not even *like* him now scared him deeply.

"Sara, sure," Clay said. "Going to work like she does. So what?"

Kevin just smiled and Clay wanted to hit him. He had, one afternoon back in the garage when he asked Clay if Sara was seeing anybody special, he'd like to ask her out. Clay surprised him enough that Kevin didn't push things too far. Maybe they would tear into each other at some square dance, maybe not. Tourists' cars, flushed out by the bright morning, shot by. Clay felt dizzy, exposed. How did he appear to them, if they bothered to glance? A young man in loud orange squinting at the wind, an upkeeper of the bridge, some Cape Breton guy spotting up the scenery, waiting for divorce, watching his wife drive by like he was part of the superstructure? A Massachusetts car sped past, snapping the cloth of his coveralls. Suddenly he was thinking about a drink. He had never phrased it just that way. I want a drink of water, yes, he'd said that on a hot day, or Jesus, I'd like a cold beer. But now there was this way of saying it: I need, I want, Jesus, I could do with a drink. A whole jug of water sat not six feet away but it wasn't that thirst at all.

"You ought to get below," Kevin said. "They're waiting."

"When I'm ready." Clay took another hit of Tommy's cigarette. "You look like a rocket," he said to him. "The coveralls were new."

"Jesus," Tommy said. "If they can't spot us now, nothing will save us."

The bridge seemed to inhale when a car passed, and deeper when a tractor trailer downgeared behind it. Clay watched a train of cars tailing a familiar white Rabbit, its fenders and panels burned with rust. Knox, heading for Sydney. And wasn't that George sitting in the back seat like Knox was a cabbie? George

didn't wave, didn't so much as look in Clay's direction, and that
stung him so hard he felt hot. Clay leaned over the railing as if
he were sick. The water, greened deeply from the dark mountain
trees this time of the morning, was slashed with currents. The
lone buoy beneath the bridge cut a wake like a tiny boat.

"What *would* save us?" Clay said. "Who from?"

"Yes, dear, he'd prefer lamplight," Nora said. Clay walked with
his cousin along the edge of Wentworth Park pond. Ducks gathered near them, then dispersed when they saw no bread.

"That was a month ago," Clay said. "I haven't seen him."

"No, you haven't." Nora had angry black hair Clay liked,
always mussed from combing it with her nervous, slender fingers.
"You touch him?"

"What?"

"Bone. Skin the color of an old sheet. Some days he can't
piss. He blacks out and he can't remember what he did, what he
said. Just as well sometimes. See him in daylight, dear."

"I aim to. I got something on my mind."

Nora blew out smoke impatiently, flicking her cigarette
away, a sharp hiss in the dull green water. She had a pretty mouth
and Clay was distracted by her lips. Her face was faintly freckled
like a girl's.

"George's candle is about burned, and vodka burns good,"
she said.

"Jesus, Nora, you got him on skid row already? No, go 'way."

"Clay, dear. Go up to the Keltic Tavern, go on. It's afternoon.
You might find him there with his cronies, splitting pension
checks, cadging drinks from each other when they're broke."

"I will, I'll do that." But the Keltic was not The Rock Bar and
Grill, that he knew. It would not be George and himself but
other men, afternoon men crouched over the small disarranged

tables. Some would be quiet, some quarrelsome. George had always seemed to him a man with friends, a drinking talker who could draw company to him if company were to be had. "He could probably use a few dollars."

"You may depend."

They stopped to let two little girls dash by them crying to the ducks, waving slices of white bread like money. Their urgent shrieks struck the oily surface of the pond like glints. His head felt unfit for information, his wits thick in the sticky air. He regretted that he had come into Sydney looking for George. There were moments when he was not sure which George he was looking for or what he wanted if he found him. Clay spoke close to his cousin's face to be heard over the racket of the ducks.

"We were real pals last year, Nora, George and me. Older, younger, didn't matter. Why did it sound so far in the past, years away, like he was telling her about his youth? We could've died together that summer," he said, seized suddenly by the truth of it, the heart. "That's how it was."

Nora fixed her frank blue eyes on him. "But you *didn't* die together, or apart. Now if you want to catch up, you'd better hurry. George has a lead on you." She peered at him, patted his cheek. "I think."

"He used to box, you know," Clay said, cocking his own fists and looking at them.

"Listen, dear, George can hardly walk straight. That guy they found beaten to a pulp downtown? His body was a sight now, I'll tell you. And who did it? His drinking buddies. George has an awful tongue sometimes."

The girls were tossing, with dainty wrists, bits of bread like flowers to a crowd, their faces serious. Nora started walking and Clay let her go a ways. Why had she never married? She still had a figure, Lord. Chubbier, but hell in those jeans.

"Sara never knew him, not really," Clay said, catching her. "She didn't . . . I didn't see it myself, this what you're telling me."

"Oh, he had plenty of drinking tales to tell, didn't he. Joke about it, sure. But problems? Never. If you want to rile him, just say, look, you could still get help, you don't have to end up in the gutter. Oh, my." Nora took Clay's arm and sat them down on a bench. "George is a drunk, plump and plain. He's been one for summers and seasons. On rocks or water, it wouldn't matter. He wanted me to marry him. Sure. Years ago. When he came back from Boston, I used to let him stay over some nights. Then I had to tell him on the phone, listen, I've got one bed and I sleep in it. I'll give you a meal, and that's it. He cursed me good, finally, so I hardly see him. His nerves are raw as razors. He'll say sorry but he can't remember for what. Oh, he always had soft spots, but I can't find them anymore. Maybe you can. Take him a pint of vodka, why not. The man is dying, dear."

The soot-colored ducks, drifting like decoys and dozing now, were nudged by a warm harbor breeze. A gull glided swanlike in their midst and the girls watched it soberly, hands at their sides. Up on a side street an ice-cream cart was clanging and they ran toward the sound. Clay could feel the hot push of traffic on the main road. He would need, soon, a quiet place with beer. A man in a pedal boat pumped by, grinning, churning a wake.

"We'll have to try one of those, Clay, next time you're here," Nora said.

"I'll be on the pogey by then."

"Jesus, you didn't lose your job, did you, Clay?"

"No, no. No, I'm on leave, like. Straightening things out. You ever been to Meat Cove, Nora?"

"God, no, dear. Why would I go up there?"

"I just thought maybe you'd been."

"It's a shame about you and Sara. It is, you know."

That bookstore where she worked, it was new. Not too far from the Keltic. What would he say to her, there in those books? "There's nothing to be done," he said.

"Is that so? I don't believe it."

"Would you believe that's Knox Robertson over there?" Clay shaded his eyes, pointing across the pond. There he was, dapper in a straw hat, the brim tipped down. Nora waved to him.

"He coming over here?" Clay said. He did not fancy any kind of conversation with Knox.

"No," Nora said. "I'm going over there."

"You? Legal matters, is it?"

"It's just dinner and a drive, then I'm back to work."

"I didn't know you knew him that close, Nora."

"Oh, since a while. He's in town a lot."

"Christ, don't tell him anything bad about me."

Nora hugged him and kissed his mouth hard, a quick taste of sex lingering there, like always, and Clay had to smile. "I don't know anything bad enough to tell," she said. "I wouldn't anyway."

He watched her set off around the pond, her white blouse whiter for her coal-colored hair. George, the bastard, he'd slept with her and never said a word. And what was Knox to her? No accounting sometimes for what a woman liked and didn't. Sara doesn't want hard feelings, Knox said on the phone, she isn't asking for much. Jesus.

A young woman in shorts glanced at Clay as she pushed a stroller by, her baby, stunned by its pacifer, lolling under a white bonnet. There was an instant of contact and he knew all he had to say was hello but he looked away. On the mown grass a man in a business suit napped under a newspaper, fingers locked on his belly. Clay had always wanted to be older, but he did not want to feel like this. Not many years ago he had yearned for nothing more than the privileges of a man, the right to mess up, if it came to that, his own life. George. Up at the Keltic. Shabby, skinny, his eyes dead, like a fish on sand. George was not an old man. Clay had soared with him. They'd spread their arms like wings one night, they were feeling so good, the lights on the water like strips of lit silk and the wind warm as breath. George was flying and nothing could stop him. He did not want to be stopped, ever: keep going, b'y, another beer, higher, higher, nobody can touch us up here, to hell with them all, don't let's die with a lunch bucket. And there was no real difference between the wormlike glow in the dark hills, whatever it was (fire? spirits?) or the satellite they saw crossing against the stars, blinking out its slow incredibly fast arc, and George said at first a shooting star but then they both quit yelling and looked and knew it wasn't any sort of star, not pulsing like that, not something out of that white burst up there at all but the steady beat of their own lives and they jeered it, they whooped like dogs, they booed that arcane collection of metal and circuits clean out of sight, and then they danced, they hooked arms to Scotty Fitzgerald's violin, the cassette player turned up so loud that Ethel the retired librarian up near the woods flashed her lonely porch light angrily a few times before she gave up, and George lost his footing and disappeared off the edge of The Rock into the lion's paw juniper below, too stoned to be hurt, and then emerged staggering back up, laughing, breathless, the wind gone out of him, and then they divined women, extolled their virtues like preachers, sweetthought them into shapes and fantasies of talk, lines too outrageous for real life. Even Nora had been there in their words, but George not letting on he'd known her naked, and he and Clay wrestled clumsy as bears and George showed him how to throw a right cross, his wide white fist brushing

Clay's nose, the pot expanding Clay's notion of power as he aimed left hooks at the sky, and they heard a stag snort in the woods as the red ash of the last joint was lost in their fingertips, and Clay remembered that Sara was at home, over in Uncle Gord's bachelor house where the dry wood smelled old, in those half-hearted bedrooms, he'd never wanted a family, Uncle Gord, you could never feel kids in any corner of that house, a house an old lonely man drew around him like a blanket. And then Clay had suddenly gone quiet there on The Rock, as if he had taken in the whole evening in one gulp, its pleasure and craziness constricting to one inhalation of air, beyond talk. How easily, until that moment, had he forgotten Sara, shaping so easily other women in his mind, their mouths, their willing arms.

How could ducks flip up like that and dive into blind green water? Clay stood quickly as if a bus had arrived. Was that George over there, by the pavilion where kids were playing? No, he did not have that stiffback gait, not even drunk he didn't. In the wakes the ducks made, the sun danced sharply. Jesus. The Keltic was a long hot walk away. George would be sitting there telling stories. Like how he lost his driving license in Boston after hitting a trooper's car in a snowstorm, not his fault, he said, just weather, and if a bottle rolled under the seat, that was not the cause of anything anyone else had claim to, good or bad. But Meat Cove was not a story he knew. Not the fields of moose, the fetid wind, the dark rumps of meat scattered like a battle had gone through, skulls and antlers flung like driftwood. Sara told Clay once that the land stopped brutally there, the cliffs of streaked rock were slung back from that bare blind sea. If it caught you out when a storm was on, it would bash you to bone, boat or man, surging up those rocks white and roaring, and in that foam you would be no more than a glimpse of driftwood, a wet flash of skin. Moose die anyway, George would say, what's it matter if you can't get high, moose blood from Cape North to Sydney doesn't matter unless we get high, you and me, or you, or me.

Along the edge of the bridgewalk the railing had disappeared or had never been there. The water below was gray as dusk, an angry tide in long sinewy currents. The eddies were like living scars, white. The latticework hummed with wind, a fiddle drone, not music but urgent and ambiguous chords. Clay hesitated, sensing the sudden space, but there was a thrill to it too, and this fear he knew he could come back from. He did not jump but rather fell, unpushed and easy. The first instant of regret passed, and his horror of falling, honed by months high on the bridge, passed with it. The fall lasted so long, the luxury of its surprise, he could note that the water rushing to meet him was green as glass and that its flawed translucence he would enter, feeling it the same moment he was consumed. His clothing trembled like feathers. His eyes could not open wide enough to take in what he saw, so tiny was he becoming to the world, so rapidly. A hurtling name. A speck. A particle.

Clay sat up before he woke, before he knew he was not under water. His breath came in hoarse whispers, his heart a pump gone crazy. His hand roamed over the sheet for Sara whom nightmare had never seemed to touch, but this was not her bed. His fear, palpable as an embrace, faded slowly into the outside dark: falling, turning in air, the water arriving. And no one else anywhere detectable: it was that chill that left him weak.

At breakfast the sun seemed to stream over the table like a brook. Clay ate with the sun in his eyes and grumbled about the eggs.

"Like you always ate them," Aunt Jo said. "Scrambled like always. Scrambled like you."

Clay held his ragged head. No bridge. No trucks and cars blustering by. "Radio yesterday said rain. Where is it? Is the wind up?"

"And why?"

"I'm not in the mood for the bridge, that's why." He could not tell her. He stared into the black puddle of his coffee.

"It's no wonder, the fresh pile of bottles in the coal shed." Jo poked him gently. "You'd be wise to strap yourself to that bridge this morning, my man. They'll be dipping you out like a fish."

"I'm never bothered. I'm used to that rigmarole up there." It was something he would miss, and not miss. But it would dog him a long time.

"Is Sara liking her new job, have you heard?" Jo said from the sink, her back to him.

"What Sara likes doesn't matter," he said, surprised. "Not to me now."

Jo stopped washing his plate, the sponge in her hand. "You're a foolish man. Lord, you are."

The way she said it, he could have been ten. But he had no reply, nothing that could make him feel older or better. He stared at a streak of mist hovering like stone above the strait. Good God. And there would be no crowing about it, not on The Rock or anywhere.

Going north, he didn't have to cross the bridge, and once he was over the mountain, across Englishtown ferry and headed up the coast, his head cleared, its smoke and murk and fuss thinned away. His old pickup shuddered as he pushed it past sixty and then he had to dawdle behind the broad stern of a motorhome. He wanted beer desperately and none to be had before Ingonish. Coming on Wreck Cove, he stopped at the general store for Cokes, pausing to size up the lobsters in the tank: Jo would enjoy one, but they were hardly more than canners, a middling season nearing its end. He drank a can quickly, squeezing its cool metal as he drove, the sugar easing into his blood, and maybe the caffeine would get him to the provincial liquor store. Not a road to hurry on in any case. The second can got him over Smoky Mountain, a stretch of switchbacks where bad drivers sometimes swayed into your lane. The high drop-offs to the sea caught his nerves, beckoned, the low guardrail just a quick tumble toward the rocks. He could too easily see his truck, the wheels whacked out from under it, veering off, capsizing into space. He kept well back from the trailer ahead, wincing when its taillights brightened, braking, gearing down. Family in that rig, a boy in the rear window, palming the glass like it was his playroom while Ingonish Bay broadened out below. Clay lost the trailer to a gas station and held to a steady fifty kilometres through Ingonish. By Ingonish Village the liquor commission lay behind him and he wanted terribly to turn back, wanted the lovely jingling sound of bottled beer at his feet, but this journey had a certain rhythm to it now and that would break it, and so he drove on in a kind of sorrow, as if he had passed up a lovely hitchhiker holding a sign that said Meat Cove. Around Sugarloaf and through that valley that leafed out like crazy in the fall, his thirst was real and threatening, Cokes thrumming in his blood. Sara had taken him through here one Sunday before they married, October, the long thin light of autumn, all the sun seeming to gather into leaves bright as flowers. Sara and the mood and the light of those trees he would have liked to have again, but all that greened out into the wooded slopes of the mountains. They hadn't gone as far as Meat Cove that day, he and Sara, it was at the end of the last road and they had no reason then, no desire to go. Born there I was, she said, but it's too far for a Sunday like this one.

He was well into the north mountains and then out of them, the ocean coming up so vast he squinted, and he was climbing up and down a coast road, across a brook bridge, and then high again, no cars coming toward him. Was Meat Cove as far as anyone had wanted to live, wanted to dig their hearts into? Who first took this place seriously, who said there's enough meadow up here to hold a small farm, to cling to for all you're worth? Shipwrecked men?

Clay pulled over where a grassy run of ground spilled toward the cliff. The ocean lay quiet, a steep look down. A yellow boat bobbed small as a kid's, a lobsterman moving from trap to trap, spurts of wake in the gray sea, the engine clear as conversation when it revved. Out in the northeast, St. Paul's Island was a hazy blue object, the last rock and earth before sea claimed everything. Lightkeepers had lived there once. Uncle Charlie told Clay about a family whose girl, sick with appendix, had been plucked off the rocks in stormy morning hours by a cutter crew: they had to lay their boat in close so a good wave would carry it up in the dark and set it down on flat rock, not crush it but set it there high enough until the girl was aboard and the next high sea could lift them away free. Clay had loved the story, the joy of rescue, the danger, the cool skill, the girl going off in a roaring sea, safe. Sara must have looked out into these misty distances, little as she was, must have seen what Clay was seeing. Even children would remember this out their windows, the angry weather on the way. The lobster boat barely rose and fell. Clay wondered where Sara's house had been, he'd seen so few.

As he turned back to his truck, a big Mercury, lumpy with rusted chrome, stopped in the middle of the road. An elderly man at the wheel yelled out was anything the matter, was he broke down? "No, no," Clay said. When he raised his hand to wave him off, he caught sight of an odd little house sitting a ways above the road. Clay glanced quickly behind him at the view that site would enjoy: a long expanse of sea, and the Cape North headlands.

"Say, who lives up *there?*" he said.

The man removed his baseball cap and leaned out the driver's window. "That? Nobody. Squatter fella had it once. Built her." He rolled a cigarette in one smooth motion, closing it with a lick and a twirl of fingers. "Hippie," he said, but neutrally, as he would say *crow* or *spruce* because it was there in his landscape. But he let the word sink in, become specific. "Had a purple shirt, with beads sewn in it. Sure could see him coming. Harmless. But odd, you know. Odd."

"Christ, it's a strange rig," Clay said, shading his eyes. Homemade, for sure. From here, it seemed all points and angles, something out of a folktale. "Where's he got to?"

The old man turned off his crackling radio. "This young fella was from the States, way down there someplace, I forget. Some years back. Got a girl pregnant and it troubled him so awful he come way up here. Something, eh? Guess it was a burden to him." The man glanced up at the house. "Vexed him so, he started starving himself. A penance like, I guess. Put that funny little house together with stones and wood and starved in it. Found him too late they did, took him off to Baddeck and he died there. Right in that little hospital they have. Never woke up."

"How come nobody knew?" Clay said, frowning at the man like he'd had a hand in it. "Nobody knew he wasn't eating anything?"

The man put the cigarette in his pocket and the car in gear, checking its lurch with the brake. "Was thin when he got here. Just got thinner, that fella, far as I could see. He was some religious. No kind of religious we knew."

The car rattled carefully away and was gone over the next bend. Clay swayed in a sudden wind. Into a rising swell the lobster boat raised and dipped its prow. Rain had begun out at sea, stippling the metallic water, a long light sigh sweeping toward him.

Clay drove on, the paved road turned to dirt and began to wind into the dense green height of the mountain, down into a switchback and through a cove issuing from a deep valley, past a house near the road. Maybe Sara's? Her kin? What would he say if he knocked on the door anyway, and what would they tell him? She's long gone from here, boy, from this rugged spot. The road curved up and he could see the end, the last house, a mown field where you could picnic near the cliffs, and beyond there was a trail into the tree-darkened slopes. The cliffs leaned back, pushed by the sheer weight of what they'd been through. The ocean bore upon them. Their steepness plunged to pinnacled rock, to strewn and fractured boulders the water was slowly covering and revealing. In the cove an open boat had been hauled up the black sand. Up on the headland the woods leveled into clear spaces. Maybe the moose had been routed there. You needed open ground for that. But Sara was not here. He could not feel anything about her in this place, not what she'd left, not what she'd started with. She was in another house now, her own. She had made it that. Clay had never met her Uncle Gord but could see him nevertheless sitting at that square maple table in the kitchen, nearly the only thing housebreakers hadn't smashed or carted off before Sara and Clay saved it, and the house. Gord had to have been lonely, good God, talking to himself in Gaelic, no one to respond. In the soil around that house Clay's pick had punctured bottles, fished out dirty brown necks of glass, frosted shards that for a second excited him. No, they were no kind of treasure. Still, he had worked on that house, with Sara and himself inside it. Now he wouldn't even know what to say if he knocked at the door.

He started back, trying to recall where he'd passed the last Liquor Commission, how many miles, but when he saw the squatter's place he eased the truck up close to the roadbank and stopped. He only meant to look but he shut off the engine. There was only the rain striking the windshield in gusts, the queer house dimming and clearing, dimming and clearing in the glass. When Clay's breath and heat fogged it over, he got out and walked up a path of tramped grass. People had come and gone here, curious like him. The house (was it a house at all, or a vision of something in its builder's head?) sat in a level clearing, the point of its tower thrusting up like a spear. One section of it logs, the rest was of mortared stone, a mix of steep roof lines and little gables. Rain sizzled from its eaves. The man had been some kind of hippie, hadn't he, to have cobbled up wood and stone into this eccentric shape, the small turrets and the square tower, the odd-sized windows with no glass? Why this when a plain cabin would do a man to die in? Clay peered into the tower room: Maybe you could starve better in a small space, reach more easily, if the need arose, the other chambers of the house. Apart from the stone fireplace that took up one wall, there was no sign of stove or utensils, no strewn pathetic things like you always found in abandoned houses. No cupboards, no larder. In corners Clay couldn't see, rain spattered on stone.

How old had he been? Old enough to mortar rocks into walls and chimney, to shingle the crazy roofs, to put together what he saw in his own head. And he was religious. Was it that side of him that caused him pain? A girl carrying his kid, his, and he had to atone for it somewhere so far away from his home nobody would have heard of it, or of him, or known about a baby born in shame.

But he arrived here, and he put this structure together. He starved himself, to death.

Clay tried to see him, to hear him at work. The sharp slice of a shovel. The strokes of his saw. He must have been a good way along before he allowed himself to go hungry. Jesus, there was just too much hard work here. You didn't climb twelve feet up with stones in your arms and your belly empty for very many days. Maybe when the roofs were ready for the wood shingles he was weaker then, his hands shaky, his head lighter as he looked out: he had some sea out there, and the long, dark, lying-down shape of Cape North. Think of leading a wake-up-go-to-work life without food. The increasing weight of every single object he lifted—hammer, nails, a piece of wood, a cup of water. Water kept him for a while, just that. That outsized stone hearth, he must have lain there, curled up like a kid in bed, colder now that he ate nothing, his strength mainly in his mind, his will. Without meals or the worry of their making, he would have dozed, prayed, daydreamed. How long? And the girl. Did he see her as she had been at first, undressed with him, naked in his arms, or did she grow different in his mind as the baby grew inside her? All that time, his thoughts burning down with the fire, flickering like his body, wood to ember to ash, and then one morning (or was it night, just a cold numb darkness?) he could not get up, could not fetch wood even if wood were cut and waiting. The grate was cold, the stones he lay on. He could concentrate then on the one thing that made him do this. He had already passed a point, there had been a night when he lay with his eyes open as they had never been open, and the ache and the yearning slipped away and food was something he had left behind any need for, like sex, like that warm girl who had ignited his sin.

Clay was thirsty. There was probably a well or a brook some-where in the trees crowding the rear of the house but he couldn't search for it now. He sipped a palmful of rain from the eaves. He circled the strange structure again, touching it. In the grass under a turret he found a plain brass buckle, a bit of hard leather still attached. He took it in his fist and crossed the road, down through a wild meadow where cow parsnips bloomed high as his chin. Near the cliff edge a cluster of harebells stopped him, blue in the grass. He stepped back. He could not, without leaning forward, see how the turf turned down toward the sea, but when he closed his eyes it filled him, that great ocean crashing and climbing below, and he took it deep into his heart and held it until it beat in his own quick blood.

ALL THE MEN ARE SLEEPING

For Patrice

I

Isobel could barely open her eyes, the wind burned so, but the slits of her sight were furious with attention. Through the dizzying snow the horse's black rump, straining against its fear, against Blair's grip on the reins, disappeared again and again. Its instincts might or might not keep the sleigh clear of what they all were afraid of, she, Blair, the horse: tender ice, a wide crack of open water. Anger ran through Isobel like a chill: she'd been drawn into Blair's bravado. Reckless to reach a patient, never mind the weather or distance or risk. Already he had that reputation in this part of Cape Breton, call Dr. MacKenna, he'll come if it kills him. He had lost one horse in the ice, a lovely animal, he'd told Isobel, a hobbled pacer, longlegged, she glided over snow, and then he'd had to look on helplessly as that horse reared up and drowned in an ice pond, trapped in the shafts of the sleigh, her legs a white thrashing in black water before they went stiff and sank. Could a horse *smell* water flowing under ice, under snow?

Last night Isobel had said, not many hours after she'd arrived here, Do you want to be a legend or something? The heroic physician? Legends take time, Blair. You have to live for a while.

I don't think about how long I'll live. Do you?

Sometimes. As I watched my school burn down. After making love. Those kinds of times.

He gave her a tired smile and continued packing medical equipment into a large leather bag, whispering out its inventory. He'd seen patients since early morning, here and out on calls. If he couldn't reach this distant farmhouse via the ice, it would mean miles more on snowbanked roads, taking to the fields, hours of struggling with his horse, shoveling through vales so drifted and slowgoing he had to fling his coat off in a sweat. Sometimes no one was near enough to help him or even know he was there, digging like a miner.

You don't really want to come, he said. The ice is chancy at night. In conditions like this, unpredictable.

I'm acquainted with winter. I've seen dirtier weather than this.

It's not just weather. It's cracks. Ponds. Losing your way.

Ponds?

A low patch of water that freezes over, but thin. Usually shallow, sometimes not. At night you can't see it until it breaks. In the day, you can see black in the ice.

Gusts of snow pressed against the windowpane, subsided. Isobel could see the frozen bay, dusk-white. To the east, hills darker than the deep grey sky.

I didn't come all the way from Halifax, she said, to read magazines in your waiting room. I'm not keeping house these days, Blair. I'm traveling.

He was latching up his coat of some thick fur, festooned with extra clasps he'd had sewn on against the wind. Wrapped in it, he seemed immense to her, but still, except for his face weathered beyond his years, like the college boy she had known. And he still had that beautiful hair, dark as mahogany. Hair whose distraction he had once been so conscious of that he wore it nearly shorn. The big coat seemed to close him away and Isobel grabbed up her gloves, her woolen scarf from the chair.

Dress as heavy as you can, he said. Take my sweater there. This isn't Halifax.

No, she said. I've realized that.

A phone rang, startling her. There it was on the wall, an oak box with visible bells. Blair hunched over the speaker, doodling on the wallpaper. He was abrupt with the other party, a confinement case, not rude but edgy as he told them he had an emergency over toward MacKay's Point but he would see to her as soon as he could get a fresh horse. I never know just what I'm going to find when I get there, he'd told Isobel last night as they drank bootleg rum. It might take me hours to work through the drifts, and then I discover they need medication I'm out of or some instrument I couldn't bring. I can't get everything in two bags anyway, and I'm the only doctor for, Christ Almighty, miles around. Miles.

The bushes, he said, turning his mouth into the cowl of her hood. Watch for the bushes. His warm breath was gone in an instant, and he was bulk again, weight at her side. The horse halted, shied, but Isobel could see no open cracks (what was a crack *like*, the word carried an odd horror), and of course there was the water you couldn't see, merely veneered with ice, its color lost in snow and darkness. Blair snapped the reins and the sleigh lurched on, the tail of the horse disembodied, a dark whisk, dark hank of hair. The ice has been bushed, he told her back in his office, we'll have markers to follow. And for awhile they had, stumpy spruce appearing like stains in the whirling dark, snow captured in their branches, and she was childishly happy to spot each one, it said safety somehow, teetering in the wind, homely for a moment like something you'd see in a backyard, and then it was gone, and she felt herself yearning forward for the next one, leaning, urging the horse, just a little tree, that's all we have to locate, one bush at a time. But where was *ahead?* They were still moving, the horse pushing on, she could feel its halting steps in the sleigh's uncertain motion. Don't worry, he's a smart animal, Blair had said, and he wants to get off the ice worse than we do.

It would go in first, its hooves would break through and there would be those first sickening sounds of ice splitting, like gunshots, like huge windowpanes collapsing, a breath's pause, then the plunge of water, and all its alarms, the awful whinnying of the horse as the cold strikes. She could see this and her body was rigid with it. A deep pond had drowned Blair's horse and nearly drowned him too. I had to keep breaking the ice, he'd told her last night, I couldn't seem to pull myself onto it. Sapped all the strength I had left to get myself laid out on that ice. I threw up, I was that worn out.

The sleigh stopped fully and snow rushed to enclose them.

Where are you going? Blair!

Got to find the bush! he yelled. Don't want to hit water! Hold the reins! Answer me when I shout so I don't lose you!

Then he was gone along with his voice, something dark in the snow one moment and then erased. The horse stamped and Isobel cried out, tightening the reins, and it lurched once and then quit. If Blair didn't come back, where would this horse lead them? She'd have to sit here stupid, blind. She would freeze first, sleepily, and then the horse. Better a slow numbness than the agony of water, so cold it would be like fire. Christ, her students would think this a foolish venture, the very thing she'd scold them for, you took the ice at night in a sleigh, and a snowstorm blowing up: you must be mad, madder than the man you went with. *Semel insanivimus omnes*, girls. But she had no students anymore since the school fire, and her common sense seemed to desert her at times, coming up here suddenly by train to this far eastern end of the province, a large island whose beauty you always heard about no matter where in Nova Scotia you lived, a hard and lovely place, even in winter, Johnny said, born here himself, but in Arichat, miles away up the great sea-fed lake she had watched from the train, white and still, save for dark slashes of water here and there. But Blair had never been mad, not even at Dalhousie. She had wished sometimes that he was, like Johnny LeBlanc. The only men she'd ever cared about. Johnny from Arichat.

She heard Blair calling her, *Is-o-bel*, drawing it out. Not ahead but off to the side somewhere in the white hypnotic darkness. She swept the scarf away from her face and answered him, once, twice. Then she wasn't sure if she had heard him because the wind turned and howled, pitched to her name. She stood up and yelled Blair Blair and it sounded so thin she thought for a moment she would cry, every helpless feeling she'd ever had ran down a wire to her heart, but instead she swore and yelled out again, Damn it where are you?

Bring it here! he said, bring the horse toward me! She sat. She hadn't driven a horse since she was a girl but he kept shouting here, this way, over here, and she got the horse moving and it seemed eager to find him too and soon there he was, bigger than the bush, their shapes merging into one until he beat the snow off his shoulders. The bones in her hands ached, she'd gripped the reins so hard.

II

Isobel had never been to a farm in winter and its immobility oppressed her, the huddled, darkened outbuildings, cowering in deep snow. The wind thrashed about, powdery, stinging. A lantern dangled from the front gate and she wanted to cup its dim glow to her breast. She was unbelievably tired already. Cold and the tension, she told herself. She could hear the steel runners slicing snow, the brittle creak of harness, the chugging breath of the horse.

Is there another way back? she said. Her lips seemed to skim dreamily over the words.

If you've got a day to burn, Blair said. I don't.

He urged the horse to the rear of the house where a man in shirtsleeves rushed from the back door, snow crunching under his feet, his hair wild in the lantern light. He grabbed the bridle.

Droch shìde! he said.

Suarach, Jack!

You go right in, Doctor, and get yourself warm. I'll see to the horse. Is that a nurse there with you?

She's an old friend, Jack, visiting. I guess she could nurse if she had to.

I could have doctored too, given the chance.

She felt numb and cramped, and a flash of shame at her bitterness in front of this stranger, a man with illness in his home. A window upstairs, dimmer than the lantern. A shadow inside passed across its frosty light.

Last night by oil lamp they had drunk Blair's Demerrara rum, given to him in fee, smooth and dark and thick. It loosened them into talk. They had both forgotten how hungry they were to talk to each other, how much they had once enjoyed it at Dalhousie despite all else, Johnny LeBlanc and after. Late into the evening they lit memories like matches, watched them burn.

He had said, A May rain, remember? It was *you* who took *me* to a flat you borrowed for the afternoon. From Johnny . . . Johnny . . .

Leblanc. From Arichat, Isle Madame. This very Cape Breton. Yes. It was his sheets we fucked on. The first time.

Your language seems to have a country flavor these days, Blair.

Listen, I've arranged for you to stay with a widow down the street. Mrs. MacFarlane. Nice old soul.

The bachelor physician. A pillar of the village. You weren't always.

Nor you. It wasn't a village. Johnny Lilac, we called him. His cologne smelled like lilacs. Like those June bushes in my mother's yard.

Johnny made me laugh when I didn't feel like it.

Women and laughter. They're suckers for it.

You could be moody, Blair. The Celtic Cloud we called you.

Oh, Johnny. I could smell him in the sheets.

Isobel's cheekbones burned as a young woman called Josie steered her close to the kitchen stove. A big kettle simmered steam and she leaned toward it to clear her breath. Her nose ran thinly like water but she could no more extract her hankie from her coat than she could a pill of fluff. A blur of wool socks and a red wool shirt, draped on a line above the stove. A sweetish smell. Soap? Something cooking? She studied the stove's Victorian trim, nickel incised ornately, polished. The engine of the house. Sturdy pots. A match scar on the black metal surface. Blair was handling the conversation, first with Josie, then the man Jack when he came in from the barn, stamping. Isobel could feel at her back the commotion around Blair, solicitous, almost tender, the woman helping him out of his big coat like a kid who'd come in from the snow, exchanging remarks Isobel could not pick up. Isobel's mouth, her jaw were stiff. She spread her fingers over the heat: sometimes Johnny's fingers had been cold and he huffed on them before he touched her. Snow depressed him.

You put a good blanket over him, did you, Jack? Blair said.

I rubbed that horse and covered him, Doctor, and I thought he could do with oats and a drink. Hard going in this, eh? But better than an automobile, better legs than wheels in this.

I wore out two Fords, Jack. Beat the hell out of them. A horse knows where danger is. How long has Hector had fever?

I couldn't but guess, Doctor, the woman said. He kept on his feet so long, you know, dragging himself around. He drank juniper tea. Just a cold in the chest, he said. You will eat, you and the lady?

That's Isobel. We were students at Dalhousie together, for a while.

He joined Isobel at the stove, washing his large hands in the warmth. Hands she remembered, quiet, as if they knew what was occurring under her flesh. Was that a gift she lacked? She had been smarter than he at university, her marks higher, her papers praised. But that seemed to have no application anymore, none. Or her excellence in Latin. She had loved its unreality, its sonorous precision. Lines she had incanted alone she loved to hear recited in her class, by some shy but intelligent girl. It had the fearsome privilege of always sounding *right*, Latin, of looking permanent: like a venerable and beautiful building.

I didn't know you spoke Gaelic, she said.

It's useful to know a little. Some things you can only say in Gaelic, so they tell me.

The woman reached between them for the teapot and poured them both a cup.

You recovering? he said gently.

I'm fine. Cold to the bone, but fine.

Nearby a daybed sat against the wall, rumpled, a fiddle lying on a pillow, the bow placed almost formally across its strings.

Does he play? Isobel said, pointing.

Jack? I never heard of it. Wouldn't be playing tonight anyway. Josie, you have a fiddler visiting?

Angus Ban, from down Deepdale. He's with Hector now.

They went up the narrow stairway, Josie leading them with a kerosene lamp. Blair had assumed Isobel wanted to come upstairs and told Josie, She's assisting me temporarily, she's from Halifax—investing her vaguely with a medical authority she did not have but which she had once desired more than anything, and when the medical school had turned her down, she closed it all away: she would not be a nurse instead, she would be nothing to do with medicine. She would teach the Latin she had won a medal for. But Blair had said it only to simplify her being here and she went along, drowsy from the kitchen warmth they'd left behind. On the small landing they met the fiddler, his face grotesquely sad in the lamplight. He had short white hair and a white moustache trimmed neatly and he slid past them without speaking. Outside the sick man's door they halted as if his breathing, rapid and insistent, required them to stop.

Under the slanted ceiling, its roof swept by wind, Blair bent over the patient. He looked hurled down, the blankets disarranged, torn from his body. The black, bristly hair of his chest shone with sweat.

Oh look at him, Josie said. Hector, behind his dark eyelids, did not resist as she straightened his limbs, toweled his body. She tugged taut the damp sheet, fluffed out blankets and quilts.

Should it be so cold in here? Isobel said.

The bedrooms here are always cold, Blair said, holding the man's wrist in his fingers, it's a cold house. Josie, could we stuff something around that window? I don't like the draft. He's so hot he could be outside, but still.

I've an old sheet I'll tear up. She touched Hector's face as she left the room.

Ah, what's this? Blair said, lifting the bedclothes. Something was bound with a bandage to the sole of Hector's foot. Blair sniffed, frowned.

What is it? Isobel said.

Dried cod. An old remedy. The salt fish draws off the fever. When it cooks the fish . . . Blair pressed his stethoscope to the man's chest, listened to the tap of his finger. He thumped another spot, another.

You're not leaving the fish on his feet? Isobel caught the sharp salt smell of his body, salt of the sea.

What's the harm? Their cures work sometimes. We can't say much better about ours, can we.

Blair rubbed alcohol on the man's chest, then inserted a long hypodermic from his bag. The needle filled slowly with fluid tinged a faint red and he bent close to the lamp.

Pus, he said. Pleural effusion, sure as hell. Christ.

Empyema? Isobel could hear the sharp rip of cotton in the hallway. You might have guessed, she said, even on the phone.

Blair looked at her. Isobel, he said, tapping his temple. No one's a doctor just up *here*. Not in this place.

That's where we all start, isn't it? Head, then hands?

Josie returned to caulk the windowsill, talking as she pressed in the strips of sheet. Hector, he wouldn't listen to me, she said. I told him, you're sick, something's wrong.

Pneumonia, Josie. Pleurisy, I'm afraid. We'd have to put him on the train for Sydney. Better part of a night right there. It would be awful hard.

Yes, she said. It would anyway. She bit the rag, tore it away from her teeth. Why am I doing this then? she cried.

I'll make him comfortable. Josie, dear, that's all I can do, Blair said. His voice had such tenderness in it Isobel looked up.

What do you mean? Isobel said. Comfortable?

Listen. He needs an operation but we can't get him across the ice to the train, not in time. You know the outdoors, you've been outdoors, Isobel. Blair dug his nails down the window frost.

Look at that wind. Jesus, the drifts! This is our winter, Isobel. Back in the nineteenth century, that's where it puts us.

III

Isobel sat down even though the dishes of boiled potatoes and turnips and salt herring did not excite her hunger. Blair had gone to the outhouse. She imagined snow whistling through the cracks like smoke. Lord, she'd have to be bursting. What she dearly wanted now was the taste of a cigarette, silky, warm. A packet in her small handbag but she knew she could not light one, not even with the smell of tobacco already in the air. Whose? Jack had left the house, well-bundled. There, the fiddler, on the edge of the daybed. He'd been watching her, drawing quietly on his pipe.

Who would you be? he said.

She wanted to talk. She told him about the private girls' school and then about the fire. She'd stood out by the road, under a big oak tree apart from the other teachers, her face lashed by the ravenous light. The ferocity of the heat had stunned her, breezing madly through leaves overhead. She heard windows explode, the incendiary whoosh of chemicals. Slack hoses, shrivelled from a frozen water main, laced the hard ground, the firemen watching, like her, the school burn, the magnificent flames clawing the brick, the gothic embellishments, as if the whole structure had been designed to burn dramatically. The fire, she said, sort of turned me out, and I came up this way from the mainland. To visit.

Terrible to lose all that, your work, the fiddler said. You don't look old for an old friend of the Doctor's.

He asked me why I showed up here and I said, to see you, the country doctor at work. I stopped to see a man in Arichat. But he wasn't there.

The fiddler said in a loud whisper, A hospital would save Hector's life. Death doesn't need to come here like it used to. Still, there's no money in the country. Do you know what I'm saying? None.

I'm sorry, she said.

I'm sorry too, dear, he said. I can't begin to tell you.

Josie lugged in a pail from the pantry and began pouring water into the stove tank. You wouldn't get much of a bath from that, and what a wait. Isobel loved a hot bath at home, the feathery warmth afterward. She ached for one. She hadn't washed, only her hands in the pantry, the water cold as the outdoors, and no wonder: two buckets of broken ice from the frozen well, barely melted, sat near the small trapdoor, open to the musky smell of clay, potatoes, winter apples. With only one oil lamp, the kitchen seemed dusky now, its light so toned down she felt sleepy. Was it late? She could see no clock nor hear one.

Oh, do eat, Miss, Josie said, wiping her hands on her apron. It will warm you.

Isobel did not want to be hovered over. Could Blair have found that bush in the storm without her? Was he glad, was he grateful she'd been with him? Not likely he would ever say.

How is he now? Angus Ban nodded at the ceiling.

He was out of his head, you know, but it passed. He's resting. I'll get up there soon.

Josie stared into the empty pail she was holding, then went back to the pantry. Isobel thought she could hear sobs and fought the urge to go to her, to comfort her. Angus Ban tapped out his pipe in the coal scuttle.

I can't disturb my dear friend upstairs, you see. Got to get his strength up. Oh God, yes.

Is that what you do, play the fiddle? Is that your work?

Angus Ban frowned. I'm not a barefoot man. I make tunes, and I play them. That's what God wanted.

But he shouldered the fiddle as if to demonstrate what he did. After a few bars he quit.

Losing the Bushes, he said, is what I called that tune.

The doctor and I, we lost the bushes tonight, Isobel said.

God help you, Angus Ban said, placing his fiddle in a battered black case. You could end up in open water but here you are in this kitchen.

Open water. Isobel did not know what to say and the kitchen fell silent. Soon the outside door opened in a blast of wind and stomping and Blair appeared, his eyes streaming tears, snow in his hair. He'd looked in on the horse, that's what kept him. He exchanged a broad joke with Angus Ban and sat down. Isobel was amazed at how quickly he could put his food away, drawing it in with his breath, his eyes gone stupid, no conversation in them at all. But then he was often in a rush, wasn't he, often did not eat for many hours, and on those snowdrifted roads and trails he burned energy like a horse himself. And sometimes he had to find a bushline in blinding snow. Under the right conditions, he had said, ice is sensible, it is speed, directness, a marvelous highway. Isobel buttered a biscuit, nibbled it.

Are we going back over the ice? she said calmly.

Not soon. Daylight. *Sa'mhadainn.*

Josie set the teapot on the table between them. Her eyes looked black and bright but she smiled at Isobel.

You'll stay here the night. Jack has gone to a telephone. He'll let them know you're here.

There's a big rocker in Hector's room. I'll doze in that, Blair said.

No, no, you take our bed, Doctor. Jack will be late and he's got a pallet. The lady can sleep with Mother in her big warm bed. Off the parlor there.

Your mother? Isobel said.

Jack's, but she's the mother in this house. She hardly walks and she sleeps quiet. I'll show you where when you're ready.

Oh, I couldn't. Please. No.

Bed was a very private place and Isobel could not crawl into a stranger's, old woman or not, into its fragrant heat.

In the country, sometimes you're glad for any bed you can find, Josie said. Eh, Doctor?

Oh, my, yes. I've been in some odd ones and I never complained. I've slept on the floor with Indian women, waiting for a birth, all night. I can fall asleep in one breath. Not so, Josie?

Indeed, Josie said comfortably, pouring her own tea and sipping it as she stood. Known you to sleep while talking to you. Known you to talk a sick woman out of her bed, so bad did you want it.

He didn't, said Isobel, her eyes moving from Josie to Blair.

Yes, didn't he tell old Mabel Fraser she should get up and walk around the house for a little while, it would be good for her. Her feet hadn't hit the floor before the Doctor was snoring. True?

Didn't hurt her a bit, Blair said. She's living still. I was so tired I was punch-drunk.

He smiled at Josie and she returned it warmly over her steaming teacup, a deep look into him that said she appreciated this man, *knew* this man. The weary lines seemed to disappear from her face.

I came in a house one time, Angus Ban said, loudly as if they'd forgotten he was there, and I see a great big dog on the kitchen bed. My God, I said. But wasn't it the doctor here snoozing in his big fur coat?

They all laughed but Isobel. She observed them, how Blair leaned into their little circle as he might to a fire. Heartened,

Angus Ban was working up a story, its principal character, whom they all knew, cued only by his nickname, Johnny Needle. It had to do with him and his outhouse, having to visit it in terrible weather. Angus Ban paused to get the accent right, broader and more exaggerated than his own: It's a mean arsehole that would send a man out in a night like this. Laughter, more tea.

Wasn't that needle still in him somewhere? Blair said. You know, Josie said, it traveled along his bones and came out years later, not long before he died. They all went quiet and then Josie turned away toward the stove.

Isobel closed her eyes, sore from squinting into the wind, from smoky heat. She wanted to pretend she could leave when she liked, could walk outside and get into a car and drive home, wake in the ordinary morning of a school day. She wanted a summer road, dry and clear. Her Uncle Stan had owned a farm some distance from Halifax, in the Annapolis Valley, and she had been there in the summer, the open days of hay and the rattle of harness and wagon, the stench of cow stalls that set her reeling after she stepped blinking into the ammoniac gloom of manure and hooves and raw planking. Her cousins chased her, their shouts over the stubbled field, and then the sweet cloying flavor of fresh milk, her heavy Aunt Mae as florid before her kitchen stove as a stoker in a mill. Heat and sun and flies, many small motions against long slow rhythms, horseflies the size of bumblebees piercing the hide of a mare until her flanks were laced with blood. The juice of timothy between her teeth, the itch of straw on her skin, a horse whose rolling musculature she'd tried to control, clutching the coarse hair of its mane. How easily she would sleep right now in a sultry, summer room. God, warm feet and a bed. But a farm in winter, no. In winter, you were on the moon, lost in the whiteness. Beyond the house, so much blinding space, a vertigo of snow, the darkness of trees, water, ice.

Blair was touching her shoulder, leaning near her face. You must lie down, Isobel. Josie will show you the room. Her mother won't mind.

And you?

I'll wrap up in the rocker, after I see to Hector.

What is there to see to?

Blair leaned nearer, lowering his voice. I can sit there with him and feel helpless. That's all I can see to, Miss Isobel, on this particular night. That's what God decided, I guess. I just come when these people call me, if I can. I don't figure in the grand designs.

I'll doze off down here, where it's warm.

You're welcome in my lap. He smiled, his eyes dull with fatigue, the lids trembling a moment as if he were drunk.

The rocker wouldn't hold us, she said. Do you suppose I could smoke? I won't if they mind.

Jesus, go ahead. Good night then.

There's more blankets up there! Josie called after him, lifting a stove lid and pokering the coals into flame. Don't be cold!

Am I ever, dear? Blair said, ducking up the stairway. Isobel listened to his weight fall slowly on each step: more tired than herself, and she was wilting. Were she a familiar visitor in this house, she'd accept any bed offered just to lie down. She envied Angus Ban his tousled couch, here in the open kitchen. When Jack returned, would he say, Doctor, there was a call and they want you over to the other side, so-and-so's in labor or her brother's put an ax in his foot? Blair would not hesitate, he might even welcome a summons away from that humbling vigil upstairs. But could *Isobel* go, Isobel who had been so happy to get off that ice she had all but wept? Could she pull herself up and get behind a horse in weather like this when her toes still burned and her ears ached from straining to hear ice in the wind and her mind kept falling into bed? Yes, yes, if she were the doctor in this house, yes, she would, if they said her name the way they said Blair's, she would.

Can I look in your cup?

Josie was swirling Isobel's nearly-empty teacup. The leaves, she said. Josie inverted the cup in a saucer to drain the last drops, then took it near the lamp, turning and tilting it.

It takes a bit, she said, for the signs to come clear. But I see an L, for sure an L. Journey line is long, and it doesn't return here. You wouldn't want to come back to this house anyway, would you?

Josie peered deeper. A small cross, a delay. Some trouble but who hasn't had that? A big flower on the bottom, can't tell what kind. Luck . . .

Can we leave it at that? Isobel said.

There's more. Well . . . others are better at it than me.

In the pantry Josie emptied the kettle into a sink of dishes. Isobel wanted to help her with something, with anything, but the stove's warmth was almost stupefying. Dusty snow drove against the windowpane and she shut her eyes and soon saw blank white ice suddenly open, jagged, black, more like sky than water, through which you could fall or fly. She shook herself awake.

Drops from a flowered towel, drooping on a line, stung the stovetop in measured hisses. She patted through her coat until she felt the packet of Exports. Just the sweet smell seemed to revive her. She tamped one out on the table, struck a stove match, a sharp rasp in the room, and drew the flare into smoke, exhaling a delicious stream above her head. She wouldn't need to sleep now, not for awhile anyway.

We might as well be in Siberia, eh? Angus Ban said.

She'd forgotten he was back there beyond the stove. The rooms of the house were all chiaroscuro, a single lamp, an island of light grading away into shadow. She pulled the cigarette from her mouth.

Hard times everywhere, I guess, Isobel said. She adored the taste of the cigarette, but why did she think it made her look monied? Her but a schoolteacher, her salary so low it brought her a kind of dignity and little else? Blair often got no fee at all, or he got a chicken or meat or whatever they could offer. What would Jack and Josie give him? What would he expect? After one more long puff she mashed the cigarette in a saucer.

She'd crossed the stormy ice, in a sleigh, this very evening. She had not spent it on a daybed.

Angus Ban set his fiddle case on the floor and stretched out slowly, facing the wall with a deep sigh.

I'll warm the bed for you when you're ready. Josie stood in the hall doorway, wearing a white cardigan and a fresh blue apron. She cradled two stout sticks, as long as her forearm, in a towel, their wood sleek and dark from use.

I'm very much awake, Isobel said.

Josie placed the warming sticks in the oven, then she spread blankets over Angus Ban.

Is that a cigarette smell? God, I'd love one. Mother wouldn't have it. She'd put me out first.

Have what?

Smoking. Anything.

Josie glanced at Angus Ban. She was more than decent to me, once, Josie said. Still, it's never really your house, is it? Nothing gets past her.

Should something?

Your own life!

Yes. Of course. And hadn't Isobel fought her own mother, especially over men? She would never have liked Johnny, his quiet, black-eyed charm, the ways he made love, the small things he turned into occasions.

Are you alone here a lot? Isobel said.

Not much. Not enough. Herself in there, and . . . the usual coming and going of people. Oh, I've been alone. Sure.

Josie rubbed at the window frost. Jack's got the heavy sled. But he might just stay till morning.

You've known Dr. MacKenna a good while? Isobel said.

One of the first calls he made, this house. We liked him from the start, you know. He's right plain. No airs ever, with him. Och, he's a man. He'd go through hell to get to you. You wouldn't have heard of the time he walked from Kempt Head to Washabuckt when his horse came up lame, and a storm on, a terrible wind, he walked right into the teeth of that and was near frozen to death when he arrived there? But he arrived. I swear you couldn't kill him.

No, Isobel said. I hadn't heard that. But I'm glad he's invincible.

He can walk into any house, any time the day or night, eat what he finds there, sleep wherever he can. He can take a fresh horse without asking. He sees to us and we see to him, as we can. Like you do.

Me?

You crossed the ice with him. This night. Any woman can go in a sleigh when the sun is shining. Did you know a car went under there last week? The doctor went over by horse, and they figured, well, okay. But the cracks were widening.

As the horse went under, Blair told Isobel last night, late, she rose herself up, a great splashing heave for breath, and the sleigh pulling her down. In a little while he could see a dark shade in the water, in the hole. Awful to see the horse come back up, so slowly, not moving at all.

The doctor and yourself, Josie said, you're to be married, are you?

God, no. Blair would find that very funny. No, no, it's been years.

What's been years?

Absence. And everything we've done during it, every little thing in our lives.

Josie scraped a match under the table and lit their cigarettes, holding the flame like a teacup. She drew on hers elaborately, a parody of women in magazines, and yet she looked lovely doing so, her slender, hopeful, dark-eyed face, alight, wary, as if something terrible and welcome was in the air.

You're wearing his sweater, she said.

Isobel pulled at the baggy brown wool. And a good thing I am. To be plain with you, Josie, I need to pee.

I'll put a pot out for you in Mother's room.

No, please. I can't do that. I'll wake her.

Wake her you won't. She's a sleeper, that one, when she wants.

The window near Isobel was black, silvered with veins of frost. She'd find a corner outside, quick and private. She caped her coat around her and stepped out the back door, closing off the house. The brutal air made her moan, and the night. The snow seemed alive, restless, whorled around fenceposts, the long aching curls of drifts, dark blue, from which the wind spun crystals, a sharp, soft spray on her face. A low, black ridge behind the barns was edged with the cold silver of a set moon. The fields extended harmlessly over the ice, one white surface, snow billowing up like veils, then settling. Somewhere underneath, a tide was running, out or in, she didn't know, currents heard more than seen, an exposed purling in some widening crack. A pond. Skating on a pond: how benign, and she'd done that, the shore-bank always near, reachable, a bonfire burning. Skating, you could always be saved. A friend had survived that, the ice caving under her in one wide teetering cake, water coming not in a gush but an upwelling, an overflowing, cold cold water in her shoes, sliding up her leg. Isobel backed away into the kitchen.

She followed Josie into a room dimmed by the dark quilts of a large bed. She hesitated as the door shut softly behind her. An alarm clock ticked metallically. The mother seemed lost in the bedcovers, still and childlike. Isobel waited. When she discerned an unmistakable snore, she tugged down her wool slacks and her underpants, pausing a beat before she squatted above the white chamberpot. The air cooled her naked skin. She clutched her knees and tried to hurry. How absurd she looked, blushing, her face hot. When the pot hissed she looked toward the bed. Oh! she said, tottering: the old woman lay facing her, her dark eyes moist and gleaming in the low lamplight. Angry, ridiculous, Isobel stood up quickly, her back to the woman, but her clothing twisted on her legs. I'm sorry I woke you, she said, too loud, lidding the chamberpot clumsily. The old woman cut her off, Gaelic words more spat than spoke, and Isobel felt instantly small. As she reached for the lamp she detected a dry, cold, distinct scent: a small bowl of potpourri on the table. The warm, welcome bloom of her mother's lilacs, lush in summer windows. Johnny LeBlanc's cologne, a sweet, slightly dizzying, mysterious musk. His lips, his mouth touching her skin. A kiss in a cold hallway, warm, strange, muscular. Johnny LeBlanc took her to his room and on his dresser were sprigs from home, that pale heartbreaking lavender, and when on his bed she drew her breath, she tasted it, the scent was him, was everything. But what had she wanted, approaching that old house in Arichat where his sister now lived? An impossible desire, carried from Halifax, from after the burning. She found only the house in Arichat, its street and number from the only letter he ever wrote to her, distant and wooden, like a translation. Johnny? *Il est parti!* his sister said, in her Acadian French, vehement, suspicious.

Blair knew nothing, nothing real, about those afternoons in Halifax, only that she'd been with Johnny LeBlanc.

In the hallway Isobel warmed her hand over the lamp. Imagine being ill in this house, lying in that room, waking to see a strange woman pissing in your own pot! Blair, he'd only laugh, he'd love to hear about this. Fastidious Isobel, you're too squeamish to be an M.D. No, she had insisted, no, that has nothing to do with it. I'll take the blood when it comes.

She brought the lamp into the dark kitchen and Josie took it from her, set it on the table.

Why don't you take our bed now? Jack won't be back till morning.

I'm not sleepy, Josie.

She *wanted* to be awake. The darkened rooms of the house, the snow whirling thinly across the soft white fields—no, she was afraid of sleep, of its awful comfort.

Maybe Doctor MacKenna would like the bed.

He's asleep in the rocker, dear, Josie said. Don't you call him Blair? I do.

Then she covered her eyes with her hands and Isobel sat her down, glad to attend to her.

I'm sorry to act foolish, Josie said. Hector upstairs and nothing to be done for him. She smeared her tears angrily. I'm afraid to touch him, he's so still. Why wake the doctor anyway? Let him sleep. It's to punish me, all this, she said with calm bitterness.

Punish you?

Jack's mother in there, that's what she said. I'd done something wicked, she said. Hector. Somebody. Don't ask me how she'd know the like of that.

Angus Ban's breathing fluttered. The heated sigh of coals, shifting, sinking.

Hector would have married me once, if he'd had the means to, Josie said. I should never have come to this house. I shouldn't be telling you this. Jack's been good to me. As good as a man can when you live like this in the country. But it's nothing to do with that, is it? I'd have loved Hector anyway. I loved touching him, putting my hands on him.

But his mother knew?

If knowing is seeing, no. I have to move her everywhere she goes. Her mind roams all over. She said she saw a white deer yesterday, out on the ice, but I don't believe her. Even before she was too sick to walk she'd never lift a hand to help me. No. It was once her house, you see, *her* kitchen, and so she'd let me do it all, tell me what was lacking. Except if I went away for a day or two, went to Sydney say. She'd do everything that needed doing, but when I got back here she was in her bed again like she'd never been out of it. In it she'd stay, me bringing her tea. It's *warm*, she'd say, it's *warm*, the tea fair boiling on her lips. Oh God, I've got some long dark looks ahead of me!

Josie reached across the table and took Isobel's hand. She spoke so low Isobel had to lean to hear her.

Jack was away off in town. Mother could still go visiting then. He'd dropped her off at her sister's, I think it was, yes. Over at Little Mary's. A warm day, lovely. Breezes, all through the house. You could hear the curtains, swish. We didn't say much at all to each other. Less said, the better, eh? It was like we'd been waiting but we didn't know it. That's how smooth it was between us, like we sort of danced up the stairs, but quiet and slow. Do you know how hard it is to keep a secret like that?

I know something about secrets, yes.

She released Isobel's hand and sat up, smoothing her hair. Her eyes were dry now. She looked once around the kitchen where everything had been put by her own hand.

Listen, she said, raising her chin: all the men are sleeping.

IV

At the top of the stairs the cold seemed sharper now. The wood creaked brittlely under her step. At the door to Hector's room she could see the spool posts of the bed and Blair's legs stretched into the gloom beneath it. Josie had come up here on a hot summer afternoon, into that bed. The wind had caressed them through that window, flung high. Inside, Isobel pressed her back to the cold forget-me-nots of the wallpaper. Hector seemed calmed by the quilts that lay neatly over him, stilled, his face to one side, frowning as if he'd been asked to listen. Blair, big and disheveled under blankets, like a traveler in a station, his head thrown back in sleep. The Doctor. *Idoneus homo.* Isobel touched his hair, his face, and he lurched awake: he seemed not to see her at all, then he fell back in the rocker.

Josie, he said, his voice hoarse, ravaged by fits of sleep. Last night he'd walked Isobel down the street to Mrs. MacFarlane's unrespectably late, the snow so cold it squeaked, then risen early. He closed his eyes, rocking the chair in slight, quick motions. I'm not sure I can go on.

Isobel turned up the lamp. Go on with what? she said.

Blair stared at her, dazed. I'll be all right. I'm just tired. Are you cold, Isobel? You must be cold. God. He smiled. How did you get here? I can't believe I'm looking at you.

You were dreaming, Isobel said. Your foot was jumping.

The blankets fell away as he sat up and pressed his hands tightly through his hair. I was dreaming, yes, of the horse I lost. So fast and beautiful. And I had to go tell Sam Alan MacAskill, who raised her, your lovely horse is under the ice.

Isobel hugged her arms. Snow slashed across the window like sand. You must have been close to her.

Ah, Isobel. What am I to do with you?

I'm sorry. I should know what a horse means out here. I'm sorry.

I don't remember you sorry about much, ever.

Did I need to be? I can't remember that I did.

Johnny Lilac. You went for him so.

It's not as if we were engaged, Blair, you and me.

Blair got up slowly and felt Hector's brow. He took hold of the man's wrist. Jesus, he said.

Is he gone? Isobel said, almost to herself.

He's on his way somewhere. Girl, you're shivering.

Blair snatched up a blanket from the floor, swept it around himself and then took her into it, into his arms. She felt for the first time the sheer bulk of him that had carried him across this country in winter for nine years, arriving, with or without his healing skills, in houses like this one where there was nothing left but faith and salt codfish, juniper tea. Isobel touched his eyes and felt tears there. He pushed his lips to her hand, her face, whispering nonsense, her name. Underneath her sweater, his hand found her skin, her breast, touching her nipple as if it were the very center he sought, and the breath went out of her. His warm hands moved down and up the taut muscles of her back, softening them, up under her hair, and in his hand the nape of her neck felt bare, intimate. What had horrified her watching the fire was that she might have willed it, as if only a calamity could make her leave the life she led there. It was like being burned out of your house. She kissed the cool sweat of his neck as she murmured no, not here, we can't. Beneath the blanket the warmth was sweet, but her eyes fixed for a moment on the wooden ceiling: above the lamp a nail-head glinted with frost. Isobel ground her face into his chest, pushed against the slow cold of the room. Blair could not undo the buttons of her slacks and she helped him, and the blanket slid away and she worried would Josie hear, would Josie come up.

V

The morning light pained her eyes. Across the whitening ice a light wind cut, whisking snow. Isobel, waiting in the sleigh, could see where broad sheens had been swept, so polished her eyes teared. The shore they'd be making for was a ridge of tree-dark hills, mottled with white meadows. The horse stood trembling, huffing, a jittery engine. Jack held the bridle tight and stroked the horse's neck while Blair fussed over the harnessry, tugging at the belly girth, the hames.

He won't mind it so much now, Blair said. He looked hearty, clapping his gloved hands, his face ruddied by a day's beard. This horse prefers the daylight. But don't we all, eh Jack? *Fad an la?*

La sam bith, Jack said. He'd returned at first light with three phone messages for the doctor. He knew his brother was dead, he told them, why hurry the horse.

Isobel had slept through his arrival, alone in Jack and Josie's bed where Blair had carried her and set her down. She woke to talking downstairs, unsure at first where she was. She stretched her legs deeper, her toes flinching on the warming sticks, their smooth cool wood. The frail window light seemed soulless and she'd pulled the covers closer around her and waited. At breakfast the others had eaten and were dressing for the outdoors, except Angus Ban whose hands seemed dead in his lap. Josie was quiet, and when Isobel heard her speaking Gaelic to the mother, giving her tea in her room, their swift, familiar conversation, it was if they had never talked, she and Isobel: there was no way Josie would tell in that language what she had told Isobel last night.

The sleigh listed toward Blair as he climbed aboard and Isobel spread his share of the buffalo robe over his lap. In the upper window Josie's face appeared, obscured by frost, the soft blue of her apron. Soon she would wash Hector for the wake, dress him, and they would lay him out on boards for whatever remained to him, whatever attention, love, curiosity.

Blair tightened his hands and the reins cut into the leather of his gloves.

Now you follow the bushes, Doctor, Jack said.

There's got to be a faster way, Jack. I mean, look at all that light.

They left the white fields of the farm, dropped down a bank onto the snow of the lake, the horse pausing, then putting his strength into the shafts. Angus Ban's fiddle keened behind them, slowly, then sharp, like sun hitting snow, and Blair looked back once before he hunched forward, his face set and shut. Isobel feared now, more than anything, a sudden release of sound. The horse broke through a shallow drift, picking up speed, sending up a snowy spray as exhilarating as water, and Blair urged him on.

The first crack seemed to shoot backward from the runners as if the sleigh discharged a bolt of lightning, but dark, and the horse snorted and reared, then plunged harder forward as Blair snapped the reins, shouting as she had never heard him before. Isobel turned and saw water, the awful color of it seeping into snow like blood in a cut, into the thin grooves playing out behind them, but she said nothing. She wanted to seize Blair's arm, infuse its tense, solid life with her own, but she didn't. She held onto the seat. She was here, and she would be here as long as this horse kept moving, kept churning snow into the bright morning air.

EYESTONE

An ancient chill is rippling the dark brooks.
ELIZABETH BISHOP, "CAPE BRETON"

Royce is about to enter the barn when Mrs. Corbett comes into the edge of his vision. He does not wave to her anymore: she would only shade her eyes in his direction, as she is doing now, and then drop her hand as if he were a ship passing on the horizon. He watches her arrange laundry along the line that runs from her back door to the woodshed. The white sheets, bright against the green of the overgrown meadow, fill slowly like flags, their patches darkened by the light behind them. He does not understand why an old widow need wash every sheet she owns. Her men are gone—her sons, her husband. But there is much about Mrs. Corbett he does not understand. Sometimes when he strolled through the pasture, rich with wildflowers he sought to identify, he could feel her watching from behind the kitchen curtains and he would flush with anger. How was it she could make him feel like a trespasser? He wants to shout, that's *my* house you're standing in. But she is old. Sometimes in the woods he glimpses her as she forages for plants: suddenly she is there, and then not. She is a folk healer, or was. She takes her clothesbasket into the house, looking his way once before she closes the door. Is it callous to think she might die to oblige him? Maybe Royce's wife was right: Mrs. Corbett will outlive everything.

Even inside the barn Royce can feel her eyes. Nearly a year has passed since her husband, from the milkcan in the middle of the threshing floor, took his last step into space. From the high vaulted ceiling the hayfork sways almost imperceptibly like a rung bell coming to rest. Poor devil. He barely knew the man, but during the first months after Royce purchased the farm, old Corbett sat propped on his cot in the kitchen, staring out the east window at the weather, at the barn he built himself, the last of its red paint scoured away in salt winds and the driven ice of storms. The day Royce brought the papers around for him to sign, Mrs. Corbett, whispering to herself in Gaelic, sat glumly in one corner of the parlor as if her husband were selling not the land but her. Nonetheless, Corbett extracted from Royce the promise that she be allowed to live on in the house until her death—a concession Royce gladly granted, wanting only the land at that time, others being after it. "The cottage across the road will do for myself, and my wife," Royce said. "When she joins me." A rash statement, but perhaps rashness characterized everything he'd done since he met that woman, that girl. Corbett, obviously ill, pointed to the ceiling: "Upstairs there, my mother and my dad died, in the same year. No running water then, and we nursed them all that long time they were sick. You'll never see me in a hospital, or my wife either."

Afterward, Royce gave Corbett hardly a thought, absorbed as he was in his hundred acres of woods, fields, and shore. He did not know that Corbett was sitting out his nights in the kitchen struggling for breath, sleeping in fits and snatches with his chin on his breast, or that sometimes his wife fixed a strand of red yarn around his neck. And then one warm morning when the untilled fields burgeoned with hay and flowers and weeds,

Corbett, his wife away in town, hobbled out to the barn and hung himself in a loop of the hayfork rope, swinging from a ridgepole that bore the scars of his own ax.

On the planks of the threshing floor Royce tests his weight. A few have stove in, pattered into rot from leaks. "I'm going to make something new here, when the old lady is gone," he'd said to his wife not long after she arrived. A shingle or two have sloughed away, seams have spread some. Wind pries at the aluminum roofing, but the handhewn posts are solid, the beams and purlins true. He foresaw this barn, in his daydreams back in Boston, as a big lodge which, to bring in money, he might let out to artists in the summer, easterners seeking rural peace, and, since he was a painter himself, offer instruction even though he didn't want to teach anymore. It was one of several schemes he brought with him, and with which he passed his first winter here, sketching rooms and windows and furniture through dark housebound afternoons, showing to his wife their ever-increasing elaborateness as if the detail alone might counter her growing indifference. She chided him for not painting anymore, for giving up. "You might have noticed," he said, "there are no galleries around here." Her own pale but happy watercolors she'd filled her summer with turned into the harsh shades of late autumn, then into the loneliness of snow and cold. "This could be a hut in Labrador," she said one evening. "We have no friends. We're always running out of things, all kinds of things." He was stir-crazy too by then but determined not to go back to Boston, not yet. "We'll make this place ours, even in the winter," he said. She said, "Never. We're summer people, Royce. That's the part of you I loved." He told her no, you have to take the country in all seasons and that doesn't come easy. "Maybe you're too young for the country," he said. "I thought you could handle it." She looked at him. "Handle what? What are we handling?"

Spring came so late it was hardly spring at all, mid-May and shadowsnow still blue at the edge of the woods. "She has a fireplace down there," his wife said, looking out the window at Mrs. Corbett's house. Royce got up and stood behind her. "She comes with the place," he said. On the pane were fish spines of frost. After two days of wind and freezing rains, his wife packed and he drove her to the airport in Sydney. "It was a bad idea from the start, wasn't it?" she said. "For me?" He kissed her and stepped back, already missing her. "I guess I've used up my ideas," he told her. "I'll see this one through."

He pokes around the barn, touching things he owns but that never seem his. Rusting machinery lies forlornly about. Someday he'll paint them bright colors. A tooth harrow, a hayrake, the last harvest its graceful tines have gathered tumbling out of the lofts, bales broken, the mildewed hay scattered. He smells the dried manure in the raw, browned wood of the stalls: underneath their collapsed planks he once found a cow skull gaping from the soft earth and took it home to his wife who delighted in such objects. On a doorpost there is a dark sheen where Corbett's hand so many times took hold. When Royce is inside the barn, his careful, exact drawings seem to have no connection at all to it. The sharp warmth, the worn surfaces have an intimacy he longs to feel on canvas but cannot.

He turns to the milkcan and pushes it over with his foot. It crunches along the planks a short distance and stops. One afternoon he sketched her by the light of the back door, a fine dust rising from the dry hay and settling lightly on her skin, moist in the barn's heat, skin he can taste now, vividly. Overhead at the tiny gable window a swallow, defeated by glass, assails the dusty pane again and again. He tries to scare it out with stones from his pocket, pegging them at the roof, but the bird will not quit. Leaving, he props open the door so the swallow and its ill-luck can leave with him. In the barn's foundation there is a new crack. His wife would stoop and run her fingers over the small shells embedded in its concrete—periwinkles and snails, bits of scallop, oyster, clam.

Royce squints up at the white-grey sky. The sun burns somewhere. He can feel its heat, and for a moment a sudden aimlessness comes over him. He looks quickly at the fading white shingles of the house: a curtain moves in the kitchen.

It is with some weariness that he pushes himself into thickets that obliterate paths he found, or made, only the summer before, vowing then not only to draw everything on wings, legs, or roots but to learn their identities as well. Now heavy spring rains have left the meadows lush and soggy, sheer growth which, in June, swept green and rapid over the fields. Dense grass he stomped down is combed back by the wind as if he never passed there. In any case, his hikes have become more random, pointless, their only objective to eat up time before he must return to the cottage. As he moves through browntop grass, he trails his fingers in its kinky silk and smiles: it feels like her hair.

He follows a deer path into a sea of ferns, waist-high fronds that have raced into summer in the shade of birches, hiding stumps and deadfalls. Under them lies a humid ferny scent, warm when you fall into it, like under a skirt. His wife had hiked to places that did not attract him, and she would stay there drawing as long as blackflies and the weather allowed. Her landscapes, though never from a perspective he would have chosen, he praised despite their lack of risk, their melodrama. The rattling croak of a raven passes overhead. "Corvus corax," Royce whispers. He had recited her the Latin names of things they encountered. Most of the birds he could recognize now, having offered themselves easily in the spring, bits of color in the dun days of dead hay and bare trees but now just teasing sounds in the leaves. He speaks the names of flowers as he walks. "*Achillea millefolium. Eupatorium perfoliatum. Aletris farinosa. Prunella vulgaris.*" He rolls the Latin on his tongue, but Mrs. Corbett would know them by their common names—yarrow, boneset, heal-all, colic-root—evoking broken limbs, fevers, writhing infants. And yet one windy afternoon last summer, taking them to his wife, he approached Mrs Corbett holding out a cluster of what he now knew as spotted touch-me-nots. Bundled in her late husband's tattered sweater and seated on a milking stool, its legs trussed with wire, she had continued slicing seed potatoes for her little plot. "Goldenrod," she said, barely glancing. "No," he said. "Even I know goldenrod." She tossed the bad part of a potato into a battered pail, the good into a basket. "There's some here that wasn't here before," she said finally, never looking at him. "She draws flowers. Ask your wife." Royce bid her good day, and before he reached the cottage door, the blooms were withered petals of orange and red.

Feeling rank with repellant and sweat, he squats down by the purling coolness of a brook. He remembers his wife trying to sketch him here. "I can never do you," she said, scowling him over with scribbles. It was true. Her drawings of him were always off the mark, as if she were unwilling to see what he really looked like.

Before he raises his head, he knows that Mrs. Corbett is there, somewhere up among the trees. Just above a bend in the ravine, she is working her hand over the trunk of a fir, stroking its bark for pitch. Her white hair stands out against the needled branches and she holds a pint basket. If she is aware of him she gives no sign. She is singing in a soft, cooing rill a Gaelic song he has heard her sing before, "*Tha mo chùl riut, Tha mo chùl riut. . . .*" Is it some charm for gathering balsam, for urging sap from the tree? Often he has come across her trail, sometimes no more than a faint cleavage through fern, a cloudy footprint in brookside mud. When he looks up again she is gone.

My wife, he thinks, is with another man now. A new teacher.

The brook disappears into a marsh which he skirts to reach the nearly sandless shore (a disappointment to his wife who liked beaches). Its short slope is strewn with large rounded stones, and when the east wind blows up a storm you can hear their liquid clack and rumble under the spreading foam. He kicks over driftwood as he goes. A cormorant, straining its reptilian neck, skims the grey sea toward the Bird Islands, bleak tables in the distance. He tugs at a lobster trap partly buried in the sand until the old manila line snaps. He still reaches for gifts on his hikes, even though his wife has left, and he takes them home—a broken antler, a shed snakeskin, the intact skeleton of a cat he lifted bone by bone from a bed of moss. He pockets two spikes that have rusted together and climbs a short bank, pushing his way through the spruce. A bird, one he's been after for months, calls somewhere above him, but as he fumbles for the glasses a held branch slips and strikes him in the face. Hunched and swearing he touches his eye, but the wet is tears, not blood. He protects it with his arm and beats aside the tough spruce until he reaches an old path that leads up to Mrs. Corbett's lower pasture. The pain subsides but something scratches at his eyeball, a bit of needle or bark. A narrow stream crosses the path and he kneels beside it, scooping water over his face, wincing. "You saw this place in your dreams, Royce," his wife said. "Nothing will come of that barn down there. And that house. You're not even a painter anymore. All you have are plans on paper." What did she know, really? That he was only reaching from one handhold to the next?

The path opens out into a rise and he gets his bearings from the barn roof, from its weathervane made of handsawn boards. Skewed by the wind, it resembles some species of drunken fowl, leaning north, pointing east. He breaks off a maple sapling to whisk away the flies.

Mrs. Corbett appears along the ridge of haytops above him, first her head, then her shoulders as she crosses from the barn. On other afternoons he has seen her on that path, a kerchief clasped to her chin, her gait slow and absorbed as if she were returning from church. He does not know what she does in there. Stand where her husband died perhaps, conjure him. Telling his wife about his plans, Royce had always prefaced them by saying, "When the old lady leaves . . ." But one day in that wintry spring his wife cut him short: "Mrs. Corbett isn't going anywhere. That's like saying, wait until the trees leave, wait until the rocks go away." Suddenly his irritation converges upon her—the pain in his eye, the itch and sweat of tramping his own land with nothing to show for it but a solitary meal and another night in a cottage. If he takes the house, she will be gone.

When he shouts her name the air seems to smother his voice. But she stops and turns. The nearer he gets to her, the less certain he is as to how he will put it. She stands calmly on the pathway as he staggers through the ripe hay. He wonders if she has looked like this always, gaunt, straight, her eyes pale as beach shells. He has tried to sketch her in the past, but always at a distance or from memory, the versions as varied as his moods.

"Listen," he says. His eye squints tears. "There's this . . . this bird, Mrs. Corbett. I hear it all the time. Just after dark even." When he can draw a good breath he whistles a reasonable imitation of its call.

"The Bridal Bird, is what my sister Mary used to call it," she says.

"I've never heard of that one."

"She was a little foolish, my sister." Mrs. Corbett pulls the flowered scarf off her head and tucks it into her hands. Her hair is very white and he feels dizzied by it. The rims of his eye tremble.

"Mrs. Corbett. I know I said you could stay in the house. But it's not in writing, there's nothing legally binding to me."

"What is it you want?"

"The house. My wife went back to Boston, as you know, this spring. She can't live in the cottage. I . . . to get her back, I must have the house. That, you see . . . would be a new start. I'll give you time, lots of time."

"Time I've been given."

"Surely you have a place to go? Relatives?"

"I have a place to go, yes. If it's the house you want, you shall have it. All of it."

She looks into his face, not with shock or hurt but as if she is trying to identify him. "You've hurt your eye, have you? Come down to me after dinner. We have a cure for that. Not for everything, but for that we do." She steps past him and goes on toward her back door.

"Six months?" he says. "Is that time enough? By the end of winter?" But she doesn't reply. Through his shimmering vision she seems already to be disappearing.

Royce sits in the old stuffed chair pulled close to the window, a bottle of rum on the floor beside him. Between blasts of static the radio murmurs. In his wife's absence he lets it play even while he is out so that he might return to music or a voice, any voice or any music. After dinner sometimes he watches the evening weather, the color and light above the shoreline trees. He used to sketch it in pastels but he doesn't bother anymore. Even his good eye is getting sore from the strain. And evicting the old lady bothers him. She and her husband, they courted in buggy and sleigh. He squints glumly at clouds low to the sea, a bluish ridge streaked like agate from the sun where a storm is building over the water, clouds bruising and swelling. Lightning blinks harmlessly in the distance. In the rising wind the cottage crackles like ice, the air suddenly cool in the room. He and his wife had laughed that summer—nervously at first—about the tickings and creakings, lying wide-eyed in bed while the stairs released sounds of foot-steps stored in their wood. Under the covers they joked about ghosts, about the retired minister who'd died here, and then made love, safe in its heat. But they kept a lamp burning downstairs throughout the nights until they were used to the profoundly quiet darkness, so deep the whole world might be dark.

He hears the bird again, far away, fainter as it shelters from the coming storm. Whitecaps leap and flicker in the sea, and though the woods behind Mrs. Corbett's barn hide the shore, he knows waves are beginning to break and reach, stirring the beach stones. He wipes the sticky dampness from his cheek. The eye throbs. Too late now to find a doctor. He can't drive through rain with his sight cut in two. Her house darkens against the wild fields, the swaying trees. Three weeks ago he flew to Boston to see his wife. There was a look to her he hadn't seen in a long time. She had resumed graduate study, but was now praising a potter, a talented and crazy man ten years her senior (drunk, he'd crawled across the floor at a party, removed one of her sandals, and caressed her foot with kisses) though not too crazy to be tenured. Ceramics, she told Royce, was what she needed all along, their tactility, their sensuousness. Around her apartment sat free-form pots, organic, suggestive. Royce begged off a party they'd been invited to, so she went alone. Sitting in the dark, he called up an old colleague, a man he'd knocked around with, but the man's fires were all banked now, his affairs behind him, and he talked as if Royce were calling from Antarctica. After Royce hung up, there was no one else he cared to talk to. Late at night in the cottage he and his wife had listened to the marine weather report just to hear the flow of the names . . . Bay of Fundy, Banqero Bank, Sable Island, Fourchu, East Scotia Slope, Cabot Strait, Gulf Magdalen, Anticosti . . . seas two to four feet. . . . He had come to Cape Breton, so he'd thought, for a last chance to find something original in himself. But he had come as well to keep a woman, to sustain her ardor. Hadn't his break with the past impressed her at first, the very gesture of it? But it was only his past he'd broken from, not hers. And in that setting, she came to appraise him differently. He had nothing more to teach her, only more to learn. The next morning while she slept, he left her apartment and flew back to Sydney.

And now he owns this land. Does he not? He has not stolen it. Didn't they let so much of their land slip away, these people, let it go to so many strangers like himself that even the government got alarmed? Dead farms, and distant indifferent heirs selling out to Americans, Western Canadians, Germans, whoever had the cash. Not Mrs. Corbett. He raises his rum to her, and drinks.

But Mrs. Corbett, have I not risked a great deal? I chucked a college job, cashed my pension. I *left* Boston, left that place your kin fled to over the generations, the Boston States, land of plenty. I was forty. Do you remember that age? Did you fret over it? I fell in love. I thought what I needed was to be foolish. I swept her away into the country. Country? What did we know? There were drives through rural landscapes on autumn Sundays, through those miracles of leaves. And on that summer trip to Cape Breton, even the bad weather looked good to us. I subscribed to a country magazine and looked at pictures of people burning wood in Swedish stoves and getting endeared to draft horses and goats. Maybe I should have arrived on horseback, Mrs. Corbett. I couldn't have come less prepared, or more deluded. But no one could have told me how you pass the hours here, or what a truly dark night is like, even with a woman sleeping in your arms, her watercolors taped to the walls.

He touches his eye: gritty, inflamed. He'll need to finish the rum before he sleeps. He glances at the cat skull under the lamp, its cheekbones flaring like small wings. Wind cracks sharply in the walls. Across the road Mrs. Corbett's kitchen has become a solitary veil of light, and east of it the metal roof of the barn shines with rain. There'd be a wind blowing through the rafters now, scattering hay, tolling the hayfork. Is the swallow roosting or is it free?

Rain hits sudden and hard, peppering the windowpane. Sears of lightning strike the sea, their tendrils bright, and he tenses for thunder. It comes, like stone splitting. In its wake the radio quits and the tablelamp winks out. He gets up and feels for a wall switch. Nothing. A good Cape Breton blackout. That could last for hours. He moves his chair further back from the window which has begun to leak as it always does when windward. He fetches towels and applies them to the sill, wringing them out and replacing them as if the house has a fever. He holds one, chilly with rain, against his face. Remembering a bedroom, he runs upstairs to the single gabled room where a wet curtain slaps against the wall and slams the window shut. Lightning flares off the white canvasses strewn about. Mrs. Corbett's house has been reduced to the rain-hazy glow of her kitchen. She'd be using candles or kerosene now. But his unlit cottage is soothing and he likes the sounds of the storm. Recalling from his youth rules for survival, he stands back from the window. Don't shelter under trees. Don't court a lightning bolt with your nose to a windowpane. He could add another to that list now: don't love a young woman, and don't take her to a place like this. Ah, but Mrs. Corbett, she has survived hazards and dangers. She knows about ailments far more grave than a bit of bark in the eye. She has washed her own dead for burial. That she used leaves and resins to make medicine Royce knows from old Ranald who keeps a store at the highway. And that she tried to save her husband with a salve she rubbed at night into his ribs. "A blood charmer, the best—seventh daughter of a seventh son," Ranald said. "She can stop you bleeding with just your name, just the saying of it." She once healed a festering foot that Ranald wounded on a two-handed scythe. Ranald believes in her cures—a coin to ease the agony of diseased bone, a drawing poultice, healing water from a hidden spring. From his cottage last summer Royce saw occasional visitors come, all elderly. But this year none. Maybe her husband's death has sapped her powers, or left a pall.

Downstairs, he works away at the rum, his back to the wall. Thunder passes into rumbles further west but the rain stays heavy. His eye clenches like a hot fist. The woods will be cool now, taking in the sea. He goes outdoors and turns his face up to the rain. In the gravel of the driveway a large toad leaps with a sound like a tossed beanbag. He is used to them now. They can bring luck, Ranald says, but somehow you must extract, without killing them, their potent bones—one like a fork, the other a spoon. Do you know the secret of that, Mrs. Corbett? He presses his palm to his face: the eye beats like a heart.

He feels his way back inside and begins to pull wildflowers from bottles and jars arranged on the windowsills. He stuffs charcoal sticks into his pocket and shelters the bouquet under a sketchpad as he crosses the road to her house. The barn is a dim stain in the mist that streams and eddies around him. The back door opens to his knock and she is there in the faint light of the kitchen.

"It's for your eye you're here," she says.

He cannot find in her voice any suggestion of how she feels. Scorn, pity, indifference—any of them are possible.

"Come inside then." She holds the screendoor open and waits.

It's been a long time since he was in her house, and never at night. The silence seems fixed under the steady rain. There is a smell of ashes from the stove. An old kerosene lamp, a hairline crack in its chimney, burns on the table, and under its soft white light are set two china dishes. The small bowl, its glaze patterned with bluebells, holds something like sugar, the matching saucer a liquid, water perhaps. She goes into the pantry and comes back with a towel which she hands to him. He rubs it over his face and thanks her.

"I don't mind the rain, to tell you the truth," he says.

She stares at his fistful of ragged flowers.

"For you." He fluffs them with his fingers, the purple loose-strife, the closed blooms of hawkweed. "They used to think this gave hawks their sharp sight. But probably you knew that. Probably your husband called it devil's paintbrush."

"It doesn't matter now," she says. "Nice of you to bring them." She takes the flowers and puts them into a canning jar on the table. She points to the threadbare cot by the east window where on the tartan blanket her husband dozed and sat out his last months. "You lie there."

"No, I only came down for candles, Mrs. Corbett. And to draw you. I want to draw your portrait."

"Oh, there'll be no pictures of me, and this is no kind of light for doing them."

He cannot see her face clearly, as he had not that afternoon Corbett signed over the land. He feels oddly helpless and tired. He sits on the very edge of the cot, listening to the storm revive, the tremors of thunder in the roof.

"No, I'll drive to the doctor tomorrow," he says. "It's nothing. I was careless in the woods. I deserved it."

But her long thin hands are moving under the lamplight,

lifting some object from the bowl. She puffs on it, then rinses it in the saucer. She bears it carefully toward him between finger and thumb. It looks like a tiny white pebble.

"You've come to where the eyestone is," she says. "It cannot travel but in the eye. Lie back now. Let the stone work."

"I don't think I need this," he says, trying to rise, but she presses him down. When she lifts his eyelid, he sucks in his breath and grips her by the wrist, releasing it as she lowers the lid over the stone.

"What is it?" he whispers. Yet he can barely feel it.

"Lie still. You mustn't move about. Let the stone move. It's very old in my family, the stone, very old."

"I have to get back to the cottage. I can't stay."

"Not much to be done in the dark," she says.

"I have a lot to do. But listen . . ."

"You can't do what you can't see."

"Listen, Mrs. Corbett. You don't have to leave the house. Stay. Stay as long as you like."

"I have done that," she says. She seats herself by the table, her back to the lamp. He cannot remember what she looks like. Just her white hair, her freckled hands. A key hangs on a nail above the cot. Attached to it with a bit of red yarn is a crudely whittled bird, its wings spread as in flight. Tired, he begins to talk, afraid of sleep.

"There's a tribe somewhere, in Sumatra, I think," he says. "They cut effigies of birds out of wood, with their machetes. They carve a body and soaring wings. The souls of these people are always flying, and now they have to beckon them home or they'll fly too far away and die. They hang the wooden birds up high on poles, to draw their souls back home. . . ." He smiles. "Forgive me. I used to be a teacher. It was your weathervane I was thinking of. . . ."

"It shows the wind different now."

He poises his hand above his eye but refrains from touching it. The stone is there. But soft, cool.

"Tell me what this is, Mrs. Corbett."

She waits until a run of thunder has bowled through the house, shivering windowpanes and the lamp. The cot gives off an old smell of tobacco.

"The very tip of a conch," she says. "So my father told me. But even to him it was old, carried and cared for since a long time. Nobody knows where it came from, or where it will go. It's alive. It knows the eye."

Rain sweeps over the window like hail. He raises his head. "How long?"

She motions him still.

"I can't sleep here," he says. "Don't let me sleep."

"She's not coming back, is she. Your wife."

He sits up and looks at her. He lies slowly back.

"The bird you're after finding," she says. "It would be a white-throated sparrow, from the sound of it."

"A sparrow? I'd hoped for something grander." He closes his eyes. "I've heard you singing sometimes. What words are they? What do they mean?"

She shifts in her chair. "Just the song of a bird."

"But they're words, aren't they? Don't they say something?"

"They say, 'My back to you, My back to you . . . You're not of my kin. . . . ' It's only a song that pigeons make. The birds knew Gaelic once."

The rain has come back heavy. It sings over the windows.

"Were you pretty, Mrs. Corbett, when you were young?"

She touches her cheekbone, then lays her hand out flat on the table. "Some thought so," she says. "But you get weathered. There's no shelter from that."

The wind coos in the stove flue. She is standing beside him. "Royce Simmons," she says. "The house is yours."

He turns his head and glimpses the flowers, drooping from their journey in the rain. But Mrs. Corbett is gone. The kitchen has a final tidiness about it, everything arranged and at rest. "Mrs. Corbett?" His voice drifts into the recesses of the house. . . .

He feared it would press like a stone, the eye so tender, but instead it meanders softly, caressing the inflamed flesh like the mouth of a snail as it slips through his dream. He is climbing a stairway at night but the going is hard, slow. He lugs a pail and its weight staggers him, the water soaking his feet as he struggles up toward the landing. From some upstairs room an old man calls out for a drink of water, and then a woman too, their cries mingling into a single terrifying sound. He is afraid to find their rooms in the dark, their neatly made beds. He fears their faces are white as moons. Fever is in the air, it is hard to breathe and he wants to wake. He dips his hand into the bucket but the water too is warm. A woman's mouth closes on his own, sliding away. In the pungent warmth of the barn, hay and flowers, withered and stiff, rustle under his steps. The barn seems so huge and high with light streaming like rain through the open rafters. He stands over the threshing floor, fixed by an eye, small, a bird's, a white throat beating like an artery. He wants to take it in his hands, feel it there viscous, but instead the coarse scratch of hemp constricts him and his mouth widens. The warped boards of the weather-vane reel in the wind. The rope is red, he knows it is red though he cannot see it, and when the bird, its wings beating, moves for his eye in the dark of the hayloft, he falls away into the grass. In the deep grass someone bends to him and she holds the bone like a spoon and he must drink from it, taste the tears that burn in his eye. When the spoon touches his lips, he turns away, but the taste is sweet like water from a spring.

VIKINGS

Holding the wheel wide like a helmsman, Captain MacCuaig drives fast. The valley is long, with mountains of heavy green woods on either side, and it chills him a little how the woods have come, with their old darkness his grandfather feared. His people once lived here in numbers, and Cameron Gunn is still here, somewhere up north. The river beside him, a torrent in spring, is quiet water and khaki rocks. He's a bad driver, he knows that, sidling over the center line. He can take a thousand-foot freighter through the eye of a needle, but cars are nervous things. His son Calum used to chide him, Dad, you're on a city street, not Lake Superior. When Calum was small he took him and Jean back to Cape Breton in their first automobile, leaving it stuck on a shoulder to ride down to the old farmhouse in his brother Malcolm's big sled, the horse blowing and stepping high in the drifts. Calum got a turn at the reins. Later, MacCuaig watched his son roam the frozen pastures, footprints paying out behind him in the snow. He broke ice on the brook and carried water for his grandmother but complained that only the kitchen was warm, not like his house in Ohio with heat everywhere.

"Aren't you the soft boy, then," Jean said. Calum learned to like tea with rich milk, and his grandmother would pat his hands and exclaim to him in Gaelic, which MacCuaig did not encourage since he was a second mate on the Great Lakes and Gaelic was country to him now. What would Calum need of Gaelic? But of course the time would come when he wouldn't know just what his son needed. On that same trip he didn't even know what his wife needed, not deep inside her. A good Cape Breton blizzard shut them all up in the house for two days, and he came upon Jean in an upstairs bedroom where she was turning a spinning wheel slowly with the tip of her finger. Her long, blue-black hair was gathered under pins MacCuaig longed to remove. Snow whirled against the windowpane and she seemed barely aware of him. "Snow brings it all back," she said. "What back? Cameron Gunn?" All he could think to say was, "That's my mother's, that wheel." He had happily watched her at it as a boy. The soft clack of its treadle had been a warm sound. Every part of it, even the smallest, had a Gaelic name and she would recite them for him. *Teic*, the flyer. *Piorna*, the reel. His wife's sadness bothered him, there in a room he'd felt good in. The wheel went round, spinning nothing.

He turns up the coastal road, the Atlantic an occasional glimpse through birch groves. Passing a road cut seaward, he catches sight of campers on a beach, then the overgrowth of spruce and fir resumes. A name on a mailbox: he and Cameron had fancied a girl up there once, before Jean Beaton. Why had they always gone for the same women? For a while it seemed fun, but Jean changed all that. Ah, Lord. Wasn't leaving here the best move he ever made? Wouldn't he have little or nothing now if he had stayed on? Yet he wants to see the cleared fields, the houses standing, the old names waiting for mail. This morning he sat in Willena MacKenzie's kitchen while he probed her sharp

94-year-old memory. Unbidden, she recounted how Cameron Gunn once stopped a frightened horse, seizing it by the mane, Jean Beaton pulling helplessly on the reins. MacCuaig listened and said nothing, preferring that to talk about death. "I always thought they'd marry, those two," Willena said innocently, as if they had. Since MacCuaig's arrival yesterday he has been working Cameron back into his mind. He runs over again and again the times they went around together, first he and Cam, then the three of them, and the things he saw and didn't see. And that day in the cove.

Going through North Shore he thinks, what shore, you can't find the damn thing now, and his impatience for the sea increases through Breton Cove, Skir Dhu, Birch Plain. But soon the mountains, which had moved off to the west, close in again above him and the highway becomes one with the coast. Up ahead Cape Smoky looms, its barren nap grayed from an old fire. Suddenly a stretch of shore opens out and he eases onto the shoulder for a look. Out of the wide sea waves break without sound, dissolving over driftwood and stones. A small boy kneels on the beach, plowing a wooden boat through the sand. MacCuaig envies the grave absorption of his play. Yet in his own mind lies the hulk of the *Edmund Fitzgerald*, battered beyond belief ninety fathoms down. He has thought about it a long time and it would have felt, MacCuaig is sure, like a deep stumble, the ship's first frightening failure, a sensation no seaman, sleeping or awake, could mistake for anything else: she is not rising to meet the next sea but rather plunging beneath it, suddenly alien, submarining through Lake Superior's darkness with undiminished speed until she ploughs into the bottom silt with such force the anchor windlass will pierce the steel plating of the bow like a huge ragged cannonball. To a man already long awake, so tense he can't finish a letter to his wife because the barest outline of his existence lies right there on the page, pathetic words convey none of the enormity he feels gathering inside him, truth so brilliant only death can absorb it. He knows everything about water but this: how it comes through your door in the dark. Nightmares are not even close. For some seconds more a few men might still be finding air, until water fills the final mouthful of breath. MacCuaig dwells on this before he leaves—the ship utterly still, dark, and ruined.

The wind is up now, the late afternoon sun, lidded with long clouds, is down along the mountains. Cameron was the strongest man he ever knew, not tall but squarely built, whereas MacCuaig, like all the men in his family, was just big, someone who took up room. When Cam laid hold of you, it could stop your breath. He could hug the bones out of you and at dances he was a man to stand with. Dances always had fights. People expected them, even the women, and some liked a good fight though they would never admit it. Jean did, and her a schoolteacher. Her eyes would get bright when the men flared up. They went to a dance up Ingonish once, he and Cameron and Jean, and of course everyone knew about the Ingonish boys, some tough monkeys up there, but George MacCuaig didn't give a damn because Jean Beaton wanted to go and Cameron Gunn was going with them. They took some lumps before they even got in the door, but the men soon stood away from Cameron. Cam had a bloody mouth when it was over, and Jean put her hankie to it and held it there. Things began to change right then, MacCuaig thinks, when she looked at the blood on her white hankie.

On a grassy driveway that narrows toward a gray shingled house he stops the car. An old rural gothic with a steep gable, it's set alone against the ocean as if, in a stately way, it washed up there. A man stands at the porch railing. He holds an open book and MacCuaig hopes it's not the Bible, that Cameron hasn't, in his old age, got religious. Behind the house the sea is a deep gray, flecked by a wind that staggers MacCuaig as he steps from the car. Clouds are roiling over Smoky Head to the north, darkening it down, and everything feels heated and cooled and rushed. But Cameron has come down from the porch, and they grip hands and step back, surprised by each other, unprepared.

"You look fit, Cam. It's not fair."

"Very little is fair, George. Captain MacCuaig, eh? I know that much. You look prosperous. You look like you got where you needed to go."

Embarrassed by the three-piece suit he wears now instead of a uniform, MacCuaig plucks at the cloth. "I'm a pilot now. I take foreign ships through the rivers, so I have to look important."

"You do."

"A lonely place here, Cam."

"Some MacAulay fella owned it. Son's gone and didn't want it, so he sold it to me."

"You got a woman in there with you?"

"It wouldn't suit a woman. It's an old man's house, George."

Cameron Gunn is nearly bald, his head tanned and strong, set deep in his shoulders. He wears a loose white shirt, the sleeves rolled up his long arms. He doesn't look even sixty, MacCuaig thinks, and damn him.

"You're a reader now, Cam?" MacCuaig peers through the porch rails at books scattered about the chair. He can smell the floor's new paint, a ship-deck red. "I don't remember you with books."

"What do you remember, then?"

MacCuaig knows he couldn't answer that question, not yet. He smiles and holds up his hands. "Women on your arm."

"Untrue, but good enough. I always liked books. I just kept them to myself. 'From Ymir's flesh the earth was formed, the boulders from his bones, the sky from the frost-cold giant's skull, the billows from his blood.' "

"Christ."

"A Viking, George. Eh? Poetry. They weren't all swords and sailing."

"I never said they were. It's all news to me, Cam."

"Jean liked poetry. Do you remember that?"

Her name seems to change the air around them, to shift the very wind.

"With bones and blood in it?" MacCuaig tries to recall a time when she mentioned poetry, but he cannot. He tilts his head at the book Cameron is holding. *The Saga of Grettir the Strong.* "Jesus, that's your own story, boy."

"Not really." Cameron slides the book back onto the porch. "But I've read everything about Vikings a man like me can know. Sagas, everything. I think they must have landed here, on Cape Breton Island, I'm sure of it. Signs point to it, if you know this part of the world."

"Sagas." MacCuaig tastes the word on his tongue. "The ocean behind the old fields, always coming, coming," he says. He can hear the soft concussion of the waves. "Are you keeping a boat?"

"I'd be left with kindling. It's the wild, white water here, George."

"You had the first boat, before any of us. We were going to be sea captains, we said, go off sailing together."

"We sailed all right. But not together."

"You were a helluva boatman. You could have gone where I went, did what I did."

"I didn't want to do what you did, George. There's some fine seafaring right here, and the land drew the Vikings in, into the Great Bras D'Eau. Good shelter there and they knew it . . . long before there were any women to row into coves with."

"I wouldn't know."

Wind rustles through the books open on the porch.

"I stopped at the old school," MacCuaig says.

"Which? Ours is gone."

"The one with the leftover hippie in it, down Rock River."

"He's a good fella. Runs that craft shop when he isn't fishing."

"I just didn't like some of the junk there. A cartoon moose with a Cape Breton necktie? It was a school once, you know . . . with a good teacher."

"Yes. Sure. Jean taught the whole damn bunch, eh? God."

Cameron sits on the steps. He looks out over the front field where wind surges like water through the weed-ruined hay.

"Somehow I can't see her gone," he says. "I remember her only young, you know. She had a tongue like a razor sometimes. Didn't she? But nothing like her. Jesus, no. Not up and down this island."

MacCuaig reaches out his hand, then withdraws it, embarrassed. As if Cameron needs comforting. "Whose woman was she, whose wife?"

"When Willena called me that day," Cameron goes on, "I thought, how long since I've seen Jean Beaton? I'm sorry, George. You're grieved, I know. I'm hurt myself, hard. And there's nothing we can say that's any use."

"What's to say? All been said." But at her funeral almost nothing was said that mattered. She could just as well have arrived the day before, so little did that minister in Ohio know about her.

"You wouldn't want tea, George?"

"I'm tea'd up. You know how they are with the tea."

"We'll have a look around then."

They wind down a narrow path behind the house, leaning into the wind as if heading somewhere definite, like a dance, MacCuaig's coat whipping behind him. He thinks, yes, does Cameron have the strength he used to, when we all talked about it, men and women alike? What is it about a strong man we can't resist? Most of Cameron's land is open, the few trees wind-stunted, little higher than the goldenrod luxurious in its first blush out of which small birds scatter. Cameron comments on the stony soil, the old, carefully-laid piles of fieldstone, gray and lichened. Some farmer cursed them out of the dirt, he says, and MacCuaig remembers his own dad carrying stones on his back and setting them down so consciously you'd think he was building a cathedral. Everybody was strong in those days, up to a point: then there was the likes of Cam, who bends for a handful of blueberries without breaking stride, popping them into his mouth. He points out bull thistle and the tight white blossoms of pearly everlasting. The path dips and the property ends abruptly along a steep, wave-bitten bank. Below them lies a stony shore, not a patch of sand to be seen up or down it. The Atlantic stretches for miles, the waves breaking over low and random rocks along the tideline. The water is shot with afternoon light like flexing metal. The two men stop and gaze out.

"She'd be a lively ride out there, Cam."

"Jesus, she would, big boat or little. A tough haul at the oars, eh?"

But it's Cameron who was the rower, and it's the slow limber of long ships that MacCuaig knows, their decks awash or bare. When he was a deckhand on his first lakeboat scrubbing down, he would see the captain, "Silent John" Campbell, playing solitaire in his cabin. Sometimes he was at the cards all afternoon if they were on a run, with fair weather and no rivers. Silent John was a Cape Breton man, but the sight of him there at his desk, turning those cards out, stayed with MacCuaig a long time. I'll never be that alone, he told himself. Years later when he made first mate he was allowed to have his wife along for a trip, but Jean refused. What was iron ore to her, the dirty docks, the officers' mess with its tiresome scuttlebutt? Just once he wanted to close his cabin door behind him and see her there waiting: that meant something so deep he couldn't even bring it up to her. Instead the heart went out of his letters. When he wrote, it was we went here, there, the weather was good, bad, dangerous. He had wanted to give her some of the sea's excitement, but it was too late to delight her with that. He'd lost her to another man in a quiet cove years before, not on the sea at all. He got his own ship eventually and his own cabin on the Texas deck, and he broke out his own pack of bumboat cards and dealt them to himself. Sometimes he would imagine her at home, waiting. But she was not waiting for anything he could put on paper or bring to her. She was filling spaces he couldn't fill in a winter's time, not in any time.

"That day in your boat, Cam," MacCuaig says. "You remember it? You bent Jean's head to the water."

"What? Good Lord, man, what dredged that up?"

"She never forgot it."

"Then she forgave it, at least. She wasn't petty. Look, we were young, full of feelings. That's all it was."

"Feelings, yes." MacCuaig returns to that afternoon like a tongue to a sore tooth. He can still see Cameron at the oars, pulling without effort. He was a rower in a thousand. The cove was sheltered around by trees whose bare smooth roots reached down the clay banks and disappeared in cloudy silt. Fleeing bootleggers sometimes dumped booze into the deep still water. No bottom to it, the locals had gladly believed. But MacCuaig had seen the true depth on charts, knew what the bootleggers knew. Jean sat in the bow thwart, trailing a wake with her fingers, MacCuaig in the transom, thinking ahead, wondering what her dark blue eyes would tell him when later he was alone with her. But now neither she nor Cam said a word, and MacCuaig felt outside them both, as if he were not in the boat at all. It was a feeling he would remember, its exact weight and touch.

"What's it matter now?" Cameron says. "You went off with her."

"Not that day."

Cameron picks up gravel from the path and tosses it pebble by pebble to the shore. "She was going away, so I kept her company for awhile. Isn't that what marriage is? Company?"

"That's part of it," MacCuaig says, hoping he won't ask him what the other parts are. He adds quickly, "It takes a rare kind of woman to be a skipper's wife." But he hears the false rhythm of his voice.

"What kind of rare?" Cameron says.

MacCuaig persists, going where he doesn't want to go. "Not every woman can stand the separation, for one thing. It's not natural."

"Of course it isn't. Did she? Did Jean?"

"She was there when I came home." This is as much truth as he can share. The words are dry in his mouth.

"What's so rare about sitting home alone most of her life, getting old by herself?"

"We get old anyway. She had her eyes wide open when she took up with me."

"No eyes were open wider than Jean Beaton's, believe me. But she didn't see herself pacing a widow's walk either."

"Jesus, what do you know about it? Never married, never gone the way I was gone. If she loves a man, she waits."

"A woman can wait and still hate the sight of you. Or she can love you like hell and wait in her own kind of way. Which is rare? Eh? You don't know a goddamn thing about women, George. You never did."

"That's possible." He wants to ask Cameron where in hell he got so smart about them, but he gives it up. The wind has shifted. Clouds move like thick smoke. Closed into themselves, the men watch the weather as it forms, reading the cold smell of rain, the deepening rhythm of the swells. The only light in the sea seems the sudden foam spilling white through the rocks below them.

"That wind'll give courage to the tide," MacCuaig says, glad to steer another course. "They'd want to shelter from that, your Vikings."

"Aw, they were great seamen. Coasting, most of it, toughest sailing there is. You know and I know. I fished these waters for Oh God how many years, all the way from Scaterie to Flint Island. But I had motor and compass. A Viking had landmarks and such, and when he didn't it was just the clouds, kinds of light, seabirds. And Lord, that beautiful boat."

"It was all of that."

MacCuaig had sailed season after season in his own unbeautiful ships. You would never think of a Viking boat going down, such a wonderful vessel, eyesweet, all grace. But when he saw the underwater photos of the *Fitz* lying in calm, silty darkness, it shook him, the awful state of her. He'd wondered what McSorley her captain had felt when he knew what was coming, and when it came, and all that time to think about it, helpless, *We're holding our own.*

"Did your Vikings leave wives behind, Cam?"

"Wives ran the farms when their men were off raiding. Oh, very capable and strong, yes."

When MacCuaig decided to retire early and take up piloting, he'd told his wife, I can be home more now, I'll be working the rivers. But in their house they would sometimes flinch with surprise when they came upon each other in a hallway or a room. Jean read books he couldn't talk about. All he had was Lake talk. She didn't believe he had done this for her, and having him there in those seasons was all wrong. "It's too late anyway," she said, already ill. No, he was no Viking coming home, just a stranger boarding ships he was not captain of. And he'd never ride one down, like McSorley and the *Fitz*.

"You don't know the Lakes, Cam. One Lake Erie squall'd have you reeling."

"Go 'way, George. Puddles."

"I'll show you some photos that'd . . . well. Twenty-nine men under that iron." He had wanted somehow to be nearer his wife than it seemed possible to be, than he had been ever. But yes, it was too late. "Takes some sea to bring down a boat that size. Drove her down like a submarine."

"The *Fitzgerald?* I read about her, and there was a song on the radio. Yes. Terrible."

Cameron starts down a path that cuts the bank. He stops partway and points toward the ocean. "They had to run with the wind, you see, Vikings couldn't beat to windward. Running before a nor'easter, Leif Ericson, well he could have landed here. Vinland. If you know how a boat goes, and how the land looks from it, things fit." He plunges on, descending.

"Did he get into Dix's Cove by any chance?" MacCuaig, conscious of his weight, watches where he puts his feet.

"Maybe, yes. Might have rowed in there like we did," Cameron says.

"No, not like we did," but MacCuaig's voice is lost in the wind.

"There's whiskey there yet, you know, on the bottom of that cove," Cameron calls back to him. "But it'd take a diver with real balls to get it."

You? MacCuaig thinks.

Close to the sea, in the direct zone of its power, the air is stronger, the wind cooler. Cameron moves nimbly along the shore despite the loose stones the sea has worried into roundness. They extend like dishevelled cobblestones in each direction. Come evening, rivers of foam will rearrange them. There is none of the safe leisure of a beach here, no promise of warm sand, just the soft wet slide of stone and gravel as the sea washes through.

The big, dry rocks, dulled by the day's sun, make decent walking and Cameron picks his way, his shirt billowing. MacCuaig, breathing too hard, curses the man's stamina. He swam the Great Bras D'Eau once, currents and all, Jean waiting on her family's beach, MacCuaig rowing the skiff this time, alongside him. Jean wore a yellow dress pulled above her knees and he couldn't tell who she was watching when she shaded her eyes. Now MacCuaig struggles to follow but the stones teeter and slip underfoot and he doesn't want to turn an ankle, have to use Cam for a crutch. Hard enough to climb that damn Jacob's ladder as it is, up from a bobbing pilot boat. Where the hell is Cameron going anyway, Bay St. Lawrence?

MacCuaig sits down on a boulder and rips his tie loose. He wishes desperately for a cigar, can taste it, but a doctor made him quit. *I like that smoke,* Jean said once, looking fresh and pretty and happy to see him. *It means you're home.* Jesus.

Cameron rowed them across the sandy bar that ran under the narrow entrance, the sand coming up suddenly beneath the hull, bearing the boat's shadow, then the water just as quick went dark and they were in the cove. Cameron shipped the oars and they drifted quietly. Drops from the blades patted rings on the water. They'd had words, Cam and Jean, MacCuaig knew that, home for a week from the Lakes. But he had already asked her to marry him, and that made him stand clear. Whatever simmered between those two, let them handle it. Cameron jigged a fishing line over the gunnel, slowly, lazily. *No fish here you want to catch, boy,* MacCuaig said. *Not with that rig.* Cameron said nothing. Jean was combing her hair in long, thoughtful strokes, her head tilted so it draped down her arm. *I'm going over to the falls,* MacCuaig said. *There's been rain.* But she never gave him a glance. He took up an oar and poled the skiff nearer the bank. He muddied and soaked his new black shoes but he put his back to the boat and headed up into the trees. Let her and Cameron have it out, whatever had to be got out. MacCuaig was going to take her away. Cameron Gunn, strong as a bear, would never keep her here. Distance. Separation. MacCuaig, even then, knew what that could do. She'd be sixteen hundred miles from this place, long miles, train miles. MacCuaig had asked Cameron many times, Cam, come down sailing, I can get you on the Lakes, lots of our men are down there on the ore boats. But he was glad later that Cam had said maybe, said it in a way that meant no, it wasn't what he wanted. The waterfalls coursed down the end of a long ravine, through sprung and upcurved trees, their leaves and needles turning the air damp, the moss lush, almost bright. The rocks were sheened with algae, like green silk. She'd said when he took her here, *Such air! It's like a tropical place.* He told her how he found it years before, chasing a dog. There were small white flowers on thin stalks and she gathered a handful, clutching them to her face. *We must come back.* But they hadn't. He washed mud from his shoes in the cold water and walked back barefooted, shocked at the tenderness of his feet. Close to the cove, other footprints crowded his own and went off up a path. The empty boat, tied to a tree, swung slowly on its slack line. He sat on the bank, his shoes foolishly in his lap, and watched a kingfisher strike the water and fly up, an eel in its beak. He felt their feet on the path behind him, and then they passed him on either side. *The falls are roaring,* MacCuaig said. *You went the wrong way.* Cameron hauled the boat in and held the bow while they climbed aboard. He seemed grim and powerful, yet he smiled at MacCuaig, just for a moment, not meanly but as if he'd suddenly remembered there had once been something between them.

Cameron approaches, a piece of varnished wood in his hand. "See this?" One end is badly splintered. "A small boat come ashore here a while ago and that's all that's left of her. Ground up."

"Jean said that. I can't stay here. It'll grind me up."

"She said that? Where?"

"Here. Before we left. Some spot, I don't remember." MacCuaig looks at the waves milling toward them, breaking with a crisp release of white.

"You look tired, George."

Cameron sits down beside him. With his teeth he opens the blade of a jackknife and begins paring splinters from the wood.

"You have a boy, don't you?" he says. His hands work the knife deeply but carefully.

"Hardly a boy now."

"Seaman?"

MacCuaig laughs. "You wouldn't get him near a boat. He works in Europe, for a newspaper. He's in Rome."

"Is he big? Is he a MacCuaig?"

"Like Jean's people, lanky. He was her boy really. She brought him up." The last time he saw Calum he wore a leather headband and an arrogant shirt. "He was a strong kid, you know. Skinny but strong." MacCuaig remembers the winter night he was dressing for the Shipmasters' Ball, fiddling with his best braid and blue in front of the closet mirror. He liked himself in that uniform, maybe too much. Aware of someone behind him, he turned to see his son in the doorway, looking him over. He thought, My God, he looks like Cameron Gunn.

"While he was growing up, I used to see you in him sometimes."

Cameron stops his knife over the wood. "Why?"

MacCuaig is tempted to tell him, to fracture things and see where pieces fall. But the risk, for himself, is too great.

"I mean your nature. You took no guff."

"I took a good bit from Jean Beaton."

"Maybe you should've had the family, Cam, not me."

"A seaman's life is hard on a family, true enough." Cameron frowns as he digs a rough shape into the wood. "A fisherman is home most evenings. I could have done that, for a wife and a son."

Home in the evenings. When Calum was older, in his teens, MacCuaig so angered him one Friday night, refusing him the car because he'd been drinking, that he blurted out, *A man comes here when you're gone, so who do you think you are?* MacCuaig didn't know whether to believe such meanness or even if he wanted to, but it ate away at him. Jean was pretty, but she was his wife. And after all, they had left Cameron Gunn behind. On a muggy July evening his ship tied up at a slow dock ninety miles from home and he bummed a ride with the third engineer whose wife was waiting at the gate. During the long drive MacCuaig kept telling himself this is a mistake, that he didn't want to know, yet he didn't say stop, let me out. They dropped him off at the end of his street, and in front of the house he saw not his own car but a dusty maroon Pontiac under the streetlamp. Music from a radio played through the screendoor and he stood behind a hedge in the darkened driveway and watched them dancing in the back den. Their eyes were closed and they held each other the way people do who are going away, but they didn't let go, not even after the music quit and the announcer came on, just swayed dreamily, smiling over each other's shoulders at no one. It was like looking into someone else's house, like he was a prowler or a peeping Tom. If he walked in, she might give him the look she gave him in the boat so many years before: why are you here? Now? So what was called for? Storming in with raised fists? Whatever consequences he imagined only depressed him. The man was slight and sandy-haired. He danced well, held his partner as if she were light and lovely in his hands. The air was rich with roses along that side of the house and MacCuaig had never smelled them before, never seen them in their prime, luminous in the summer dark. Jean and flowers. He turned away toward his ship, fled toward its familiarity. How might things have been if he had a shore job, like the man dancing? Maybe the same, maybe she would still have needed another man on some hot and fragrant night. He caught a Greyhound back to port. Aboard ship he told the first mate he wasn't feeling good, something he ate, and lay in his bunk listening to the unloading rigs grind in and out of the holds, their lights flaring in his curtains. The hot, dead air spread over him. It hurt that his son, this boy of hers, had known, and thrown it at him. The feeling in the cove came back, but now there was no future to heal it with. He didn't want to know the sandy-haired man in his dapper slacks: he was not Cameron after all, and they hadn't loved her together on some common ground. Months later Jean wrote him about a car wreck in which a man was killed she'd met in the library. She told him this news in unusual detail. For awhile she didn't write. Was Calum a comfort to her, he who shared her secrets? MacCuaig let her grieve, gave her time, his only gift to her, time of her own. While he was away she could keep her other life: he was not even sitting in the same boat with her now. He would have to settle for winter, for having her when the months were cold, the rivers frozen, the ships still. That was a hard time to be alone.

"Tell me, Cam. Were your Vikings afraid out there ever?"

"They weren't fools." Parings of tan wood flutter over his shoes. Cameron looks at the sky where clouds are spreading like long dark feathers. "You know, the Viking skipper hauled rope like the rest of them. He ate from the same pot, slept under the weather. Who sails that close to the water anymore?"

"You wanted to be a Viking, Cam, is that it? Raise hell with your sword?"

"I never had much in the way of money, George. But I wouldn't have left here all the same."

Waves rise, curl white and spinning. The sea washes further

in, rolls back. MacCuaig smells rain on the cooling wind. The sea is coming to meet them. It is always coming. In a while it will overwhelm the shore, this day perhaps more violently than others, hurling and tumbling, and the raw wet clay of the seabank will disgorge more stones and they will join the restless stones of the beach. He picks up a chunk of orange styrofoam wedged in among them. Not much of the Fitz was ever found on the beaches. A lifejacket or two, slick with bunker oil.

"She more than liked you, Cam. I know that much."

Cameron folds his knife and tosses the wood into the surf where a swell rises, concealing the offshore rocks.

"You always knew that, George."

"But don't you remember the three of us? Even . . . well, I knew you were alone with her at times. I didn't mind. I don't know, maybe there was even a little excitement there. But that summer when I came back from the Lakes, things were different. Like only one of us could have her. Something like that."

"Of course things were different." Cameron squints at the sea. On the horizon a fishing boat dips and rises in its work-manlike way, going home. "Odd what one day can do, when a man has hopes. If I'd've been a goddamn Viking, I'd have taken her off. Eh? Life was short and hard and they went after what they wanted. Me, I just took what came my way. She was a bright woman, our Jean. That's what put the hook right into me. I've never talked to a woman like her before or since. Talked! But she wanted out of here." Cameron gets up. The wind works at the loose folds of his shirt, his collar. "Those were hard times, harder than the usual run. You had a job on the lakeboats. You came home in the winter with money in your pockets and the promise of more. I don't think you know what that can mean, how it can affect the way people look at each other, all of it. You were the man of means, George."

"What are you telling me?"

"We carried on without you. You were gone. Then there you were, wanting her for good."

"People have a way of carrying on without me. Would she have been better off with you than me, is that it?"

"Foolish to think about it now, George. Remember the good you had with her, and be glad for that. It was far more and far longer than mine."

Cameron starts up the beach, unsteady against the growing wind. MacCuaig shouts at him, "Longer maybe, but was it *more?*"

When he came home on a week's leave that summer and saw them together, their affection was like a charged field, it could have spun a compass dizzy. But still he asked her to marry him. Wasn't he a third mate with a big steel company that would run boats Depression or not? And as long as they did, they'd have a berth for George MacCuaig because he'd come there young and he had a way with ships like some men had with horses. If you want her, go get her, his dad had told him, Cam Gunn can barely keep a boat these days, what would he do with a wife? Two days after Cameron rowed them out of the rumrunners' cove she told MacCuaig yes, she would go back to the States with him, they could marry quickly in Sydney with no fuss. But some change had come over her. She seemed quieter, even older somehow, and he knew it was a change he'd had nothing to do with. He never asked her if she loved him: he had time now to win her on his own. She'd be in a house with a new baby, a new life. No Cameron in it, anywhere. On their few trips back to Cape Breton, Cam seemed always to be off somewhere, fishing, out of touch, and soon she stopped asking about him. Yet, had it been Cameron Gunn dancing with her in that summer window with the smell of roses in the air, George would not have been shocked.

The wind has stiffened and the sky is as dark as Smoky Head to the north. The waves break over the shore, clattering through the slack stone. After the Fitzgerald went under, he felt he could quit then, for a reason no one but him need know about. He'd hoped she might want him to come home, but she never said, so he came partway. Even the worst storms end. The sea subsides, grows calm, the sun fills it with color again. Ships ride easy. People come outdoors. But they don't remember the men who are gone. What does Cameron know about any of this, an old bachelor and his dead Vikings?

Cameron stands off up the beach, solitary, still a man a woman would like. MacCuaig remembers the sound of his breath as he took up the oars and turned them out of the cove, Jean wringing water from the black rope of her hair. When they were out in the strait, they saw a wind had come up hard against the tide. Whitecaps bounded toward them in the dusk. *I could row for days,* Cam said, his back to her. It was like he was ferrying them somewhere none of them knew about. The boat rolled and bucked. Jean gripped the gunnels with both hands. *The waves look like sheep,* she said.

When MacCuaig reaches him, Cameron is looking down at a grey rock. Its flat surface is mottled with dark mica in a shape that at first glance could be anything.

"Is that Viking's work, Cam? Something they left for us?"

"Just stone." He kneels and rubs his hand over the figure that resembles maybe a leaping deer, or a ship with sail, if you angled your sight a certain way. "Vikings loved to decorate stone. But this lies in the stone itself. They buried their dead sometimes in graves shaped like boats."

"We used to discuss your strength a lot," MacCuaig says. "Everybody had a story about Cam Gunn, lifting something, breaking something in half. We all wanted a bit of that. The women too."

"You're a big man yourself, George."

"But I could never lift the like of that rock. You could. You'd have done it once, easy, like a bale of hay."

"Lots of things I'd have done once easy. They'd only be foolish now."

"Jesus, look at us. Two old men by the sea, waiting for the tide to come in. Aw, lift that for us, boy. For all of us."

Cameron stands up. He looks at MacCuaig hard. "I don't do that anymore."

"We dared you so much in the old days sometimes you said no. Remember? 'Cam can do it,' they'd say. 'Do it, Cam.' Jean said that too. Didn't she?"

"Do you think I'm Giant MacAskill or what?"

"What's wrong with Giant MacAskill?"

"He's dead, for one thing."

"Now there was a strong man. He gave meaning to the word. Aw, it's a sad day if Cameron Gunn can't lift that."

"It's a sad day anyway."

The stone lies between them. Cameron kicks it lightly and lets out a deep breath. "Will you leave me alone, then, George? You bring too much back, boy."

"I've only begun."

"Then we'll end it here."

He squats down slowly and pats the stone like the flank of an animal. MacCuaig raises his hands but he doesn't stop him. His heart is already filling his chest. He knows nothing about the true weight of stones but this one looks impossibly inert, embedded. Cameron waits. His dark eyes look blind, reaching toward some other place. "This is for Jean Beaton," he says. From the south a black squall is advancing, peppering the sea with rain. He embraces the stone carefully, almost tenderly as his fingers work around it for the purchase he needs. His bare head shines with mist. Then with a sharp grunt, muted in the growing clamor of the surf, he hugs the stone into him, rocking gently on his haunches. No, not at his age, he might have the arms but the legs never, no, goddamnit, MacCuaig wants to see him crumple just this one time. There is a low agonized sound as Cameron begins to rise. His legs shudder, his neck swells with cords of muscle, baring his teeth. He staggers, rights himself, his legs slowly straighten and he bears the gray stone against him as if he has carried it a long distance. He turns to MacCuaig, his eyes wide with what could be fury or hate but maybe it's only the strain that twists his face. MacCuaig backs away. "That's okay, Cam, that's enough," he says. Cameron shakes his head fiercely. His whole body trembles and MacCuaig is afraid for him, for both of them. "Were you the man for her, Cam? Not me?" He asks this as he has many times to himself, in different voices and different moods, but now the answer is as open as the sea itself and he feels gutted. The stone falls from Cameron's hands. Splinters of rock fly as it hits, the pale smoke of impact caught quickly in the wind. Cameron fumbles with his torn shirt and there is blood in the grizzled hair of his chest, on the palms of his hands.

"Cam, here."

MacCuaig has pulled a hankie from his pocket. His hand is shaking. Cameron takes the hankie and dabs inside his shirt, his breath rough. He looks down at the overturned stone. A hard sea will move it, MacCuaig thinks, a storm that will wake Cameron and he will lie there listening.

"Those ship pictures, Cam. I have them in the car."

"The ship . . . on the bottom of the Lake?"

"It's more than that, Cam. You'll see, you'll understand, a boatman like you."

"Goodbye, George."

"Look at them with me, Cam. I want to talk about them." But Cameron moves off toward the water. MacCuaig yells after him, "She never left me! Never!"

A short climb up the bank the air is warmer and MacCuaig stops to get his breath. Up here where the salt wind smells of balsam from the hedge-high spruce, a man could believe in a farm. A farmer plowed but the sea was at the edge of his eyes, always. He combed stone from the furrows and felt safe, even with his back to that water. Let it howl at the end of his land. He had a house, he had wife and children. What was a storm to him? Unless there had been a drowning. Then he might stand here looking out. The light would hurt and the waves would sound strange as they rustled through the shore. He might see a man kneeling at the tide-line where the sea meanders to his hands, as MacCuaig sees now. Cameron scoops out water before the wash recedes, rubbing it slowly over his hands. It seems as if they have not met, that they are two men arrived by chance, their purposes separate, mysterious. Cameron waits for the next wave, his bent back catching the troubled light of the sky. Against the vast flickers of ocean he seems small, reduced. They might have talked about the good times from their youth, all those days before Jean Beaton.

By the time MacCuaig is on the highway a skittering rain has thickened the dusk. He'll have missed supper at Malcolm's. Yesterday he told his nephew's kids about lakeboats, about the great inland seas and how saltwater men are fooled by them. The Indians knew: Seas of Sweetwater they called them, for their taste and their beauty.

As he nears the turn-off that would take him around the bay, his headlights pick out a sign nailed to a tree: "Little Schoolhouse on the Hill: Five Miles," and he considers that he might stop there again and explain that his wife taught in that school and what it was like in those days when her pay was so poor she could barely keep her board, and some days the snow was deep up against the windows and she wore her coat and gloves, the fingers white with chalk when MacCuaig came to get her. But instead he stays on the highway: The cable ferry will get him home sooner, and he wants to get home.

As the ferry road reaches into the bay he passes a lobster boat beached on the gravel. The mountain ridge beyond is growing dark.

When Cam turned away from the oars and took Jean's face in his hands as if for a kiss, instead he slowly forced her head back over the gunnel until her hair hung in the water, held her there, her eyes burning, and then let her go. Something was happening, and MacCuaig let it. He should have intervened. But is was as if he was not there.

MacCuaig's car is the first one at the wharf, a wide concrete ramp running down to the channel. He shuts off the engine and rolls his window down, welcoming the gust of rain on his face. A small boat is working up the bay. He can just make out the tiny lights, the spray punching up white from her bow.

The wreckage of the *Edmund Fitzgerald* lies at five hundred thirty feet, in eastern Lake Superior, in Canadian waters. The lake floor where she has settled—in two widely separated parts, the after section, its rudder at midships position, bottom up— shows extensive disruption. The forward section, upright, is holed on the starboard side and badly damaged. Shell plating is distorted and laid in toward the centerline. Areas of separation show ductile failure of severe proportions. MacCuaig has read the reports, in all their detail. But the photographs took over where the imagination could not go: the thick deck plates are torn like tin in the smoky light of the underwater camera, the blown windows of the pilothouse just black holes, their steel frames crumpled, like those of a stepped-on toy. The bow has plowed deep into bottom mud from the speed and weight of her descent. But when, still blazing with lights, she first plunged beneath that night-black water, someone, safe in his cabin, would have been puzzled a moment by the giddy angle of incline before the new noise reached him: the sea is *in,* and it is roaring into every room and chamber. And then maybe a deep rumble as the boilers blow, his bunklight winking harmlessly out like a puffed candle, his mind a streak of memory in the sudden blackness, and at his door he hears the sea arriving with sounds he has never heard before, and the porthole bursts, water he knows is white rushing him cold against the dark ceiling, up, up, toward a last kiss of air.

Areas of separation. MacCuaig lays his head back on the seat. Cameron broke her spirit that afternoon, broke it and kept it. Something like that. Something. He closes his eyes.

There is a long row of cars behind him now and their engines are starting up. The white ferry rocks slowly toward them, along the taut cable that disappears beneath its hull. How could they call this a ship, this graceless barge with bulwarks, the bridge on one side like an afterthought? Broke loose from its cable last year, his brother told him, just helpless, running clear out to sea before they could get a line on it.

The ferry grinds into its mooring and discharges a pulp-wood truck. MacCuaig drives aboard, directed snug to a bulwark by a woman deckhand. Her yellow slicker flashes with rain behind the red arc of her light and soon he is hemmed in by other cars. The sea ramp closes up and the ferry lurches forward on its cable, drawing them toward Englishtown.

What time is it in Rome? In a few days he will be a voice on a darkened bridge. *See that light? Put your bow right on it.* And he will hear behind him the easy turn of a wheel as spokes pass hand to hand. He will guide them through unfamiliar waters, he knows the rivers, he knows the seas.

Car lights, diffused in the rainy dark, shine out from the other shore. His hands lie in his lap. "Vikings," he says, just to hear the sound of the word.

WHATEVER'S OUT THERE

How can you live alone like you do, way up there? they still wrote
to her, friends in the States, women. She did not know many
women here, but living alone would be one of their accepted
realities, though they might not, as Enita was, be walking this
calm, hot shore on a weekday morning. After the storm two days
ago the beach seemed dull, a disruption of stones and sand, and
she had no interest in toeing out of its moist coolness whatever
the storm had left, flotsam for her windowsills, bits of elsewhere
driven here by the sea. Or for the junk sculptures she pieced
together, funky arrangements that said something, she hoped,
about this little jut of Cape Breton she'd come to know. She
kicked, to hear its rattle, a rusted chain on a ruined post. And,
ah, the lobster traps. One or two at least, somewhere here, after
that big blow. She could tell the rare handmade one now, every
piece of it wood, no plastic rings in the eyes but neat circles of
bark-covered twig. Red Murdock had explained it to her: This
one's by an old-timer, you see, he makes it all but the netting.
Murdock, all his kindly help when she arrived here to a mad
March house, bitterly cold. She could hear his voice, even when

she hadn't seen him in a while: a soft brogue, a boat being rowed slowly. She wanted to anticipate just what he would say when she showed him the bale wrapped in plastic, puddling the linoleum of her kitchen floor, but she did not know him well enough to put those words in his mouth. He combed this shore too, but for useful things. He was her only near neighbor, his weathered house hidden around a spit just east of her, a conifer woods between them.

Every morning Enita walked, regardless of the weather, from the rounded rocks to the flat, to the shingle of stony mix, pebble to gravel to sand. She glanced back at her odd, veering tracks, then pushed on into her routine morning, about which an old friend back home had exclaimed, Five months of *that?* Enita hadn't cared. She didn't even *want* news from home, not then, not about Chet certainly or the familiar events of the college town they'd lived in. Yet, news had come, in a way, from somewhere, and she had dragged it to her house.

The night before last the tail of a hurricane lashed through (a woman's name or a man's, she could not remember), winds of slashing rain. Shingles had flapped away like wings. Murdock would replace them. Spray on the roof made her imagine waves swelling from the shore, not sixty yards away in any case, a white surf crashing through beach stones. Herding their clatter up the shorebank she now stood under, a low cliff of clay disgorging granite the sea would smoothe and round. Under a bare sun the water was an undulating glare, the stones dry, faded. Along the hightide line seaweed crunched underfoot, burned black, brittle and sharp to the touch. Some kind of grasshopper in a clump of beach grass, a thin snapping sound. More like a desert than a northeastern shore today, the sun hot in her black hair, hotter, she thought, than the pale blonde of Chet's lover would be, under this sun. How did you compete with a young body, with energy that overrode all flaws, as it once had Enita's? Short of making yourself look foolish, foolishly young, there was no way. And Chet had been busy looking foolish enough for both of them, wringing his thinning gray hair into a ponytail that gave to his face the strained profile of a hood ornament.

She'd welcome now that storm's eerie, cooling wind. It had wailed in the great tumble of driftwood gathered in the point's windward arm as through some tangled wreck. That had bothered her, not the sound itself but the force it was announcing, the breadth of oceans. Aren't you afraid there? a friend had written, get a dog at least. A dog? The storm's thrilling racket had not unnerved her as it might have once, gasps of lightning lighting her room, the sounds from old movies, country-house terror in the rain, groaning woodwork, flailing curtains, moans in the eaves. She could even have turned it into fun had someone been next to her. The sea had seemed too near, yet coming from so far away, hurling its gray and frightening weight up the shore. She'd picked up the telephone, needing to hear that familiar, homely, leveling buzz in the receiver, nothing more. Who would she have called anyway, about what? The mysterious bundle in her kitchen? Red Murdock had no phone. And what could he have done for her? She was just the woman around the point. As for the Mounties, busy and miles away, they did not answer calls regarding states of mind. Besides, the line was dead, a loud silence in the windy noise.

As soon as he saw the skiff, laden with water, near to drowning in the swells, Red Murdock felt his father's panic, what the sight of an empty, drifting boat must have done to him all that long time ago. The clarity stunned him for a step or two, and then he calmed himself and thought of the woman, she'd been on his mind anyway. He would get this boat for her, yes. No oars or nothing. He waded into the surf still washing high and whirled a small grappling hook over its gunnel, hauling it near enough to grab and drag clear. He tipped the water out, turned it keel up on the rocks: she'd taken a knocking but not a bad little boat. A busted thwart, a spread plank here and there. Sound, on the whole. Some refastening, caulking, a coat of good paint. Must've got away from somebody in the storm. He hadn't seen a small boat like it around here since he'd given up his own after his father died. Trim it up and give it to her, why not. Enita. He liked her name. Lately he'd had the feeling she was going to leave, go back home. Just a feeling. She never said she wanted a boat of course, but that would make it more a surprise, turning it over to her. She seemed the sort who'd want it, a quiet pulling boat. A set of good oars and he'd show her how to row. She took care of herself, and if he showed her how to do something, to get her water pump going or fillet a fish, she remembered.

You could row here safe enough, if you watched the weather. If you knew the tricks of it, of the water itself.

How had she fared in the storm? He wanted to know, but she liked her privacy. A few days ago she told him she'd like to see his still, and that had him smiling as he walked. He'd given her a taste, last spring's good batch, smooth and clear as springwater. Brought it to her when she was down with a cold. Warm you in two heartbeats, he'd said. Then she asked him straight out one day, Do you have a still, Murdock, are you moonshining? I mine a little silver, he'd told her, surprised that he answered at all. Jesus, he had only known her a couple months when she dropped that on him. Not prying, more a nudge in the ribs. And he'd said, Going to turn me in now, are you? but smiling, rising to the coy danger he had not felt in so long he wasn't sure he detected it, that kind of play. Sometimes she stepped right into his mind, something she'd said or how she looked. Bittersweet, all of it, this time of life.

He dragged the boat into the edge of the woods so she would not see it.

At Red Murdock's temples there was still a blush of his nickname, and in the grizzled hair of his chest. He was sixty-three, his face a reddish tan and freckled because he liked the sun. He ate only what he called natural meat, any animal not found in a supermarket, and though he didn't care for hunting himself, for the killing, he bartered his liquor for the carcass of a deer, a portion of moose, a few partridge or rabbits. He had eaten everything from bear to crow, he told Enita, and considered himself the better for it, and there wasn't much in the sea he had not tried, though some of it he wouldn't try again. He baked his own bread and flavored his cooking with herbs he grew or picked wild. His potatoes and turnips and carrots, stored in an old deep cellar, got him from one summer to the next. He'd helped Enita put in a small garden, twice, glad to work alongside her another afternoon after a June frost had killed her seedlings. In earlier years he had fished these waters, here along the north side of the Great Bras D'Eau where the channel opened wide into the Atlantic. His father had known all the raw rocks, where current and wave combined against you, had laid traps until heart trouble forced him ashore, later to quit laboring altogether, and finally into a chair, by a window.

The storm had pushed a trap up the beach, clogged it with stony seaweed. Could be the man lost a good few of them in that blow the other night, lost money and lobster and time. He looked up the beach but she wasn't in sight. She wore her black hair in a braid down her back, black braid of hemp. She'd been married to a professor of some kind, he knew that, somewhere down in the States, but he left that side of her alone.

The Dutchman's tour boat was heading out to the Bird Islands, a sign the seas were down. Still, be a seasick few before they got to the birds. Binoculars flashed at the shore where Red Murdock was standing. All he could see was a string of sunglasses and caps along the bulwarks, sometimes the mirror flare of a panning lens. Just lookers, not watchers. They didn't see much really, nothing they could keep but snapshots. He'd been here so long, and the house longer. His dad had seen sail here, schooners, and local rigs of their own. A boat could come in right off the point there, riding the tide, and you wouldn't hear a thing but maybe a voice, the soft shaking of canvas.

In the spare bedroom Enita sat in the old rocker near the window, placed as it was when she arrived. She liked the soft bowl of the seat, compressed into the shape of haunches. She would look first southeast toward the sea, and then swing west along the channel, the cliffs of Black Rock, a few houses tiny and white above them. East, if she leaned a little, she could see just above the treeline the mossy ridge of Red Murdock's roof. Anyone in this chair would have seen her trundle that bale up her path, push it with her foot, winded. Her eyes shifted side-wise to the dresser mirror whose cheap glass, rippled in a yellowish mist, reflected little but the black braid on her breast, the sallow shadows of her face. About Chet she was both glad and bitter. Sometimes she hated him because he had shown her too well what she already knew—that she was getting older and that she could do nothing about it that would matter. Her frowns and smiles were deeper, indelible. She joked about them. She looked okay. But someday, if she lived long enough, her face might, if she were to glimpse it now, terrify her. Youth was so relentless. In a university town, it just kept coming at you. They were always fresh, always turning over, the students, and within those few years some of them became as beautiful as they would ever be, an intelligent loveliness. Not hard to imagine how Chet could have fallen for one, the whole foolish trip.

"A Mountie showed up at the wharf last week," Red Murdock said as he ducked down a set of narrow wooden stairs, directing Enita by the hand into the cool, sharp, fermenting smell of the cellar. "The man wanted our help, he said, you fishermen, beachcombers, anybody near the water. More drugs than ever coming into Nova Scotia now by water, he said."

"The Coastal Watch Program," Enita said. "I read about it in *The Post.*"

Enita could see cracks of sunlight back under the sills. Red Murdock groped for a string cord and lit a bulb dangling above a crock. It sat on long, flat stones like the foundation's. He lifted the lid and sniffed.

"What's in this batch?" Enita said, peering in.

"Oranges, pineapples, odd fruit. It's a good one, I think. After it's wine, I cook it, see? The still there, with the coil coming out of her? Spring water cools the vapor. You see, the steam condenses down like, drips out here. Then you got a liquor."

"Lovely."

"We need your eyes and your ears, the constable said, in this fight against drugs. Nobody on the wharf knew a thing about it."

"So they said."

"But they'd keep an eye out, they did say that."

"For what?" Enita pushed her palm against the cold clay wall of the cellar.

"Suspicious activity, in particular at night. Say a boat running without lights, that kind of thing. Strange, not known along here, is what he meant."

Enita ran her fingertip slowly down the coil's spiral, down to a bead glistening at its tip which she plucked and tasted: alcohol slightly sweet, warm on the tongue. The bale had arrived on the evening tide, slow swells crashing up through the stones, stirring them into a dull clatter, and there, a slowly tumbling thing. A flash of raingear? She'd expected any moment to see skin, a face, limbs skewing as the waves pushed it clear. She was afraid of its touch, of what she'd have to attest to. But it turned out to be a small bale, bound in the dark green plastic of garbage bags. She had kicked it as if it were faking, then pulled it higher up where the stones were dry. She'd walked off a ways before returning, hoping somehow it might be gone, swept magically out into the tidal currents to a further beach, turned up by someone more innocent than she. The light had been in that strange, bright zone of a coming storm. There were no boats in the channel or heading in from the sea, and as usual that time of the week, no one along the shore but herself. So she'd dragged it home, assessing the heft and feel of it along the way, her heart beating so fast she laughed: her kill.

"Wouldn't the Mountie be interested in *this?*" she said, tapping a lidded jar of clear liquor.

"No. He means *drugs.* This isn't rumrunning. They wouldn't be looking for me now, not for mine. My dad did some of that, back in the thirties, twenties, before he took sick. But they never found so much as a pint around here."

"What was wrong with him?"

"Well . . . his heart, I guess. That was most of it."

Red Murdock put the light out. Sun sketched seams of light under the house. "I never sell what I make," he said, his voice somehow intimate though he didn't intend it to be. "I give it, I trade it."

"Oh, I see," Enita said softly into the dark.

Upstairs Red Murdock conducted her through his collection of beachcombed things. She turned a teakwood goblet in her hands. "Odd item to wash up here," he said, "we drink more plain than that. Tipped off of a fancy boat, I suppose." Enita sniffed the rim for an odor of wine. "Let's hope he didn't fall overboard along with it," she said. "Or she," Red Murdock said. Bottles, some from the beach, others from ash pits, he had blended along a wide windowsill, shades from a bitters molasses brown rising to an old golden beer bottle, an aqua cough syrup beginning a run of blue that concluded in a cobalt jar. "My grandfather was great for the patent medicines," he said. "Any with alcohol." Enita aimed at the shoreline a pair of German binoculars, the lenses clouded with mist. There was also a seized-up clock, its face gone but revealing a rich collection of brass gears and wheels. A carbide miner's lamp, its brass polished, sat in the bight of a small harpoon.

"My dad's things."

"I don't find stuff nearly as nice as yours," Enita said. Of course what she found yesterday was easily as nice as Red Murdock's collectibles, possibly more so, more interesting, more desirable, unsettling.

"Eyes and luck," he said.

"Did anyone ever drown there?"

"No drowned body on the sand, if that's what you mean. Young fella from Englishtown died out there near the Islands only this month, but the sea was so bad he knew better, just saucy. Hell, I'll haul traps there anyway, what do the old fellas know? That's the kind he was. Too near the rocks where the sea builds up and one knocked him overboard, him afloat all right, paddling, but his own boat reared up over him and slammed down on his head. His dad warned him, was out that day too, saw it all happen. Pulled him out, but the boy's neck was broke. Water has the last word. Some don't believe it."

"I want your opinion on something, Murdock. Could you come over?"

"Over when?" He wanted her to stay longer, to sit down with him in his house, but he could see she was up on her toes.

"Soon. This evening."

She would have invited him for supper but there it would be, in the way of their meal.

Enita toweled up the linoleum, wrung the saltwater out the back door. Salt had dried in the dark creases of the bale. Maybe a drowned body would have been better than this, less complicated. She wanted to lie. No, it was nothing special, Murdock, just a dead animal in my garden, and now something must have carried it away. . . .

She went outside to pull green onions but kept straightening up in the garden and gazing toward the Atlantic as she beat dirt from the bulbs. She had come across this place in a magazine, remote and beautiful, as far east on the continent as you could get, and she'd written immediately to a cousin of Red Murdock, a man gone prosperous in Massachusetts. She soon took a leave from her computer screen, from the university press she'd done years of editing for. When she first arrived, any feeling of idleness here had worried her. Random, unfocused activity had no place. Nor would Red Murdock's circumscribed ambitions, his sense of days and hours, a casual carpenter. Enita had told friends, Look, new things every day, and a fresh place. Lying in bed on a foggy morning and listening to the mournful bleep of the Black Rock lighthouse came to be okay, just that. No Chet. No flighty enthusiasms. Weekend merged into weekday.

She flung the onions away, turned down toward the shore, through the ancient apple trees bearing stubbornly their hard green fruit, through the tall grasses shot with the pink of wild roses, once pasture, years ago, cows grazing right up to the stones. The cliffs along Black Rock caught sun, about to disappear above the long mountain behind her. Waves mixed calmly through the stones. Chet. Odd how, even from this distance, his name could prod her. Man and wife too long. She could not blame him terribly for falling in love with a girl of twenty-two. Who wouldn't want those kinds of emotions? But he squandered on that affair all the passion and attention and money—some of it Enita's—he could muster. Ah, youthyearning. She would have thought that a man with a PhD could have avoided it, but in fact he flung himself into it headfirst. Perhaps it was mean of her to exult when simple mathematics dawned upon his girlfriend, clouding his possibilities. Poor girl. His decline must have seemed suddenly imminent, her own inconceivable. She shied away into the frequent lovemaking of a boy her own age, confirming it's what she'd needed all along, not a man of forty-eight. And not poetry, neither directly nor discursively, insisting, as Chet's poetry often did, that youth was brief, love perilous, and death everywhere. Enita would come upon him staring into mirrors in different parts of the house but she did not ask him what he was seeing there. I thought she had a deep side to her, he told Enita, she loved difficult poetry, I read to her, we talked and talked. But you were both stoned, Enita said.

Where she could see Red Murdock's house up above the beach, she turned back toward the pond, unwilling to meet him on his way. Even when the sea was rough and pounding the strip of shore that diked it, the pond was smoothly dark, another mood entirely, enclosed by tall spruce trees that plunged almost into the water where gulls clustered and dozed, immobile in their precise reflections. She'd come across a dead beaver on her first cold walk here, strangled in a snare, thrashed to death, its comical teeth bared. The witless cruelty of that wire, more so when she later found where the beaver had lived, how easily had the trapper determined the beaver's path up the bank to its comfortable bachelor's den in the rooty cave of a collapsed tree, intent upon its innocent and driven enterprise, alone, unaware that another world, another logic, overshadowed its own. Whoever set it won't trap again until winter, Red Murdock had told her. You won't be here in winter, though, will you. She tried to recall the exact tone he'd said that in, whether it had been simply fact, or slightly questioning, or even regretful.

She pitched pebbles into the pond, scattering the gulls from their rest, then returned to the house to wait for him.

"Whatever it is, she's wrapped good," Red Murdock said. Wearing a dark blue cotton shirt, neatly pressed, and khaki trousers, he looked formal almost, like a congenial officer here, by invitiation, to get to the bottom of things. He slid his hands over the bale, its plastic, its thick twine and tape. "Been in the sea a while."

"I wonder how long," Enita said. Because the bale took up much of the table, they stood side by side, regarding it. Enita did not know how to tell him what was probably inside and that she knew how it would look, smell, taste, what kind of ambience it could bring to a room. Or that she might want to hang on to at least a portion of it. How big or how small varied with her moods, the consequences she imagined. Perhaps too he saw her in some simpler, womanly way. It was all a risk. She took up the bread knife and sawed at the cords until they snapped.

"That could use a stone," Red Murdock said.

"A *stone?*" She slashed through layers of plastic.

"I meant the knife."

Enita withdrew a brick-shaped packet, sliced it open. Exposed, the long compact strands were immediately fragrant. Tops, all flowers. *Sinsemilla.* Expensive as gold now, but someone at parties might have had a little in the old days, days for which she felt a sentimental rush—the nickel bags, cleaning ten bucks worth of pot in the lid of a shoebox, seeds dense as BBs sliding back and forth (I could start a plantation with these, Chet would say, disgusted), gathering with a few grad student friends on the floor of someone's room, a candle guttering in sandal-wood scent, passing a joint around and talking talking talking about their peeves and joys, about a war they were removed from, going quiet by turns, distracted by music in the room and in their heads, by the constantly shifting sexual attention, who you were with, who you would like to be with when circum-stances allowed.

"What is it?" Red Murdock said, stepping back.

"It's what the Mounties asked us to watch for, Murdock. It's worth some money all right. But you *can* touch it. It will not explode."

When he made no move, Enita untangled a long colla, sticky with resin, and put it to his nose like a flower. "Marijuana. Pot, grass, weed, boo, tea. Whacky tabacky."

"You know about this stuff then?"

"Part of my era, Murdock. College days, and after. Like liquor for you, I guess."

He sniffed it. "What's it do, in your opinion?"

"You feel better than you would without it. Some people overdo it, but that's always the way, isn't it. No bigger deal than moonshine, believe me. And it's much kinder to your head."

"It won't be kind if they catch you."

"Who would come here for me?"

"I couldn't say anyone would. But you might've been seen hauling it home."

"Unlikely, don't you think? Late in the day, a storm coming on?"

He sat down slowly, pulled out a cigarette and lit it. "Well. Maybe they'll give you a medal when you turn it in."

"Possible." Enita looked out the door window where green onions hung in a bunch from the porch post, beating in the wind. He'd brought her a small basket of beach peas he'd picked from the shore. Her pickling cucumbers were coming in. She hadn't read a good newspaper in a month.

"Suppose I didn't," she said. "Suppose I held on to it, hid it away."

"My Lord, that's a whack of drugs you're looking at there, girl. What do you mean to do with it?"

"I don't exactly know, Murdock." Perhaps into her morning walks, into the routine of cooking and tending to herself, studying moods of sky and sea and self, even into the reading and sketching she so much enjoyed, there had crept a tinge of boredom she was afraid of because it seemed wrong, so against what she valued here. The old house and its wild sea fields, the small discoveries, the lovely yellow-red irises that suddenly bloomed below the kitchen window where their bladed leaves had been lost in grass, the twisted apple trees, the black fox that strolled past her back steps as casually as a neighborhood dog, a dead rabbit in its muzzle. But there it was, sometimes, a hint of ennui, her staring off at a blank rainy ocean, a book as limp in her hands as the rabbit in the fox's mouth. Did she really miss flea markets, art films, concerts on campus, a small party with old friends with whom she could get pleasantly loose and gabby and high? She had persuaded herself she wanted to get by on this shore, alone. Not because of its simplicity or purity since it was not simple or pure, but rather its old complexities which she sometimes sensed acutely.

"You wouldn't want them to think you were after selling it," Red Murdock said solemnly. "They'd hang you for that."

"Oh, no, sell it never. But surely they wouldn't hang me, Murdock." She stuffed the brick into the bale, folded the plastic shut. His attitude made her stubborn, knowing she could not explain herself to him. "Look, it just . . . washed up. Where did it come from? For who? Did the boat sink? Did they toss it overboard? It's had a long journey, maybe from Asia or South America. It's a story we don't usually get, Murdock."

Red Murdock got up and flipped his cigarette out the door, holding it open, staring at ocean light turning the color of slate.

"Suppose them who owns it come looking for it?" he said.

"How would they know?"

"People like that know more than you think."

"I guess I'd have to call on you, then, Murdock."

He turned to her with a slight smile, reflecting her own. "Listen, put it away somewhere, eh? God, you can't leave it on your kitchen table."

He followed her upstairs, bearing the bale in his arms, but when she turned into the spare bedroom, he stopped in the doorway. "Not here," he said. 'Don't put it in here."

Enita was already kneeling inside the closet, yanking clothes from a deep, camphorous trunk, heaping behind her a dark wool suit, trousers, shirts, a blanket. She beckoned impatiently to him. "Bring it here," she said. "This is perfect."

He dropped the bale inside with a disapproving grunt and stepped away. Enita covered it with the old clothing, shut the lid, the closet door. They stood in the waning light without speaking.

"You sit in that chair?" Red Murdock said. The varnish of the rocker was nearly black in the evening light. Enita raised the window slightly, a breeze quickly on her skin cooler than she'd expected.

"It was set that way. I just like to look out."

He tugged at the bed's thin coverlet. Under it, Enita knew, was a hard, bare mattress.

"What do you look at?" he said.

"Whatever's out there, "she said. "You know what's out there."

In the rear of his work shed Red Murdock planed a board he'd cut for the thwart. The boat lay bottom up out back. Shavings, releasing a scent of spruce, curled out of the plane and dropped like hair to the hard dirt floor. Five cigarettes a day he'd been keeping himself to, for the cost and because he was tired of the packets' bold warnings about strokes and heart disease and death, thank God he had his mother's arteries. But today he was smoking one after the other. He was trying to hold on to the Enita he knew before yesterday, and while he worked at his toolbench, he almost could. But what had he known of her anyway? Some days she had seemed permanent, like she had no future but here, just the way she was living now. Other times her mind was moving her somewhere else and she did not intend to tell him about it. Any pause today brought her kitchen to mind, the dull knife sawing the plastic, the stuff inside clumped like old hay. Jesus, it was over there in the old house right now. He knew how polite a Mountie could be just before he collared you. Predicted rain had not come but the air was sticky, windless, the sea pressed flat by the gray weight of the sky. He unvised the board and sighted along its edge toward the open door. He'd seen a fiberglass boat with a red hull this morning. No insignia but he was sure it was the Mounties. They didn't patrol often, and they wouldn't chase much down with that rig if the weather got rough, just a big outboard.

If she were not pretty, if she were small or mean or a bad neighbor, would he report her? Probably not. He was not high-minded about this drug business, had not paid it much notice except when it appeared in the newspaper, its lurid causes and effects. He'd seen drunkenness all his life, seen it good and seen it crazy, been whacked out himself with it, swinging into stupid fights, woken up face down in his own dirt. But he'd sung with it too, danced, drawn out some lovely talk he would never hear again. It was just what you knew, a young man in the country, you got half-cut and you let whatever happened happen. The house Enita was in had been his family's once, his father's. The bed she slept in Red Murdock had slept in until he moved over here. Her bare feet padded over the same floor. Her house, and this, had been part of all the life along the road, every property a small farm, the ferry traffic, the two churches, made now into houses too. Since a long while closed off by new woods and most of the old houses owned by summer people wanting a piece of shore-front. But before last night, except for a fella he'd traded some moonshine to offering him a smoke and Red Murdock saying no, thanks, whatever it does I'm too old for it, he had never *seen* drugs. Now he'd seen it in her hands, smelled it, heard her talk about it. Upstairs now, under his dad's moth-holed suit, shiny in the seat, the elbows, the knees. Didn't the white iron bedstead look more frail than he remembered? He was disgusted that he had tightened up in front of her, that the whole business had shaken him some.

The new thwart fit snug and he fastened it with brass screws. She would sit on this when she learned to row. Of course she might not want to row, not even a boat of her own. That was a responsibility, even if you rowed by yourself. She watched the boats coming and going, she'd remarked on them. This boat had good lines, and she would sit in it sweetly. Or so he'd imagined. Her name on the transom. Her boat, not his. And wasn't she right to wonder what kind of boat they'd pitched that bale off? Maybe others had been fired over the side, washed ashore too somewhere along these waters, people puzzling over them, maybe wrestling with what they'd found. Some would turn them in, some wouldn't, if they knew there was money to be had. Hard to blame them, jobs scarce as crow's teeth. Still it bothered him that Enita wanted to keep the stuff, there in the old home. He liked having her around the point, seeing her suddenly on the shore on a warm day, her feet, pale and graceful, stepping from rock to rock, the brief visits back and forth, not frequent—he knew she liked to be left alone—but enough to lift his day a notch or two. Now it was like a stranger had moved in with her and it gave him a knotted feeling in his gut.

Red Murdock lit another cigarette and turned the boat over so he could start scraping the hull. He would paint it white, a fresh clean white. Trim the gunnels in blue. Blue was her color, he thought. Blue was her eyes.

They still had legal things to discuss, she and Chet, but that was not what she'd bought the card for, a bright view of Cape Breton Island's east coast, rocky in a grand way that would remind him of Big Sur. Just an impression or two. She owed him no special language anymore, that energy and love that once filled her letters when she'd tried to bring him, in words, to wherever she was. She could tell him the tide has left kelp, cinnamon and dark yellow, like bands of thick, shed skin. The sea is finely corrugated, calm. But would he appreciate that term, *calm?* The swells were faint shadows on the metallic surface, breaking softly and falling back, crackling through the shoreline gravel, small, polite versions of the waves of last week. Should she mention to Chet the incredible stash that had washed into her arms? His delight would, for a few moments, be spontaneous, genuine, shared, out of their past, but later, unhinged with envy, he would find her number somehow and his excited, insincere voice would be on the phone, fascinated suddenly by this place she was living in, freshly curious, offering to take this windfall off her hands, to do a deal. And that was a cupboard best left closed. Leave him alone, and then she could leave herself alone. Leave him busy far away, refurbishing his ego with a woman nearer his own age, though not uncomfortably near. Civility would do. Calm. The slow rustle and slide of stones.

Around the point to the west of her lay a sandy beach, a shallow cove protected from the tidal currents, and she could hear swimmers, their voices and play seeming much further off than they were. Enita liked to swim there when it was abandoned, the fine buff sand sensual on her feet. There was the red boat again, the one she'd noticed yesterday, meandering along the channel, stopping now and then. They weren't fishing and they didn't seem to be heading in or out but they did cast a heavy line, pull something up, toss it back. She would ask Red Murdock about it. Her binoculars were back in the kitchen but she thought that underneath their orange lifejackets the two men were wearing khaki. She had never seen a fisherman in a lifejacket. The boat rose and fell lazily, like the afternoon, as if the red boat were merely part of its motion, a daub of color against the bluffs of Black Rock Head toward which it now turned, cutting a wake. Enita fished in her jacket for the cigarettes Red Murdock forgot the other night, two of which she had smoked. She lit a third, certain she wouldn't crave them again. There was no reason to suppose any connection between the red boat and herself, between what they might be searching for and what she'd hid in her house. Had they suspected, they would be on her shore right now, but they never even looked her way. She turned the cigarette packet over in her hand, read the stark white-on-black warnings, English one side, French the other, strokes and heart disease, then *des maladies du coeur.* No wonder she quit. In French at least, not just organs were involved but sickness of the heart. The red boat was now just that, someone fishing in the distance perhaps or messing about. Behind her, above the mountain, the sun had turned the water blue and friendly. Her shoulders were warmed, her hair. Red Murdock hadn't been around since they stuffed the bale in that heavy well-traveled trunk with N. MacL. stenciled on it. He had said to her, No, when she flung out the clothing it contained. Who was N. MacL.? The sea looked benign now, everything—water, cliffs, the low tables of the Bird Islands. Flat, calmed, leveled. Enita closed the card to Chet without adding another line. Her greeting-card voice was gone, the resolve she'd opened it with. She didn't know what she wanted to write to him now, on a pictorial scene of Cape Breton. Long swells that Murdock called rollers had arisen, as if some great vessel had passed behind the horizon, and the waves spread higher and louder through the stones.

"In the days before the bridge went up people'd row from one side to the other," Red Murdock said, "if the weather wasn't too rough or foggy, and there was a young fella who kept a small boat he took back and forth because he had work in the summer, over there. His father was old, you see, and anxious about him and so he'd watch for him late every afternoon until he was in sight, rowing home, and one day the young fella, a few drinks in him and fed up with his dad always watching like an old woman, lay himself down in his boat when it got near where his father could see it, hid himself in the bottom and let the boat drift so his father would think he'd drowned. But the man is so struck by the empty boat that his heart just quits, and he dies in his rocker, there by the window."

"That was cruel," Enita said.

"He didn't mean it. You don't think when you're young."

Red Murdock had been pleased to see Enita at his back door after supper, holding out his cigarettes, one of which she was smoking. But she'd been so quiet since she arrived, staring out the back window in which a green spider, big as a grape, was knitting up its web, trembling in the wind, that he told her a story with a window in it.

"Would you like a drink?" he said.

"Of that hootch?"

"It's bad, is it?" he said. She'd never used that tone with him, sarcastic.

"No, Murdock, but it's not what I need." But then she turned toward him, smiling, that smile with shades to it. "Listen, I'll have a drink of your stuff with you, if you'll share some of mine with me."

"Yours?"

Enita took from the pocket of her blouse a joint she had carefully rolled, amused that she could still do it so neatly, in her bedroom with the blind drawn, twisting it in her awkward fingers. Last night she'd opened the trunk and teased out a single flower top, like lifting a coin from a treasure chest, then sealed the bale up again. Red Murdock looked at the joint with the twirl on one end.

"Ah," he said. "*That* stuff." He sighed. This was not the same as sharing a drink of his liquor, not at all. They had, he and this woman, shared a few simple things these last months and it often surprised him that they shared them so well. But her eyes were dark now, sizing him up, and he did not want her to see him as timid, as just country. "Why?" he said.

"Why do you drink, Murdock?"

"I don't go overboard, not anymore."

"But it must give you something you like, you enjoy. Doesn't it? And you like drinking with other people?"

"Well, not so much now."

"Thanks."

"I didn't mean you."

Enita reached into his breast pocket and he caught his breath as she fished out a book of matches. She lit the joint, inhaled, held it, breathed it out. "Don't look at me as if I were plucking out my eyeballs, Murdock. It isn't anything wild."

"I wouldn't know just what it was."

"Here."

"You go ahead yourself."

"No, listen, I mean it. Don't be silly now. *You*, and *me*."

He accepted it, scowling as he puffed.

"It's not a cigar," she said. "Take a couple more and hold them a little. There. That's the way."

He told her he didn't feel a thing, that an unfiltered Export did more than this, but down in the cellar his head suddenly went light and his feet wandered a bit before he set them carefully down. He studied the lightbulb swaying at eye-level and his mind seemed to sway as well, slowly, broadly, everything clear but demanding more attention than he would usually give it. He listened to a drop of water, a single distinct spat somewhere in the dark crawlspace, and for a few moments it magnified into a leak but his sense told him no, it's condensation from a water pipe or a little weeping around a joint, nothing for worry. He smiled, and then more widely. How did her funny cigarette get that name? For connecting things together? He started up the stairs but had to back down because he forgot the jar of liquor. Up we go. He couldn't seem to quit grinning. His eyes burned a little, like he'd been on the water in the sun, but he didn't say anything to Enita. He remembered that she would take his moonshine mixed with pop and he poked noisily around the kitchen for his homemade ginger ale until he could stop smiling. He had no idea if anything was amusing at all or just everything, but did not care so long as he didn't look foolish. He measured out the drinks, held each one to the light, frowning like a chemist. It seemed important that all this be done exactly right, without rush, and he almost forgot Enita was in the room.

"Murdock, for God's sake," she said. "You're not much company. I thought you'd died in that basement."

"I'm old enough. I could've."

"You wouldn't do that. You're not the sort. You don't *feel* old, do you?" She'd pulled him into the flow of her mind, it seemed like, and he didn't care, was glad. Things sang in his head. The shape of her name was her somehow, a ripple of light, of sound. A good while ago the drums in his own life had quit, he knew that. There had always been some music he'd hummed to without thinking, danced to. Down there in the grassy field of the point they used to knock together a wooden platform for dances, and they danced the nails out of her. They had bonfires and there were good fiddlers up and down the island, and in the wee dark hours men stepdanced in the headlights of the last car until the lights went yellow and the car had to be pushed to get it a start home. That was gone, but he could taste the excitement of it. He didn't know what to say to her while he was feeling this way, so he looked out the back door at Black Rock Head, blunt, stolid in the sea's blue darkness. When a good sou'easter was on, the sea reached high up Red Murdock's shore, scattering stone and wood far back into the rough sand, trees and limbs and trunks, sometimes as far as the woods pond where, bone bare, they tangled in the irontinted water. Down the channel to the west the steady light of a boat. There was an early star, solid as the head of a spike. He wanted to know more about her, he wanted to talk, he wanted to touch her.

He said, reeling back a little but catching himself, "This makes me your partner in crime. We're in this together, eh?" His voice was joking, he smiled, but his heart seemed to be beating loud enough to hear: she was from away, and she had brought that thing into the old kitchen, that homely place he'd known all his life.

Enita smiled. "Anyway, what are we *in?* Something deep and mysterious, I hope."

Suddenly he was unsure of her tone, her intentions. Was she pulling his leg?

"We should haul that bale back where it came from," he said, then hearing his own gruffness, went on more lightly, "we could row her out and drop her, you know, let somebody else have the headache of it."

"But I *want* the headache of it, Murdock. I want to see what it's like."

"It isn't just you."

"Murdock, please, don't be such a granny. It's in my house, not yours." She touched his hand. "Anyway, I'd never implicate you, for God's sake."

"I know that, but that *was* my house, you see. I was born there and I lived there."

"You said it was your Uncle Frank's."

"No, this one was. I traded with his son. Long time ago."

"Why?"

"Prefer it here."

He drank his liquor quickly, eager for its masking heat. It was different from the smoke and he wanted to tell her how. He wanted to tell her a detail of his father's suit, that in the black gabardine cloth its pinstripe was all but invisible.

"Suppose we dumped that bale and it simply washed back up here?" Enita said. "Now *that* would be funny. Where would we get a boat anyway? You don't have one, but you don't need one, I guess. Chet, don't you know, sold his Volvo sedan and bought a Harley-Davidson motorcycle. Don't ask why." She could see it, smell its exhaust. A simple-minded Freudian machine, gleaming between his thighs. From those high handlebars he'd slung his slight physique. On a downtown street one morning she had suddenly seen him blare by, hearing the Harley first, the chesty accelerating crack of its engine, then looking up to spot his ponytail flying, his chin high, and she had actually admired him for those two or three seconds, that rushed grainy image of him, a person he might have been, braver, bolder in some way that mattered, but could never be except for mere moments in his wife's eyes, she who had been his lover once, at maybe the best time of her life, of his life. Had the girl known that? Enita knew things the girl would never notice because she wasn't looking for them. "But you know, Murdock, that same afternoon he pulls up to a traffic light and he finds himself center attraction to a dozen Hells Angels. They sneered at him, as you might guess, but Chet thought, somehow, the jibes they flung at him were ironic. At heart, he said, at heart. They did admire his Harley Springer, but only to imply they would soon rip it out from under his puny legs. Your 'shine tastes good, thanks. Now, he knew he looked silly on that bike, melodramatic. Nervous drivers eyeing him in their rearview mirrors. That girl had enough sense not to ride with him, she did have that".

"I could find the lend of a boat, don't you worry," Red Murdock said, his mind running over the water with her, rowing. He'd have to show her the oars, but it was night. In his boat alone sometimes he had felt like pulling toward the ocean, heading out there, taking the rollers alone. He wouldn't let the boat drift, not this time. He wouldn't lie in the bottom, not ever like he did that day, the boat like a needle in a compass.

"Where did you get your tattoo?" Enita said. She had hold of his forearm, touching the faded red maple leaf.

He rolled his sleeve up further. The tattoo looked somehow fresh to him, new. The air seemed warm, even the breeze from the window.

"Halifax. I worked a cargo boat for a while."

"Chet got one, at his age. Can you imagine? A phoenix with an arrow through its heart." She pulled out another of his cigarettes and lit it. "He and his girlfriend, high on pot and dinner wine. Romantic, you see, and maybe it was. You know, a little thrill. Sly glances from students and secretaries. He liked that, for a while. Then a colleague said, You never did time, did you? And the feminist theorist in the office next door told him it was aggressive, like drumming your chest, she said. I told him it was sexy in a ratty sort of way. The girl's was a little butterfly."

Red Murdock nearly blurted out, as a link of information, that the bosun he'd sailed with had had a green horsefly tattooed smack on the head of his prick. Instead he just thought, it must have hurt like blazes, the man was not that big. He poured himself half a glass. Rough silk. It sat warm inside him a while and then spread quietly into his head, seeped into his tongue. *Tha'm pathadh orm.* He was losing the Gaelic. Dad had it good. Nobody now but old Malcolm at the Cape and sometimes Red Murdock would go down there. No long talks, just the tossing of a line to each other, a phrase, words clustering around a name, comforting sounds they made at each other. So much had slipped through his fingers.

"Chet's seeing a therapist now," Enita said, as if she were talking to someone else.

"Why, did he hurt himself?"

She smiled. "Well, yes. Yes he did."

Red Murdock smiled politely. Frigging Chet. Who the hell cared? The sea was rushing the stones, a loud stirring.

It was the way the man was stepping that caught Enita's eye, as if he had never walked on a stony beach. He'd appeared around the lower point, his arms teetering out like a kid's on skates. A fine rain glistened over everything and that made it strange to see him here, midweek, an afternoon of gray damp. He crept near the water to yank at a piece of dark plastic in the sand. She wanted to run, to be out of sight, but held herself erect, an air of proprietorship about her even though she knew the shoreline was owned by no one. She regretted she could not drive him off with a shout, a threat. She endured his approach when he spotted her, his hands coming down to his sides. By the time he reached her he had a cigarette lit in his mouth.

"This your place?" he said, through smoke. She glanced behind her where he was looking: just her house, the wide path, the vegetables blooming in her garden.

"For a while." She might have said I'll be leaving tomorrow, just to cut off talk.

"How long is a while?"

She measured his insolence, rain inching down her face. His hair was nearly shaven, but not that or his nose ring or his opaque spectacles conveyed the menace he'd intended. The grim convict baldness was too contrived, as if he were the victim of a prank. He was slim, perhaps athletic once, belied by the small potbelly he seemed to be inflating for her benefit. She could never understand the pride men took in that, lugging it around like a sack, oof, check *this* out.

"When my husband and I are ready."

She knelt down and resumed unwinding fishing line from a driftwood piece she'd fancied. She hated his standing there: he'd made her lie, and suddenly he was another man to deal with. He rearranged his foothold so he could stand relaxed. Binoculars hung like a pendant against his chest.

"You spend a lot of time on the beach here? Nice view. Shit, I wouldn't want to *swim* here."

"Are you watching birds?" she said. "The Islands are full of them."

"No, I'm not after birds."

She uncircled the string from the wood more slowly.

"You're not much for the gab, are you?" he said.

He clattered carefully off, stopping now and then to squat over something, but she could tell his attention remained on her, so she was not surprised when he looped back. She stood up with the driftwood under her arm, fingering its satiny grain. She wouldn't mind seeing the red boat out there. Canadian law and order. A Mountie in a scarlet coat.

"My buddy lost something off his boat," he said. This time he stood further back. "He fishes out there." He waved vaguely toward the Atlantic, the Bird Islands, staring through lenses of inky violet.

"I haven't found anything. But if I do."

"What's that then?"

She held it out to him. "Did you lose it? Here."

He unsnapped the last button of his denim jacket. "No, it's sort of a big box, wrapped in plastic. You know, gear."

She took a long slow breath, afraid of details or lies. She smiled, tilted her head at him. "Art is all I'm interested in. Natural objects."

"Art what?"

"Pieces of old metal. Sometimes wood. Junk sculpture. I hope you find what you're looking for. Lots of people use this beach."

He looked slowly in both directions. "All I've seen is you."

"Sorry."

All the way up her path, lingering casually to stroke the leaves of a potato plant, her knees were weak. She'd been so certain that the bale had drifted from a long way off, to see a man on the beach who was linked to it constricted everything dizzily. When she was inside her kitchen and wheeled around to confront the sight of him, he was gone. The rain had thick-ened, without wind. Runoff from the eave streamed across the window. Murdock should be told. They had neither of them met up since she weaved home three nights ago, sweeping her way with a borrowed flashlight, too aware of her visibility. They, she and Red Murdock, had seemed to sheer off from each other that evening, and maybe they both realized at a certain point what they needed was to be alone, that they had nothing at that moment to offer each other, and by then he was not talking at all. Enita felt it was the grass, and of course Murdock had put away a good deal of his liquor. She had hoped, while heading to his house, that something would resolve itself, but by the time she left for home she'd had no idea what could have been resolved, needed to be, only that she'd believed the grass would do it, like a potient, that all would dissolve into laughter and openness and something new. Instead they both got stoned and slipped away into their own minds.

She walked the long driveway through the woods to reach her mailbox at the road. How normal this was, fetching mail. Lowering the lid, she reached inside and felt nothing, not even a flyer. Her hair was dense with rain and she pulled her hood up around her face. She could leave this very day if she wanted to. She had the means. She could close the house up fast and get tomorrow's flight out of Sydney. But toward what? A town with attractive comforts, run through with her married life, and Chet still there to be seen, on the street, in a bookstore, in line for a movie.

A pickup truck passed, slow like a local, its windows fogged, but she couldn't tell anything by its license plate, just another Nova Scotia number. Should she phone up Kirsty Horton, the woman not far up the road, tell her she'd seen a truck she didn't recognize? There'd been a rash of break-ins. True enough, but they'd spared Enita: she was home too much, her lights burning, her radio playing the CBC's eclectic menu, her car parked under the silver poplar tree. No, Kirsty would want to come by, smoke cigarettes, share small, hopeless grievances. Her husband was away down the province somewhere, seeking work. The young man on the beach, his chest was naked, hairless. Had he shaved that too? Was bare skin frightening now?

She took the dirt road around the bend, the clay muddy in spots, and followed Red Murdock's driveway that twisted through woods, then opened out to the old house, the first time she'd seen it straight on. Behind Murdock's shed there was an upturned boat, its hull brilliant white. The house had a small porch but everything within the house, as she imagined it, would be turned toward the sea, and if she rapped on the door, Murdock too would be somewhere in the house with his back to the road. From the open shed, smells of oil, and fresh wood, and turpentine. His yard was familiar enough, the high grass it encroached upon. But she startled him when she put her nose against his kitchen window.

"Jesus," he said, "I'm old now if I wasn't before!"

He beckoned her inside. In the sink lay fish, scaled and cleaned. She could smell them on his hand as he offered her a smoke.

"What's up?" she said. "Why the hush?"

"You took me by surprise. I pulled in a few sculpin this morning, from the shore. Ugly little bastards, sculpin, but they're good when you get to the meat of them. Listen, I don't know, just the weather maybe feels odd. Don't you feel something?"

"Feel what?" This was not what she wanted to hear from him, a tone of superstition. She needed him to be as normal as the mail, not give her gooseflesh.

"Look at the sea out there, Enita. You'd think it had stopped moving at all. Dead still. Everything's coming straight down, the rain."

"Rain usually does."

His kitchen seemed so decent in the daylight, clean and spare, though liquor drifted among his words. That night she'd been here, there was a while when the room was like a deckhouse, like they were at sea, lights out in the watery darkness, fascinating, beacons or boats or whatever.

"Had a conversation with a young man on the beach," she said.

"Beachcombing like yourself, was he?" Murdock had partly hid his jar of moonshine behind the teapot.

"He was combing for what I already have. For the bale."

Red Murdock winced. "And what might this beachcombing young fella look like?"

"Punkish, but not real young punkish. He might've come to it late."

"Jesus."

"No, I don't think it was him. Not really."

"You're in fine trim this morning. What kind of talk did you have with this fella?"

"Brief. What could he suspect about me? He doesn't know anything."

"Your house, you know, it isn't hard to break into."

"A good shoulder on the door, Murdock. But it is daylight." She wanted to run, just a mindless fleeing into the woods, up the side of the mountain, out of breath, lost. "I'm going into town. I'm out of things, necessities."

"We all get out of things. Lock up good, eh? I'll wander down the shore and see what we got there."

"Can I bring you anything back?" She was already out the door, looking back through the screen.

In rain, that old house could have been almost any time in his life. Except for the truck idling under him, he could be coming on it a young man, toward its familiar face in rain, the spruce shingles weathered gray, the green-trimmed windows, the steep gables that shed all but the thickest snow. The silver poplar, towering now, had popped up wild and his dad had left it because it looked good in the wind. He did not want this house broken into, by anyone.

She was right, the back door gave to his shoulder, the latch-plate tearing easily out of the wood, and, tense in her privacy, he moved quickly to the stairs, but struck with her things lying about, he held up. She'd tidied nothing, put nothing out of sight, just went, took herself out of here. That stopped him, that she would do that now when maybe some real danger was at her doorstep. Yet as he walked the rooms downstairs he felt a tenderness for her: something of herself she always put away before she met him, before she came to his door, even on the beach he'd seen her, when she noticed him a ways off, collect herself so she could talk to him about anything but what was on her mind. One of her sculptures sat in windowlight, in angles of anger or confusion, it seemed to him. She'd taken it inside from the backyard, rusted scraps epoxied together. A long barn-door hinge, a buggy iron or two, a small plow blade, wheel rims, a copper skuttle handle, other bits that had caught her fancy. Joined together they must have meant something to her that he could not see, could not describe. I'll show you how to weld if you like, he'd told her, and then you can do bigger pieces, but they hadn't got around to it. He turned a few pages in the book she'd been reading, not noticing the words, they didn't matter.

He'd get the bale in the truck, under a tarp, and he'd take it up North River where he knew deep pools that would hold it until it rot. Riskier than the sea but.

Passing her bedroom he glanced inside, sheets flung spilling, her bed gaping with windowlight, a pillow crumpled on the floor. To think on a woman this way, again, was almost new, almost mysterious. Last night was hot. Upstairs here it had always been hot in summer. He was afraid to enter her room, to touch her tossed clothing. He was sure that she'd know, that he'd leave something of himself she would detect. Maybe she'd turn against him anyway for what he was about to do. He could hear her saying, It wasn't your business, Murdock, to get rid of it.

He opened the spare room closet. The trunk was draped in the hems of clothing she'd recently hung there. Whose initials on the trunk? she'd asked him. My mother's. But where are *her* things then? Oh she left us too long ago to have clothes here, she went away in a hurry to be with a man in Boston, and that's all I can tell you about her. And my sisters, too, the three of them went down to the States as soon as they could, and I was left with my dad, the two of us, so he looked to me for a lot, I guess. Red Murdock could easily see him, the back of him there, rocking slightly but fast as if that was the last of his motion, winding down. Then the sight of a boat seized him, nobody at the oars. Red Murdock would have taken that rocker and put it in another room, any room, but that Enita liked it as it was.

At first the voices seemed to come from the shore, but when he rushed to the window there was a young man, and a girl, in the yard already, she laughing at Enita's drenched, limp scarecrow, and before Red Murdock could duck the man saw him and turned by instinct to run. Catching himself, he gave a false and hearty wave.

Red Murdock stepped out back into the soft rain just as he would have at his own door. He didn't want to fuss about private property, there was too much of that now. Trespassing signs nailed all over the trees.

"You're her husband, are you?" he said to Red Murdock, "the woman who lives here?" The friendliness of his voice had an urgent strain to it. His sunglasses were huge pupils of color. "I met her on the beach there."

"She'll be back in a little while. Just having a walk, are you?"

"Me and Rita there, yeah."

The girl wore a pink jacket, its hood down, her red hair streaming over her eyes. A smile touched her lips for a moment. "We took a break from fishing."

"What're you getting?" Red Murdock said. He just noticed the Black Rock lighthouse, a deep wail every thirty seconds, a stab of light in mist.

"Pollock," the man said, too quickly. "Off the wharf back there."

"Pollock have a lot of blood in them. But you get that blood out quick, and they're a good fish."

"She said it was all right to cut through your property. Your wife."

"No harm there. You're not dressed for the rain much."

"Doesn't matter." The man tilted his head up, taking in the house. "You got a nice spot here. What a view, eh, Rita?"

"Terrific. You must see a lot out there." She leaned her head gracefully to the side, squeezing her hair into a dripping braid. "Stuff washes ashore, I bet."

"Well, you walk as you wish," Red Murdock said. "I'm busy in the house."

He watched the couple back away before they turned onto the path to the shore. Had no intention of cutting through, neither of them. The man scooped up a stone and baseballed it into the apple trees. The girl was older than Red Murdock had thought, her walk was a woman's, content with how she looked. He heard Enita's car, the rattling diesel. Not this soon back from town?

"I just had to drive, I had to get some *air*. I'm all right." She threw her raincoat on the chair. "How come you're in here? What's wrong?"

"Your friend from the beach was here. The one with the blind eyeglasses. I put myself in the house to defend it, you could say."

Enita ran the sink tap hard while she looked out the window. The shore, what she could see of it, was deserted, but of course below the bank anyone could be walking. "Thanks, Murdock. I should've been here. I'm the one who met him. I'm the one who . . . "

"You can meet anything on the shore and not be blamed for it. He thinks I belong to the place, that I live here, and maybe that's suitable for now, you know. It won't hurt."

"Yes. I wouldn't want him to think it was just me here. Not at the moment."

"He won't think what we want him to for long. That bale, Enita, you got to get rid of it."

"It's not a shipment of heroin. Really."

"It's all the same as far as the others are concerned. There isn't anybody looking for it what thinks it's a bale of hay. Is there, now?"

"Suddenly everything is so serious."

"Somebody knows it's along this shore, our shore. They don't know that they're right about it, but that doesn't make things any better for you."

"I never said I wanted them better."

"Just after dark tonight I'll come by. It's supposed to clear some later, so. Then we'll get rid of that, eh? Keep some for yourself but. I'll keep a lookout on the beach till then."

The steak she had thawed did not raise her appetite, but she did open the expensive bottle of California wine she'd been saving to go with it. From the kitchen table she could keep an eye on the back field, the shore, the path. The rain grew fainter and fainter until it was just still, moist air, and then a wind came up out of the west, exhilarating, cool, full of sound, waggling the sticks of her scarecrow, its denim shirt sluggish as a sail. Yesterday she'd put out in the grass a bowl of leftover dessert and the ravens were at it immediately, their beaks tipped with whipped cream like kids at a party. No one would come here now, this time of day. Looking for what, exactly? That kid with a ring in his nose, nosing around. But what kind of life was this, keeping sentry, her back to a house that needed her attention. She had let things slide, she'd read two novels this week, curled up in a chair, but the words streamed by like water. Still, she was glad to lose herself in someone else's language, even as her own letters trailed away now after a few scrawled lines. The bale seemed to dull her wit, her invention when she wrote to friends. She did not want money, she still had savings. Yet, the bale was a kind of wealth, a hoard. She had spent a bit of it, sure, a luxury to have that sweet smoke available, all hers, but there were people out there, maybe not even very far away, who would love to get their hands on it.

She smoked half a joint, killing it in a yellow-rose teacup she'd filled with sand. Then she pored, as she had the last three evenings, through an old photograph album she'd found moldering in a bureau. Histories she imagined for its faces could only be vague but she looked hard for Red Murdock and thought he was there in a few dim black-and-whites, a young man on a boat, maybe the old ferry, arms crossed firmly over his chest, not out of arrogance (his smile cancelled that) but because he was entirely at ease with himself: there was nothing about him that said I need your help to know who I am. Enita turned the brittle, black pages slowly, absorbed: was that his philandering mother, her 1930s dress pulled up to reveal her good legs to the camera? Who the handsome guy, dark as an Italian, holding a baby girl? The four elderly men in black suits, soberly graying, seated on a row of chairs placed in a field, lovely deciduous trees behind them and, further on, the sea: everything about it said Sunday afternoon. Did she hear a car? She did not get up but simply willed the sound away. The rattling call of a kingfisher came from the pond. When she looked up from the table, the back field was dark, the trees swaying shapes in the wind, and she was frightened.

In her car, she rocked slowly down the road to Red Murdock's, feeling a splash here and there in the floorboards, her headlights asking something to lurch out of the trees, but she had a locked vehicle to defend herself, an accelerator, a horn. She almost wished for commotion, a noisy confrontation that would shake loose the solemn, soaking weight of the evening. The joint she could have done without, its paranoid intensity. But cool, without alarm.

"I would have come over to you," Red Murdock said, letting her in, an edge of impatience in his voice that depressed her. He was wearing a yellow rain jumper, open in front, its rubber slick with damp like his face.

"Nothing's wrong," she said, "I haven't seen a soul over there. There's no hurry."

"How would you know that?" He finished coiling a thin rope he'd been holding and set it on the table where an oil lamp burned.

"That's romantic," she said. "Or is the power gone out?"

"Neither one. I like that kind of light sometimes is all. And it doesn't attract much attention."

"Well, it attracts mine, Murdock. Can I sit down or are we off into the night so soon?"

Before he answered he looked through binoculars toward the shore. "It's clear enough to row if the sea doesn't get dirty. I've

got the lend of a boat up the beach a way, fifteen or twenty minutes, maybe more without a flashlight."

"It's Saturday night, Murdock. I don't want to go out in a boat."

"Won't be easier on Sunday, or Monday either. Anyway, I didn't
mean you had to come with me. I'll need your eyes on the shore."

"Murdock, sit down. Please. It's presumptuous of you to . . .
to . . . you haven't even asked me if I want that bale dumped in
the ocean. Am I not capable of disposing of it? I have a car. We're
surrounded by country, by water and woods. I can take care of it.
Sit down." She realized her voice was shaking and she groped in
her pocket for the stub of the joint. "Could I have a light, please?"

Red Murdock sighed. He pulled off his jumper and let it
drop to the floor behind him. He poured himself a glass of
liquor and sat across from her, reaching over the table with a flaring wooden match. When she offered him a hit, he calmly raised
his hand, tapped his glass. "I'm fine," he said.

"I just want to sit here for a while. All right? It's a nice
evening. That breeze is wonderful now."

"If you don't think I like you sitting here, you're mistaken."

She thought he looked older this evening, tired perhaps.
Maybe it was the red-gray stubble.

"You must've been hot in that jumper," she said. "Your
shirt is soaked."

"*Slainte mhath!*" He raised his glass to her and emptied it in
two long swallows. He smiled. "I got to keep up with you."

"No, no. I'm just drifting, Murdock. I don't want to think
about anything but what's around me here, right now. What was
your mother's name?"

"Marsaili. Gaelic for . . . for what? Marjory, I guess, since
that's what she called herself in Boston. Maybe we should walk
up the beach, eh? While we can? Get some air? I'll just show you
where the boat is lying. That's all. In case . . . well, in case."

"Marsaili. Pretty. Did you enjoy your fish?"

"They were fair. You know what I miss?"

"What?"

"Swordfish hearts. Been a long while since I've had me some hearts. Almost big as a deer heart. He hunted swordfish, my dad. He could fling a harpoon, I'll tell you. Sometimes they got tuna they couldn't give away, in those days."

They set off through the sea field, the tall grass, into the moonless dark. Wet beach stones, awkward even in daylight, teetered and slipped under their shoes. Enita trailed behind him, laughing. She wasn't serious about this, was she? What was he to do? A breeze off the sea cooled his face and he wiped it over his eyes. You got feelings at night you never got in the daytime, here on the shore, the water always doing something, even in its calmness beating like a big, slow heart. Enita was waving her arms at him in mock distress and he turned away, suddenly sober. In the old cemetery above the point a set of car lights latticed the spruce trees and went out. Just parkers, lovers, maybe kids. Maybe. The swells were coming in like long sighs, sifting the fine stone. He was aware of a star, dim as a nailhead, and then a light moving in the slow surge not far offshore. Small boat, an outboard at trolling speed, but they wouldn't be fishing. His eyes open to the darkness, he turned back and found Enita sitting on a big stone.

"That boat out there," he said. "It's the Mountie boat, I'm almost sure. Doesn't mean . . ."

"Murdock," she whispered, squeezing his hand. "I just wanted to get stoned, you see? Lonesome for old times is what I was. I wanted to feel young, or feel how I *felt* when I was young. You don't know what I mean."

He glanced at the boat. Something splashed near its hull. Maybe a grappling hook.

"No," he said. "Probably I don't."

"I'm sorry. Are they coming ashore do you think?" She kept hold of his hand and stood up. "God, getting busted here would be awful, truly awful. It would ruin everything."

"Easy. They're not after you, or me either."

He led her back over the familiar stones, sliding and rolling and shifting all these years, old ones, new ones, always on the move, different configurations every day and still he could step without falling, even in the dark he never fell. The sea seemed louder, long breaths of water suspended, a gasp of stones, a pause, another. Who was this woman whose hand was in his? Where was he taking her, or she him? He had never walked this beach linked to a woman, it was like he had caught hold of something lovely flying by and he was taking it back, taking it home. The boat, whatever it was, whoever, didn't matter. They weren't coming for him or for anything he cared about.

"We're going to my house," Enita said, question, confirmation.

Red Murdock helped her up the short bank and they crossed her field, the path he'd mown for her, the shorn patch of lawn behind her house where monkshead bloomed like bits of blue and white china under the backdoor light. He had never known her scared before, but he could feel it dry and cool in her skin and he pulled her hand to his mouth and kissed it. It was what he felt like doing, no other act at that moment seemed a better thing to do. But Enita seemed hardly to notice and at the door she disengaged her hand from his and pushed inside, and he thought, God, this is another age of spurning, yanked back to his youth when he hardly knew how a girl would take him, when he was dumb enough sometimes to put himself in harm's way of a pretty woman who scorned the sight and the sound of him, and then he got smarter and maybe a little better looking and that passed, but here it was again full circle, and what kind of contempt was he in for now. He turned toward the water. The boat—yes, they had a small searchlight going now, a shaft of light driven down into the water, not aimed at the beach, and he heard her voice behind him saying come inside, Murdock, they'll see you.

They stood at her window as they had in his cellar, just the sound of their breathing in the darkness, even her backdoor light out now, a few moths clinging like petals to the screen. Why had his father's vigil grated on him so? The man had done it because he loved him, because he was all he had left, but Red Murdock had wanted to cross the water alone, unwatched, unaccounted for, it made him grind his teeth to be waited for by an old man who worried too much. Wasn't that one dispiriting consequence of being old? Worry and easy fright? And he had said, even as he wept over his father and his own foolishness, I will never be frightened like that, if I live to a hundred, not by anyone I love or hate. But fear was part of love anyway. Fear gave it its point, its cut: fear of death, long before you knew its embrace included yourself. Even as a boy it was there, he had felt it in the earliest kinds of separation. A night in his bed loft, his mother suddenly gone from the room below. A closed door, the parlor an oil-lamp hush, his own heart sick. His dad, those afternoons at the window, willing him home. How could you love without risk, how could you stir your heart in that way?

"They've moved off," he said, touching her shoulder. "It's not us, not you. We can't do it tonight but we'll get rid of it tomorrow."

Enita switched on the kitchen light just long enough to look at him.

The next morning Enita walked west instead of east, around the upper point, where the ebb cut deep and fast-flowing, to the gentle arm of beach, its fine sand cool in a misted air that was like looking through ground glass. She nudged the charred spokes of a driftwood fire, raising a weak smoke. Mashed beer cans, a few butts. But for that the deserted shore was clean, the grass of the point, drooping with finespun moisture, running brilliantly through the gray air back to alder bushes and rushes that edged the pond. During the night she had not thought of the bale in the closet, under the old clothes of Murdock's father. She undressed slowly, blouse, jeans, feeling pale in her black swimsuit. A white scallop shell turned out to be a piece of styrofoam. A soda can flashed in the bottom sand. The heel of a wine bottle had abraded into foggy green stone. A wine-colored jellyfish pulsed in the shallows but she waded past it, the water moving in cold circles up her legs. She stood, lifting water slowly through her hands. She didn't remember when Murdock left. He was awake a long time. Maybe he didn't sleep at all. Sometime before morning he was gone. She had half-woke once or twice; it seemed so odd to feel his body next to hers, her skin against his skin, his hair, shock almost, who is this, who has the right to be here, until her mind relaxed. Earlier he had touched her face, a gentle tarry smell on his hands, like old rope in a boat. The peaty whiskey she'd given him was on his lips. Any whiskey will do, he'd said, a little something for courage. Why courage? she'd said, used to the dark room, and she took from the dresser drawer the single malt whiskey Chet had urged on her before she left, Here, you'll need this in the cold weather. Listen, Murdock said, I'm not young, I might not be any good for you. I don't care, Murdock, she said, unless someone breaks down the door. The boat's gone, he said. If I wanted what they call hot sex, she said, I suppose I could find it somewhere. You could, he said, God knows you're pretty enough. Do you think so, Murdock? Well, it's just you and me now. Is it? he said. That's fine then. He unbuttoned his shirt somberly and draped it over the back of the rocker, then his trousers, slowly unclothing himself, as if he were preparing to bathe or swim. She expected him to go only to his shorts and socks, but there he was, pale but for his darker face and arms, turning toward the window, lean, oddly chaste. Remember I told you about the old man always watching for his son come rowing across there, and the rotten trick he played on his dad? Yes, well he was young then. He laid down in the bottom of that boat, grinning up at the sky. He could paint a picture of it for you if you asked him. Rocking there, big clouds sailing overhead. He wanted to let loose, but he was hiding too. Maybe his dad was ready to die anyway, maybe it was that his time had come, empty boat or no. But it was the son that pushed him, him that come up from the shore and as soon as he stepped in the kitchen door, he knew what he'd done. All while he put the boat up he was smiling, smiling at his clever trick, but even then I think he knew because his heart was beating so hard. He was afraid already. He'd forgot about his dad, you see, just long enough to do that in the boat. Enita moved the palm of her hand in circles over the muscles of his shoulders, felt him tremble along the hard ridge of his back. He turned calmly and hugged her to him, his delight flowing through her, out of his own unself-pitying solitude. Yet if she saw him today, tomorrow, along the rocks, would she tell him okay, all right, take the bale away?

She dove, groaning in the cold water, but after a few hard strokes it felt good and she turned on her back and floated, breathing in the pearl-white sky. She could not hear the footsteps, shoes slashing into sand.

Red Murdock dragged the skiff to the shore, slipped it down on the loose stones above the highwater mark. The white hull he had accented with a strip of royal blue along the gunnels. Looking sharp for a derelict. If she liked it, he would put her name on the stern. His hand was steady even yet. He said her name aloud and all of her appeal seemed to rush his heart, staggering him for a moment, then he closed that feeling off, cinched it, and went about his work.

After supper when the long sun stretched across the Black Rock bluffs, he was sure he would spot her soon from his kitchen window, see her pause at the boat, circle it slowly, running her finger over it the way she did over things she found. Last night would never happen again. But he had thought that already over with before he met her, and so last night was a gift. They would push off in her boat, their secret cargo weighted with a stone, under the blanket he was folding now, and he would row them slowly out toward the islands, his oars dipping rings in the calm sea. He could feel the rhythm of it now, feel his body lean toward her and back, toward her and back.

HOLY ANNIE

"He might've made something fine of his life," Rhoda MacCrimmon said to her sister.

Annie, whose lips had been moving daintily over the Psalms, lifted her eyes. "Yes, and handsome he was," she said, picking up her cue. "Smart as a whip."

"He loved rum more than living, and how many times did I tell him so." Rhoda stilled the tips of her knitting needles for an instant. "But those women, they were bad for him. They dragged him down."

"Dressed up, he looked professional. Like a doctor or a solicitor."

"Ah, he cut a figure, that man!"

The two women had sung this litany around their brother for so many years that to Annie its truth seemed as eternal as the verses under her fingertips. But Roderick had been buried a week now, dead of heart failure. She wished there were more to say about him, that his final absence would have brought more than their old loving lamentations of him. No, it seemed that Roderick was said out, God rest his soul.

Rhoda glared at the misted kitchen window and then at the wall clock. "And where is that Dan Alec? His dad home three hours already." She was a florid woman and her plump face seemed to burn hotter at the mention of her son's name. "Had to come back without him, Angus did. How is that boy to get home from Sydney now, the last bus gone?"

"I suppose he'll hitchhike, dear," Annie said placidly. "He's a man, you know."

"Then he'll be a right soaked man." Her lips formed into a grouchy pout which as she gazed at her knitting dissolved into a faint affectionate smile. She lifted out of her lap the torso of a black sweater. "Was for him, this. Was for Roderick."

They both drew their breaths in a whisper of sadness. Then Rhoda's needles flashed faster among the strands of wool and Annie went back to her reading. But her eyes kept straying from the words tonight, fixing instead upon some mark on the page. A dark smudge. A nick in the paper's grain. The lacy stain of faded liquid. Had they happened in Africa? Who made them? She could not remember. The Bible, it seemed, had been with her since she was the girl who wanted to be a missionary. She had carried it everywhere, tucked in her arm like a crippled bird, quoting passages by heart. Behind her back they had called her Holy Annie and they shook their heads when the Presbyterian Church posted her to Ghana. She suffered thirteen months in the climate and then returned home to Cape Breton and her widowed dad. After his death she often crossed the fields to sit with Rhoda, and when the thin gossip of New Skye was exhausted she read her Bible, bending intensely over it as if her own life were recorded somewhere amongst the words. But this evening the lines flitted about like sparrows, settling nowhere in her mind.

From the bedroom overhead a snore rose and fell like the creaking timbers of a ship. Rhoda jammed her knitting down.

"Angus? Angus for the love of God stop that racket!" She cocked an ear until a loud snuffle shattered her husband's sleep. "Lord in heaven, he wakes the dead."

"He's tired out, dear. He had lots of errands in Sydney, tidying up Roderick's affairs and all."

"He didn't have to tidy up the tavern. That's one errand I didn't list."

"Now, it's not often he does that."

"Never's too often for me."

Annie sighed, blaming the day-long rain for a dismal feeling she could not shake. The wind was still out of the east, carrying in mist from the ocean that moved like vaporous airships slow and steady over the strait. She looked out at the last of a queer twilight glowing in the spirea bush by the window, its small white blossoms trembling beneath a leaky gutter. In the distance, streaks of hidden sun cut briefly through the smoky air along the ridge of the mountain, then they were smothered, and darkness settled fast. She was staring at the snow-white blossoms when she heard a thump at the back door followed quickly by an amiable curse. Dan Alec appeared in the dusk of the entryway, grinning widely under dripping hair.

"Sailor home from the sea," Rhoda said acidly to her sister, not looking at him. Her needles picked up speed.

"A sea of sorts," Dan Alec said roughly, then turned to his aunt. "Hullo, Annie. How're you t'day?"

"Fine, dear. We were worried a bit."

"No need. Ma likes to worry." Dan Alec crossed his arms and leaned against the doorframe regarding his mother with studied amusement. "Eh, Ma? What people think. That's her main worry."

"Talk nonsense, go ahead. All I might expect in that breeze of whiskey blowing out your mouth."

"Rum, Ma. Uncle Rod's rum, matter of fact."

She stopped knitting and looked hard at him.

"Uncle Roderick is dead. Have some respect for him at least."

"I do, Ma, I do. More now than ever."

He winked at his aunt and swaggered into the kitchen. The rain had tightened his reddish hair into dense curls that made him look boyish in spite of his heavy features and the fisherman's squintlines around his eyes. A denim shirttail poked from the hem of his sweater, black like the one growing furiously beneath his mother's fingers. He raised the lid of the skillet and sniffed.

"Supper's cold and cold it'll stay," Rhoda said. "Your dad waited better than two hours for you."

"Then he wasted no time. Not in the Keltic Tavern he didn't."

"You're a pair, him snoring upstairs like a sick horse."

Ignoring her, Dan Alec lifted the skillet and spooned stew into his mouth. He weaved slightly as if the wind outside were moving him.

"Use a plate, for heaven's sake!" his mother hissed.

He paused in his chewing and narrowed his eyes at her. "I'll eat as I like."

"Not in this house you won't. You never have and you never will."

They stared each other down, Rhoda's back arched in her chair. Annie smiled between them. She was fond of her nephew and knew that Rhoda had been severe with him over the years. Oh, he had acted the devil more than once but there was nothing grave in it. She wished she had the power to end their bickering, and sometimes just her presence was enough, as if she were some sort of nun. But tonight their electricity arced over her.

Dan Alec set the skillet back on the stove. He rubbed his hands over the heat and then reached under his sweater as for a weapon, drawing out a pint of rum he'd tucked behind his buckle.

"Get rid of that!" his mother said sharply. "There's no liquor in this house!"

"You're after sounding like a sergeant, Ma, all rules and regulations." He held the bottle up to the light. "Uncle Rod's. A bit of his legacy, eh? There's another one in his trashcan, empty. Now Dan Alec'll kill this one too, every drop. You wouldn't want me to chuck it out, not Uncle Rod's last pint."

Rhoda lay her hands in her lap as if to calm herself, but there was a tremor in her voice.

"What business had you in Roderick's house picking over his things? If Dad let you in, he had no right. It's to be shut up til it's sold."

Dan Alec took a tumbler from the cupboard and casually filled it with rum.

"Well, there's another has a key." He smiled at Annie as if she were in on the mystery, and she smiled innocently back.

"Who?" his mother demanded. "No one's to have a key but your Dad."

"Go easy, dear," Annie said, touching her arm. Rhoda's face was aflame. "Don't get excited so."

"Yes, Ma, go easy." Dan Alec gulped rum from the glass and wiped his mouth on his sleeve. "It's only Peg MacIvor what has a key."

"*Her?* That trash?"

Dan Alec inclined his head toward Annie. "Must excuse my mother, dear. The lady in question has always been 'that trash,' so far as Ma is concerned. Not respectable, no. Loose. She liked to drink and snuggle up with our Uncle Roderick. Of course he was fit only for a preacher's daughter."

Annie blushed and looked down at her Bible. Yes, she had now and then joined Rhoda in some headshaking over Peg MacIvor. Not that Annie had anything specific against the woman or knew much about her, only that she was the last in a string of them who had provided good company to her brother's bad habits. The few times he did stop drinking he had started up again, it seemed, as soon as another woman came along.

"And what were *you* doing there with that woman, your uncle barely in his grave?"

"Nothing Uncle Rod would disapprove of, Ma. Nothing himself didn't do many's an evening."

"What would you know of his evenings?"

Dan Alec only grinned at her. She settled back in her chair and looked away as if she suddenly was afraid of an answer. Dan Alec was talking reckless, and there was Annie to consider.

"All I know is Peg MacIvor dragged him down like the rest," she said finally. "And that's a fact."

Annie thought back to the woman at the funeral, the one who'd stayed off to the side. She had looked haggard, too weary for a woman in her forties, even with a permanent fresh in her auburn hair. At the wake Rhoda would not speak to her, knowing Peg MacIvor had been with him when he was stricken. But Annie had felt a pang of sorrow for her. Sometimes she had tried to imagine Roderick with his women: her brother, for he was a soft-spoken man, sipping quietly on an iced drink in a dim room, the woman—any one of them—seated beside him talking loud and coarse. Beyond that she could not imagine his iniquities. But seeing that MacIvor woman in the shadows of the churchyard birches, Annie had imagined something quite different between them and felt a remorse she could not explain. And what had she known about his life, after all? Far less than this woman. Living twenty-five miles away he had kept it from her and from Rhoda except for the spare details that drifted like scraps of newspaper back to New Skye. When he did visit he listened patiently, a slight smile under his thin moustache as the sisters urged him to find a good wife. He would get up and look out the parlor window toward the Atlantic and say, "I miss the country. The air is better here." But as there was no liquor to be had in Rhoda's house, he would soon grow restless, kiss them goodbye and drive back to Sydney. Weeks would pass before they saw him but his name was forever coming up as if he had just stepped out the door.

"That middle-aged tramp!" Rhoda's voice had risen to a shout that smothered what her son was saying.

Dan Alec moved to the table and set his rum in front of her. She swiped at the glass but he kept his grip on it and thumped it back down. "Now you listen to me, girl. Uncle Rod was down long before Peg MacIvor came by, and with women far worse. 'Give me a drinkin' lady anytime, Dan Alec,' he used to say. And you who thinks she knows every wicked corner in the county never got wind of his wild parties, day and night sometimes, four people to a bed the . . ."

"You're drunk and a liar!" Rhoda tried to rise but Dan Alec held her down by the shoulder.

"Drunk maybe, but no liar." He licked spilled rum from the back of his hand. "And here's more truth for you. I met Peg on Princes Street today. Some things led to others and off we went to Uncle Rod's place. We found his bottles quick enough, and we tumbled around in his bed besides. With his blessing, if I'm not mistaken."

"You dirt!"

"That man had a cock this long, Ma." Dan Alec expanded his hands like a fisherman sizing his catch. "And he was tuckin' it in the day he died."

From upstairs came a loud bark of laughter that seemed to vibrate through every room in the house. As if punched in the midriff Annie let out her held breath in a short cry and slowly closed her Bible. Rhoda shouted at the ceiling, "You shut up, Angus MacCrimmon! Laugh at this son of yours! Yes, you're a pair, the two of you!" But her voice was hoarse and distraught. She pushed damp strands of hair from her brow and looked beseechingly at her sister. "Oh, Annie, do you see what a torment he is! Thank the Lord he's the last child home and not the first or I'd never had another, and me giving him all I could . . ."

"Lord Jesus!" Dan Alec bawled. "You gave me the back of your hand!" His mother sank into her chair. Her breast heaved as she fought for words to combat him, her eyes angry and bright with tears.

"But that's all passed," he said evenly as he stood over her.

"This is my house too and I'll stay in it. You rail at Dad, if he'll take it. But leave Dan Alec alone."

He went into the adjoining parlor and stretched out on the sofa, propping his boots insolently on the armrest. Annie patted her sister's hand. She pitied her, Rhoda looked so dazed, but she was not sure what comfort to give. True, Dan Alec had no right to be so crude but he had too long been treated like a misbehaving boy. Men were rough sometimes, and they had to have their bluster.

"He shouldn't have talked that dirt, you sitting in the middle of it," Rhoda said, wiping her eyes in her apron.

"Never mind, dear. I'm not a child in a white Sunday dress."

Angus's snoring had resumed full volume, rising and falling under the slow swells of his dreams. The rain had quit. The roof gutter leaked its last drops like ticks of a clock. In the parlor Dan Alec chuckled and then sighed with exaggerated contentment. "Uncle Rod indeed," he said loud enough to be heard in the kitchen. "By Jesus, that was a tough act to follow!"

His mother picked up her knitting from the floor and got to her feet slowly, agedly, cradling the balled wool up to her breast.

"I'll listen to no more of him!" she whispered fiercely to her sister. Annie could not recall her ever whispering in this kitchen, about anything. "Forgive me, dear, I'm going upstairs."

"Yes, you go rest. This won't be so bad in the morning."

"Not that I'll sleep, no, not with what I've put up with today. Will you take the path home, dear? Use the flashlight, won't you, and be careful, the ground is wet."

"I'll be fine, dear. Don't be too hard on Dan Alec. He's a young man yet."

"No, Annie. Right this hour he's as old as he'll ever be. Never change a hair of him." She stared into the parlor where his wet rubber boots shone in the light of the table lamp. "Oh, he'll go gray, yes, gray and sodden and snoring like his father. But what he is now he is for all his life." Pausing in the little hallway she looked back at her sister. "He could have been someone important, he really could have, you know."

"Who, dear?"

"Could take him for the prime minister in his dark blue suit. Sixty-one and a full head of hair, dark and wavy. . . ."

"Yes, dear. He was a bonny man."

Annie listened to her sister's heavy steps marking the stairs. The snoring had stopped. Murmurs, loud, then soft, played about the ceiling. The bed creaked deeply and the house was quiet again. Annie felt quite alone, more than she did in her own empty house. The evening had swirled around her and here she was rooted in the chair with her Bible. She looked around the kitchen helplessly. It was such a man's place. The work clothes of father and son hung on hooks by the stove. They gave off a faint smell of damp and sweat and warm rubber. Two hunting rifles were propped in a corner like brooms and a heap of stubbed-out cigarettes rested among the coal in the scuttle. Funny how Roderick was so different, elegant almost, even though he worked at the steel mill. Yet she remembered his eyes, how they looked his last visit: as if he were tired of sight.

She opened the Bible whose pages had so often filled her loneliness. Leafing slowly through the Psalms she settled on the Nineteenth. Only her lips moved at first, then her soft voice she had read to her dad in, " . . . Day to day pours forth speech, and night to night declares knowledge. There is no speech nor are there words; their voice is not heard; yet their voice goes out through all the earth, and their words to the end of the world. . . ." But the verses did not soothe her and she closed the well-thumbed pages, the black cover smooth and stained from her hands in Africa. She recalled that place now like a hot light she had squinted into day after day without comprehension.

In the parlor, smoke from Dan Alec's cigarette crept into the air. He was clapping his boots together slowly like hands. "Damn," he said aloud but to himself, "I'm not sure if she was laughin' or cryin.'"

Annie sat looking at the glass of rum. She took it in her hands gently like an antique vase and turned it around and around, finally shutting her eyes as she sipped from the rim. A harsh warmth shuddered through her. She ran her tongue slowly over her lips: this is what women tasted on her brother. She remembered that his words were tinged with this sour-sweetness when he said close to her face, "See you in a while, Annie, dear." He had always been kind.

She listened to Dan Alec's slow breathing in the next room. She wanted to go in and talk to him, but what would she say? For much of her life she had dealt out bits of the Bible, if diffidently, more often to herself than to others. Now her mind roamed chapter and verse in vain. There was no comfort, no hope in the way she felt in this kitchen. If she walked into that other room and her nephew looked up at her he would think, though he wouldn't speak it, "Holy Annie," and then they both would have to talk in a certain way. She did not want that. She wanted to ask him something that might surprise him, that he would never expect from this woman who always had a Bible open before her as if it spoke all her mind and heart.

But standing at the door to the parlor she saw Dan Alec asleep, his cigarette fagging out in a saucer. He looked so harmless now, susceptible, merely a man. She crushed out the cigarette and returned to the kitchen.

After tidying up for Rhoda she put on her tan raincoat and tied a plastic scarf carefully around her hair. Then she noticed the rum in the center of the table. Without hesitation she seized the glass and raised it quickly to her lips, drinking what was left in a long swallow. There. That was the last of it. Heat swelled like a wave through her body and she reeled backwards against the wall. Giddy, she was. Heat always made her giddy and faint. Her eyes blurred with tears and her hands trembled like strummed wires but she gathered up the Bible and felt her way out the back door into a cool damp darkness. The rum wasn't so bad, once the fire died. It seemed to be melting now into her limbs, lightening them. A soft mist fanned her flushed cheeks. She smiled up at the sky. The wind had gone round to the west and was ferrying great clouds toward the sea. Moving fast, they rolled enormous over the ridge, an unseen moon writhing white in the gauzy spaces among them. More awesome than space-ships, they were, churning so silently, and where were they going? "The heavens are telling the glory of God," she whispered, and she realized she was laughing as if someone had told her a joke in her sleep. She clapped a hand to her mouth for this silliness, swaying wide-eyed now in hay to her waist. The path home ran like a dark stream through the old pasture. The grasses parted and closed as though under a sea, languid and waved with shadows. She waded toward the woods out of whose branches blew a rich smell of balsam. Everything was in motion, it seemed, for her, for Annie, even though the old footpath was narrow that had once been wide enough for two. Only a trickle of feet now drip drip to her door. Her coat had come open and her dress was getting wet but she didn't care. She remembered walking out in Africa through tall grass one early morning, the dew so heavy she raised her skirt, but the grasses, cool against her skin, had soaked her stockings through. . . . Startled that she was so suddenly face down in wet hay, she got up with difficulty and set her eyes again for home. But her hands felt light and she stopped to ponder. Her Bible. Couldn't go on without that, no. She went back a few steps and knelt where her body had pressed down the hay. The Bible was slippery with damp and she rubbed her hands over it. Hadn't it seen worse weathers though? Terrible suns, and rains to drown you? She sang now as she walked but the words made no sense. Oh this was nice whatever it was, turning her around and around with a fistful of clover. Any direction would do when you spun like a top. No need rushing, and nobody waiting besides. Dad had rum hidden somewhere, that she knew. She would search for it tonight. Fun to swing from room to room, turning out trunks and cupboards, then finding it, a secret. Did Rod do that ever? Dan Alec did, and shame on him too. When she neared the stand of spruce that divided her dad's land from MacCrimmon's, she looked up at the black trees. What if she had lost her Bible here? Didn't she know this meadow like the veins on her hand, all its crossings and crisscrossings? She would have found it in the morning. Like the stones in the field it would be waiting. . . .

THE SNOWS, THEY MELT THE SOONEST

Duncan yanked the bucket up from the well and carried it splashing toward the back door of the trailer. Hauling water for a priest, if you could believe it. The man was inside right now. No crucifixes had Duncan, on the wall or on his neck, but there he was. The man was a pal from her girlhood, so what could you say? A priest was a priest.

In the kitchen Duncan set the bucket down and dipped his fingers in the water. Not cold enough for a decent drink, and the weather so damned sticky, a sack of wet sand. The man just showed up, came huffing slowly up through the trees taking things in, flowers in his hand he'd picked on his way up from the road, blue lupines, as if Holly hadn't seen a million of them by now, and Duncan had thought, who the hell is this on the step, daubing his face with a hanky?

The trailer had absorbed the afternoon heat spitefully, another irritant to Duncan's wife. Metal and plastic, she liked to say, what can you expect? She was away at the ash pit, him having to greet the priest alone and make talk. He rinsed their lunch dishes quietly in the sink, killing time, and filled the water jug in the fridge. She'd mentioned him many times, this priest, but never that he might arrive. Duncan had imagined a man Holly's age, maybe a high school boyfriend in his forties whose heartbreak had sent him off to seminary, the warmth in the way she spoke of him, but he was more like sixty. A stout man, a big man gone soft, big hands and girth. Well, a priest wouldn't stay late. Priests had things to do at night, didn't they, duties, obligations? Pray or whatever, tend to their spiritual affairs. Probably went to bed early, early mass in the morning and all that, rolling out with the sun. Priesting was a full-time job. But this man was a teacher, so maybe it was different for him.

So you drove all the way down from Antigonish, did you, Father? Duncan said from the kitchen doorway.

I have friends there, Duncan. St. FX. A lovely drive were it not for this awful heat. When I was young I could bear it.

I'm a winter man myself. I'd rather shiver than sweat.

The priest was sunk deeply into their one stuffed chair, near the rear window that Holly said belonged on a large bus, going nowhere. That vinyl would cook him, his sky-blue shirt already plastered to his skin. Where was the black? Duncan would have preferred the black clothing, the high collar, the whole uniform, if you were having a priest in the house.

Duncan, the priest said. Brown warrior. You knew that's your name in Gaelic.

I'll take the warrior part, Duncan said. The rest doesn't fit. My dad, he knew the Gaelic but he never passed a letter of it on to me.

A *damh ursainn*, there. The priest pointed his dusty black shoe at the cast-iron cow they used for a doorstop.

Not if I can help it, Duncan said, thinking he meant something religious.

The priest smiled. Highland people, way back, they kept

their best beast nearest the door. The Door Ox they called it. When they died, it went to the landlord.

More's the worse for them. That's why my great-grandfather came to Cape Breton.

And a wise move, too. My mother and dad prayed in Gaelic, joked in it. Gaelic was the real song of their lives, not English, the priest said. You're a printer.

Barely. My shop's up for sale.

Hard times?

Computers. They stole my bread and butter, I'm afraid. People bang out their own stuff at home. It's not a mystery anymore.

But you could still set, say, a book of poems? A small book. Maybe fifty copies or so.

Hand-set, you mean? I have the old equipment, sure.

And I have a book of poems. Not mine, a friend's. She's doing a good thing, she's composing them in Gaelic and then in English, facing page. Some are quite good, in both tongues, and that's heartening, a young person involved in the language that way. I'd like to do it, just bring them out for her. A gift.

I'm not Catholic, Duncan said to keep things clear.

All I want is a printer, and Holly said you were good.

Did she? She must've said it a long time ago. It's terrible warm in here, Father, but outside the flies would kill us.

Listen, how did we all manage before? the priest said. Of course we did. Weather is life.

Still, the man looked to be suffering, and Duncan, though he'd sobered up fast, felt shaky himself. He fetched the priest water with an ice cube already shrinking in the glass, and when he turned, there was his wife inside the front door. The priest had not seen her but she was taking him in, a bit stunned, as if she'd had something else on her mind entirely.

Hugh, she said, and the priest glanced up, smiling. He struggled to rise but she pushed him gently back and kissed his temple. She would have hugged him, Duncan was sure, hugging was in now, on TV people hugged anything that moved. I'm a wreck, she said, if only I'd known the day. Her face was raked with dirt from the gloves she'd dug with and had tossed to the floor. The flies were bad, I hate them near my eyes, she said.

Did you find anything glorious? the priest said to her.

It's just a rockpile down the bank, Father. The old farm up the hill, they threw their bottles and things there for years. She breathed as if she'd been running, her thick brown bangs damp with sweat. She smelled of repellent, keroseney.

Duncan, can you get Father a real drink? He's come a distance.

I wouldn't mind a whiskey, the priest said. I'm not fussy either. A little more water with it would be fine.

We have all the necessary things, Duncan said. Even water.

Holly shot him a hard look but he just smiled at her.

He should have known the padre would take a drink, they all liked it, he knew that much. Fine. Pick up where we left off. He took his time in the kitchen while Holly had a quick wash. When he brought the whiskeys in she said, The toilet needs water, Duncan, the tank is empty. She wore a skirt now, a fresh blouse. We have a poor water situation, Father. We failed the perc test.

The ground failed it, Duncan said.

They make a small hole and fill it with water, Father.

They want to see how long it takes to percolate into the soil, Duncan said. Ours has problems.

When he told me about it first, Father, I thought he said *perk* with a *k*.

Duncan wanted to say something mean, but he didn't. She had come to suspect there was another woman in their life, that he'd done something that hurt, but she didn't know exactly what or the woman herself. A week ago, in the old house up above them, he'd already been with that woman and it was a secret he wanted to hold on to, go back to, so he said nothing.

Holly lit a cigarette and seemed to relax.

Father reads handwriting, Duncan.

So do I, Duncan said.

She turned away from him, jerking her thick hair the way she had the first time he ever spoke to her, at a dance, a fling of dismissal he should have remembered but over the years she had made him forget.

I interpret handwriting, is what she means, the priest said, smiling. What's there in the loops and slants and so on. But I won't bore you with that.

It doesn't sound like your kind of work, Father.

The priest, perspiring amiably, knit his fingers over his big waist. His weight seemed calming somehow. So much mystery in the world, Duncan, he said. More than enough to go around.

You should hear the roof when it rains, Holly said to the priest, it sounds like a cattle shed.

Yes. And then there's the doorstop, Duncan said. Makes no noise at all.

Do you have any idea how big the skull of a horse is, Duncan? his wife said. Of course you don't. I uncovered one this afternoon, Father, but I left it where it was, believe me.

Thanks, Duncan said. All over the trailer there were odd pieces of bones and broken glassware she'd unearthed at the pit, displayed like archaeological findings. He did not understand their fascination, and Holly so neat and tight in other ways. He emptied his glass, glad to be drinking again.

We won't bother you with handwriting, Holly said. It's too warm, Hugh. Father.

I didn't used to mind heat this way. Give me snow and I don't care how cold it is. No, you go ahead, dear, as you wish. Write out a paragraph or so, in your natural hand. The priest removed his glasses, thumbing moisture from the lens. His eyes looked suddenly larger and young. I won't peek, I won't say a word.

The trailer grew so still Duncan did not move except to rattle the tiny ice cubes in his glass. His wife's hand whispered across the paper. She sat almost primly at the table, her legs tucked back, nice legs they were, too. Once, every little thing about her had been attractive, nothing at all then that wasn't fine, whatever she spoke or did or wore, her straight brown hair, thick and short, baring the nape of her neck he'd always wanted to kiss. He had never watched her write more than a list, never a letter, though he knew she had written them. Maybe that's the way she'd written to him years ago, not a priest in sight. Before Duncan took up type-setting, he'd worked three seasons on the Great Lakes after they were married, on the iron ore boats, and she had no idea, then or now, what it meant to catch sight of her handwriting when the mate passed out the mail. No one's eyes but his would have cared. Every warm thing about her curved through the lines of that writing. And it had just been for him, for him. But there would be no love on that page anymore, no yearning for Duncan. Still, that's what she must have looked like when she wrote him, when she missed him. What sins of hers did the priest know about?

When Holly was finished, the priest studied the paper in the window light while she stared at the kelly green rug on the floor, smiling, shaking her head. She glanced up at Duncan. It looks like a rug in an Irish whorehouse, she whispered. Never been in one, Duncan whispered back. Yes you have, that and worse, she said. Could you leave for a little while? Father MacVarish has things to tell me.

Maybe I have things to tell you.

He took the metal pail out to the old well and flung it down the hole. She hated the trailer, its tan siding and chocolate trim, like a cheap cake, she said, and then there was the cost of having it hauled here from North Sydney, the legal fuss about drilling a proper well and piping it indoors because their piece of land wasn't legally big enough, after he'd had a friend drop in a septic that wasn't legal either. Weekends and summers, away from their house in town was all he cared about, but she'd wanted a proper cottage, right down at the shore, not here above the road with woods around it. Waterfront had grown pricey, and his printing shop had sagged steadily the last few years. Word processing, what a term. That book for the priest, Duncan would never do it, they were just making conversation. He was finding that he didn't care much anymore. A little job here or there, another hockey program, another auction announcement, what the hell. And now there was the woman up the hill.

The pail bobbed in the well, brown bits of needles whirling slowly into its mouth. The spruce trees pressed thickly around him. God, you'd never get a breeze here! And how could he get away? Holly'd been on him over the inconveniences, the lack of hot showers, of a tap for dishes. They had both been drinking this afternoon, for the heat at first. Then he'd flung an old affair at her, a doctor at the hospital, all the particulars are there, he'd told her, and you don't have any facts at all on me, just a feeling about some woman, come on. She knew that was true, but off to the ash pit she went. Tiffs made them drink, and liquor made them irritable, and neither of them liked irritability, which only made them worse. There came the priest into their foul air. That's what Duncan should have said at the door, we were just having a drink, Father, with lots of ice, and she's away to the ash pit. Not easy to put on a good face for a priest with your hackles still up, but Duncan had made the transformation.

He lingered outside, yanking at weeds in the tiny lawn he'd carved out of the scrubby spruce, the grass studded with nasty little stumps that tripped him in the dark. This had all been a pasture once, part of the old farm. The woman, Brenda, came weekends to the old house up behind the trees. Her husband, an airline pilot, was not home much. Right now she was up there alone. What timing. Duncan could've slipped away, surprised her. Let Holly have the priest to herself. Jesus. Duncan had bumped into Brenda on the wharf one Saturday, he at the trailer by himself, Holly on night shift. Brenda was from years back, Sydney Academy, when they'd run in the same crowd. Pretty girl but nothing between them. He could barely remember what she'd looked like. She was fishing for cod, she said, and he told her the cod here in the channel were wormy, all that he'd ever caught, and she'd shivered at that but kept casting. He'd crushed a few snails from under the wharf and baited her line. She had a few beers in her cooler and soon they were laughing with each other, like they had never met before. Dusk found them up in the old house, rain tickling the windows, all night, Holly having stayed in town, soured by the weather. Despite everything, despite every bit of common sense, Brenda struck some fire in him he didn't want to go out. She was not really pretty anymore, not like his wife. But yet, something in the configurations of her he liked, the shape and feel of her in his hands. There was no history between them, no cold-hearted resentments, no disappointments, no measures of each other except the most immediate kind. A hard cock, full of joy. Was that too much to ask for? Without hesitation, they had driven up there and had fun. He had no defense for it really, not desperation or loneliness or revenge. Just pleasure, a betrayal he could keep a secret but never hide.

Duncan listened to the priest's voice, a deep and steady sound inside the trailer. Small talk. What else? They weren't in church or a glebe house. What was she telling him? She'd never wanted Duncan to remove the trailer's wheels, deflated now, nearly obscured by weedy grass. I feel better, she said, knowing this place is ready to roll. Don't worry, he said, it's staying where it is. Except for the ash pit, she preferred the shore, looking for sun, a sandy spot for a swim. What did she want from the priest? Nostalgia? His blessing? She hadn't been to mass in years. She had a few things to confess, if that was in the back of her mind. Forgive me, Father.

On the trunk lid of Duncan's Buick, old enough now to embarrass her, someone had written letters in the dust, but the writing was fake, it didn't even say wash me. All you needed to be a printer now was a keyboard, any bonehead could do it, punching up letters on a screen, moving mice around. If they found it on their hands they wouldn't recognize it, ink, and metal, the real setting and shaping of text. As he passed under the rear window Duncan heard his wife rap smartly on the wall. Listen to that! she said. You can't even hang a picture in this place! He wanted to call into her, of what, The Virgin? Trouble with a nurse, she was not a woman of secrets. She knew too much about the body, how it worked, why it didn't. She was still sexy in that uniform, she never lost that, those white hose whistling down a hallway. Could he find the ways to live without her?

A gypsum freighter was passing up the strait, a trail of smoke above the trees, a pulse of engines. He wished he were inhumanly strong, that he could lift the trailer off its blocks and haul it up the hill like an ox, lumber along not a thought in his head, her inside talking away, maybe about things Duncan would not absolve her of, but the priest would incline his ear sympathetically toward her distress. Duncan had come upon her one morning working the rosary through her fingers, one sensuous black bead at a time, like the necklace of someone dear, and he'd had all he could do to keep from shouting stop.

He would have to go in soon, the blackflies were feasting. Nothing a priest could do about them either. But Duncan turned instead toward the woods where a short way in he had knocked together a scrapwood shed, its interior, in these hot days, smelling woody as an old stump. He wiped the webs off a pint of rum stashed in a corner and drank. There was his old hockey gear he'd stored, his battered skates, his favorite stick, sweetly curved, taped, he could feel the puck alive in the blade all the way up the handle. Maybe in the winter he'd do a few turns on the pond up above. He missed the clashing heat, the gear on his body like he was another being, winged and gloved. He'd kept at it through his forties, the old-timers league, and then fifty loomed and a knee went out and he couldn't skate the way he needed. He could talk to the priest about hockey all right.

Why was he getting drunk again late in the day, skidding along? Sometimes he wanted to close everything down and start over. He was not any goddamned good at the arguments, he could only shout things that made no sense, just angry sound. Now Holly wanted to move out, live on her own, she said. Well. He capped the bottle with a hard twist. If he got toasted in front of the priest, her tongue would make him pay. He didn't care. You reached a point. Something far bigger was at work in the world, he knew that much, he'd lived long enough to figure that out. Three sheets to the wind could sail you over it, if over it you'd get at all.

He pushed through thick fir and spruce along a narrow path Holly did not know about because he'd tramped it down himself. It ended behind long boughs of hemlock. Beyond them he could see the big, slightly rundown house the woman lived in. A field, recently mown and heady with a sweet grass smell, ran out of sight to the road. Duncan parted the branches just enough to keep himself concealed. Lord, there she was in a raised window, brushing her hair and not even dressed. Her bare breasts, a startling white in the long shadows of the afternoon, moved with the slow strokes of the brush. When Duncan had met her on the wharf, unsnarling her fishing reel, blond hair mussed by the wind, it never occurred to him they'd soon be undressed together, or she bare and calm like this in the window of her old house. Holly would never show herself like that, no matter what. In the grass below the window a dog was staring up at her, its tail thrumming. Old Mabel's dog who followed people home from the wharf. Not a dumb animal, that, all he needed right now was a guitar. Duncan had kissed her behind that very window. What was she thinking of now? Not him, not Duncan. Some idea of herself in the world. The kind of moments you can have only when you're naked and by yourself. He wanted to pick up where they'd left off, but this was not the day. She wouldn't be pleased to see him coming across the grass.

Back down the path, a humid tunnel of needles and leaves. For the priest, all this business had been long over with. He'd woke up with a stiff one in the morning like the rest of us, and a sin just to take it in his hand. Vows and all that. A spider web veiled Duncan's face like soft hair and he clawed it away. Sweating out the rum now. The priest would still be there, in that smothering heat.

What I was wondering about, Father, Duncan said, two quick whiskeys in the kitchen humming in his brain, is the absence of the sexual side of things.

Father MacVarish's eyebrows remained high for a few moments, then he smiled. Of what things?

Dun*can*, Holly said, two unmistakable notes.

That's all right, the priest said. If it's on his mind.

If what's on my mind? It's on everybody's mind, and maybe you can read that, too.

I'm sorry to hear you're splitting up, Holly and you. I'm sorry to hear that.

No need, Father. We'll be free as birds. I've got no church after me, for one thing. Eh? I won't be asking anybody's permission, for anything. No confessions. Lots of eligible partners floating around. That's the whole idea.

Duncan, Holly said, you haven't had a whole idea in a long time. Sit down.

You see, Father? Would you like to wake up to that on a winter morning, in February, say? It was all there in the handwriting, I guess. I just couldn't see it.

Duncan, isn't there water to haul or something?

I've hauled yours.

Don't you wish, dear.

Please, the priest said.

Duncan was standing, his back arched ridiculously against the wall. Father, I'll fix your glass there. No? He took two steady paces toward the bathroom but stopped: he'd already filled the tank, he'd been to the well enough, enough, but she'd want the priest to flush, she'd tell him don't worry about it, Father, Hugh, please, just pull the handle, I've got this houseboy who'll fill it up again right quick. But they had the whole outdoors, didn't they all? Hadn't the priest said he'd been raised in the country, he knew a good tree, he'd milked cows, heard his mother singing Gaelic songs when she worked, he'd plowed with his father's ox, followed the dung cart, tasted the sweaty dust of the fields, cranked the grinding stone while his father's scythe bit and sparked? Duncan had never known much about the country except the funny way people talked. And here the old farm was, hidden all around him. Even the old house.

Listen, he said. I want to take you somewhere.

You? Holly said. The mind reels.

To the cold spot. It's up north a way, and don't tell me you've ever been there.

You seem a little out of your head, Duncan. It's the heat. Sit down. Please. Father MacVarish said he'd do your handwriting.

It's entirely up to you, Duncan, the priest said.

He doesn't sugar it, Holly said. He sure didn't sweeten mine. Go on, Duncan, do it. Aren't you curious? You're afraid.

Afraid of how I write my own name?

He wants more than your name, Duncan.

I need a good sample, Duncan. Copy a paragraph out of something, whatever you want.

Something I like?

Doesn't matter. Just write the way you always do.

Duncan felt feverish, the trailer was more than warm, it was close, suffocating. The priest seemed to have sunk deeper into his chair, his shirt stained with damp, his glasses misty.

Come on, Duncan said. The cold spot on a hot day. Doesn't that make sense to all of us?

I don't swim, the priest said, if it's water you mean.

He doesn't swim either, Holly said. He means a tavern, I think.

Anybody around here, *anybody*, could take you to water, Father. But not to the cold spot.

You're afraid, Holly said. Yourself, right there on the page.

There's some things I'm afraid of. Not that, I think. But okay, fine. Suppose I just crack the Bible there and write whatever comes up.

But that's a *Biobull*, the priest said. Would you write from it naturally, not knowing the Gaelic? That's the question, I guess.

He never touches that Bible, Holly said. His mother sent that to him after his dad died. It keeps the coffee table steady, that's all.

It's got an English section in it, Duncan said. Just words with a pen, anyway. What's the difference? Then I'll take us all to a place that's beautifully cool. We could use that. All of us.

An air-conditioned bar? Holly said. No thanks.

No. No, no. It isn't anything like that.

Duncan opened the *Biobull* onto the table and sat himself down, glancing over at the paragraph his wife had copied from a magazine. He smoothed out a page of notepaper. He was damned if he'd make a fool of himself. He would write neatly, not all over the page. He felt oddly steady, the liquor gone, for the moment, into some other part of him. Whiskey was like that. He held out his hand: not a tremor.

Does God have handwriting, Father? he said.

Everywhere.

Ah!

Duncan followed his finger from word to word. Gothic. Six point. Not easy on the eyes but it had religion all over it. Listening to the priest fanning the air with Holly's magazine, he considered disguising his hand, slanting it strangely and dressing it out. But Holly seemed too serious for games, and she'd see the way he was putting it down. Drunk, she'd say, that's all that says. Okay. He whispered as he wrote, they were not words people used every day. He didn't care what these lines referred to, or where in the Bible they occurred. It was a long document, and where he fit into its words, he did not know. Sweat blurred a few letters but he kept on. Had they been lovers sometime way back, she and the priest? He wasn't that old. Too bad he wasn't young enough to test her, Jesus, a priest, then she could say something, her sin would be magnificent. Duncan's handwriting slowly unfurled, he was proud of it, the way it filled the page, a triumph. It was just copying of course, no thoughts of his own were there. Not like they'd be in a letter to someone. And what was this fuss about handwriting anyway, with all its quirky acrobatics? Type, on the page, it was more than words, it could cast a spell, all its beautiful proportions, but not this. He tore the sheet of paper off and held it out to Father MacVarish.

I'd like to hear what you have to say about him, Holly said. He owes me that.

The priest folded the sheet of paper twice and slipped it into his breast pocket like a hanky. Weren't we going somewhere? I think we were.

The priest sat in the front, Holly in back blowing angry smoke at Duncan's head. But he was driving better than he had hoped. In this lucid zone of drinking, certain things on the road were unnervingly clear, even grave. The wind blasted warmly through the window, whipping his hair. He lapsed into a serene examination of the water passing bright below them, then the other roadside, graffiti on granite rocks blurred past, exclamations of identity or love. The priest grabbed his arm, not pushy but firm, and Duncan corrected the wheel. I'm fine, Father. Steering was a breeze, that part of it. Cars ground past him up the mountain in the passing lane. He leaned toward the window and yelled, Rev it up, you bastards, not a goddamn one of you knows where the cold spot is, you . . . Holly pressed her nails into his shoulder and he said okay okay I'm okay. Jesus, he didn't want to lose it, Father and all right here with him, now that they were really going somewhere. He dug into his driving and got them over the mountain and down the long run of highway that seemed to intoxicate him dangerously for a stretch, the momentum and the easy curves, the old car gliding heavily and fast, but he teased the brake until he turned off, so splendidly under control he didn't mind the tighter curves along the bay, he was practically sober, for Christ's sake.

Holly and the priest murmured about the landscape they were not familiar with, and on a dirt road Duncan pointed things out breezily, inventing names, That's Old Rory's Brook right there, yes, and that's Benn Slagis, if I'm not mistaken, that mountain there. He had to concentrate, it was just memory taking him back, and he slowed down, studying landmarks. They passed a house the color of driftwood in a ragged clearing, all that was left of a farm, the rest thickened in with trees and brush, and he felt a stab of sadness for the stark, sagging dwelling, eaten by weather. You wouldn't find a woman in a window there, naked or dressed. Had he missed his chance? But what chance?

The mountains he drove between were not high but their slopes were steep, dense like fleece you could run your hand through, and they seemed to cradle the valley, the late sun, poised to set early, a faint swatch of light along the peaks. Shadows were already rising into the higher woods. He crept the car along until he reached a small bridge, and remembering the water underneath it, he stopped. Leaving the engine running, he leaned over the railing: the river was summer narrow, its dry rocks almost white on either bank, the shallows an amber light that shaded dark as wine into pools beneath the bridge, traced with gentle whorls and eddies. The priest came up beside him.

Holly is getting anxious, I'm afraid.

Is she waiting for me to jump? Duncan said.

She isn't keen about this cold spot, whatever it is. She thinks you're making it up, Duncan.

She's never been there, Father.

Yes, well, he said mildly, leaning for a better look below. A man could jump here easily. More than deep enough for a nice dive.

I swam here once with friends. Too many years ago. I leapt all right, feet first. It was deeper than I thought, that odd iron color, and I really went down into it, Father. It scared me good.

It looks so cool I wish I were a swimmer.

The woman you want the poems printed for, is she more than a friend, Father?

She is what I told you, Duncan.

It's not far from here, Father, where we're going. What did Holly say?

About you or about herself?

Either or both.

There's a streak of properness in you, Duncan, I can tell you that. You want to do the right thing. It's in your handwriting. I read it on the way.

Okay. Go ahead.

You don't like responsibility. That's one thing. You lack drive.

Tell Holly. It would really cheer her up. Go on, Father.

You're emotional, and sometimes your emotions get control over you. I'm just telling you what I see. Something unsettled in your character, even yet.

I can't even remember what I wrote down. I was just copying words.

Yes. *Thus saith the Lord, thy redeemer, and he that formed thee from the womb, I am the Lord that maketh all things. . . .*

Duncan fished out a thin flask from his hip pocket. The priest shook his head, then relented. He took a polite nip, then another, longer.

You know, when they age barrels of Scotch, he said, handing it back, a little evaporates year by year. It's called the angel's share.

We get the best of it.

By some measures we do. Shall we go to this spot then, Duncan? I think we're ready.

As they got into the car, Holly directed a black look at Duncan, but he didn't mind. He was going where he wanted to go, and it wasn't an ash pit.

The roadsides were looking equally familiar, ditch and brush and trees, then ah, a small barn he remembered, comically buttoned up now and boarded shut, weatherspread up roof and wall. He stopped the car. Yes, it certainly feels colder, it really does, Holly said acidly. Wait, you'll have to follow me, Duncan said, getting out. He panicked—had he forgotten, *had* he made it up?—but then he found the cleft in the brush, the path behind it. How wonderful that the day was humid, cloying. Perfect. He listened to the priest heaving himself out of the car, a huff, a groan, the old Buick had doors like a bank vault. Duncan's eyes fixed on a pale white spot on tree bark, so perfectly round it could have been painted. Only a kind of lichen, on a tree with red berries. He heard Holly's muffled voice say she'd wait where she was.

No, you come, too, the priest said. It wouldn't be right.

This way! Duncan called out.

He wanted it to be as it had been the first time he'd moved through these trees, hot and a little depressed from an afternoon of drinking and carousing with friends. He'd left them swimming in the river and wandered off on his own down this dirt road and found this, the air so cool and inexplicable he had touched everything, looking for its source, branches and bark, spreading his hands, his arms, and then the path cut into rocks that seemed to bathe him in coolness, and here it was again and he reached his hand into the colder air of a fissure, its captured snow gray as glass. Behind him the priest was saying yes, yes, I can feel it, can't you, Holly?

Look at this, she said, coming between them. She had tugged out a piece of icy snow, coarse as rock salt. She handed it to the priest and he rubbed it over his face, his eyes closed.

Isn't it cool, Father? Duncan said. Isn't it cooler here than anywhere else we could be?

It makes you want to stay. The priest laughed, moving his hands slowly as if he were scooping the air to his face. This must come from way down, he said, deep in the earth somewhere, Duncan.

Only at this very place, right here. Go the length and breadth of this island, you won't find it anywhere else.

Duncan, Holly said. We should go back now. I can barely see your face.

It's the same face. I'm hurt that you can't remember it.

It's getting dark here, Duncan. And cold.

Not dark yet, the priest said, looking up the steep mountain where a patch of dim sun was dissolving. Just valley darkness, that's all it is. *And I have put my words in thy mouth, and I have covered thee in the shadow of mine hand. . . .*

Duncan felt the sweat cooling his face, his arms. Everywhere else, he said, the sky is heating up. Ozone. Strange word, isn't it? Ancient kind of word.

You're drunk, Duncan.

No, dear, I'm not. Am I, Father?

I don't think you are.

Holly likes ash pits. Where the farm people threw things away.

I'll bring it home to you, Duncan, that skull. Big flat teeth, ground down. The big dirty bones of its head.

Animals might come here at night to get cool, Duncan said. At night. Not horses, the horses are gone.

They know a lot more than we think, the animals, the priest said.

We'll wait. We'll see what comes down in the dark, eh, Father?

I'll wait at the road, Holly said, and she stepped off into the trees. Wind gusted above their heads, trailing an eddy of warmth.

We shouldn't leave her for long, the priest said. He seated himself on a large stone and was reaching toward a crack in the granite where the air was coolest, his palms spread as if it were fire. I saw a horse shot when I was a boy. I was awed by it, how it fell and shook the ground. My father told me why it had to be done. It bothered me anyway.

They exchanged the flask, a polished flicker between them.

A little grotto here, Duncan said. An altar. A shrine to Ozone.

I wouldn't go that far. But it's fine. Lovely. Holly's waiting on us.

She'll be all right. There's worse places than this to be waiting.

Berries, did you see them? That ash tree back there? Sprigs of red, the priest said, inhaling. All this evening green, and that.

It gets dark fast when that sun slips away. That book you want printed, Father, tell me a poem from it.

I'd have to call one up. I need a little time. I'm breathing better now, the air is thin and cool.

I'll do it on the finest paper I can find.

Sooner or later the world eats us up, Duncan.

Duncan could see only the pale shape of the priest's face, his hands moving gracefully in the air.

When I was a boy, the priest said, in woods like these, I felt all kinds of spirits. I never thought . . .

Go on, Father, Duncan said. Go on.

ASHES

Roderick felt the faint line crease his middle as he emerged from the brook path, not strong like wire but enough, even in its give, to vex him. He thought it no more than a strand of vine and he twisted it in his fist, but it bit and didn't break: tough white twine and it stretching almost invisibly down the wooded hill behind him, toward that hidden turn of the brook where light swayed the thick crowns of trees. A soft wave of alarm rose in his chest. This was marker line, strung by someone he did not know, or for what purpose. He drew the string back slowly until it snapped and leaped like flyline into the leaves. But this did not comfort him long and his breathing was louder as he climbed further up into the high and shady birches he had encouraged all the years he owned, and did not own, this land. Along the contours of the hill grasses and ferns and wildflowers grew, not scrub, not thickets of spruce and alder. Up where he could see through the red maples to the road, there was some yellow thing on the meadow and he stumbled toward it. He didn't know any yellow truck or car, but Jesus yes, sure, it was a dozer, a great hunk of yellow iron down off the road, careened there.

Parked. Who'd been at the levers, a drunk? Christ, it was a serious machine. Blade higher than his head. Roderick placed his foot ankle-deep into a rut its treads had channeled, the clay laid slick and bare. In some way it seemed worse sitting than running, its silence immense, more disturbing than sound. He had worked in the roar of machinery years ago, in the steel plant, immersed in the hot ringing din of the rod mill. But here on the old land, the noise of his life was done with. He'd never been in war but surely somewhere between battles a tank had sat just as this dozer was, under summer leaves, waiting. He put his hand on the cool steel tread, polished and scarred. Lord, what this metal could do to the bits of flowers down in his clay soil shade, its thin kind of grasses good for nothing but their soft greenness, no, he wouldn't have it. No iron down there. He did not love that place exactly, that was not what he would say if he were to tell someone about it. Love was too careful a word. Something akin, but no matter: that particular spot he did need, and he had claimed it a long time ago.

Maybe the bulldozer was here to dig a foundation, here near the road. Maybe the owner of the property was building a summerhouse at last? Unless there was a new owner. Bad enough, but surely he wouldn't have this big rig marauding down the hill, for God's sake, with sixty acres to play with? Then again, would he have even seen it? People these days bought country land from a book, from a picture, from nothing at all but a sales pitch and a good price.

The brook place you had to seek out since no path would take you near it. Who could it matter to but himself, Roderick John MacRae?

His dinner was on the table but Roderick stood at the kitchen window and ran his eye again and again from the road, from that yellow streak in the shadows, down through the wooded hill to the shore woods, to the water behind them. All that land had once been his family's, his. Father's, grandfather's. Although his dad had moved them into Sydney when he went to work for the steel mill, they had held on to the place, kept the house up as best they could, summers and time off, until his dad died, and Roderick came into it. Twenty-four years ago, Roderick, himself ill and out of work, sold all but the house and a few acres to a Toronto man because he wanted it only for summers. Just that, the man said, the shore and the pastures to roam in, the cove where he could keep a boat. New woods had taken over much pasture and field but there was still a path to the beach. I might put a cottage somewhere, Roderick, he said, nothing bigger, look, I wouldn't spoil this for a second. And he hadn't, hadn't put so much as a cabin there, a lean-to. A big silver trailer had sat a while, and there were a few summers of expensive tents, beach fires, hollering and firecrackers around Dominion Day, the speedboat humming off up the strait on calm, fine afternoons, and some odd noises in the woods at night, the shrieks and laughter of drinking and drunken pursuits, from what Roderick could tell. He was never part of that. Then no one came, no one showed up any time of year and he had it alone, all seasons, all summer. And he'd kept it the way he wished, thinning the softwood out so hardwoods could thrive, an open woods, curving along the hills and gullies to the shore. And of course, the brook spot. Even beech had come back, if not the grand trees of his youth, but there anyway, tall and yellow in autumn. The man who bought the land always sent a Christmas card, nothing religious, just a humorous one of holiday pratfalls and excess. Roderick remembered the broad handwriting: It had seemed reliable, frank, good-natured, nothing sly or deceptive there. But no card had arrived in three years. You're the caretaker, the man had told him, keep it looking fine, I've been a bit sick.

Roderick sat down to his salt cod, good cod. Lord it wasn't easy to get it anymore, the fish he'd fed on as a kid, fresh, salted, the fish every poor soul had fed on, that and herring, no matter what else failed you had salt fish. Once you could jig them from your boat on bare hooks, dozens, haul them in clear to the gunnels. What cod would you find in the waters here now, when offshore the catch was so poor there was talk of shutting it down, the whole show? Factories had their place, but not out there on the ocean. The fishery was wrecked.

Roderick didn't eat. The plate cooled.

Maddocks. That was the owner's name. He wondered, were the man dead and buried, what sort of stone they'd have put over him. Where would he have wanted his name set down, what words under it? Something comical maybe, like his cards at Christmas.

"So," Archie Bugle said, resting his chin on his cane handle. "You've got yellow iron on your old land, eh?"

Archie's porch faced nicely toward the water, grayer now than the afternoon sky, white-flecked. Archie's sister Peg, with whom he lived, did not join them but stood just inside the hallway, looking out like a cook at a galley door.

"It is mine and it isn't mine, as you know," Roderick said. He had given Archie Bugle the bare bones of his situation and was regretting it already. "Somebody new owns it, I'm thinking. I fear their plans."

"Well, they're in the tank of that bulldozer, you can be damn sure of that."

"He made me a promise, that man I sold it to. A long time ago we shook hands." Roderick extended his own large hand and closed it. "Yes, you can be buried there, he told me. Pick your site and it won't be touched."

"Buried down there? In the woods?" Archie raised his shaggy white eyebrows. "What for, Roderick John, when there's a cemetery not two miles down the road?"

Roderick wished he had not mentioned the gravesite. It was like releasing something he had captured in his hands and watching it fly away. He was superstitious, besides. He did not want to be thought peculiar, but was it morbid and foolish, choosing a grave on family land that went back 170 years? Was it simply normal to let somebody tuck you away in the back corner of Man O' War Point, under another piece of polished red granite chiseled with scant particulars? How was that preferable, if any man stopped to think about it, to a lovely secluded hollow of your own, the water a stone's throw from your feet, the mountain beyond and sun setting over it? Whether the bones of your family were ten feet away or two miles could hardly matter. Death, so they said, was not just a reckoning but a gathering together.

"It's a personal thing," Roderick said.

"It's a queer thing, if you ask me. You've got people on Man O' War Point and you want to plant yourself where there's nobody at all?"

"There *was* people there."

"Not *in* the ground, Roderick John. Anyway, a verbal agreement is what you got, boy. A new owner, all he says is I never heard tell of it. Worthless. Got to be on paper."

"Maybe it isn't a new owner," Roderick said, without conviction. A man's word worthless? Not around here. But it seemed that today wherever he stepped, there was the bulldozer. Whatever was on his mind, there it sat, latent destruction. He found he was listening, even this far away, for the sound of a diesel.

Archie Bugle said, "That's not a local dozer, is it."

"Not hardly."

"Well now, here's Corry, here comes our man." Archie drummed his cane. He loved Corry's salacious conversation, a certain kind of talk that was all but gone among them. Peg was always in earshot of Archie's life, but Corry said what he pleased, Peg or no. "He'll know something."

"He always knows *something*." Roderick found the man good company, there being damn little of that this part of his life. But he could get on your nerves sometimes, and here was Roderick seeing bulldozers left and right.

Corry's vast brown Cougar eased up the driveway like a ship toward a dock, waxed finish gleaming. He had moved to St. Aubin Island after retiring from the steel plant, bought himself a little house near the shore. People knew the car even if they didn't know him.

"Don't tell Corry anything about this," Roderick said.

"Why? He worked at the coke ovens over twenty years." Archie Bugle, in the country all his life, had always been awed by the smoky clangor of the mill, the corrosive fumes of the coke plant.

"Yes, he should be dead."

"There you are. He's held up to everything."

Corry roamed the island in that huge old car, a California vehicle some summer widow had brought here not long before she died, coated with expensive paint, wide enough to sleep in, a hood like a foredeck, sidewalls whiter than a piper's spats. Corry emerged from it slowly, appraising it as he closed the door. He stood for a few moments brushing the vinyl roof, then locked it and approached the porch in his stiff, careful gait that could be taken for a drunk's if you didn't know him.

"Will you look at him lock her up?" Archie Bugle said loudly.

Corry placed his polished shoe on the first step of the porch. He winked. "It's not what I'm locking out, Archie B., but in."

"For instance what?"

"Things drifting around in there, California things." He noticed Peg behind the screen and gave her a sarcastic little bow. "Pleasures of the flesh. It's not a hearse, you know."

"Make a good one," Roderick said.

"Roderick John's got a dozer problem, you see, on the old place," Archie Bugle said. "Don't know the why of it."

Corry, slashing at a deerfly, took his chair between the two men. He shook the crease in his trousers. Their coppery sheen resembled his Cougar's and he was looking at it now, his squint tight but favorable. He had a fierce red face, thin and alert. Age and the coke plant: they burned you down. But he believed in keeping up the fires of sex, as he liked to say, and wherever he found any smoke at all, he blew on it. "Didn't I see it. I thought, construction. Digging a septic. Foundation for somebody, and not for Roderick John."

"Of course it wouldn't be for myself. I got nothing to build. The point is, over what ground is it going?"

"No ground, this day." Corry lit a long thin cigarette. He was dressed up smartly in a dark tartan sportcoat and clashing tie. When he had a date, he often stopped here first, especially if Peg was at the door. "Whoever owns it got better things to do. Three days just sitting. Makes you wonder, yes."

"Roderick John's afraid . . . "

"Never mind about that, Archie Bugle," Roderick said. "I'll figure it out."

"Well, God, man, you never should've sold the place," Archie said, "if you wanted to be laid out in a piece of it."

"He seemed like a good fella. I thought it wouldn't be bad."

"What wouldn't be bad?" Corry said. "Everything gets bad if you live long enough."

"The land, the arrangement, me looking after things."

Corry smacked a blackfly off the back of his hand. "But the

land is his, you see. Don't matter how many years he don't show up there."

"Roderick John's got a plot down there," Archie Bugle said.

"Plot of what? A book?"

Roderick closed his eyes. "Burial," he said. "Mine."

"Jesus, Roderick John, I didn't know you were so shy," Corry said, turning to him. "But you, you won't need much of a spot in any case. They won't let you lay your big body in the ground, boy. Ashes it's got to be."

"Ashes?"

"Dust to dust. Cremation, if it's burial on private land. That's the law now."

Roderick had never considered cremation, not for himself, not ever what it might be like. That he should be forced into it angered him: he'd had that part thought out. Now he had to imagine fire, and himself a handful of ashes. Cremation. High class, something educated and clean, and they could stow you afterward in a nice container, out of the way, shelved. And wasn't the fire gas, blue flame, neat and cold? Hot, God yes, but burning down did not appeal to him, putting his remains in the hands of stokers in white coats, sliding you into a furnace. He knew furnaces. He had seen a man tumble into molten iron, as bright and dancing as a pool of lava, and he was quickly no more than another plume of smoke. No. Too fast, bone and powder, no chance to let death know what you look like, what life has made of you: The man lying there had to be the same man who stood. Ashes were stuff you shook out of the kitchen stove, clinkers and grit. Nothing to find, if ever they dug, those people who studied graves. Could sift till doomsday for him. He wanted to be face up, hands folded, everything at rest, in one piece, down there by the brook, like the way they found people in the *National Geographic* magazine.

There would be no mistaking that shape was him, not a handful of fertilizer or something you scattered across an icy sidewalk to keep from falling.

"It's not cheap, you know, Roderick John," Corry said. "You can't have it done out back, with a few pals and gasoline. Regulations is what we live by now."

"If that's the law, then . . ." Roderick said. He felt a little hot, embarrassed. How could he not have known about this? When was it law?

"Little pot of your ash," Corry said. "Put it in a nice dish with a cover on it. Good for the soil. Won't harm the water. Who could say no to that? New owner, old owner, he might not care. Just don't set one of those goddamn monuments on it, those big granite pricks. Tourist attraction he might not like."

"Then again he might go for it," Archie Bugle said, urging Corry on. "You know, the idea of it like."

"*Idea* of what? Of Roderick John MacRae? Or his prick? I like the man but you'd have to do better than that. Peg? Come out here, girl. Give us your opinion."

"Corry, hush." A long time ago Archie Bugle had brought a young wife here to live, and in less than a year she had left him. Corry referred to Peg as Miss Primpot, the Holy Old Maid. I could certainly buckle her knees, he claimed once, if ever I could get near her.

"You only talk dirt," Peg said firmly. She had stepped back from the doorway.

"Archie B., was it Peg your sister that scared your young wife away? Did she listen in?"

"God, no, Peg had nothing to do with it."

"Damned foolish thing, Archie B., bringing a young wife here with a spinster sister in the house. You upstairs in that old creaky bed of yours, bumpety-bump."

"But this was my *house*," Archie Bugle said, flaring up, not amused about his wife. "So I took her *to* it."

"Peg's always been here," Roderick said, "as if she were a rock or a tree."

From somewhere behind the screen door, in the dusk of the hallway, Peg stirred. She didn't move near the door but she said, "I wouldn't listen to you if I could hear, Corry Matheson."

Corry did not look around but he smiled. "It's not just talk, Peggy Mary. Mysterious things do happen. Look at Roderick John here. Perplexed by a big machine."

"All that's going to happen to you has happened." She had moved further back in the hallway and her voice was dimmer. "As for Roderick John, he might try praying."

"Like I pray for you, Peggy Mary John Archie MacLean," Corry said. "Some day I'm coming in there to see you. I'm coming in like a dirty story, all done up like chocolates."

"You're an awful man."

"That's what they tell me, dear. I'm going to see a lady this very afternoon, and awful I'm going to be. Awful's what they want, and what I want too. Enough talk about ashes and graves."

Somewhere in the house a door closed.

A breeze trembled through the field grass where the Cougar rested in the laziness of the afternoon. "Good as new," Corry said. "Seats still *smell* new, for Lord's sake. The leather of money."

"Maybe you could tow that dozer out," Archie Bugle said. "A lot of wasted horsepower there. The lady can wait."

But Corry didn't seem to hear. "What do you suppose makes a woman talk like that?"

"Like what?" Archie Bugle said.

"Harrying a man, raising questions about his character."

"You had a wife a long time, Corry," Roderick said. "You should know, if anybody."

"We didn't talk much, my friend. She wouldn't shed any light on it."

They watched the weather coming east, long easy clouds, rolling shades of gray in an unencumbered sky. Down in the woods, the flies would be light in a breeze like this. Roderick had things to do. More than ever his foot was tapping but he stayed in the chair, in the company of these men, listening for a sound, not sure what he would do when he heard it. When dark came he'd have to sleep and what if he didn't wake early enough to plant himself in front of that dozer in the morning and demand what it intended, where it was to go. He was not afraid of any man driving, he'd wrestle him down off that seat if he had to. He'd always been strong, a catcher in the rod mill had to be strong. It still came back to him easily, all its heat and exertion, he loved remembering it. Fifteen minutes on, fifteen off, that's how hot and hard the work was. Sometimes you could stay at it a half-hour if the rod was thin. Walk out in the factory yard, get the air. This breeze carried for a moment that pleasure, that possibility of relief. Then back into the loud heat, poised in your thick leather apron, gripping tongs, waiting to spot the reflection the rod, glowing and sparking in the gloom, cast ahead of it, coming steady and fast, and when it bloomed on the wall, you counted: *one, two,* and then *catch,* and you clamped your tongs to the nose of that rushing, looping rod and whipped it around and thrust it into the next mill that would reduce it yet further. An athlete's timing, you had to have that. If you missed, you were catching nothing, and the mill had to be stopped and tangled coils of rod balled up for the scrap machine, and they did not allow you many misses. But if you were quick and strong, you caught every rod, you didn't miss. You were young then, they all were, the catchers, sometimes they'd scream above the noise, Get 'em out Get 'em out, they were so keyed up, the pressure right there end to end, one molten rod after another wheeling toward you to be snatched and turned like a living thing. Dust, smoke, 120 Fahrenheit, white-hot steel, there was nothing else that made any difference when you were really moving, in the hot center of it, blazing through, proof that, because you had brawn, you needed to know only this much about the world, and the noise of your life was loud.

"Intercourse," Corry said precisely. He lowered the long cigarette he was smoking and tapped its tip between the decking. "Was made for it, that car."

The whetstone rasped into the scythe's curve, a calming singsong of metal and stone. Roderick wanted it sharp, sharp. His grandpa at eighty had swung into a hayfield on a hot afternoon, sleeves of his white shirt rolled, his torso swaying as he cut and stepped, his wind good even then, a slow but still-useful machine. Two months before he died, he was loading hay bales all afternoon. If I can still grab it, I can lift it. Roderick had the same build, thick through the middle, nothing could dent his belly or back, and what made his grandpa a good reaper had made Roderick a good catcher, big shoulders, handy down the ages if you swung a sword or a pick or a catcher's tongs. All he needed to live and to keep himself in trim were tools like this one with the stamp of family on them, a good double-bitted ax, a crosscut saw. When the blade drew a little blood from his thumb, Roderick sliced the air, wishing the scythe still mattered, that it was a needed thing. He set out through the old pasture running west toward the woods. It was not harvest he was after or the cosmetics of mown grass, but motion and sweat. He cut a slow circle into the hay, widening it neatly, sucking wind and perspiring as he had years ago, in a rhythm not unlike this, not in a hayfield but a mill. Yes, he'd been sick but he'd beaten the TB, he'd come back from that. He still

had power in the stroke, he had the long good arms and the
strong back and he could swing that scythe flat and full, and
the hay, run through with bull thistle and goldenrod and wild
plants he didn't even know, fell, every stalk of it. He cleared out
a space until his shoulders ached and his muscles burned, leaving
this swath to dry in the sun. There. Whatever wanted to fill this
circle could, spirit or motor or some whim of weather. He had
turned it out, its juices were sweet in the air. Catching his breath,
he blinked at the afternoon sky, a dizzying calm blue in which a
contrail was dissolving, the high faint cloud of a plane's passage.
They crossed this piece of country at such an altitude he rarely
noticed them. So far were they separated from their sound, the
airplanes, small and silver and silent, they seemed to be leaving it
for good, casting it off.

What folly to have believed the land was his again, and that
he could be planted in it, like a tree, a rock.

He crisscrossed restlessly the trails he'd cut and cleaned over
the years and where he often walked in good weather or bad,
turning eventually to the place near the brook. He whacked at
weeds of scrub spruce, or the tenacious alder, one deft swipe of
the scythe. But he could not destroy the hints of yellow everywhere. Light on leaves, on water. A ragged birch stump embla-
zoned with yellow fungus. A dozer that big could go anywhere,
anywhere on this land, up hill or down dale, clear to the beach
and back, there was not a goddamn tree big enough or deep
enough to halt it. A hundred years worth of root wouldn't do it.
He did not want to think what that machine could do, or the way
it just sat up there, left behind, more dangerous than dynamite.
Men he knew, he'd laughed at their love of yellow iron. The
young fella up the road who bought the MacNeil place thought
he'd rout the alders once and for all because some fool from town
cleared a great patch of them with a dozer, its big toothed blade

ripping them out by the roots, and all so easily, shoving them into huge mounds to burn. Sure, it cleared the land like he'd wanted it, he'd beaten the alders and won back a field. But it won't work, Roderick told him, that's just a big iron version of what we do with a pick and a shovel, dig them out one summer and curse them again the next until their roots are tough as cable. No, no, the man said, it gets the roots and everything, you see, the dozer does. Yes, Roderick said, and the topsoil along with it. And he'd sat in his kitchen and listened to the bulldozer grinding back and forth over the young man's land, scooping out, with its ferocious efficiency, bladefuls of alders, their brittle branches crunching and snapping like gunshots. And by nightfall the trees were rubbish and during the cold weeks of January the man burned the alder piles one by one, their hot cores glowing in the early dusks, ash coiling up gray into the windy snow, and in his bed, near sleep, Roderick sometimes sniffed the smoke and it surprised him, the wild smell of it coming in the crack of his window. Alder good wood to burn, hot, hot. Melt iron, ruin grates. But by summer that bare waste ground, oh Jesus, he knew the alders would love it, they couldn't wait, they were ready with suitcases, and move in they did. By fall that field was so thick with them, you'd think they'd been sown, and the next summer too dense to walk through, roots knotted like fists. How Roderick had laughed to see them crowding there. But ashes, the ashes.

Roderick held the receiver like a hammer.

"I didn't hear from Mr. Maddocks for a couple years," he said to the unresponsive voice. "It's just that I was wondering about him."

"You're the what, the caretaker?"

"I looked after his property here. For him. Many years."

"Where's here?"

"St. Aubin. Cape Breton. Nova Scotia."

"Oh, yes. Yes. Well, I forgot your name. He told me to drop you a line. I thought you were a bill collector or somebody for Jesus. He's dead and gone. Awful sick. Went quickly."

"A blessing, I guess."

"What? He didn't owe you money, did he?"

"Listen, on the property, there's a bulldozer there. Parked since a couple days, maybe three." Roderick's mouth was dry. "What's up with it?"

"Up? It's not us, not ours. Tell them to beat it. We'll be out there sometime, but this summer, well. Sometime."

Roderick could detect nothing of Maddocks in his son's voice. It seemed to promise, in its vagueness, nothing good. But the dozer was not part of that, not now. He could order it away, climb into that damn seat and drive it off if he had to, the Mounties couldn't touch him. Still, he was more uneasy than before. The man he'd just talked to knew not stick nor stone of this place.

That night through the dark fields, through the woods he knew so well, every root and hazard, Roderick needed no flashlight. The spaces lit with moon cast deep shadows, a groping darkness Roderick moved through as if it were day, skirting the spot where he, in one form or other, would someday lie. He just glanced down there at the shrouded trees, moonwashed, then headed up until he saw the rectangular hulk of the bulldozer, its yellow bleached by moon. Like a thief he clambered over its metal, cool with dew, and sat himself in the steel seat. Jesus, you were high up here: it made you think you could take any land you liked. Trees might slow you up but never stop you, and what rocks were there you couldn't lift or shove? What a beast. No wonder the drivers looked dazed sometimes, like they couldn't hear anything but the diesel and the dangerous clangor of treads, just them and the machine and the levers, nothing outside all that. Destruction, and that was what all clearing and leveling was, wasn't it, gouging out, scraping clean, like you'd dig out a sod hump. He felt the instruments for a key but there was none. God, how he would love to roar it into life, direct it, clanking and grinding, into some ditch down the road and whoever owned it could get it out, their problem. He tugged at the levers, worked the pedals. There was no way he would rouse this thing on his own. The driver would come, and then they'd have it out. Roderick would set him straight: the owner doesn't want your services, doesn't need them, you've got the wrong place, shove off. Yet he could imagine a kind of satisfaction, having this machine under you, blasting trees out of your path, scooping up rocks like pebbles, mashing a landscape into whatever. *You catch it at the seventh roller coming off, grab it and swing it around into the rollers of number eight. Nearly end to end, they were, coming at you, a white molten snake, looping and narrowing from mill to mill, and you could see it brighten the dark mill wall and you knew it was arriving steady as a train and would appear with a smooth, contained, fiery light, sudden but expected, and you whirled in a splash of sparks and you captured the rod and you passed it on into the rollers eagerly spinning, always spinning.*

Roderick slumped in the seat. A foot pedal squeaked as he pumped it in and out, in and out. When the moon eased behind the hill, there was only one dark shape in the field, big and silent.

It did not occur to Roderick that he might resort to prayer even after another day and another went by with the dozer unclaimed and unmoving, as if it had been left there deliberately to absorb momentum. Peg could pray for him, churchgoer that she was. Late in the afternoon he stood where his grave was to be. Columbines were just now giving up petals for seed, dropping one by one their purple blossoms. The brook nearby purled faintly with the low, narrow water of summer. Beech trees and maples gentled the light. He had to think about this part of death all over again and he hadn't the heart for it. He had thought that taken care of, since the burial was the only portion of it he had any say in: He believed that if you were laid out in just the right place, your spirit, the only thing that lived, had something your own going for it. A site consecrated by four generations, not by their interment, for most of them lay on Man O' War Point, but by their passing over this land for a long time in the comings and goings of their lives. But here, no visitors. Just the blue-eyed grass, the wild iris. Just Roderick. And a girl once, right here. He had brought her, or had they brought each other, her hand in his, warm as light. Why did he keep thinking now that the bulldozer would come down here for sure? Rooted up, scooped and scattered. The ground, damp from a night shower, gave slightly underfoot as he paced it, back and forth, printing the sod with his boots.

He had thought that he would sit up, if there was a sitting up when the time came, toward the mountain across the water along whose ridge he'd seen many suns disappear, many kinds. In the Catholic cemetery over on the south side of the island the graves were directed eastward toward the rising of Judgment Day. So it had to matter, did it not? And that was a day he'd heard about plenty, growing up, and the necessity, or impossibility, of being saved from damnation. Roderick had chafed at all that but the questions still troubled him. Are the fires of hell hotter than the rod mill? he'd asked his dad finally, old enough to distance himself from The Gospel Hall, and the man had said, Hotter than any agony you can imagine, you young pup. A hard man in a rigid denomination: it made Knox Presbyterians sound like libertines. The Gospel Hall wouldn't let you pee if they thought it would make you feel good. Roderick couldn't go to a dance or a party, and when movies came along he was forbidden them as well. When his dad relented eventually and brought a phonograph home, the only records he allowed were Gaelic hymns and devotionals, not the sort of thing that would get you up for a Saturday night. There were endless Sundays in hard chairs in rooms bare of church trappings, hours of preaching, one lay-brother after another it seemed, until he was dazed with the heat and the gravity of voices whose weight seemed to grow until he was bowed down with fatigue. When Roderick got old enough to think through some of the things he heard, the notion of being saved seemed to have worrisome holes in it, and what shone through them was not sunshine. After they took him on at the steel mill, Roderick left the Gospel Hall and his dad feared for his soul, loudly at first but finally just shaking his head when Roderick did not get up for Sunday but lay deliciously in bed. In later years his dad would sit bent over a radio, his arthritic hands deformed at the shapes they'd worked in, listening to broadcasts of the Gospel Hall in the weak kitchen sun because he couldn't travel to meetings anymore, convinced though he was of his own salvation. Roderick did not want to, could not, determine whether he was among the elect, those whom God had already, somehow, selected to be saved, or among the damned, do what he might to correct it. What occured after dying was—spin out what you would—baffling. But he did want his own burial, here. It was all in his will, the careful instructions written out in ink, a little map. All he had known, after all, was how to be ready, how to present himself.

He knew there would come a point when nothing would be far away, going or coming. Last night he listened to another high, solitary airplane, already over the sea when he heard that long fading whisper, like letting out breath. What would shape him out of ashes? What would care to?

When you see it on the wall, you count one, two, *and then catch. You never say* three *because she's gone, you're catching nothing.*

Was that a whiff of exhaust somewhere? The beat of an idling engine? Suddenly Roderick seized a young birch tree by its trunk and struggled to bring its crown to the ground, but it was too strong and sprang away in a slash of leaves, quivering upright. The air was warm and dizzy and clouds lumbered in from the ocean, solemn with rain. He had liked the moistness here, the moss a slick green on rock, and further up thick enough to lie on, dry, if there hadn't been rain. He hastened up an old back trail, winding through a dense, gloomy stand of slender spruce, so crowded their trunks were grayed with lichen, their branches, bare and brittle as sticks where the sun hardly reached. He breathed with a tense, quickening panic: the dark, good God, he was afraid of the dark. He laughed and moaned at himself—what, you fool, could any dark be compared to the big dark you know nothing about? This was nothing, night was nothing. Branches prodded his face and arms as he pushed ahead, snapping them off brutally, hurrying, but there where the path ended like a tall door someone was waiting in the field, looking his way, backlit. "Whoa!" Roderick yelled, angry to be surprised here, scratched and perspiring as if he were lost. "Who's up there?"

"Easy, boy. I was only up looking at your dozer."

"Corry, you bastard. You know, I never run into anybody here." Roderick felt oddly glad to see him, relieved somehow. "Where's your hat? I'd have known the hat."

"With the feather? In my car. I was needing a little walk." Corry looked hot himself, his white shirt wilted, his necktie yanked loose.

"Let's walk toward whiskey."

"A mind-reading man."

In the kitchen Roderick set down a bottle of rye he'd barely touched in months and two small glasses, wiped clean. He was getting untidy but he didn't much care, him who were so neat all these years. Neither spoke while Roderick, amazed at his own eagerness to be drunk, poured generously. He wanted to hear, for once, just what Corry and that woman had done this afternoon. He would listen to every nasty detail, and if Corry wanted to dress it all up a little, that was all right with Roderick too. He had forgotten what drink was capable of if you didn't sip it but simply squared up to it.

"My great-uncle Dougal prospered in California," he said, looking down the front hall to the Cougar parked beyond the front porch. "Rushing for gold like a lot of fools out there in the 1850s, in bigger mountains than these, snow to your rooftops in wintertime. But Dougal, he opened an inn there in the Sierra foothills, and his son years later got on me to come out, lots of work, he said. My dad said, you'd better take it, nothing going here but Depression. But the next day I got a joyful call: the steel plant had a place for me. That night I drank rum glass after glass and they put me to bed insensible. You know, the thought of packing my things and really leaving for California made me light in the gut, like coming over a wave in a small boat. I was more pleased I didn't have to go than being there could ever make me."

"Slainte!" Corry toasted and they drank, clean and quick. When Corry got tight, there was no ranting and roaring, no Sundays stupid with Saturday night. Roderick liked that about him.

"Funny how the dozer looks like she's there for good," Corry said.

"I'll get a man to fire her up pretty soon. Run her clean to the shore and watch her sink. Goodbye dozer."

"Wouldn't be legal."

"Legal got nothing to do with it."

"Yes. I know."

"You're going to be buried in that automobile," Roderick said. The quick glass of rye settled a strange calm into him, though his heart seemed to beat quietly fast.

Corry laughed. "I'd need the dozer for that. But why not? I don't want that car junked in somebody's woods, spruce pushing up the floorboards. Look at that paint. No rust, not a pinhole."

"No salt out there in California."

"Not a lot here either."

"What, the winter roads?"

"No, this man's summer. The salt's gone out of it." Corry tamped a long cigarette on the tabletop, lit it. "You ever think of the first woman you laid down with, Roderick John?"

"Wouldn't do me a bit of good."

"Lord, I can taste her sometimes. I can feel the hem of her dress, her slip. That little noise the satin makes. They always wore dresses, remember? The perfume was nothing special, dime-store stuff, but Jesus. I could tell you every inch of her."

"Don't."

"Might. Just for the hell of it." Corry sighed deeply. "For God's sake, Roderick John, I used to drive all around the island and half the time there'd be a woman in the seat beside me."

"Which half was better?"

"Do you know what I'm talking about at all, man? When were you with a woman last?"

"It's pretty dim, I admit. But there's another time, much earlier time. I'd been working in the mill a while and I brought a woman home, just into the driveway, late, driving my dad's old Ford, and we went at it in the front seat, pretty well juiced and ready for each other, the both of us, and later I stumble out of the car for a piss but I wander upstairs when I'm done, to bed somehow, passed out. In the morning my dad, up at daybreak wouldn't you know, discovers the poor girl asleep where I left her, her skirt to her waist and her underpants snagged on the gear shift. It was a sight you and me would've gladly exaggerated, but he told it straight, my dad. He'd woke her up as gently as he could and turned his back while she dressed, and then he sat her in the kitchen and cooked her eggs and baloney and poured coffee until she felt better. Long before I woke up he drove her home, or as close to it as she wanted to be left. But he did not preach to me about it, not a word of that. He just told me it was time I got myself a room somewhere, and that it was a mean thing to leave a girl out there in the cold. He could surprise me sometimes. But I didn't love his religion. It's no good to me now."

"All I remember of church is, no, you can't do that. All out of whack to the comfort it gave, anyway. Still, that Presbyterian love, it can fool you. That same fire they scare you with can heat up your blood."

"Works that well, does it?"

"Not anymore. You have to do what's required," Corry said, looking away out the back window. "That's what it comes down to and they only have so much patience, boy. Used to be *we* couldn't wait, our foot to the floor, a few squirts and a cigarette, eh? And now there I am in the drugstore with my arm in the blood pressure machine, grinning like a fish because my heart's still beating, toting up my score. If those things gave nickels, I'd be rich. Christ."

"You've had a disappointment, Corry, boy. I'll fill your glass."

"That doesn't half describe it, my friend." Corry's voice dropped to a note Roderick hadn't heard before, sad and smoky. "No ailments, I said. I told her, let's talk about what still works, even if it doesn't work so good as it used to. But she was fixed on the broken, the pains, the aches, the threats and dangers and what's to be done about them. It's a medical world, boy. So. I'm pulling up my trousers, and her, she's vacuuming the room. She's shaking out the curtains."

"I'm glad to be free of that," Roderick said. He let the rye heat on his tongue, then swallowed.

"You're never free of that till you're dead. My God, there's nothing sadder than a soft dick."

The back field was flowing with early goldenrod on which brown butterflies trembled, then blew about like tiny leaves. Thistle seeds scattered past the window, bits of feather. Through the screen they could hear the aspens hiss. Roderick squinted at the shades of leaves, their different rhythms of green. Truth was, he did remember that girl. He was not immune. They'd known each other as summer neighbors, knew the woods and paths to the beach, the brook: all seemed to lead to water, and they both had a thirst. As keen as he was, she was, church or no church, and they'd both spent many a Sunday in those hard pews. They knew the language of sin, they'd heard it, the rules and the risks of it. But he led her down to that spot by the brook, to that leafy privacy where their nakedness seemed so easy they laughed. But ashes?

He had never wanted marriage, to her or any that came after. They had their ways and he had his. Any fit man could cook his meals, mend his clothes, clean up after his own body. And of course a point comes when you know you're alone, that it's too late for that kind of company day by day. And there was Corry to consider, living in silence with a woman who refused to talk to him because he had taken church money she was in charge of and gone on a binge.

"How long was it, Corry, that Willena wouldn't speak?"

"Seven years," he said quickly, as if they'd been discussing her all along. "Some might say that was a blessing, but of course that's an easy thing to say. I could have left. But you know I didn't want to, and she knew it, and she punished the shit out of me. No talk but just the necessary yes or no. But it's the bits of conversation that you like in a woman and they knit you together in a way, after a while, because it's not quite like the talk you have with anybody else. The silence, well, it was queer. I never knew what to do about it. I was proud too, you know. After a while it was just wills, hers and mine. I never stopped thinking about her. Without her voice, I was always wondering about her, harder than before. She died suddenly, as they say, too quick to tell me anything at all—yes, no, or maybe."

"Without talk, I don't see it."

"Hard to explain, and since she's gone, there's no point in that either."

Against the mountain an eagle, a brilliant white bit, was drifting, high over the water, its black lost in the dark green shadows of trees.

"Sunday tomorrow," Roderick said. "I haven't been to church in fifty years."

"No black suit for me, boy."

"Was my dad's idea of heaven—one Sunday after another."

"No room for women, I suppose?"

"Not the way you're thinking, Corry, my man. That's all over with up there, so they tell us."

"I suppose. And ashes, they're so damned unreliable."

"You too?"

"They don't so much burn you as bake you. Twenty-five hundred degrees. Three hours. There's bits left, but not the bits we care about."

Corry topped his glass and Roderick's. Above the mountain, sun burned a few moments deep in cloud before it swelled and darkened.

"Be blazes in the mill today, eh?" Corry said.

"Lord. Basic rate plus tonnage. Always on edge. Rolled a thousand billets a day without a rejection. Rolled all sizes, right down to wire, just a weaving glowing filament."

"Chase that wire to hell and back, eh? Whiskey makes me want to dance, Roderick John. You got music here, Scotch music anywhere?"

"None on the radio, not this day and hour. Plenty of other racket, that stuff that sounds like a scrapyard."

"I'll jig my own tune then." Corry rapped out a beat with a spoon, humming, and then he stood up slowly and picked it up with the heel and toe of his shiny black shoes, his back straight, arms at his side. Roderick was surprised at the supple swiftness of his footwork, neat and close to the floor, a good stepdancer in the old style.

"I knew men could dance that all night," he said.

"They cleared the floor for me more than once, boy." Corry stepped off a few more bars and then stopped. He breathed deeply like a runner and sat down. "Short night," he said.

"That was good, boy. I'm weary just watching."

"I never liked watching. I wanted to be in there."

"Yes, yes." In the early years after he sold the land, Roderick had gotten up from bed for no reason but restlessness, a summer night dark and bright at the same time, the moon as brilliant as snow. His illness had passed and he was strong again but in the old house living alone, and that night there seemed to be nothing ahead of him, no one close to him: everyone had gone away for good. The burden of the old house was his, every room, and the land. Then out in an old pasture, succumbing already to woods, he saw three people stepping tenderly across the chilly, dewy grass, things dangling from their arms. Two men and a woman, he could hear their laughter, their murmured remarks. In the middle of the field they flung away the clothes they were carrying and joined hands, moving slowly in a circle, cooing at the moon. They were naked, moon-white, and as soon as Roderick apprehended that, he felt leaden with yearning. Never before or since had he so much wanted to be taken in, and he did not even know into what. When the circle of revelers parted and were soon gone toward the shore, he listened to their calls in the woods, their howls as they waded into the midnight water, keeping him awake.

"Listen," Corry said, "We'll go up there and get that damn dozer started, get it out of your life."

"No. I don't think so."

"Something else on your mind?"

"Yes. I'm going to die."

"Most certainly."

"No, I mean soon."

"Ah. At least you know. Some of us wait, some of us run. Me, I have a car with a big engine."

"I'm not afraid of it. I just thought if they could put me under a piece of my own ground, I'd get over the tough part, the surprises."

"But we don't know what the surprises are, Roderick John. Are you sick, do you have something terminal?"

"I haven't. It's got nothing to do with being sick. Now it's ashes I have to think about, and worse."

"Have another drink then, seeing as you're going to die."

"I didn't mean this afternoon. I'll wait till you leave anyway."

"That's decent of you, Roderick John. I've had enough dying for one day." Corry's gaunt face was flushed with whiskey and he blew out smoke with a long exhaling that seemed to merge with wind flowing through the back field, through the kitchen. Then rain brought down a sudden dusk.

"The peepers have stopped, have you noticed?" Roderick

said, but Corry did not answer. Yes, the small frogs that in the night woods cheeped like birds. They'd quit, suddenly. But of course it was July and they should be finished mating anyway. Nothing odd about their silence except that Roderick was aware of it and missed them. He did not remember just when Corry left, did not recall even the engine of his car, only the kitchen growing darker, and on the water a brief light like ice, silvery. The room grew cooler with the evening breeze but Roderick made no move toward a supper. He watched a moon appear, large, low and richly yellow, but turning white as porcelain as it rose. He took the last of the whiskey in sips because it seemed to hone his attention in some necessary way. The deep darkness of country night. Someone's wharf at the foot of the mountain, one solitary light in a wide, high blackness. Well, he would lie some way under leaf or snow. Rabbits would cross, fast if they sensed a fox in the cold air, a dust of flakes following their tracks, or they might pause, listening. The fox would move dainty, swift at the right moments, clearheaded with hunger, not panic, unless the snow were deep and the lynx, on its big soft feet, were running him calmly down. Deer hooves to the brook, marking the sod deep. He'd shot his share when he was young, skinned out their steaming insides. Meat he'd wanted, needed. Birds would brush the ground for bugs, for seeds. A grouse would scoot through the summer grass, diverting danger from her young. But that danger would not be human. He did not remember either when he slept, when his head lay on the table, and his dreams were rapid and confused, as if his sleeping consciousness dismissed everything parading across it, all enticements, fantasies, regrets, and when sun lit the back field in a sudden flicker of russet, the grasses still cool, faintly smoking, he was already hearing an engine, the clattering of tread, dirt gorging against steel, the stones tumbling, screeching, and as he got to his feet he was already counting, *one, two.*

WORK

As Jack MacBain was struggling once again to get beyond the first few bars of "Devil in the Kitchen," Little Norman wanted to tell him the dream. He had dreamed of the quarry again last night—the high white gypsum cliff trembling with heat, and under its blazing face hunks of white rock that Jack and him had split. But now Jack was driving his fiddle hard and close to the floor, as he had earlier that evening down at the Fire Hall where dancers, to that deep Cape Breton stroke, beat the floorboards like the skin of a drum. Then Jack had faltered—not that the dancers cared so long as he caught it up again—but he'd slowed up and slowed up and then lost it, lost the tune like you'd step in a hole, his ruddy face redder and his eyes bright with embarrassment. In mid-stroke he'd had to quit, just as he was quitting now.

"No use to this," Jack said. He stared down at the fiddle on his lap and scratched the bow along the side of his neck as if this might draw the tune from his memory. "Jesus, boy. I think I'm done out."

"And you, Norman," Jack's wife called from the corner where her anger had placed her. "You had to encourage him, eh? Not for a minute was he fit to play a dance, everyone looking on."

"I *was* fit," Jack said hotly. "You got to play for dances. Dancers *make* you play, make you good." He lay the fiddle and bow on the kitchen table beside the open lid of the case. "All I needed was a little rum. And you didn't give me any."

"Sure, Dalena," Norman said, feeling miserable enough without the blame. "It was a farewell, like, and maybe just a splash . . ."

"Some farewell, that," Dalena said. She frowned. "He don't need to be remembered that way, the tunes leaving him." She sat on a box and hugged herself, surrounded by the belongings they would take to the Senior Citizens Home in the morning. Norman looked at her hands: girl's hands they were, even yet. And her hair still mostly black when it had every reason to be white. She it was, small and busy, had waited on Jack when he was home, put him to bed when he was drunk and roaring. But the rest of the time when he was away it had been Norman who'd seen to him, wherever they worked—mines, mill, lumberwoods. The quarry too.

"We'll remember how he *played*, Dal," Norman said, hurt, "not how he quit." Shame enough to see a big man go back, and a fine fiddler to boot. Lungs choking up, kidneys half-shot. But the *mind*—that struck him hard, poor Jack, not knowing the tunes anymore, a man who, many a time, had driven his fiddle down right to the last dancer reeling at sunrise.

"Take it, Norman," Jack said. "Take it with you home tonight, that fiddle. I'm done."

"Aw, I'm no fiddler. Come on, boy, don't be so glum."

"Dal?" Jack said gravely. "For sure I'm needing a little rum." He stared at the floor and let a few deep breaths rattle in his lungs for pity. But Dalena was running her bifocals along a row of small plastic bottles on the window sill.

"You know what Dr. Fraser told you," she said, stern as a nurse. "Time for your medicine anyway."

"A little celebration," Jack said. "Look at it like that, girl, not like Dr. Fraser."

"And what are we celebrating then?" she said, her back to them.

"Don't be so hard, Dal," Little Norman said. "You two off and away in the morning, and me back up the road without a soul."

"Rum won't change any of that, Norman. And you've got your health and no worries. Like you say, a fiddler you're not."

Norman had his scars, sure, and pains now and then to go with them. And some days his blood seemed to go slack like he'd just done two shifts in a mine. A bit of sleep cured that. And hard work. Work could make him forget most anything—a damn good knack to have, so his dad once told him. As for his eye blinded in the pit, it was like coming on a corner he could never quite turn and sometimes he had to cock his head like a rooster. But these were not worries, true, not worries the way Dalena meant. Anyway, it wasn't her sympathy he was after tonight: he just wished she were feeling more easy. Goodbyes were hard enough.

Jack had seized the fiddle and bow again and was cutting into "The Black Sporran," but it soon tapered off into a groping whine. He whacked the instrument back onto the table.

"Give us a drink, Dal," he said. "For the love of Jesus." He was breathing in a kind of growl but without much steam behind it.

"Your cuts are sharp as ever, Jack," Little Norman said quietly.

"Aw, frig, might as well give that bow back to the fairies where it came from."

"Jack," Dalena said, counting the pills in her palm. "There's lemonade in the icebox."

There was a time when Norman would have seen his pal, with the back of that big hand, sweep those pills to the floor. Not now. Dal didn't fear his storms anymore. She was seeing to him now, up one side and down the other, just like Little Norman had through sixty-odd years of work, not only in the lumberwoods but in the steel mill too when they shared rooms in Sydney and had one hell of a time out on the town, racketing about.

"I don't want pills," Jack said. "And I don't want iced piss either. I'll buy my *own* rum when we get to that goddamn home. I'll get a taxi."

Dalena would have ducked and whispered in the old days but now she held the pills tight and stood in his face.

"There's a new chapter in your life tomorrow, Jack," she said. "And there's no rum in it."

"Last frigging chapter, then. You can shut the damn book too. Norman, tell this woman about rum. Tell her what it *means*, boy."

"I know what it means," Dalena said.

Norman slid to the edge of his chair. He cleared his throat. "You talk about sick? Jack and me, well now, we *worked* our way through sick spells, for Jesus sake, our eyes so hot with fever they'd glow in the dark. It was all the medicine we had, eh? A good slug of Demerara? Now that was rum, by God."

Jack smiled. "You could dip it with a spoon. Like molasses. Smooth as a kiss, that."

"Drink it all night and no harm the next morning. Roll out like a baby. Rumrunning days, best rum in the world. Triple X Black Diamond, and a right jewel it was."

Flushed with the memory, Jack picked up the bow like a stick from the ground and tapped it on his knee, leaving a faint mark like chalk.

"We rummed up a lot that summer of the steel strike."

"'22 was it? '23?"

"Bloody Sunday I'm taking about. We broke the Sabbath good with the bottle Rod MacLeod gave us. But we didn't scamper, did we? You get good Black Diamond under your belt, the provincial police can go hang, and everything else." He looked darkly at Dalena.

"Terrible work anyway, that mill. Fires in your face. Rather break rock," Little Norman said.

"Sure, cut wood. Out in the air, good air. Give us a sharp crosscut and we'd do seven cord a day, eh, Norman? And what cut the cold? *Rum.* Not too much, now, no. Just a snapper."

"And no goddamn provincials there, boy. But you was never scared of them, Jack. Didn't care who it was or where the hell or what."

"They cracked you good too, Norman, chased you down."

"Oh, Jesus, them hardwood batons." Little Norman fingered a hard ridge of flesh that parted his spiky hair. "Skullbusters." But it was a horse he remembered most. Coalhaulers' horses they were, nags, most of them, mounts commandeered by the provincial police who'd somehow suffocated fourteen of their own en route from Halifax to Sydney in a box car. Drunk, the whole gang of them, charging churchgoers, anybody—striker or not—on the sidewalk that fine June evening. Norman had felt the horse behind him, its breath and its bulk, heard the creak and strain of leather. And when he turned around, it was to see that horse's eye rolling white and dirty, and the horse's bared, worn teeth champing, and then higher up a four-foot baton was already descending through a dangerous whiff of rum that was not his own. The wood opened up his head like you'd put a razor to it. But he'd never forgot the look in that horse's eye—some old torment that Little Norman instantly understood.

"Policemen? Drunken bastards!" Jack said, stroking his thighs so rapidly the provincials might have been on the road outside. "Bloody Sunday, boy!" He glared at his fiddle as though he would smash it.

Dalena said nothing. When they went on like this she ignored them, like an old soldier's wife who'd too often heard battle songs she never had the urge to sing.

"And what did we get from that strike anyway?" Jack went on.

"A few frigging pennies," Norman answered, "nothing more. A bit of free coal."

"God, we needed that rum to stay *alive*. Dal doesn't know."

"I know more than you think," Dalena said wearily. She held out a tumbler of water which Jack ignored, looking around her at his chum.

"Try the lumberwoods in winter without rum," he said, louder. "Smash a finger or a toe and no doctor at all!"

Norman smiled. Sounding like the old Jack, he was. How many days had Norman roused him out of his bunk, those mornings in the lumberwoods, cold and dark, coaxing him to the cookroom where a big breakfast finally got him out of the dumps? The rest of the day they could outwork any men, big or little, even if it took some rum on the side. But there in the Senior Citizens Home, how would Dalena get the man moving? How would she raise his spirits on a dreary winter morning, no work and no rum ahead of him?

"What difference would a taste of it make?" Jack shouted. His huge head, nearly bald now, was damp with sweat. "Well, I'll tell you," he answered, more evenly. "Life and death!"

"Don't get heated up, Jack," Dalena said. "There's none of it in the house anyway. But this you have to take. Now open."

Jack accepted the pills on his tongue like poison and took a mouthful of water, scowling. "Dr. Yango'd let me have rum."

Dalena glanced out the window at the cottage next door. A Filipino doctor from Sydney Mines had built it for summers and brought his family down on weekends.

"He'd never," she said. "Don't kid yourself."

"They were at the dance, and having a good time too," Little Norman said. He wished Dalena would have a good time, or go tend to something like she used to and leave him and Jack alone. They hadn't a chance to talk much this night, not like they did with just the two of them. On the Yangos' front porch facing the water hung a cylinder of vivid, humming blue. Norman knew she liked the doctor, an important man, in a way she could never like him.

"Strange, that bug light," he said. "Singes flies like hair in a candle, but the flies are all gone."

"Well, it's a comfort to me when the Doctor is down, I can tell you," Dalena said. "If Jack was to have a turn, I'd only need shout and . . ."

"Norman!" Jack yelled, his hands on his ears. "Got anything on your hip?"

"I do, Jack. Good stuff, too."

Dalena turned her furious eyes on Norman. "And *you* his friend?"

"Aw, Dal, the man needs a lift. Just a taste wouldn't hurt, the size of him."

"Size got nothing to do with it, Norman. He's sick."

Jack was looking down at his hands, opening and closing them slowly as if he wanted to grab something. "I'll get a taxi," he mumbled, "when we're there. You wait."

Dalena shivered and rubbed her arms. "We need a fire in that stove, then I'll make tea. Could you fetch some wood, Norman?"

"What, am I crippled?" Jack said, rising. "Can't split wood? God almighty, I'm man enough for that. Let's go, Norman, give me a hand, boy."

"Now wait. . . ." Dalena appealed to Norman, but he gave her a solemn nod and she relented.

Jack eased himself down the back steps and shambled to the woodpile, Norman just behind him, glad to be free of Dalena. Under the faint light from the kitchen window Jack waited with the ax while Norman set up a short log on the chopping block.

"Might as well do this with the fiddle," Jack said as he split the log clean. "She'd burn nice."

"No, Jack, no. You'll get the tunes again, boy."

"A time comes, Norman, when the well she don't fill up no more. Maybe I got to go on a machine pretty soon." He raised the ax high above his head and brought it down with such force the halved wood flew. "A goddamn machine."

Norman did not want the details. He glanced up at the pill bottles silhouetted in the window, then reached down for another log and set it up, watching Jack bring the ax down with a grunt. The dull crack of the wood sounded fine to Norman, the power of it.

"Not like that fourteen pound sledgehammer, Jack," he said. "Eh?"

"Ten cents more a day they paid you at the quarry. You could swing that goddamn big sledge, Jack. You were a breaker, boy."

"Was I now?" He sank the ax head hard into the block and stood back, his breath shooting into the cold air of an east wind. Leaves hustled in eddies around their feet, and through spruce trees across the road the surface of the strait shivered with light from the opposite shore. Norman liked it here by the water. He himself lived back up in the rear near the old mine where the mountain levelled out and trees shut you away from the sea. Boston people owned the place and kept him on there to look out for it. They only came for a month in the summer and he was glad when they left. All he'd needed since a long time was a room and a bed, and Jack down the road.

"God," Jack whispered hoarsely. "Give us a taste, Norman. What the hell, eh? Quick now or she'll be at the door."

Norman worked the pint of rum out of his back pocket and drank, sighing with a satisfaction deeper than the rum itself. Then he put it in Jack's hand like a corpsman. "This is the medicine. Take it slow, let it work awhile, boy." He rubbed his hands together and the heat of his palms brought back the first time they'd shared a bottle, yowling their way home through the woods.

"Kind of rips at me now." Jack shuddered. "Had none for weeks." He took another long draw. "You know, Norman, I swear the fairies were up in the trees there one night. Lord Jesus, they were pale too, white like." He stared at the dark spruce that ran thickly up the mountainside. "They want my bow back. They know I'm done with it, you see."

"Aw, the fairies are gone, gone, Jack. Don't get started on that."

"You think I'm foolish."

"Pass the bottle, boy. Let's go on a tear."

They exchanged the pint quietly like conspirators. Norman settled down on the woodpile, his head pleasantly warm.

"Jack? You recall that quarry we worked in a while? Just lads then."

Jack pulled the ax out and sat down on the chopping block. He held the rum with both hands, staring down at it. "Eh?"

"It was long ago, Jack, long ago. We was walking high up over the face one evening, just about dark. The railroad tracks fanned out down below there, all shined up. Like silver, in that last light of the day going. Now there's something, you said. Beauty there, says Jack, and I says, yes, boy, there is. We stood up there watching till dark."

"Drinking too?" said Jack dully. He was checking the rum in the bottle against the light of the kitchen. He upended it and drank.

"No, no, not the night I'm talking about. . . . Strange, you know. I've had this dream about the quarry. Sometimes it's day and the heat's fierce. Then night, and the cliffs all lit up with them carbide flares. Damn it, but there's a pile of rock behind us and all around everywhere. And I can hear your sledge going, and them lights hissing the way they did. We'd been breaking stone in that place since day one, it seemed like. Just a dream, you know."

But Jack was swaying back and forth and humming with a strong beat, something that sounded like "Farewell to Whiskey," Jack clogging heavily with one foot, stamping it down again and again. And then he stopped. He drank at the rum so long that Norman, with an eye toward the kitchen, carefully pulled it away. "Easy, boy. Let's rest a spell." But without wiping it he hastened the bottle to his own lips and took a swallow that set him coughing. Next door the bug lamp was extinguished but he could still see a faint bluish after-light where it had hung and that bothered him. "Jack, you remember up Marble Mountain, that quarry there. . . . ?"

"Bloody *Sunday!*" Jack roared, and there was Dalena's shadow at the door and she calling them. Just for a moment Norman hated her, the suddenness of her voice.

Jack, protesting, wavered to his feet and started for the house in a determined stagger. Christ, the man was half-cut already! Norman rushed after him grabbing for his arm as he climbed the back steps like rungs on a ladder, but Jack yanked it away and pushed into the kitchen, blurting bits of melody he'd ripped from one tune or another, Norman feeling hot from the rum but a little fearful when he saw Dalena rolling her eyes in disgust. Aw, girl, give us a grin. "Back from the lumberwoods, are you?" she said. Jack was whirling around like a bear, his rags of song getting smaller and smaller until they were no more than sounds, rising and falling. Dizzied, he fell into a chair and Dalena bent to look at his face. "Jesus, Norman," she said. "What were you drinking out there, gasoline?" Dal never said things like "Jesus."

"Just a little Captain Morgan, and not much of it either. He's after getting sensitive to it, I guess, eh?"

She looked at him in wonderment. "How can you be so old, Norman, and still so dumb? Help me get him to bed."

Jack did not resist, slumping his arms around them as they guided him into the bedroom and sat him on the edge of the mattress. Norman had never seen him like this, never in the longest or hardest work they'd done. He reached down to unlace his pal's shoes but Dalena took his arm and walked him to the doorway. "Listen, Norman, dear," she said gently, still holding his arm. "You had the best of his life. Did you know that? You, not me. Now leave him like he is. I'll tend to him."

Norman stepped back from her, troubled by her sudden tenderness. He had rather she'd slapped him, harped at him, and he didn't know why. He looked desperately at Jack, but the man was lost in a mutter of rum.

"He'll want the fiddle again, Dal," Norman said, almost in a whisper. "He'll be wanting that."

"No. Take it. Maybe that's finished now. Can't you see?"

"He just gets in those moods, you know, and. . . ." Dalena smiled but she was not listening. "Aw, well . . . you'll need a fire, girl. I'll get the wood in."

But when he returned with an armload of kindling she was gone into the bedroom. He listened to her through the closed door weaving her voice softly around her husband. She would be taking off his shoes, helping him out of his big wool shirt. Norman set the wood by the stove. He looked again at the bedroom door.

"See you in the morning, eh, Jack?" he called out, as he had so many times in the past, though never had he posed it like a question. Hearing no answer, he left, the fiddle case tucked under his arm like a lunchpail.

Children's voices, pitched high with excitement, drifted out an open window of the doctor's cottage. Little Norman thought it might be nice to stop in, but he went on down the road, walking in the middle until a car honked him over to the shoulder. He did not wave, knowing they were strangers. Strangers outnumbered the old families now in New Skye. "Great for leaving, these Cape Bretoners," his dad used to say when someone he liked had picked up and gone. And there was Jack leaving at last, and laying his fiddle down too. Seemed you laid this thing down and that, and then yourself. After that, God took care of it, so they said. But it troubled him to think of Jack. He'd heard about people who faded fast once they went off to the Home. Looked forward to it, others had said, what with the new building and the new apartments right downtown where you were handy to everything. But that wasn't the whole story—games and singsongs and store windows up the street. That's what Dalena spoke of, but then she'd never had much, poor girl, growing up around the quarry where the sky above was all you saw of the world.

Weary, Norman squatted on a stone by the roadside. At his feet the bank dropped sharply to the shore of the strait. Across the water a wharf light flickered in the currents. He uncapped the rum: a sharp and sweet but lonely taste it was, just medicine. Oh God, he'd like to go on a good bat. But not alone. It's friends you want when you're flushed and gabby. He reached out to touch the cold bark of a birch tree. Winter there, and in the smell of leaves too, darkening underfoot. Soon would come that raw turn of wind, that first fiery breath in your throat that made you think of ice. They had come close to death once, him and Jack together, their last time over in the Black Country. Norman had never cared for the mines, deep in the dark. But work was precious. Sometimes he thought he could still smell it, the firedamp. No, they said, there's no odor, but oh, a word he could taste, that stink of methane or whatever it was, a bog smell. Flaring their noses in that air thick with sweat and water, they had stopped their picks in mid-swing and fixed their lamps on each other's look, Jack's eyes white as a minstrel's. Somewhere down the disappearing shaft bad air found a bit of flame. Thunder and dust then, roaring over them like a nightmare train. When he woke, there was sunlight all over the room, sun in the window. He thought he was dead, and Jack along with him. But above him a doctor said, "You're tough as a rat."

When Little Norman woke, for a moment he might've been twenty again and the quarry out there waiting for the bend of his back. But in the open closet a circle of sunlight had penetrated the gloom of his clothes. The light told him first that he had missed them, that by now they would be on their way, and then it told him he would miss them like hell.

He dressed slow as a child. Never did he sleep so late into the day, and wouldn't it have to be this one. The fiddle case lay open on the chest of drawers. He plinked the strings but their sound was only painful. Where was the bow? He knelt under bed and bureau, patted the dark: it was nowhere in the room. He swayed a little when he stood. By God, Jack, he thought, where are we, after all? He pressed his fingers along the wood of the fiddle: he could feel the music that had been there, and he wouldn't need the bow.

In the kitchen he stood with a mug of black coffee, cupping its warmth. Was that a sparkle of frost on the window? Outside the wind was stripping down the woods, driving whirls of leaves across the field. Why had so much failed out? Only a handful of

farms left now. The coal mine, pulp mills, quarries. Desperate
small wages, but work. Something should have stuck here, something they'd toiled over. No, you were left staring at your hands
and that was the end of it. No work today, boy. Nothing to cut
down or bust up, to shovel or haul or drag. You didn't have to be
a Giant MacAskill who could hoist a ton on his back. We got our
tons right enough, boy. How many did we move? Put that in our
timebook. Cut it in a gravestone. Find some of that good marble on Marble Mountain and put up a rough stone for me and
Jack, for all of us who traipsed these mountains looking for work
like sheep looking for grass. Was there a man now who would
shovel snow day and night, drifts as deep as a barn and the wind
playing the devil? Like the world was an hourglass and you digging there in the bottom of it. There was no more men like them
and no more to come like them. Aw, goddamn it, he didn't want
to be bitter.

In the woodshed where old tools were stored he located the
sledgehammer under scraps of lumber. The shaft was grey, its
grain coarsened, the head rusty. But she was still tight, couldn't
fly off if you swung her. He gripped the handle: Jesus, there'd
been times in his life when he thought just his own strength
could bring him something better, often on mornings like this,
urged by that fear of winter, a touch of frost giving way maybe
for the last time to the heat of the sun. Can I outwit you, boy?
Can I buy your mill or your mine? No, by God, I can't. But I can
outwork you to hell and back again.

He set off down the New Skye Road, the sledge on his
shoulder. Coming on Jack's house his heart quickened hoping
maybe they'd been delayed. But no one answered his knock
and he walked around outside like a burglar twisting door-
knobs and hooding his eyes at the windows. Gone. Every box
and barrel.

It was a long walk to the highway. The sun slid in and out of the morning, warming him, then leaving him to shiver in the cold gusts off the strait. The shaft of the hammer chafed him and he welcomed the rest when he put his thumb to cars gathering speed for the mountain. He waited in their backwash until a plumber's van pulled over. The young man behind the wheel grinned at the sledge but said sure, he was going that way and would leave Little Norman where he wanted. They traded ready lines about the weather but talked no further. A transistor radio lay on the seat and blared into the space between them. "Here would suit me fine," Norman said when they neared the stretch he remembered.

After he left the road and stepped into the trees he was lost. The old railroad should have been somewhere about but the newer spruce had established themselves among older birch and maple and beech whose last leaves hung sparse and papery in the wind. He wandered randomly until the sun broke free again and he could get his bearings. When he found the old railbed he kept to it despite the alders and tough, stunted spruce trying to obliterate it as they did any land a man left to them. And before long he recognized the rubble that had been dumped and spread, and sometimes it looked like a land not part of this place at all but somewhere else in the world where stone, weathered grey and fine, was the earth you planted in, where hardy trees took hold, their roots like panicked fingers in the soil. The narrow gauge rails were gone, spikes, ties, the works, taken up for scrap. But he could follow the turnings, even with the trees high up beside him, crowding, lashing his face when he was too tired to fend them off. The grade was a long, slow climb. He caught the sulphur smell of a spring, glimpsed the red stems of dogwood concealing it. His bad eye beat hard and he was thirsty. Too early for water. Not even noon yet, and he'd have to earn that first sweet cupful. Finally the bed leveled off toward the quarry. He could see the ragged cliffs and chimneys sculpted into shapes he could not recall, honeycombed by rains and run-off, the white rock creased with red bleeding down from the clay above. He had forgotten how high they ran, how deeply he had been here working among the ruck. Hummocks of scrub grass and tufts of weeds spread across the floor of the quarry. Rough heaps lay half-split and spilled like the day the last man left, though for a time kids from the valley, cousins of Dalena, had hurled their share of stones here, tussled for king of the mountain. But now the sun was weak. The faces of the cliffs were cool and darkened like old ice. From high on a rim between broken trees a deer gazed down at him. He imagined its eyes brown and very still. Over the deep walls the wind soared. So full of noise was his memory he could not believe the quiet now. An old man named Murdoch the Woods had worked along with them for awhile and was forever asking, *'De 'n uair a tha e, gille?* What time is it, lad? And Little Norman would tell him never mind the time, it passes slow enough. Now he took off his coat and folded it carefully on the ground. With a quick suck of breath he drew the hammer high behind his head, arrested its arc and brought it down swiftly. The rock at his feet broke and fell away into bits, a sharp sound echoing over the cliffs. There were many rocks waiting to be split. All around him they waited. As he swung the sledge high there was nothing in his thoughts but the remembered weight above his back, and if that was all a man allowed in his mind, he could do it, hour after hour. The sound of the hammer redoubled, rose up, but was absorbed into the trees long before it reached the highway, where it might have said, someone deep in the woods is working.

IDEAS OF NORTH

I

Ken Carmichael plays back the phone message a third time, after he has had two whiskeys and holds another in his hand. His brother Paul tells him their father has disappeared, that he was on the road in his car two nights ago, heading toward an old shipmate in the county retirement home, and he never arrived. Carmichael at first thought ice, sleet, snowy road, but Paul says again a freak December rainstorm hit. They haven't found the car. Police, everybody's looking, he says, Dad could be sick you know, wandering around. I'll try you later when I can tell you more.

But he hasn't been sick in years, Carmichael says to the empty hallway. Why would he be wandering?

He turns on more lights, the TV, feeds his sleepy red cat and frees him outdoors into a light rain. His father has a cat. Who is looking out for it? On TV it is fire and blood time, somber faces chattering into mikes. But his father has disappeared not in California but somewhere near the Pennsylvania–Ohio border, here the man is not news. He turns it off and breaks out ice for another whiskey but lets it melt on the counter as he drinks. An odd sort of helplessness has crept into him, and he has work to finish, words to process. His mother died quietly in the winter, without drama, in her own bed. It had been so long since he was home in February he slipped on sidewalk ice outside the church, a backward vaudevillian swoop, legs flying, arms flailing. He sat through the service with a sore hip, glad for the distracting pain, pressed into the pew between his father and brother, remembering winter Sundays, the rubbery smell of boots and snowmelt. The frozen ground at the cemetery was dusted with snow, a squall attended the gravesite with lightning and thunder.

He stands in his backyard under a dripping redwood. Another El Niño storm is rolling in off the Pacific. Winds have left the fresh winter grass littered with twigs and tree bits. There's talk of mudslides, flooding. The old plum tree, living off its last lopped branches, twists toward the night-gray sky. The one time his father came west he loved its plums, big as lemons, their sweet flesh tinged with the dark purple tartness of their skins. Now Carmichael sees his father gazing at a flat tire, or lifting the hood, men approaching, guns or tire irons or a knife, some act for the thrill or for money or his car, probably dumped down a gully by now—the stock scenarios he wants to dismiss.

When he was a boy, one late November night his mother asked him to walk with her to their church. A light had been installed

behind its central stained-glass window, illuminating the figure
of Christ the Shepherd, with His beard and His silky shoulder-
length hair, cradling a lamb in one arm. She wanted Carmichael
to see it but he knew this walk in early winter had to do with his
father. Snow flurried across the old and beautiful glass, haunt-
ing blues and reds, thrilling in some way, colors he had never
seen anywhere else, not at that age. Though much later he would
come to think of this Jesus as debased—parodied in the hair-
styles of hippies, bikers, jocks—that night he believed in Him.
While they looked up at the window his mother told him
quietly that his dad had been taken off ship on a stretcher at the
Soo Locks way up in Michigan. A blood clot in his bruised leg
had moved to his lungs. It was the only time Carmichael would
remember him sick, but he was in the hospital a long time and
came home a gaunt man. Carmichael had sensed the gravity of
it even though his mother didn't mention that his father might
die, or how she felt about him. Feelings were not for conversation, that was their Cape Breton way, and she hadn't walked
them to the church seeking religious counsel, just unspoken
comfort. They took their oblique solace under that window, a
cold snowy wind picked up, then they headed home, hunched
into their coats. On the way they talked about things he cannot
remember, only a strange feeling that life could be darker than
he'd ever thought.

The rain that swallowed up his father in Ohio was not like this
soaking into Carmichael's hair but a harsh winter rain that
would ease into ice. Lake Erie winters blasted down from
Canada across sixty miles of open water. As kids Carmichael
and his brother knew it was up north in Nova Scotia they came
from, Cape Breton, referred to sometimes as down home or
down east, from the old tacking patterns of sailing ships, and

his only memories are winter ones, visits by train, their father home from the Great Lakes, and always deep snow, difficult and beautiful.

Paul's first words are incoherent. Carmichael has woken him, and he thinks, irrationally, that his brother shouldn't be sleeping, even though, three hours behind him, he feels exhausted himself. Listen, Paul, I have to come home, he tells him, I should be helping search for Dad. Yet he is relieved when his brother says, his voice thin and distant, No, no, don't fly here now, what could you do? The police are tracking him, it's on TV, radio. You got your job to think about. There isn't anything you could do that's not being done already. Aren't people out searching for him right now? Carmichael says. It's late as hell, Ken, his brother says, daylight they'll be out there. I was checking his fridge this morning. . . . His brother's voice catches, a brief hitch and he pauses, then continues. There was salt cod in a bowl of water. Everything was neatly wrapped, even the cat food. I have to get some sleep. It's snowing, Ken.

It comes to Carmichael, suddenly and with a shame that makes him flush, that he had hoped his father would die quietly in his sleep like their mother had, wasn't that best for everyone?

His mother first encountered his dad on a Cape Breton country road after a winter storm. At the reins of his sleigh, he saw her approaching on foot along the beaten-down snow in the center of the road, and he expected her to step to the side, into the deeper snow so his sleigh could pass, but she refused. He had to take his horse up into the bank, his mother wouldn't move for him, I'm not going up in the deep snow for you, she said, you can forget that. But he didn't forget her, and by the next winter it was clear they would go into the deep snow together. When his father told him this story, he was already an old man.

The rain has picked up, the wind, brittle oak leaves scatter across the roof shakes. Before he heard Paul's message he had been about to call Celeste, the woman he had shared this small house with and who left him weeks ago, taking most of its warmth with her. He wanted to hear her voice, her talk. But his father's disappearance is something he couldn't talk to her about. That kind of failing made her leave.

He listens to his computer boot up, but turns it off before the last icon snaps into view. In the old house in Ohio the refrigerator is humming, his dad's things lie where he left them, everything there expects him back, his cat, the mail on the hallway floor, his eight-day clock that needs winding. The air in Carmichael's open window is cold but nothing cold like Ohio, like Nova Scotia, down home.

II

At work Carmichael holes up in his cubicle. He hasn't slept, he went walking early and his shoes are wet, his clothes still damp. The atmosphere of this workplace seems insane and he can only gaze stupidly at the screen. The words seem not written but cast there like bits. His brother called at five A.M. to tell him that they found Dad's car at the end of a short road to a creek where there'd been a bridge once. Raining like hell the other night, his brother said. Dad took three wrong turns and dead-ended there at the bridge barrier, got stuck in the muddy shoulder trying to turn around. But where is he now? Carmichael said. They don't know what direction he went off in, his brother said, they're fanning out from the car.

Carmichael has been thinking about this creek all morning. Headlights picking out a defunct bridge, rusting girders in rainy darkness. The sound of high water, moving. His father there near it, or beyond it, in some disturbing way.

He senses Dennis, a programmer, slouching in the doorway. Carmichael likes Dennis, despite his callow faith in technology, because he has the pale, innocent face of a novitiate and good manners, rare among young techies. Carmichael is the geezer here, after years as a freelance technical writer, trying now to provide for his old age, remain relevant to a dot-com company where, amid disdain for written language, he has turned muddy jargon into prose. Soon they won't need a man like him for another frantic project, the venture capitalists are not venturesome, layoffs are whispered about. He wants to e-mail Paul but his brother hates computers. The nervous patter of his keyboard makes Carmichael feel foolish and he quits.

Dennis. Hello.

You hear about that guy they're looking for up north? Dennis says. It's raining really hard up in the mountains.

I did. Some people think he's a hero.

He shot a game warden but he knows the terrain so good the cops just can't catch him. They'll have to rely on us before long, Ken.

Dennis leans close and explains, as if it were a company secret, that it will soon be possible to insert into a computer the spoor of a disappeared man, the imprint of his DNA, any idiosyncratic profile of his habits, gait, scent, voice, brain waves, and locate him by scanning wherever he's disappeared, like an infallible tracking dog picking up every clue at unheard-of speed, no matter where he's hiding.

Sounds like a sinister device, Dennis. I prefer humans and dogs.

Dennis cracks his knuckles one by one, his imagination stubbornly in the future, always within reach. They went out to dinner once, Carmichael and Celeste, Dennis and a girl he said he was in love with, but Dennis cut the evening short. Work, he said. No sleep.

You don't believe in this stuff, do you, Ken? He nods toward the ceiling lit by little high-tech suns.

Cyberspace is a religious realm, Dennis, and you are one of its robed disciples.

Tell my girlfriend, she needs to know that. Coffee?

There's something I have to do first.

Later, then. Ciao.

Carmichael shuts his eyes. His mother is holding a large piece of hail up to her eye, like a spyglass. On their old back porch, in the gray light of a stormy afternoon, they have delighted in the hailstorm, from the first clatter on the slate roof, to the surprise of stones leaping like popcorn in the grass, drumming on the metal of their first car, a pale green Chevrolet parked behind the plum tree because only his dad knows how to drive it and he is away on the Great Lakes until winter. His mother and he exclaim over the pummeling its paint takes, but what can they do? During those same moments greenhouses outside of town are imploding pane by pane. The size of the hail awes them, how it pierces a muggy August day, crazy bits of ice that, after it is over, lie like tufts of cotton in the grass. She hands him the Brownie box camera and says, Your dad will never believe this, take a snap of it, and she holds the hailstone up like a rough pearl and in the photo it will bleed into the dark white of the sky and years later he will have to outline it with a fine pen. Of the greenhouses she says, All those flowers, full of glass.

He will plead illness, go home. He won't mention his father. He doesn't want breezy sympathies from his boss, a woman half his age hyped with Silicon Valley work ethic, as she exacts in the same breath a pledge to meet his deadline, which always seems to be now, or the word to get around to the brilliant geeks who will solve all this with software anyway.

He has typed on the screen one word: hero. He types more: true heroes . . . always saviors. Without saving . . . without the motivation of saving, no heroism.

III

The rain has fallen in a sizzling downpour since early evening. From behind the steamy glass of his front door Carmichael watches the curb gutters widen into streams nearly to the center of the street. The heavy fronds of the date palm sway overhead, flinging rain. He would call Celeste but he's afraid her voice will be cool, wary of why he called just now after so long, and he won't be able to tell her. She would hear the whiskey in his voice. You live in your habits, Ken, she told him, and this house is one of them. I didn't change a thing.

When Paul finally answers the phone, his voice has a weary authority Carmichael wishes were his own.

I been talking all day, Ken.

So talk to me. We have the same father.

He tells him that a truck-stop waitress claims she served Dad coffee the morning after he disappeared, she said he looked depressed. An old farm couple told the state police detective they saw an elderly man like Dad walking along the road. But the detective doesn't believe them, Paul says, they just want to be in on the action.

I never saw Dad depressed, Carmichael says. Grieving, yes.

You haven't seen him in a long time, Ken.

I'm coming home to look for him, I know the area. Jesus, I feel like I'm receiving dispatches from the front.

Ethel called me, his brother says. Ma's old friend from church. She's been talking to a spiritualist, a good one she says. This spritualist told her Dad is safe in a big green farmhouse, a couple miles from the car.

Carmichael remembers Ethel's house along an expensive stretch of Lake Erie. When they had no car, she would drive them there in the summer to use her beach, him in the backseat sweating, glad, his mother in front. The big brick house once had a broad lawn behind it, elms and maples tall against the water, serenely shading humid afternoons, the wind off the lake in their leaves. But the cliff behind the house eroded year by year and took most of that lawn fifty feet to the beach below until the winter storms kept her awake at night, afraid the cliff would reach her back door while she was sleeping.

So what are we waiting for? Carmichael says. You guys can't find a green farmhouse?

Ethel's an intelligent woman, Ken. She's worth a listen.

Psychics? Listen, I'm coming home.

I spent a lot of time with Dad these last years. He told me stories I don't think you heard.

You don't know what I heard. You were a kid.

There's not much you could do here, Ken. Not right now.

Your show, is it? The little brother in charge.

Dad's in charge. I'm just receiving messages.

Nothing extrasensory, I hope.

I don't rule out anything, Ken.

We were on the Lakes, Dad and me, we both sailed. The first deckhand job I got, he was coming down the ladder and I was going up. The *Ben Morrell*. Union Dock. Ashtabula. In a collision two years later. What would you know about that?

Take care of yourself, Ken.

His brother has the high ground, Carmichael knows that. Paul is *there*, on the scene. A carpenter, he is a child of their parents' middle age, and even now he seems more nephew than brother. Their mother adored him. He builds rural, one-of-a-kind houses by himself that take too long to complete, but he feels his slim profit is honorable, and he smokes good dope with clients who share his perspectives. He once worked with a gang of house framers who could frame at demonic speed as long as the amphetamines held up. Wielding hammers and circular saws like Vikings, they attacked their work with an irritable ferocity that pleased contractors but not the saner men around them. He quit meth, it made him feel like burnt wiring, he said. He scolds Carmichael for drinking, and Carmichael him for that born-again piety.

Yes, what *would* he do there? Tramp through winter fields, another trudging searcher? Drive back roads, squinting out somebody's car window? If you can't find a man, you can't save him.

He has another whiskey before he puts on a raincoat and walks downtown where water is ankle-deep on the main street, glittering with storefront light, people are stepping gingerly through it, their knees high, frightened but delighted. Cars cut through it in a slow, steady splash, there are shouts, queries: Will this get worse? Has this happened before? Carmichael could tell them, strangers like himself from other places, Yes, it has, years ago before we were here, creeks flow underneath your lives here, it's not just earthquakes you have to worry about. He continues toward the creek that defines the northern border of town, a gully of low water so harmless its El Camino bridge has for years sheltered a tiny community of squatters, but El Niño is feeding it now way up in the mountains, swelling it, flushing the homeless up its banks. A man hooded in a soaked parka passes by, clutching his bedding, a trash bag of possessions. The street twists along this creek that no one usually hears or notices. The water has swollen amazingly, he has never seen it so high, streaks of streetlight trembling in its flow. Where the banks are lower, the water has made its way onto a side street and courses purposefully toward the downtown, licking curbtops, creeping up lawns. How unnerving even shallow water looks when moving, its hungry momentum, rising. Across the creek the lights of houses are shimmery in the wet trees. He was never a good driver, their dad, into his forties when he bought his first car. The big silver maple at the end of their driveway lost a lot of bark at bumper level. He was used to ships, to a big wheel responding slowly, spoke to spoke, water he could always make sense of. Carmichael would not expect him to get lost, even in a car, even at eighty-six, and end up at the edge of a winter creek.

When he returns home, Dennis's voice is on the machine asking is Carmichael coming back, is he sick. Their boss can't get him on the phone and she really needs to talk to him. There's a long pause before Dennis asks if anything is wrong. Yes, Carmichael whispers, nothing in our work is noble.

He towels himself off and sits in his study with his whiskey and his sleeping, oblivious cat. The monitor glows, but he is visiting the narrow river he played along in Ohio, sunk in a deep gorge that meandered through the county and the heart of the town, under a high trestle where late in the 1890s a train derailed in a blizzard, pitching its passengers into the frozen valley below, many to their deaths. Though he remembers stripping naked with a pal and swimming in that river, an August afternoon, sultry, how thrilling it was to be bare, the sun on his body, he gives it a winter look now—pans of dirty ice broken by rising water, chunks caught in the ragged coils of driftwood, the turbid current, the hard dark mud of the bank exposed in the snow. And that creek in Pennsylvania? Bushes along its banks, trees? That high water must have sounded frightening at night, if his father could have heard it in the rain, seething past below, not the lazy green of a summer afternoon but a headlong, mad, swollen rush that he surely turned away from.

IV

Did I wake you up?

Christ, Ken.

He can hear his brother pushing himself up in bed, slugging a pillow. You know the time here?

You said there was a house down that road where Dad got stuck? Carmichael is watching the light blink on his answering machine, a message he doesn't want to hear. Behind him, his work on the screen has stopped in midsentence, cursor pulsing.

Old house? Yes, yes. Set back from the road, Paul says before pulling his voice away from the phone to speak with someone in the room. Is he there with a woman, damn him, upstairs in the old family house? Cars pass along the street, diverted from a flooded underpass. Tirespray, an impatient horn.

Nobody lives in it, Ken. On the other side of the creek

there's just a trailer home. They had lights on that night but didn't see a thing.

You think Dad saw their lights?

How would I know? The rain was wicked, the guy said. The creek is shallow and slow ordinarily, it wouldn't scare you at all, but a heavy rain up it comes to a roar, real quick. The banks are high. Someone found his hat. Snagged on bushes, by the old house.

That old tan rainhat? Jesus. Why didn't you tell me? Is that all?

It could have blown off in the wind, the wind was high.

Nobody's searching along the creek?

A chopper's been all over there, men on horseback checked it out, Ken.

Downstream, every goddamn step?

Ken, there's been no other sign of him there.

Or anywhere else.

That creek runs for a few miles at least before it hits Lake Erie. What are you going to do, drag it in the middle of winter? Ice and rocks and snags? He could've gone anywhere.

Exactly. But no one is hiking the creek.

It's not a massive manhunt, Ken. If they get a lead, they'll concentrate on the creek.

That's where I'd look. I'd go all the way down the banks to Lake Erie.

Jesus, Ken, get some sleep.

He's in the creek. I'm sure of it.

Then you're the only one who is.

He's been in there too long, Paul.

Are you on something? Get off the creek, we don't know that, you're giving up on him.

It's been five days, Paul.

More. Feels like a year though. Good night, Ken.

He would go for the lights, Carmichael says, but his brother has hung up.

December rain, the beating, cold, confusing rain. Glaring head-lights on wet asphalt. Black ice. Wrong turns. What drew him on? The dead end, the guardrail barrier. NO BRIDGE. Backed up, then the disheartening whine of tires in mud, spinning deeper. A house, but dark. How many times had he approached a dark house in his youth? In Cape Breton an unlit house in the coun-try meant only that people were sleeping, not that you wouldn't be welcome there, the doors were unlocked. If you needed help or shelter, you knocked, you came inside. But this house was locked and empty. The lights across the creek would have beck-oned like lights at sea, he was a seaman, after all. When did he lose the hat?

Carmichael puts on a tape of Bach's Toccatas. Gould's Bach. Why does he hum like that? Celeste asked, is he cold? That's north, Carmichael said. That passionate chiseled brilliance. On their way to Nova Scotia one winter, he and his parents stayed over at an aunt and uncle's house in Maine. His uncle delivered ice and had built a small storage building in the backyard, the blocks glis-tened damply in the dim light from the door. The cold wet smell of wood, wet straw, sawdust the walls were packed with. That ice, and other ice. Snow. Brittle mornings.

Ethel is free to believe her visions. Hers are hopeful, at least.

Rain has been misting in the bathroom window and Carmichael shuts it. A neighbor's lights are blurred in the pebbled glass. On his way to the bathroom on winter mornings, the furthest, coldest room in that big old house, he would pass his mother's bedroom and see her staring at the ceiling, bedclothes pulled to her chin, a small lamp burning. Whatever she was thinking he was not equipped then to imagine, but he never bothered her. She told him almost nothing about herself, her past was bits and pieces, anecdotes, crazy patches on a quilt. Some of us are on the waking side of life, like your dad, she told him once, others on the dreamy, it takes us longer to get back into the world.

He has cleared his desk and laid the map out over it. Paul told him the name of the creek and he's marked its route with a red pen, and the roads that would take him there. If Celeste were here, he would have to include her in this, tell her. But she is not here. Would she say, No, don't even consider doing that, what a stunt, your age, all these years sitting at a desk? He would say, I'm not in bad shape, I play racquetball three times a week, I was a Sea Scout, I can find my way, I know winters, I remember ice, I'm not afraid.

He will start where his father fell, where he stepped off the bank in the dark, not far from the house. It was a long fall in the rain, fixed as he was on reaching those lights, then pitched suddenly into space. The night gaped and took him. Carmichael does not know this particular creek but he can discern its lineaments, put features to its course, sticks of vegetation, the stark leafless trees of winter, debris snagged and trembling in its current, dirty ice ripped apart. If you started early, at first light, and the weather was not storming, you could walk the entire bank by dark. If not, you make a fire, you sleep a little if you can, start again at light, because once you are there . . .

He is anxious for daybreak. Another whiskey helps him sleep but he wakes, dozes into the night his father drove him and a pal sledding and they sledded in the moonlit dark down a long hill by Lake Erie while his father and mother walked arm in arm through the snow. Carmichael asked his mother why she told him so little about her youth. I didn't think Cape Breton mattered to you, she said. She had no one to talk to really, it's so clear now, she had no intimate friends, woman or man, when Dad was gone. In winter, his father was always up before light. He would call up from the kitchen, Kenny, time to get up, and Carmichael could feel his mother in the next room, curling, like him, deeper into that winter darkness. She did tell him one night, as if she were still turning it over in her mind, that she had been an honor student in Sydney Academy in Cape Breton, but what she remembered most was her terrible guilt over the way she and her friends had behaved toward their Latin teacher. A handsome middle-aged man they all loved, he began, in front of their eyes, a slow mental breakdown, week by week, class by class, until the girls whose names he would write on the blackboard to be punished would erase them as they filed out the door. Why did we do that? she said, torment him like that when we liked him so? The day they took him away the classroom was never so quiet, and he with his hands over his ears.

V

The rain is light when Carmichael goes to the outdoor shop. The flood has abated, though people are still shocked by its incursions. He'll have all he needs in his suitcase; as soon as he arrives and rents a car he can head for the creek. He tries on a navy parka, heavy with a fur-lined hood. Going up north? the salesman asks. Canada, Carmichael says, and the man nods sagely. Ohio he might, like many people in California, know nothing about, but Canada's consonants are hung with ice. The salesman assures him that the parka is waterproof and advises that he take the matching pants, but Carmichael doesn't want to look outfitted, so he says no and tries on boots. Good leather hikers, waterproof. He is afraid to look in the fitting mirror, to be struck with an absurd likeness of himself. But he looks as he hoped: competent in his parka and boots, dressed for serious action, not a weekend at Lake Tahoe. He works his hand slowly into the cool fur lining of a glove. He chooses a sturdy backpack, lingers over a sheath knife, gripping its handle of exotic wood. No animals to fear, but yes, he'll take this, that should do it.

The phone rings at home but he doesn't answer it. Though the volume of the machine is low he can pick out the cranky buzz of his boss, the voice of the future, he could fill its rhythms, its pitches and tones, with words if he wanted to but he lets her shrill little song play out, compressed and intense, and then it is over. His computer is unplugged, nothing running into it or out.

He was getting older at the very time Celeste wanted to be younger. Leaning different ways. His father, his mother. Passion, and aging. Celeste accused him at times of coldness, of closing his heart away.

On the chair he has draped the parka, hooded like a polar explorer's. The boots sit under the chair, at attention. The knife is on his desk next to the keyboard, its blade gleaming. He liked the leathery hiss when he pulled it from the sheath. He will arrange them in a suitcase carefully, call a cab. The creek will be low, quiet, scattered with ice. He hopes it hasn't frozen over. It hasn't rained, his brother told him, and the snow has been light.

He thinks he might do it in a day, if he's lucky. Downstream, all the way to the end. He can feel the whirling snow on his face, the bitter cold of January, ruts and footprints hard as concrete. Wet jeans, chapped skin, numbness in toes and fingers and lips, his jaw moving slowly like a fish's. Under that church window they talked a little. When you're a man, things like this happen to you, his mother said.

His father had been a good swimmer, but he was old. How awkwardly he must have fallen, thrashing the dark air. The rain was loud. He didn't hear the water until he hit.

VI

They found him, Paul says. Carmichael listens to his brother's breathing at the other end of the line. Ken?

Where?

Where the creek empties into Lake Erie. On a sandbar, lying there. A little girl saw him but she didn't know what he was. Sunday morning. Out with her dad. Drowning. He drowned.

He must be pretty beat up.

His brother doesn't answer and Carmichael doesn't need to hear him talk.

I'll be there tonight.

He will pack as he did for his mother's funeral, a topcoat, his good dark suit. But oh that he could have dressed himself against that weather. Followed those winter banks, alert to any odd sight, something hung up in stones or driftwood, cloth hooked on a branch, discarded bedding, fur of an animal. The water would have that muddy look of winter. There had to have been places where the body caught, was held, water coursing thinly over it, catching a wan break of sun, his skin, his torn clothing. Carmichael would know it was him at once, there would be no mistaking. The water would be cold to the bone as he waded in, dragging his legs through the turbid current, his arms high, bearing already the weight of what he had seen. Was there agony in that bruised face, the turbulence of his death? He would free him from the cruelty of the river, untangle his limbs. He would lift him then, grateful for the awful privilege, carry him in his arms to shore and arrange him gently out, return to him his dignity. Their wet clothes would darken the snow, the gray afternoon suddenly colder, flurries drifting loosely down, veiling his father's face. Rested, he might have borne him all the way to the road, have told them, but for a little girl with her father on a Sunday beach, I found him because I knew where he was.

He will write Celeste a letter when it's over. He will tell her what he wanted to do.

At home there will be no coronach, no pipes, no women wailing the grief men clamp inside themselves. Nothing of his father's Cape Breton will be heard in the service, none of its rhythms, its voices, its stern theology he was too good-natured to observe. The minister is young and knows nothing of the island that made this man, nothing of its qualities or its life. Once home, once embraced by the house and its memories, Carmichael will weep somewhere out of sight, in an empty room as he did for his mother, in a closet smelling of his father's clothes.

ABOUT THE AUTHOR

D. R. MacDonald was born on Cape Breton Island, and has won two Pushcart prizes, an Ingram Merrill Award, an O. Henry Award, and in 1983 was awarded an NEA Grant in Literature. He splits his time between California, where he teaches at Stanford University, and Cape Breton.